LITTLE,
BROWN

L B

LARGE
PRINT

For exclusives, trailers, and other information, visit jamespatterson.com.

Hunting PRINCE DRACULA

KERRI MANISCALCO

LITTLE, BROWN AND COMPANY

LARGE PRINT EDITION

JIMMY Patterson Books / Little, Brown and Company
Hachette Book Group
1290 Avenue of the Americas, New York, NY 10104
JimmyPatterson.org

First Edition: September 2017

JIMMY Patterson Books is an imprint of Little, Brown and Company, a division of Hachette Book Group, Inc. The Little, Brown name and logo are trademarks of Hachette Book Group, Inc. The JIMMY Patterson name and logo are trademarks of JBP Business, LLC.

The publisher is not responsible for websites (or their content) that are not owned by the publisher.

The Hachette Speakers Bureau provides a wide range of authors for speaking events. To find out more, go to hachettespeakersbureau.com or call (866) 376-6591.

Photographs courtesy of Wellcome Library, London (pp. 2, 34, 218, 256, 294, 324, 386, 440, 478); Sebastian Nicolae/Shutterstock (p. 46); public domain (pp. 176, 538).

Map by Tim Paul

Library of Congress Cataloging-in-Publication Data
Names: Maniscalco, Kerri, author.
Title: Hunting Prince Dracula / Kerri Maniscalco.
Description: First edition. | New York : Jimmy Patterson Books, 2017. | Series: Stalking Jack the Ripper ; 2 | Summary: "Bizarre murders are discovered in the castle of Prince Vlad the Impaler, otherwise known as Dracula. Could it be a copycat killer…or has the depraved prince been brought back to life?"—Provided by publisher.
Identifiers: LCCN 2017012967 | ISBN 9780316551663 (hardback) 9780316439862 (large print) | 9780316477802 (special ed.) | 9780316514828 (international pb)
Subjects: | CYAC: Mystery and detective stories. | Serial murderers—Fiction. | Dracula, Count (Fictitious character)—Fiction. | Vampires—Fiction.
Classification: LCC PZ7.1.M3648 Hu 2017 | DDC [Fic]—dc23
LC record available at https://lccn.loc.gov/2017012967

10 9 8 7 6 5 4 3 2 1

LSC-C

Printed in the United States of America

To Mom and Dad,
for teaching me that countless adventures
are found between the pages of books.

And to my sister,
for journeying with me to each mysterious land,
real and imagined.

"O proud death,
What feast is toward in thine eternal cell,
That thou so many princes at a shot
So bloodily hast struck?"
—*HAMLET,* ACT 5, SCENE 2
WILLIAM SHAKESPEARE

1. Audrey Rose's tower chambers
2. Thomas's rooms
3. basement morgue/entrance
   to underground tunnels
4. food stores
5. Radu's class
6. Percy's surgical theater
7. Anastasia's rooms
8. master library
9. underground tunnels

copyright 2017 Tim Paul

Hunting Prince Dracula

General view, Bukharest, Roumania. c. 1890.

ONE
GHOSTS OF THE PAST

ORIENT EXPRESS
KINGDOM OF ROMANIA
1 DECEMBER 1888

Our train gnashed its way along frozen tracks toward the white-capped fangs of the Carpathian Mountains. From our position outside Bucharest, the capital of Romania, the peaks were the color of fading bruises.

Judging from the heavy snow falling, they were likely as cold as dead flesh. Quite a charming thought for a blustery morning.

A knee struck the side of the carved wooden panel in my private booth once *again*. I closed my eyes, praying that my traveling companion would fall back asleep. One more jitter of his long limbs might unravel my fraying composure. I pressed my head against the plush high-backed seat, focusing on the soft velvet instead of poking his offending leg with my hat pin.

Sensing my growing annoyance, Mr. Thomas Cresswell shifted and began tapping his gloved fingers against the windowsill in our compartment. *My* compartment, actually.

Thomas had his own quarters but insisted on spending every hour the day possessed in my company, lest a career murderer board the train and unleash carnage.

At least that's the ridiculous story he'd told our chaperone, Mrs. Harvey. She was the charming, silver-haired woman who watched over Thomas while he stayed in his Piccadilly flat in London, and was currently on her fourth nap of the new day. Which was quite a feat considering it wasn't much past dawn.

Father had taken ill in Paris and had placed his trust and my virtue in both Mrs. Harvey's and Thomas's care. It spoke volumes as to how highly Father thought of Thomas, and how convincingly innocent and charming my friend could be when the mood or occasion struck. My hands were suddenly warm and damp inside my gloves.

Derailing that feeling, my focus slid from Thomas's dark brown hair and crisp cutaway coat to his discarded top hat and Romanian newspaper. I'd been studying the language enough to make out most of what it said. The headline read: HAS THE IMMORTAL PRINCE RETURNED? A body had been found staked through the heart near Brașov—the very village we were traveling to—leading the superstitious to believe in the impossible: Vlad Dracula, the centuries-dead prince of Romania, was alive. And hunting.

It was all rubbish meant to inspire fear and sell papers. There was no such thing as an immortal being. Flesh-and-blood men were the real monsters, and they could be cut down easily enough. In the end, even Jack the Ripper bled as all men did. Though papers still claimed he prowled the foggy London streets. Some even said he'd gone to America.

If only that were true.

An all-too-familiar pang hit my center, stealing my breath. It was always the same when I thought about the Ripper case and the memories it stirred within. When I stared into the looking glass, I saw the same green eyes and crimson lips; both my mother's Indian roots and father's English nobility apparent in my cheek-bones. By all outward appearances, I was still a vibrant seventeen-year-old girl.

And yet I'd taken such a devastating blow to my soul. I wondered how I could appear so whole and serene on the outside when inside I was thrashing with turbulence.

Uncle had sensed the shift in me, noticing the care-less mistakes I'd started making in his forensic labora-tory over the past few days. Carbolic acid I'd forgotten to use when cleansing our blades. Specimens I hadn't collected. A jagged tear I'd made in ice-cold flesh, so unlike my normal precision with the bodies lined up on his examination table. He'd said nothing, but I knew he was disappointed. I was supposed to have a heart that hardened in the face of death.

Perhaps I wasn't meant for a life of forensic studies after all.

Tap. Tap-tap-tap. Tap.

I gritted my teeth while Thomas *tap-tap-tapped* along to the chugging of the train. How Mrs. Harvey slept through the racket was truly incredible. At least he'd succeeded in drawing me from that deep well of emotions. They were the kind of feelings that were too still and too dark. Stagnant and putrid like swamp water, with red-eyed creatures lurking far below. An image well suited to where we were heading.

Soon we'd all disembark in Bucharest before traveling the rest of the way by carriage to Bran Castle, home to the Academy of Forensic Medicine and Science, or *Institutului Naţional de Criminalistică şi Medicină Legală,* as it was called in Romanian. Mrs. Harvey would spend a night or two in Braşov before traveling back to London. Part of me longed to return with her, though I'd never admit it aloud to Thomas.

Above our private booth, an opulent chandelier swung in time to the rhythm of the train, its crystals clinking together and adding a new layer of accompaniment to

Thomas's staccato taps. Pushing his incessant melody from my thoughts, I watched the world outside blur in puffs of steam and swishing tree limbs. Leafless branches were encased in sparkling white, their reflections shimmering against the polished near-ebony blue of our luxury train as the front cars curved ahead and carved through the frost-dusted land.

I leaned closer, realizing the branches weren't covered in snow, but ice. They caught the first light of day and were practically set ablaze in the bright reddish-orange sunrise. It was so peaceful I could almost forget—*wolves!* I stood so abruptly that Thomas jumped in his seat. Mrs. Harvey snored loudly, the sound akin to a snarl. I blinked and the creatures were gone, replaced by branches swaying as the train chugged onward.

What I had thought were glinting fangs were only wintry boughs. I exhaled. I'd been hearing phantom howls all night. Now I was seeing things that weren't there during daylight hours, too.

"I'm going to . . . stretch for a bit."

Thomas raised dark brows, no doubt wondering about—or more likely knowing him, admiring—my blatant dismissal of propriety, and leaned forward, but before he could offer to accompany me or wake our chaperone, I rushed for the door and slid it open.

"I need a few moments. Alone."

Thomas stared a beat too long before responding.

"Try not to miss me too much, Wadsworth." He sat back, his face falling slightly before his countenance was once again playful. The lightness didn't quite reach his eyes. "Though that might be an impossible task. I, for one, miss myself terribly when asleep."

"What was that, dear?" Mrs. Harvey asked, blinking behind her spectacles.

"I said you ought to try counting sheep."

"Was I sleeping again?"

I took advantage of the distraction, shutting the door behind me and grabbing my skirts. I didn't want Thomas reading the expression on my face. The one that I hadn't yet mastered in his presence.

I wandered down the narrow corridor, barely taking in the grandiosity as I made my way toward the dining car. I couldn't stay out here unchaperoned for long, but I needed an escape. If only from my own thoughts and worries.

Last week, I had seen my cousin Liza walking up the stairs in my home. A sight as normal as anything, except she'd left for the country weeks prior. Days later something a bit darker occurred. I'd been convinced a cadaver craned its head toward me in Uncle's laboratory, its unblinking gaze full of scorn at the blade in my hand, while its mouth spewed maggots onto the examination table. When I'd blinked, all was well.

I'd brought several medical journals for the journey

but hadn't had an opportunity to research my symptoms with Thomas openly studying me. He'd said I needed to confront my grief, but I wasn't willing to reopen that wound yet. One day, maybe.

A few compartments down, a door slid open, dragging me into the present. A man with primly styled hair exited the chamber, moving swiftly down the corridor. His suit was charcoal and made of fine material, apparent by the way it draped over his broad shoulders. When he tugged a silver comb from his frock coat, I nearly cried out. Something in my core twisted so violently my knees buckled.

It couldn't be. He had died weeks ago in that awful accident. My mind knew the impossibility standing before me, striding away with his perfect hair and matching clothing, yet my heart refused to listen.

I grasped my cream skirts and ran. I would've known that stride anywhere. Science could not explain the power of love or hope. There were no formulas or deductions for understanding, no matter what Thomas claimed regarding science versus humanity.

The man tipped his hat to passengers sitting down to tea. I was only half aware of their openmouthed stares as I bounded after him, my own top hat tilting to one side.

He approached the door to the cigar room, halting a moment to wrench the outer door open to travel between cars. Smoke leached from the room and mixed with an icy blast of air, the scent strong enough to make my insides roil. I reached out, tugging the man around, ready to toss my arms around him and cry. The events last month were only a nightmare. My—

"*Domnişoară?*"

Tears pricked my eyes. The hairstyle and clothing did not belong to the person I'd believed they did. I swiped the first bit of wetness that slid down my cheeks, not caring if I smudged the kohl I'd taken to wearing around my eyes.

He lifted a serpent-head walking cane, switching it to his other hand. He hadn't even been holding a comb. I was losing touch with what was real. I slowly backed away, noting the quiet chatter of the car behind us. The clink of teacups, the mixed accents of world travelers, all of it a crescendo building in my chest. Panic made breathing more difficult than the corset binding my ribs.

I panted, trying to draw in enough air to soothe my jumbling nerves. The clatter and laughter rose to a shrill pitch. Part of me wished the cacophony would drown out the pulse thrashing in my head. I was about to be sick.

"Are you all right, *domnişoară?* You appear..."

I laughed, uncaring that he jerked away from my sudden outburst. Oh, if there was such a thing as a higher power, it was having fun at my expense. "*Domnişoară*" finally registered in place of "Miss." This man wasn't even English. He spoke Romanian. And his hair wasn't blond at all. It was light brown.

"*Scuze,*" I said, forcing myself out of hysterics with a meager apology and slight incline of my head. "I mistook you for someone else."

Before I could embarrass myself further, I dipped my chin and quickly retreated to my car. I kept my head down, ignoring the whispers and giggles, though I'd heard enough.

I needed to collect myself before I saw Thomas again. I'd pretended otherwise, but I'd seen the concern crinkling his brow. The extra care in the way he'd tease or annoy me. I knew precisely what he was doing each time he irked me. After what my family had gone through, any other gentleman would have treated me as if I were a porcelain doll, easily fractured and discarded for being broken. Thomas was unlike other young men, however.

Much too quickly I came upon my compartment and threw my shoulders back. It was time to wear the cool exterior of a scientist. My tears had dried and my heart was now a solid fist in my chest. I breathed in and exhaled. Jack the Ripper was never coming back. As real a statement as any.

There were no career murderers on this train. Another fact.

The Autumn of Terror had ended last month.

Wolves were most certainly not hunting anyone on the *Orient Express*.

If I wasn't careful, I'd start believing Dracula had risen next.

I allowed myself another deep breath before I tugged the door open, banishing all thoughts of immortal princes as I entered the compartment.

TWO

IMMORTAL BELOVED

ORIENT EXPRESS
KINGDOM OF ROMANIA
1 DECEMBER 1888

Thomas kept his focus stubbornly fixed on the window, his leather-clad fingers still drumming that annoying rhythm. *Tap. Tap-tap-tap. Tap.*

Unsurprisingly, Mrs. Harvey was resting her eyes once again. Her soft snuffles indicated she'd fallen back asleep in the few moments I'd been gone. I stared at my companion, but he was either blissfully unaware or likely pretending to be as I slipped into the seat across from him. His profile was a study of perfect lines and angles, all carefully turned to the wintry world outside. I knew he sensed my attention on him, his mouth a bit too curved in delight for mindless thought.

"Must you keep up that wretched beat, Thomas?"

I asked. "It's driving me as mad as one of Poe's unfortunate characters. Plus, poor Mrs. Harvey must be dreaming awful things."

He shifted his attention to me, deep brown eyes turning thoughtful for a moment. It was that precise look—warm and inviting as a patch of sunshine on a crisp autumn day—that meant trouble. I could practically see his mind turning over brash things as one side of his mouth tugged upward. His crooked smile invited thoughts that Aunt Amelia would have found completely indecent. And the way his gaze fell to my own lips told me he knew it. Fiend.

"Poe? Will you carve my heart out and place it beneath your bed, then, Wadsworth? I must admit, it's not an ideal way of ending up in your sleeping quarters."

"You seem awfully certain of your ability to charm anything other than serpents."

"Admit it. Our last kiss was rather thrilling." He leaned forward, his handsome face coming entirely too close to my own. So much for having a chaperone. My heart sped up when I noticed tiny flecks in his irises. They were like little golden suns that drew me in with their enchanting rays. "Tell me you don't fancy the idea of another."

My gaze swiftly trailed over his hopeful features. The truth was, despite every dark thing that had happened the month before, I did indeed fancy the idea of another romantic encounter with him. Which somehow felt as if it were too much of a betrayal to my mourning period.

"First and last kiss," I reminded him. "It was the adrenaline coursing through my veins after nearly dying at the hands of those two ruffians. *Not* your powers of persuasion."

A wicked smile fully lifted the corners of his mouth. "If I found a dash of danger for us, would that entice you again?"

"You know, I much preferred you when you weren't speaking."

"Ah"—Thomas sat back, inhaling deeply—"either way, you prefer me."

I did my best to hide a grin. I should have known the scoundrel would find a way to turn our conversation to such improper topics. In fact, I was surprised it had taken him this long to be vulgar. We'd traveled from London to Paris with my father so he could see us off on the impressive *Orient Express,* and Thomas had been a beguiling gentleman the entire way. I'd barely recognized him while he chatted warmly with Father over scones and tea.

If it weren't for the mischievous tilt to his lips when Father wasn't looking, or the familiar lines of his stubborn jaw, I would have claimed he was an impostor. There was no way *this* Thomas Cresswell could possibly be the same annoyingly intelligent boy I'd grown too fond of this past autumn.

I tucked a loose wisp of raven hair behind my ear and glanced out the window again.

"Does your silence mean you're considering another kiss, then?"

"Can you not deduce my answer, Cresswell?" I stared at him, one brow raised in challenge, until he shrugged and continued rapping his gloved fingers against the windowsill.

This Thomas had also managed to persuade my father, the formidable Lord Edmund Wadsworth, to allow me to attend the Academy of Forensic Medicine and Science with him in Romania. A fact I still couldn't quite sort out in my mind; it was almost too fantastical to be real. Even as I sat on a train en route to the school.

My last week in London had been stuffed full of dress fittings and trunk packing. Which left too much time for them to become further acquainted, it seemed. When Father had announced Thomas would escort me to the academy along with Mrs. Harvey due to his illness, I'd practically choked on my soup course while Thomas winked over his.

I'd barely had time to sleep at night, let alone ponder the relationship budding between my infuriating friend and usually stern father. I was eager to leave the dreadfully silent house that ushered in too many ghosts of my recent past. A fact Thomas was all too aware of.

"Daydreaming of a new scalpel, or is that look simply to enrapture me?" Thomas asked, drawing me away from dark thoughts. His lips twitched at my scowl, but he was smart enough to not finish that grin. "Ah. An emotional dilemma, then. My favorite."

I watched him take note of the expression I was trying too hard to control, the satin gloves I couldn't stop fussing with, and the stiff way I sat in our booth, which had nothing to do with the corset binding my upper body, or the older woman taking up most of my seat. His gaze fixed itself to my own, sincere and full of compassion. I could see promises and wishes stitched across his features, the intensity of his feelings enough to make me tremble.

"Nervous about class? You'll bewitch them all, Wadsworth."

It was a mild relief that he sometimes misread the entire truth of my emotions. Let him believe the shudder was completely from nerves about class and not his growing interest in a betrothal. Thomas had admitted his love for me, but as with many things lately, I was unsure it was real. Perhaps he only felt beholden to me out of pity in the wake of all that happened.

I touched the buttons on the side of my gloves. "No. Not really."

His brow arched, but he said nothing. I turned my attention back to the window and the stark world outside. I wished to be lost in nothingness for a while longer.

According to literature I'd read in Father's grand library, our new academy was set in a rather macabre-sounding castle located atop the frigid Carpathian mountain range. It was a long way from home or civility, should any of my new classmates be less than welcoming. My sex was sure to be seen as a weakness amongst male peers—and what if Thomas abandoned our friendship once we arrived?

Perhaps he'd discover how odd it truly was for a young woman to carve open the dead and pluck out their organs as if they were new slippers to try on. It hadn't mattered while we were both apprenticing with Uncle in his laboratory. But what students at the prestigious Academy of Forensic Medicine and Science would think of me might not be as progressive.

Wrangling bodies was barely proper for a man to do, let alone a highborn girl. If Thomas left me friendless at school, I'd sink into an abyss so deep I feared I'd never resurface.

The proper society girl in me was loath to admit it,

but his flirtations kept me afloat in a sea of conflicting feelings. Passion and annoyance were fire, and fire was alive and crackling with power. Fire breathed. Grief was a vat of quicksand; the more one struggled against it, the deeper it pulled one under. I'd much rather be set ablaze than buried alive. Though the mere *thought* of being in a compromising position with Thomas was enough to make my face warm.

"Audrey Rose," Thomas began, fussing with the cuffs of his cutaway coat, then ran a hand through his dark hair, an action truly foreign to my normally arrogant friend. Mrs. Harvey stirred but didn't wake, and for once I truly wished she would.

"Yes?" I sat even straighter, forcing the boning of my corset to act as if it were armor. Thomas hardly ever called me by my first name unless something awful was about to occur. During an autopsy a few months back, we'd engaged in a battle of wits—which I'd thought I'd won at the time but now wasn't so sure—and I'd allowed him the use of my surname. A privilege he also granted me, and something I occasionally regretted whenever he'd call me Wadsworth in public. "What is it?"

I watched him take a few deep breaths, my focus straying to his finely made suit. He was rather handsomely dressed for our arrival. His midnight-blue suit was tailored to his frame in a way that made one pause and admire both it and the young man filling it out. I reached for my buttons, then caught myself.

"There's something I've been meaning to tell you," he said, moving about in his seat. "I . . . think it only fair to disclose this before we arrive."

His knee knocked into the wooden panel again, and he hesitated. Perhaps he was already realizing his association with me would pose an issue in school for him. I braced myself for it, the snip of the cord that tethered me to sanity. I would not ask him to stay and be my friend through this. No matter if it killed me. I focused on my breaths, counting the seconds between them.

Grandmama claimed the phrase "Renowned for their stubbornness" should be inscribed on all Wadsworth tombs. I didn't disagree. I lifted my chin. The chugging of the wheels now counted off each amplified beat of my heart, pumping adrenaline into my veins. I swallowed several times. If he didn't speak soon, I feared I'd be sick all over him and his handsome suit.

"Wadsworth. I'm sure you . . . perhaps I should—" He shook his head, then laughed. "You've truly possessed me. Next thing I'll be penning sonnets and making doe eyes." The unguardedness left his features abruptly as if he'd stopped himself from falling off a cliff. He cleared his throat, his voice much softer than

Forgetting about good form, Thomas reached for me across the compartment, and Mrs. Harvey finally stirred. As Thomas gripped my hands in his, I knew this was no figment of my imagination. Something very dark and very real was on this train with us.

THREE
MONSTERS AND LACE

ORIENT EXPRESS
KINGDOM OF ROMANIA
1 DECEMBER 1888

I jumped to my feet, scanning the area outside the train, and Thomas did the same. Sunlight tarnished the brassy world in sinister shades of gray, green, and black as the sun rose past the horizon.

"Stay here with Mrs. Harvey," Thomas said. My attention snapped to him. If he thought I was going to simply sit back while he investigated, he was obviously more unhinged than I was becoming.

"Since when do you believe me incapable?" I reached past him, tugging the compartment door with all my might. Blasted thing wouldn't budge. I kicked my traveling slippers off and braced myself, intent on ripping it from its hinges if necessary. I would not stay trapped in this beautiful cage a minute longer, no matter what was waiting to greet us.

I tried again, but the door refused to open. It was like everything in life; the more one struggled against it, the harder it became. The air suddenly felt too heavy to breathe. I pulled harder, my too-smooth fingers slipping over the even smoother gold plating. My breath hitched in my chest, getting caught in the stiff boning of my corset.

I had the wild urge to rip my underthings off, consequences of polite society be damned. I needed out. Straightaway. Thomas was beside me in an instant.

"I do not...think...you...incapable," he said, trying to wrench the door open with me, his leather gloves affording him a bit more control over the smooth plating. "For once, I'd like to be the hero. Or at least pretend to be. You're...always...saving...me. One more tug on the count of three, all right? One, two, three."

Together we finally heaved it open, and I thrust myself into the hallway, not caring what I looked like as a crowd of passengers stared, and slowly backed away from me. I must have appeared worse than I imagined, but I couldn't worry about that yet. Breathing was much more important. Hopefully no one from London society was traveling in this car and would recognize me. I bent over, wishing I'd gone with a corset-free gown, as I dragged in uncooperative breaths. Whispers in Romanian reached my ears: *"Teapa."*

"*Ţepeş.*"

I drew in another quick breath and stood taller, immediately recoiling when I spied the very thing the passengers were transfixed by, their faces drained of color.

There, between the narrow corridor and our door, a body lay slumped over. I'd have thought the man was intoxicated if it weren't for the blood leaking from a large chest wound, staining the Persian rug.

The stake protruding from his heart was a glaring indication of murder.

"Saints above," someone uttered, turning away. "It's the Impaler. The story is true!"

"*Voivode* of Wallachia."

"The Prince of Darkness."

A fist clenched around the area near my heart. *Voivode* of Wallachia…Prince of Wallachia. The title rolled inside my mind until it landed on history lessons and staked itself to the area where fear lived. Vlad Ţepeş. Vlad the Impaler.

Some called him Dracula. Son of the Dragon.

So many names for the medieval prince who'd slaughtered more men, women, and children than I dared to think of. His method of killing was how he received the surname Ţepeş. *Impaler.*

Outside the Kingdom of Romania, his family were rumored to be devilish creatures, immortal and bloodthirsty. But from what little I'd learned, the people of Romania felt very differently. Vlad was a folk hero who'd fought for his countrymen, using any means necessary to defeat his enemies. Something other countries and their beloved kings and queens did as well. Monsters were in the eye of the beholder. And no one wanted to discover their hero was the true villain of the story.

"It's the Immortal Prince!"

"Vlad Ţepeş lives."

HAS THE IMMORTAL PRINCE RETURNED? The newspaper headline flashed across my mind. This truly couldn't be happening again. I wasn't ready to be standing over the body of another murder victim so soon after the Ripper case. Examining a cadaver in the laboratory was different. Sterile. Less emotional. Seeing the crime where it occurred made it too human. Too real. Once it was something I'd longed for. Now it was something I wished to forget.

"This is a nightmare. Tell me this is a horrid dream, Cresswell."

For a brief moment, Thomas appeared as if he longed to take me into his arms and soothe each of my worries. Then that cool determination set in like a blizzard descending the mountains.

"You've stared Fear in its nasty face and made it tremble. You will make it through this, Wadsworth. *We* will make it through this. That is a fact more tangible than any dream or nightmare. I promised I'd never lie to you. I intend to honor my word."

I couldn't tear my gaze from the growing bloodstain. "The world is vicious."

Undeterred by the watchful passengers around us, Thomas brushed a lock of hair back from my face, his gaze thoughtful. "The world is neither kind nor is it cruel. It simply exists. We have the ability to view it however we choose."

"Is there a surgeon on board?" a dark-haired woman around my age cried out in Romanian. It was enough to yank me free of despair. "That man needs help! Someone get help!"

I couldn't bear to tell her this man was past assistance.

A man with rumpled hair clutched the side of his head, shaking it as if he could remove the body with the force of his denial. "This...this...must be an illusionist's act."

Mrs. Harvey poked her head into the corridor, her eyes wide behind her spectacles. "Oh!" she cried out. Thomas quickly escorted her back to the bench in my compartment, whispering soft words to her as they went.

If I hadn't been so stunned, I might have screamed myself. Unfortunately, this wasn't the first time I'd come across a man who'd been murdered only minutes before. I tried not to think about the corpse we'd found in a

London alley and the raging guilt that still gnawed at my insides. He'd died because of my wretched curiosity. I was a gruesome monster wrapped up in delicate lace.

And yet...I couldn't help but feel a buzzing sensation under my skin as I stared at this body, at the crude stake. Science gave me a purpose. It was something to lose myself in other than my own mad thoughts.

I took a few breaths, orienting myself to the horror before me. Now wasn't the time for emotions to cloud my judgment. Though part of me wished to cry for the slain man and whoever would be missing him tonight. I wondered whom he'd been traveling with...or traveling to.

I stopped my thoughts right there. *Focus,* I commanded myself. I knew this was not the work of a supernatural being. Vlad Dracula had died hundreds of years before.

Muttering something about the engine room, the passenger with the disheveled hair ran off in that direction, probably to have the engineer stop the train. I watched him weave through the gaggle of people, most of whom were struck motionless by horror.

"Mrs. Harvey fainted," Thomas said as he exited the compartment and smiled reassuringly. "I have smelling salts, but I think it's best to leave her until this is..."

I watched his throat bob with emotion he was suppressing. I chanced indecency—figuring the crowd was preoccupied by the corpse and not my lack of discretion—and gripped his gloved hand in my own quickly before letting go. Words needn't be said. No matter how much death and destruction one encountered, it was never easy. Initially. But he was right. We would get through this. We'd done it several times before.

Ignoring the chaos breaking out around me, I steeled myself against the abhorrent image and divorced myself from my emotions. Lessons on tending a crime scene Uncle had instilled in me were now body memory—I didn't need to think, simply act. This was a human specimen in need of study, that was all. Thoughts of the blood and gore and unfortunate loss of life were doors that closed simultaneously in my brain. The rest of the world and my fears and guilt faded away.

Science was an altar I knelt before, and it blessed me with solace.

"Remember," Thomas glanced up and down the corridor, trying to block the body from passengers' view, "it's merely an equation that needs solving, Wadsworth. Nothing more."

I nodded, then carefully removed my top hat and swept my long cream skirts behind me, folding away any extra emotions along with the soft fabric. My black and gold lace cuffs brushed against the deceased's frock coat, its delicate structure a horrible contradiction to the rough stake protruding from his chest. I tried to not be distracted by the blood splatter across his starched collar. While I checked for a pulse I knew I wouldn't find, I flicked my attention up to Thomas, noticing that his normally full lips were pressed into a thin line.

"What is it?"

Thomas opened his mouth, then shut it as a woman peered out from the adjacent compartment, a haughty tilt to her chin. "I demand to know the meaning of— o-oh. Oh, my."

She stared at the man heaped on the floor, gasping as if her bodice were suddenly restricting all airflow into her lungs. A gentleman from the adjacent booth caught her before she hit the ground.

"You all right, ma'am?" he asked in an American accent, gently slapping her cheek. "Ma'am?"

An angry cloud of steam hissed as the train screeched to a halt. My body swayed one way, then the next as the great force of propulsion stopped—the corridor chandelier clinking madly above. Its sound made my pulse race faster despite the sudden stillness of our environment.

Thomas knelt beside me, gaze fixed on the newly departed as he steadied me with his gloved hand and whispered, "Be on alert, Wadsworth. Whoever committed this act is likely in this corridor with us, watching our every move."

Hinc simile est epigramma Græcum Antipatri Sidonij de Alcimene aucupe, qui cùm arcu
& funda peteret aues in altum speculatus, ictus à Dipsade interijt, quem sic loquentem facit,

Καίμε τίς ἐτήτειρα πάρα σφυρά δίψας ἐχίδνα
Σαρκὶ τὸν ὀκ γενύων πικρὸν ἐνεῖσα χόλον
Ἠελίω χνέφασεν· ἰδί ὡς τὰ κατ αἰθέρα λεύσσων,
Τῶν ποσὶν ὀκ ἐδάλεω πῆμα κυλινδόμρμον.

30

DE DRACONE.

40

50

A serpent, a winged serpent, and a dragon, c. 1600s.

FOUR·
SOMETHING WICKED

ORIENT EXPRESS
KINGDOM OF ROMANIA
1 DECEMBER 1888

That very thought had also crossed my mind. We were aboard a moving train. Unless someone had leapt from between one of the cars and taken off running through the forest, they were still here. Waiting. Enjoying the spectacle.

I stood and glanced around, noting each face and cataloguing it for future reference. There was a mix of young and old, plain and gaudy. Male and female. My attention snagged on one person—a boy around our age with hair as black as mine—who shifted, tugging at the collar of his morning coat, his eyes flicking between the cadaver and the people surrounding him.

He appeared on the brink of a fainting spell. His nerves might have been from guilt or fear. He stopped shifting around long enough to meet my gaze, his water-filled eyes boring into mine. There was something haunted about him that set my pulse racing again. Perhaps he was acquainted with the victim at my feet.

My heart slammed into my sternum at the same time the conductor whistled a shrill warning to return to our compartments. In the seconds it'd taken to close my eyes and regain my composure, the nervous boy had gone. I stared at the spot where he'd been standing before turning away. Thomas shifted, his arm subtly brushing against my own.

We stood over the body, both silent in our own tumultuous thoughts while taking in the scene. I glanced down at the victim, stomach twisting.

"He'd already perished by the time we got our door open," Thomas said. "There's no amount of stitching that could make his heart whole again."

I knew what Thomas said was accurate, yet I could have sworn the victim's eyes fluttered. I took a deep breath to clear my mind. I thought of the newspaper article again. "The murder in Brașov was also an impalement," I said. "I doubt very highly they're two separate crimes. Perhaps the Brașov murderer was traveling to another city but found this opportunity too tantalizing to ignore."

Though why choose this person to slay? Had he been a target before boarding?

Thomas watched everyone, his gaze calculating and determined.

Now that the corridor was clearing out, I could inspect the deceased for clues. I begged myself to see the truth before us and not get swept up in another fantasy of a corpse springing back to life. Judging from his appearance, the victim couldn't have been more than twenty. Such a senseless loss. He was well dressed with polished shoes and an immaculate suit. His light brown hair had been carefully combed to one side and styled to perfection with pomade.

Nearby, a walking cane with a jeweled serpent head stared unseeingly at the lingering passengers ogling its former owner. That cane was striking. And familiar. My heart thudded as my focus trailed up to his face. I staggered against the wall, breathing deeply. I hadn't paid attention during the initial chaos, but this was the man I'd been mistaken about earlier. It couldn't have been more than ten or twenty minutes ago.

How he'd gone from alive and heading to the cigar car to dead outside my compartment was incomprehensible. Especially when he appeared so much like...

I closed my eyes, but the images stuck there were worse, so I stared at the entry wound and concentrated on the blood that was congealing and cooling.

"Wadsworth? What is it?"

I held a hand to my stomach, stalling. "Death is

never easy, but there's something...infinitely worse when someone young is taken."

"Death's not the only thing to fear. Murder is worse." Thomas searched my face, then glanced at the body, his features softening. "Audrey Rose—"

I quickly turned away before he could put words to my affliction.

"See what you're able to deduce, Cresswell. I need a moment."

I felt him hovering behind me, lingering long enough that I knew he was picking his next words with extreme care, and tried not to tense. "Are you all right?"

We both knew he was asking about more than the deceased lying at my feet. It seemed as if I could be flung into the depthless dark of my emotions at any second. I needed to control the images haunting me both day and night. I faced him, careful to keep both my voice and expression steady. "Of course. Just getting my bearings."

"Audrey Rose," Thomas said quietly, "you don't have to—"

"I am fine, Thomas," I said. "I simply need some quiet."

He pursed his lips but honored my wishes to not press the issue. I bent down once more, studying the wound and ignoring his uncanny resemblance to my brother. I needed to find my balance again. Locate that door to my emotions and seal it shut until my inspection was over. Then I could lock myself in my chambers and cry.

Someone gasped as I unbuttoned part of the victim's shirt to better inspect the stake. Civilities were clearly more important than discovering any clues, but I didn't rightly care. This young man deserved better. I ignored the people lingering in the corridor and pretended I was alone in Uncle's laboratory, surrounded by formaldehyde-scented jars filled with tissue samples. Even in my imagination, the animal specimens blinked at me with their milky dead eyes, judging each move I made.

I flexed my hands. *Focus.*

The victim's chest wound was even more gruesome up close. Bits of wood had splintered off, giving the appearance of brambles and their thorny stems. Blood dried nearly black around the stake. I also noticed two lines of dark crimson that had escaped from his mouth. Not surprising. Such an injury clearly caused massive internal bleeding.

If his heart hadn't been pierced, he'd likely have drowned in his own life force. It was an exceptionally horrid way to die.

A pungent scent that had nothing to do with the metallic tang of blood wafted around the victim. I leaned over the body, trying to locate the offending odor, while Thomas eyed the remaining passengers surrounding us. Knowing he could glean clues from the living the way I could divine information from the dead soothed me.

Something poked from the corners of the deceased's lips, catching my attention. For the love of England, I hoped this wasn't something my mind had conjured up. I nearly tumbled onto the victim as I drew even closer. There was most certainly something bulky and whitish shoved into his mouth. It appeared to be organic in nature, perhaps rootlike. If I could only get within...

"Ladies and gentlemen!" The conductor had cupped his hands around his mouth, shouting from the end of the hall. His accent hinted that he was from France. Unsurprising, as we'd departed from Paris. "Please return to your cabins. Members of the royal guard need the area free from... contamination."

He nervously glanced at the man in uniform beside him, who glared at the crowd until they crept back into their private quarters, shadows sinking into darkness.

The guard looked to be twenty-five or so. His hair was blacker than a starless night and was lacquered to his head. All angles, sharp lines, and cut features. Though he never changed his bland expression, tension coiled within him, a bow pulled taut enough to shoot and kill. I noticed hard muscle beneath his clothing and calluses on his—shockingly ungloved—hands as he lifted them and pointed for us to leave. He was a weapon honed by the Kingdom of Romania, ready to be set upon any perceived threat.

Thomas leaned close enough that his breath tickled the skin of my neck. "A man of few words, I see. Perhaps it's the size of his... weapon that's so intimidating."

"Thomas!" I whispered harshly, horrified by his impropriety.

He pointed to the oversize sword dangling from the young man's hip, amusement scrawled across his features. Right, then. My cheeks warmed as Thomas tsked. "And you say *I'm* the one whose mind is in the gutter. How very scandalous of you, Wadsworth. What *were* you thinking of?"

The guard turned a severe look on Thomas, eyes widening briefly before he reset his jaw.

I glanced between them while they sized each other up, two alpha wolves circling and nipping for dominance in a new pack. Finally, the guard inclined his head slightly. His voice was deep and rumbled like a steam-powered engine. "Please return to your rooms, *Alteță*."

Thomas stilled. It was a word I was unfamiliar with,

as I'd only recently began studying Romanian, so I'd no idea what the guard had called him. Perhaps it was something as simple as "sir" or "you arrogant fool."

Whatever the insult, my friend did not remain frozen with surprise for long. He crossed his arms as the guard stepped forward. "I think we'll stay and inspect the body. We're quite good at prying secrets from the dead. Care to find out?"

The guard's gaze drifted lazily over me, no doubt thinking a young woman in a lovely dress would be the complete opposite of useful. At least where science or amateur sleuthing was concerned. "It's not necessary. You may leave."

Thomas straightened to his full, impressive height and stared down his nose at the young man. He hadn't missed the intent behind the guard's scan either. Nothing good ever came out of his mouth when he took that stance. I chanced indecency and grabbed his hand. The guard curled his lip, but I didn't rightly care.

We were no longer in London, surrounded by people who could assist with getting us out of trouble should Thomas aggravate the wrong person by using his usual charm. Ending up in some musty Romanian dungeon didn't rank high amongst my plans for this lifetime. I'd seen the bleak interior of Bedlam—a horrid asylum in London whose name had become synonymous with chaos—and I could imagine well enough what we might encounter here. I wanted to study cadavers, not different species of rats in some forgotten, subterranean cell. Or spiders. A rivulet of fear slid down my spine at the thought. I'd rather face my hauntings than be trapped with spiders in some small, dark place.

"Let's go, Cresswell."

The young men stared at each other a beat more, silent arguing taking place in their rigid stances. I wanted to roll my eyes at their ridiculousness. I'd never understood the male need to carve out little plots of land and set up a castle to lord over them. All the posturing over every inch of space must get exhausting.

Finally, Thomas relented. "Very well." He squinted at the guard. "What's your name?"

The guard flashed a cruel smile. "Dăneşti."

"Ah. Dăneşti. That explains it, doesn't it?"

Thomas turned on his heel and disappeared inside his own compartment, leaving me to wonder not only at the body outside my door but the strange aura that had enveloped us since we'd entered Romania. Who was the menacing young guard, and why had his name evoked such aggravation in Thomas? Two more royal guards flanked Dăneşti, who was seemingly in charge, as he barked out orders in Romanian and motioned toward the body with precise movements.

I took that as my signal to leave. I closed my compartment door and halted. Mrs. Harvey was lying down, chest rising and falling in a steady rhythm that indicated a deep slumber. But it wasn't her position that startled me. A piece of crumpled parchment lay on my seat. I might be seeing phantom things every now and then, but I was certain there hadn't been any parchment in here before we'd discovered the body outside my door.

Chills took the liberty of crawling over my skin. I glanced around my compartment, but there was no one there besides my sleeping chaperone. Refusing to let fear overwhelm me, I marched over to the paper and smoothed it open. On it was the image of a dragon, its tail coiled around its thick neck. A cross formed the curve of its spine. I'd almost mistaken it for scales.

Maybe Thomas had drawn it, but I'd have noticed him doing so. Wouldn't I?

I dropped onto the seat, puzzling everything out, wishing myself back to the time when all I was concerned with was Thomas's incessant tapping. I couldn't be certain of anything, it seemed. Outside my compartment I heard the corpse being dragged down the corridor. I tried not to think about how the guards were destroying any clues that might have been present as the sounds of his shoes sliding over the carpet faded into nothing.

If someone other than Thomas had created the image of the dragon, how he had sneaked into my compartment and vanished without Thomas or me noticing was another mystery.

One that chilled me to my core.

Bran Castle, Transylvania, Romania

FIVE
LESSONS ON STRIGOI

BRAŞOV OUTSKIRTS
TRANSYLVANIA, ROMANIA
1 DECEMBER 1888

The Clarence—often called a Growler for all the noise it made—was as comfortable as a carriage could be while bumping and jostling for hours over uneven terrain and climbing the steep mountains and hills leading out of Bucharest.

Out of sheer boredom, I found myself entranced by swaying gold tassels that pinned back the deep purple curtains. Golden dragons were stitched into the fabric, their bodies serpentine and elegant. Mrs. Harvey, miraculously awake for the last half hour or so, grunted as we bounced over a particularly large dip in the road and tugged her blanket back up.

My brows practically raised to my hairline when she removed a flask from her fur-trimmed cloak and swigged deeply. Clear liquid sloshed onto her, filling the small space with a sharp scent of what could only be strong alcohol. Her cheeks flushed a vibrant red as she dabbed at the spilled liquid, then offered the engraved flask to me. I shook my head, unable to keep my lips from twitching upward. I liked this woman immensely.

"Traveling tonic. For motion-related illness," she said. "Helps with a fragile constitution. And miserable weather."

Thomas snorted, but I noticed he checked her freshly changed foot brick to be sure it still produced heat. Snow was coming down a bit heavier the higher we climbed in the mountains, and our carriage was quite frigid.

"Mrs. Harvey also uses her traveling tonic before retiring to her room. Some nights after I come in from Dr. Wadsworth's laboratory there are fresh biscuits laid out in the foyer," he said. "With little recollection on her part of how they were made."

"Oh, hush," she said, not unkindly. "I was prescribed this tonic for the trip. Don't go spreading half-truths, it's unbecoming. I always recall my baking and only take a nip afterward. And I make those biscuits because *someone* has quite the sweet tooth. Don't let him tell you otherwise, Miss Wadsworth."

I chuckled as the friendly old woman took another sip of her "traveling tonic" and shifted back beneath the thick wool covers, her lids already drooping. That explained her awe-inspiring ability to sleep through most of this journey. She would get along with my aunt Amelia quite well. Aunt was rather fond of sipping spirits before bed herself.

Thomas stretched his limbs out across the way, encroaching on my bench seat, though for once he seemed unaware of his transgression. He'd been uncharacteristically quiet most of the ride. Traveling never sat well with him, and this part of our excursion wasn't doing him any favors. Perhaps I needed to slip him some of Mrs. Harvey's tonic as well. It might offer us both a bit of peace before we arrived at the academy.

I studied him while he was otherwise preoccupied. His eyes had a far-off glaze to them—he was here with me, yet his mind wasn't anywhere close. I was having a particularly difficult time not thinking about the victim from the train myself. Or the strange drawing of the dragon. I wanted to speak to Thomas about it but didn't want to do so in front of our chaperone. The last thing poor Mrs. Harvey needed was to be exposed to any more frightful situations. When we'd stopped to refresh our horses and have a quick luncheon a short while back, she'd hardly eaten a thing and flinched at each noise from the inn's busy kitchens.

Thomas stared at the woods and the falling snow outside. I wanted to gaze out at the massive trees but was afraid of the images my disturbed mind might conjure up. Animals loping through the underbrush, decapitated heads stuck on pikes. Or other horrid tricks and illusions.

"Feeling unwell?"

He flicked his attention to me. "Is that your way of saying I don't appear my best?"

Without meaning to, I dropped my gaze to his cut-away coat. The midnight hue of both it and the matching waistcoat offset his dark features well, though I had a feeling it was something he was quite aware of. The way his own gaze lingered on my lips confirmed that thought.

"You seem off, is all." I didn't bother pointing out that it was freezing in our rented Growler and, if he wasn't sick with fever, he ought to wear his overcoat instead of using it as a blanket. Letting that observation go, I lifted a shoulder and proceeded to ignore him. He shifted forward, focus drifting away from Mrs. Harvey.

"Haven't you noticed?" He tapped his fingers along his thigh. I could have sworn he was creating some epic saga using Morse code but didn't interrupt him. "I haven't touched a smoke in days. I find the excess nervous energy to be...a nuisance."

"Why don't you try to sleep, then?"

"I can think of a few more intriguing things we

might do to pass the time other than sleep, Wadsworth. Braşov is still hours away."

I sighed heavily. "I swear, if you came up with something a bit less repetitive, I'd kiss you for the intellectual stimulation alone."

"I was speaking of something else entirely. Something of myths and legends and other noteworthy topics to assist with your Romanian studies. You're the one who assumed I was talking about kissing." He sat back with a satisfied grin and resumed his inspection of the forest as we slowly ambled by. "Makes one wonder how often you're thinking about it."

"You've discovered my secret. I think about it constantly." I didn't so much as crack a smile, enjoying the confusion playing over his features as he silently puzzled out my sincerity. "You were supposedly saying something worthy of note." He blinked at me as if I'd spoken a language he couldn't identify. "Hard to believe, I know."

"I, noble specimen that I am, was going to tell you about the *strigoi*. But I enjoy unearthing your secrets much better. Let's hear more about *your* thoughts."

He allowed himself a full scan of my person, seeming to pluck up a thousand details. A smile slowly curved his lips.

"Judging from the way you've straightened up and

the slight intake of breath, I'd say you're at least *considering* kissing me this moment. Naughty, naughty, Wadsworth. What would your pious aunt have to say?"

I kept my focus fixed on his face, avoiding the desire to glance at his full mouth. "Tell me more about the *stri-guy*. What are they?"

"*Strigoi,* like 'boy,'" Thomas said, his Romanian accent perfect, "are undead that take the form of those you trust. Those you'd be only too happy to invite into your home. Then they attack. Usually, it's a relative who's passed on. It's hard for us to turn away those we love," he added quietly, as if he knew how deeply those words might cut.

I tried—and failed—not to recall the way my mother's limbs had twitched when the electricity snaked through her body. Would I have welcomed her back from Death's Dominion, no matter how frightened I was? The answer disturbed me. I did not believe there was any line one wouldn't cross when it came to those one loved. Morals crumpled when faced with heartache. Some fissures within us would forever remain irreparable.

"There must be some explanation for this," I said. "I highly doubt Vlad Dracula has risen from the grave. Undead are simply gothic stories told to frighten and entertain."

Thomas turned his gaze to mine and held it. We

both knew that sometimes stories and reality collided, with devastating effects. "I agree. Unfortunately, some villagers do not. When *strigoi* are spotted, the entire family—or anyone who's been affected—travels to the grave of the offender, digs them up, rips their rotting heart out, and burns them on the spot. Oh," he added, leaning forward. "I almost forgot. Once they've burned the undead 'monster,' they drink the ashes. It's the only way to be sure the *strigoi* can't come back or inhabit another host."

"Sounds a bit...much," I said, scrunching my nose.

A grin slowly spread across Thomas's face. "Romanians never do anything halfheartedly, Wadsworth. Whether it's going to war, or fighting for love."

I blinked at the sincerity in his tone. Before I could comment, the driver whistled to the horses and drew back on the reins, halting the carriage. I sat forward, heart pounding as thoughts of roving bands of thieves and murderers swept through my mind. "What's happening? Why are we stopped?"

"I may have forgotten to mention"—Thomas paused and calmly donned the overcoat he'd been using as an extra blanket before adjusting the foot brick for me—"we're switching to a more appropriate carriage."

"What do you—" Neighing horses and tinkling bells interrupted my next question. Thomas peered out the window with me, our breath creating opaque swirls.

He wiped it clean with the sleeve of his overcoat and watched my reaction, a tentative grin upon his face.

"Surprise, Audrey Rose. Or at least I hope it's a pleasant surprise. I wasn't sure..."

A magnificent horse-drawn sleigh slid to a halt beside us, its muted reds, ochres, and pale blues an homage to Romanian painted eggs. Two large pure-white horses snuffed the air, their breath puffing out in little clouds in front of them while they toed the snow. They wore crowns of white ostrich-feather plumes—only slightly wilted from the unpleasant weather.

"You...you did this?"

Thomas glanced from me to the sleigh, biting his lip. "I hoped you might enjoy it."

I raised a brow. Enjoy it? It was a scene straight out of a fairy tale. I was utterly enchanted.

"I adore it."

Without another thought, I unlatched the door and accepted the coachman's outstretched hand, slipping over the slick metal rung before righting myself. Wind gusted with ferocity, but I hardly noticed as the coachman turned back to the carriage. I held fast to my hat and stared in wonder at the spectacular sight before me. The sleigh driver smiled as I moved away from the protective side of the Growler and stepped fully into the storm.

At least I believed he smiled. There was no way of

telling for sure, with most of his ruddy face and body covered to keep the harsh elements away. He waved as Thomas made his way to my side, inspecting both sleigh and driver in that calculating way of his.

"Seems a reasonable mode of transport as any. Especially since this storm doesn't appear to be giving up anytime soon. We should make excellent time. And your expression was well worth it." I turned to him, eyes watering with gratitude, and watched panic seize him as I smiled unabashedly. He poked his head back into the carriage and clapped. "Mrs. Harvey. Time to wake up. Allow me to assist you down."

A chilly breeze chose that moment to knife its way through the woods, causing the branches to whistle. I buried my face in the fur lining of my winter cloak. We were in the thick of the forest, sandwiched between warring mountain peaks. While there were still a few hours of daylight remaining, darkness wove its way around us. This elevation was as temperamental as my friend.

Thomas motioned toward our steamers as he helped our chaperone down from the carriage. She scowled at the falling snow and took a sip from her tonic.

Thomas followed my gaze as it traveled from one creaking tree to the next. There was something odd about these woods. They felt alive with a spirit of something neither good nor evil. There was an ancient aura, though, one that spoke in whispers of wars and bloodshed.

We were deep in the heart of Vlad the Impaler's land, and it was as if the earth wanted us to be warned: Respect this ground or suffer the consequences.

It was likely a trick of the light, but the few remaining leaves seemed to be the color of dried wounds. I wondered if the foliage had grown accustomed to the taste of blood after tens of thousands of lives had been lost here. A bird screeched above us, and I sucked in a cool breath.

"Easy now, Wadsworth. The forest doesn't have fangs."

"Thank you for that reminder, Cresswell," I said sweetly. "What would I do without you?"

He turned to me, expression as serious as I'd ever witnessed it. "You would miss me terribly and know it. Just as I would miss you in ways I cannot fathom, should we ever part."

Thomas took Mrs. Harvey by the arm, guiding her forward, as the sleigh driver motioned for us to take a seat. I stood there a moment, heart racing. His confessions were delivered so matter-of-factly, it stunned me each time.

Allowing myself a moment to steady my heart, I petted the velvet-soft muzzle of the horse nearest us before climbing into the sleigh. It wasn't fully enclosed like our carriage, but there were more fur throws in the small space than I'd ever before encountered. We might not have a covered roof, but we'd not freeze with all of the animal pelts to wrap ourselves in. Mrs. Harvey tottered into the sleigh and pressed herself against one side, leaving the rest of the seat open for us as she arranged the foot warmers.

My body seized up when I realized how close Thomas and I would have to sit. I hoped the headmaster wouldn't be standing outside for our arrival; it would hardly be decent to be found snuggling next to Thomas, even with a chaperone. As if that very thought were crossing his tainted mind, Thomas flashed a roguish grin and lifted the edge of a large fur-trimmed blanket, patting the space beside him. I set my jaw.

"What?" he asked, feigning innocence as I situated furs around myself, stuffing extra bulk between us with dramatic emphasis on building a fluffy barrier. Predictably, Mrs. Harvey was already nodding off. I wondered if Thomas had struck some sort of bargain with her to be present in physical form only. "I'm simply being gentlemanly, Wadsworth. No need to spear me with that glare of yours."

"I thought you wanted to be on your best behavior for my father's sake."

He held a hand to his heart. "You wound me. Wouldn't your father be angry if I let you freeze to death? Body heat is scientifically the best way to stay warm. In fact, there are studies that suggest removing your clothes entirely and pressing skin to skin is the surest means of avoiding hypothermia. Should you fall prey to that, I'll use every weapon necessary to save you. It's what any decent young gentleman would do. Seems terribly valiant, if you ask me."

My treacherous mind strayed to the image of Thomas without his clothing and drew a wide grin from my companion, as if he were privy to my scandalous thoughts.

"Perhaps I shall write to Father and find out what he thinks of that theory."

Thomas huffed and tossed the blanket about his shoulders, appearing like a wild king of beasts from some Homeric poem. I nestled into an oversize fur, breathing in the scent of tanned animal hide, and tried not to gag. It wasn't the most pleasant-smelling ride, but at least we'd make it to the academy before midnight. I'd endured worse scents while studying putrid cadavers with Uncle. A bit of earthy skin would hardly be too much to handle for another couple of hours.

Strange as it was to think about, I missed the slight smell of decay mixed with formalin most mornings. I couldn't wait to arrive at school and be surrounded by scientific study once again. A new environment might cure me of whatever I was suffering from. At least I hoped it would. I could not continue with forensic practices if I was afraid of reanimated corpses.

I glanced at all the grayish pelts, realization dragging my lips into a frown. "Isn't it odd to have so many wolf hides?"

Thomas lifted a shoulder. "Romanians aren't fond of large wolves."

Before I could have him clarify, the driver loaded up the last of our trunks and climbed aboard. He said something quickly in Romanian, and Thomas responded before leaning back to me, his breath coaxing gooseflesh to rise. I shivered at the unexpected thrill. "Next stop, Bran Castle. And all the delightful miscreants who study there."

"We're about to study there," I reminded him.

He sank into his blanket, doing a poor job at hiding his smile. "I know."

"How do you know Romanian so well?" I asked. "I was unaware you were fluent in anything other than sarcasm."

"My mother was Romanian," Thomas said. "She used to tell us all sorts of folktales growing up. We learned the language from birth."

I frowned. "Why not mention it sooner?"

"I'm full of surprises, Wadsworth." Thomas pulled

his blanket up over his head. "Expect a long life of unraveling these sort of delights. Keeps the mystery and spark alive."

With a snap of the reins we were off, gliding over the snow as new flakes whipped past us. Icy wind stung my cheeks, forcing tears out in glistening rivulets, but I couldn't stop watching the forest flash by through slitted eyes. Every once in a while I swore something was keeping pace with us just inside the woods' border, but it was becoming too dark to be sure.

When I heard a low howl, it was hard to tell if it was the wind or a pack of hungry wolves chasing their next warm meal. Perhaps the living, breathing murderer and ghosts of Vlad Dracula's victims weren't the only fear-inspiring things to worry about in this country.

Time passed in frozen minutes and darkening skies. We traveled up steep mountain slopes and down into smaller valleys. We made one stop in Brașov, where—after great debate on the questionable suitability of arriving at the academy without a chaperone—Thomas assisted Mrs. Harvey with securing a room in a tavern, and we said our good-byes to her. Then we climbed our way from the village toward the top of the greatest mountain I'd ever seen.

When we finally crested its summit a while later, the moon had fully risen. In its light I could make out the pale walls of the turreted castle that had once been home to Vlad Țepeș. A jet-black forest surrounded it, a natural fortress for the man-made one. I wondered if that was where Vlad had acquired the wood he'd needed for the victims he'd impaled.

Without worrying about being untoward, I inched closer to Thomas, leaching his warmth for several reasons. I hadn't thought about it earlier, but Brașov was very close to our school. Whoever had murdered that first victim had chosen a place near Dracula's castle.

I hoped it wasn't a sign of worse murders to come.

"Appears as if someone's left the light on for us." Thomas nodded toward two glowing lanterns that could be proclaiming they were the gates of Satan's lair, for all I knew.

"Looks...cozy."

Winding our way along the narrow path that led from the woods and across the small lawn, we finally pulled to a blessed stop outside the castle. Fingers of moonlight reached over the spires and slid down the roof, casting the shadows of the sleigh and horses in sinister shapes. This castle was eerie, and I hadn't even stepped inside.

For a brief moment, I longed to hide under the animal furs and travel back to the well-fortified, colorful town whose lights winked like fireflies in the valley below us.

Perhaps traveling back to England with Mrs. Harvey wouldn't be such a wretched thing. I could meet my cousin in the country. Spending time together talking and sewing items for our hope chests couldn't be that terrible. Liza made even the most mundane tasks a grand romantic adventure, and I missed her dearly.

A pang of homesickness hit my center, and I struggled to keep myself from doubling over. This was a mistake. I was not ready to be thrust into this academy built for young men. Bodies lining tables and surgical theaters. All of them reminders of the case I couldn't get past. A case that had destroyed my heart.

"You are going to dazzle them all, Wadsworth." Thomas gently squeezed my hand before releasing it. "I cannot wait to see you outshine everyone. Myself included. Though do be gentle with me. Pretend as if I'm wonderful."

I shoved my nerves aside and smiled. "A monumental task, but I will try to go easy on you, Cresswell."

I emerged from the sleigh with renewed strength and made my way up wide stone stairs as Thomas paid the driver and motioned for our trunks to be brought up. I waited for him to reach me, holding my skirts above the gathering snow, not wanting to step beyond that bleak threshold alone. We were here. We'd face down my demons together.

A massive oak door was flanked by two lanterns, a

giant knocker set directly in the middle. It looked as if two C-shaped serpent bodies had become one brooding face.

Thomas smiled blandly at the knocker. "Welcoming, isn't it?"

"It's one of the most ghastly things I've ever seen."

As I lifted the dreadful thing, the door groaned open, revealing a tall, thin man with silver hair that fell in a sheet about his collar and a deep-set scowl. Fire crackled behind him, gilding the edges of his narrow face. His dark skin glistened with a thin sheen of perspiration that he didn't bother dabbing away.

I didn't dare guess what he'd been doing.

"Doors lock in two minutes," he said in a thick Romanian accent. His upper lip curled as if he knew I fought the whispered urge to step back. I could have sworn his incisors were sharp enough to pierce skin. "I suggest you hurry inside and shut that mouth before something unpleasant flies in. We have a bit of a bat problem."

SIX
PLEASANT AS A ROTTEN CORPSE

*ACADEMY OF FORENSIC MEDICINE AND
SCIENCE
INSTITUTULUI NAȚIONAL DE
CRIMINALISTICĂ ȘI MEDICINĂ LEGALĂ
BRAN CASTLE
1 DECEMBER 1888*

I snapped my mouth shut, more out of shock at such an egregious welcome than compliance.

What a dreadfully rude man. He inspected Thomas with an equally patronizing sneer plastered across his face. I tore my attention from him, afraid I'd turn to stone if I stared too hard. For all I knew he was descended from the mythical Gorgons. He was certainly as charming as Medusa—which, I realized, was exactly what the door knocker had reminded me of.

We stepped through the doorway and waited quietly as the man walked over to a maid and began instructing her on something in Romanian. My friend shifted from one foot to the other but remained silent. It was both a small miracle and a blessing.

I glanced around. We were standing in a semicircular receiving chamber, and several darkened corridors stretched to our right and left. Straight ahead, a rather plain staircase split in two, leading to both upper and lower levels. An enormous fireplace offset the stairs, but even the inviting ambience of crackling wood couldn't stop gooseflesh from rising. The castle seemed to chill in our presence. I thought I'd felt a gust of arctic air blow in from the rafters. Darkness clung in areas the fire didn't reach, heavy and thick as a nightmare one couldn't wake from.

I wondered where they kept the bodies we were to study.

The man lifted his head and met my gaze, as if he'd heard my inner thoughts again and wished to mock me. I hoped trepidation didn't show through the cracks of my tarnished armor. I swallowed hard, releasing a breath once he'd looked away.

"I have the strangest feeling about him," I whispered.

Thomas allowed his focus to drift to the man and the maid, who was nodding along to whatever he was saying. "This room is equally charming. The sconces are all dragons. Look at those teeth spitting flames. Bet Vlad had them commissioned himself."

Torches were lit and spaced evenly throughout the receiving chamber. Dark wooden beams edged the ceiling and doors, reminding me of blackened gums. I couldn't help feeling like this castle enjoyed devouring fresh blood as much as its previous occupant enjoyed spilling it. It was an abysmal setting for any school, let alone one that studied the dead.

Lemon and antiseptic cut through the scents of damp stone and paraffin. Cleaning materials for two vastly different purposes. I noticed the floor in the receiving chamber was wet from—I assumed—other students arriving in the storm.

Wings flapped from the cavernous ceilings, drawing my attention upward. An arched window was set high up on the wall, cobwebs noticeable from here. I didn't notice any bats but pictured red eyes glaring down at me. I hoped to avoid seeing such creatures during my time here. I'd always been afraid of their leathery wings and sharp teeth.

The maid bobbed a curtsy and scurried down the corridor on the far left.

"We weren't expecting a spouse. You may stay two floors up to the left."

The man dismissed me with a flick of his wrist. At first I had thought him old because of his hair. Now I could see his face was mostly unlined and much younger. He was likely around my father's age, no more than forty.

"Forensic students are in the east wing. Or should I say, students vying for a spot in our forensics program are this way. Come"—he motioned toward Thomas—"I'm heading there myself. I'll show you to your chambers. You may visit your wife only after classes end."

Thomas got that obnoxious glint in his eyes, but this wasn't his battle to fight. I took a small step in front of him and cleared my throat. "Actually, we're both in the forensics program. And I'm not his wife. Sir."

The nasty man stopped abruptly. He slowly spun on his heel, a high-pitched screech issuing from the soles of his shoes. He narrowed his eyes as if he couldn't possibly have heard me correctly. "Pardon?"

"My name is Miss Audrey Rose Wadsworth. I believe the academy received a letter of recommendation from my uncle, Dr. Jonathan Wadsworth of London. I've been apprenticing under him for quite some time now. Both Mr. Cresswell and myself were present during the Ripper murders. We assisted my uncle and Scotland Yard in the forensics investigation. I'm quite sure the headmaster received the letter. He responded."

"Is that so."

The way he said it wasn't a question, but I pretended not to notice. "It is."

I watched the blankness leave the man's face. A vein in his neck jumped as if it might strangle the life from me. While it wasn't unheard of for a woman to study medicine or forensics, he clearly wasn't a progressive sort who enjoyed having this boys' club invaded by lace-wearing girls. Girls who obviously didn't know their proper place was in a home, not a medical laboratory. The very nerve of him, assuming I was there only because Thomas brought me. I hoped he wasn't a teacher. Studying under him would be a certain kind of perverse torture I should like to avoid.

I thrust my chin up, refusing to break away from his stare. He'd not intimidate me. Not after what I'd been through with Jack the Ripper this past autumn. He raised a brow in appraisal. I had the impression that few people—man or woman—ever stood up to him.

"Ah. Well, then. I didn't think you'd follow through. Welcome to the academy, Miss Wadsworth." He attempted a smile but appeared as if he'd swallowed a bat.

"You mentioned something about vying for a spot in the program?" I asked, ignoring his sour expression. "We were under the impression we'd been accepted."

"Yes. Well. What a shame for you. We have hundreds of students who wish to study here," he said, lifting his own chin with arrogance. "Not all gain admittance. Each season we host an assessment course to determine who will *actually* become a student."

Thomas drew back. "Our places aren't guaranteed?"

"Not at all." The man smiled fully. It was a truly terrible sight. "You have four weeks to prove yourselves. At the end of that trial period, we will decide who gains full-time entry."

My stomach clenched. "If all the students pass the assessment course, does everyone get accepted?"

"There are nine of you this round. Only two will make it through. Now, then. You may follow me, Miss Wadsworth. Your quarters are on the third floor in the east-wing tower. Alone. Well, not entirely. We house surplus cadavers on that level. They shouldn't bother you... much."

Despite our new circumstances, I managed a small smile. The dead were books both my uncle and I enjoyed reading. I was not afraid of spending time alone with corpses, perusing them for clues. Well... not until recently. My smile faded, but I kept my shudder locked inside. I hoped to control my emotions, and being so close to the bodies might very well cure me.

"They'd be more pleasant than some." Thomas made an obscene gesture behind the man's back, and I nearly choked on surprised laughter as he spun around, glaring.

"What was that, Mr. Cresswell?"

"If you insist upon knowing, I said you're—"

I shook my head slightly, hoping I conveyed to

Thomas the need for him to stop speaking. The last thing we needed was to make a greater enemy of this man. "I apologize, sir. I asked—"

"Address me as Headmaster Moldoveanu, or you will be sent back to whichever highbred cesspool you've both arrived from. I doubt either one of you will make it through this course. We have pupils who study for months and still aren't accepted. Tell me—if you're so good at what you do, where is Jack the Ripper, hmm? Why aren't you in London hunting him down? Could it be you're afraid of him, or did you simply run off when it became too difficult?"

The headmaster waited a beat, but I doubted he truly expected an answer from either of us. He shook his head, his expression even more pinched than before.

"Your uncle is a wise man. I find it highly suspect that he hasn't solved that crime. Has Dr. Jonathan Wadsworth given up?"

A shard of panic tore through my insides, piercing each organ in its attempt to flee, as I met Thomas's startled gaze. We had never told Uncle about the Ripper's true identity, though I knew he'd suspected well enough.

Thomas clenched his fists at his sides but kept his troublesome mouth shut. He caught on that I would be punished for either his or my insubordination.

Under different circumstances, I might have been impressed. It was the first time I could recall him containing himself.

"I didn't think you'd have an answer. Now, then. Follow me. Your trunks will be waiting in your chambers. Supper has already been served. You'll be on time for breakfast, promptly at sunrise, or you'll miss that, too." Headmaster Moldoveanu started walking toward the vast corridor of the east wing, then paused. Without turning he said, "Welcome to the Institutului Naţional de Criminalistică şi Medicină Legală. For now."

I stood immobile for a few seconds, heart hammering. It was preposterous that this loathsome man was our headmaster. His steps echoed in the cavernous room, gongs of doom sounding the hour of dread. Drawing in a deep breath, Thomas slid his gaze to mine. This was going to be a very long and torturous four weeks.

After leaving Thomas at his floor, I climbed the bare stairwell located at the end of a long, wide corridor the headmaster pointed out. The steps were made of dark wood and the walls a dismal white, lacking any of the crimson tapestries we'd walked past in the lower corridors. Shadows stretched wide between ill-placed sconces and pulsed along with my movements.

It reminded me of walking through the desolate corridors of Bedlam.

I ignored the flutter of fear in my chest, recalling the occupants of that asylum and the calculated manner in which some of them prowled behind rusted bars. Like this castle, that building reminded me of a living organism. One that had consciousness yet lacked a sense of right versus wrong. I wondered if I was simply in need of a warm bath and a good night's sleep.

Stones and wood did not equal bones and flesh.

Moldoveanu had said my quarters were the first door on the right before he'd marched off to Lord only knew where. Perhaps to go sleep upside down in the rafters with the rest of his kin. I *might* have muttered as much, and he'd spun around, glaring. Things were off to a smashing start.

I came to the small landing that contained my chambers and a second door a few feet down before the stairwell continued up. No torches were lit at that end of the hallway, and the darkness was oppressive. I stood there, frozen, convinced the shadows were watching me as intently as I stared at them.

My breath came out in rapid wisps of white. I assumed the coldness was partly due to the castle being so high in the mountains, and partly because of the bodies that were being stored up there.

Maybe that was what beckoned to me in the darkness. I briefly closed my eyes, and images of corpses rising off the examination tables, bodies half rotten with decay, assaulted my senses. Regardless of my sex, if any of my classmates suspected I was afraid of the cadavers, I'd be laughed out of the academy.

Without worrying on that more, I pushed the door open and swept my gaze around the space. First glance suggested the room acted as a sitting room or parlor. As was the case with the rest of the castle, the walls were white and edged with deep brown-black wood. I was amazed by how dark it felt even with the pale walls and a blaze crackling in the fireplace.

Bookcases took up the smallest wall, and on the left was an entrance to what I assumed was my sleeping chamber. I quickly crossed the sitting room—appointed with a brocade settee—and inspected what were indeed my sleeping quarters. They were cozy and made for a studious scholar. I had a small secretary with a matching chair, miniature armoire, single bed, nightstand, and trunk—all made of deep oak that had probably been gathered in the surrounding forest.

An image of bodies being pierced with black stakes dashed across my thoughts before I could banish it. I hoped none of those pieces of wood had been reused in the castle. I wondered if the person who'd impaled that man in town had taken branches from here as well.

I forced my thoughts away from the victim on the train and the one from the paper. There wasn't anything I could do to help. No matter how much I longed to.

After a cursory glance at the second door—the water closet Headmaster Moldoveanu had said came attached to my chambers, no doubt—I shifted my attention back to the sitting room. I spied a small window perched near the exposed beams, staring out at the vast Carpathian range. From here the mountains were all white and jagged, like broken teeth. Part of me wished to crawl up to the window and gaze upon the winter world that lay beyond, ignorant of my troubled disposition.

I couldn't wait to call for warm water for the washbasin and rinse the grit of travel away. But first I needed to find a way to speak with Thomas. I still hadn't had an opportunity to show him the dragon illustration that I'd found and was going to go mad if I didn't discuss it soon. Not to mention, I was especially curious about his strange reaction to Dǎneşti's name and wanted to inquire about it.

I touched the parchment in my pocket, assuring myself it was indeed real and not a figment of my imagination. It terrified me that it might be connected to the murder on the train. I dared not consider what message it was meant to convey by being left in my compartment. Or who might have been skulking about without my knowledge.

I stood before the fireplace, allowing its warmth to wrap itself around my bones as I considered a plan. Once we had entered the castle, Moldoveanu never stated that we had a curfew. Or that I was not permitted to wander the halls. It would be quite the scandal if discovered, but I could sneak down to Thomas's chambers in a—

Creaking floorboards somewhere inside my quarters had my heart bashing against my chest. Images of murderers creeping through train cars and leaving cryptic notes with dragons on them assaulted me. He was here. He'd followed us to this castle and now he'd impale me, too. I'd been a fool not to confide in Thomas while Mrs. Harvey was napping. *Breathe,* I commanded myself. I needed a weapon. There was a candelabra across the room, but it was too far to snatch without being seen by whoever might be lurking in the bedchamber or water closet.

Instead of drawing too close to those rooms without a weapon, I plucked a large book from the shelves, ready to swing it at someone's head. Knocking them out or stunning them was the best I could do. My focus drifted around the sitting room. It was empty. Completely and utterly void of any living thing, as I'd already determined. A quick scan of the bedchamber showed me the same result. I didn't bother with the water closet; it was likely too small to contain any real threat. The creaking noise was likely the castle settling. I sighed and placed the book back on its shelf. It was truly going to be a dreadful winter.

I was grateful for the fireplace. It thawed my nerves. Even in the cramped space, the heat made me feel as if I were on an island in the tropics as opposed to a lonely tower in an icy castle, hearing things that weren't as terrifying as my own imagination.

I rubbed small circles around the center of my brow ridge. Memories of Jack the Ripper's final moments in that godforsaken laboratory as he flipped the switch… I stopped myself right there. Grief needed to release me from its stubborn embrace. I could not keep doing this to myself night after night. Jack the Ripper was never coming back. His experiments were over. Just like his life.

The same held true for this castle. Dracula lived no more.

"Everything's so bloody difficult," I swore to myself as I plopped onto the settee. At least I thought I was alone, until someone choked back laughter from behind a closed door. My cheeks flushed as I grabbed the large candelabra and rushed to the barely lit water closet. "Hello? Who's there? I demand you show yourself at once."

"*Îmi pare rău, domnişoară.*" A young maid stood

abruptly from her place near the tub, apologizing as her cleaning rag plunked into a bucket. Gray eyes stared back at me. She wore an off-white peasant blouse tucked into a patchwork skirt with an embroidered apron. "Didn't mean to eavesdrop. My name is Ileana."

Her accent was soft and inviting—a hint of summer whispering through a desolate winter night. Black hair was braided and coiled under her maid's cap, and her apron was smudged with ashes, presumably from the blazing fireplace she'd stoked before I'd entered the room. I released a breath.

"Please don't bother calling me 'miss.' 'Audrey Rose' or just plain 'Audrey' is perfectly fine." I glanced around at the newly cleaned washroom. Liquid flames reflected off each dark surface, reminding me of spilled blood catching the moonlight. Like the bodily fluids leaking from Jack the Ripper's double-event victims. I swallowed the image away. The castle was wreaking havoc on my already morbid memory. "Are you assigned to this tower?"

Color blossomed across her skin as she nodded, noticeable even under layers of ash and grime. "Yes, *domnişoară*...Audrey Rose."

"Your English accent is excellent," I said, impressed. "I'm hoping to improve my Romanian while here. Where did you learn the language?"

I snapped my mouth shut after asking. It was a dreadfully rude thing to comment on. Ileana simply smiled. "My mother's family passed it along to each of their children."

It was an odd thing for a poor family from the village of Braşov, but I let it pass. I did not wish to insult a potential new friend any further. I caught myself fiddling with the buttons on the side of my gloves and stopped.

Ileana hoisted a bucket on her ample hip and nodded toward the door. "If I don't finish lighting fires in the boys' rooms, I'll be in a world of trouble, *dom*— Audrey Rose."

"Of course," I said, wringing my hands. I hadn't realized how lonely I was without Liza, and how much I wanted a girl friend. "Thank you for cleaning. If you leave some supplies, I can help."

"Oh, no. Headmaster Moldoveanu wouldn't approve. I'm to tend to the rooms when they're unoccupied. I wasn't expecting you for a few more moments." My face must have displayed my disappointment. Her expression softened. "If you'd like, I can bring breakfast up to your rooms. I do it for the other girl here."

"There's another girl staying this winter?"

Ileana nodded slowly, her smiling growing wide to match my own. "*Da, domnişoară*. She's the headmaster's ward. Would you like to meet her?"

"That sounds wonderful," I said. "I should like it very much."

"Do you need assistance changing for bed?"

I nodded, and Ileana got to work on my corset. Once she'd worked it off and I was standing in my chemise, I thanked her. "I'll handle it from here."

Ileana nudged the door open with her hip, then bid me good night in Romanian. *"Noapte bună."*

I glanced at the washroom, realizing that she'd also filled the tub with hot water. Steam rose in tendrils, beckoning me in. I bit my lip, contemplating the warm bath. I supposed it would be too improper to march into Thomas's chambers this late at night, and I did not wish to be ruined in society's eyes because of my impatience. And the drawing of the dragon would still be there in the morning...

I slipped out of my underclothes, feeling the warmth of both the water and friendship sink into my weary bones.

Perhaps the next few weeks wouldn't be as horrid as I'd thought.

SEVEN

FOLKTALES

Mist rose from the trees around the castle and settled over the mountains like fog in London alleyways as I perched on the settee, trying not to fidget.

Ileana said she'd return for breakfast, but it was nearly sunrise and I still hadn't seen her. For all I knew, she might have been detained in another part of the castle. My foot bounced in place. Headmaster Moldoveanu would lock me out of the dining hall if I showed up late. My stomach grumbled its own disapproval as I waited. I decided I'd give her two more minutes before setting out to the dining hall. I'd need to be fortified if I were to survive the next few weeks and keep my wits about me.

I walked into my sleeping chamber and fussed with the few personal items I'd brought with me; in particular, a photograph of Father and Mother, taken long ago. I set it on my nightstand, feeling a little less alone in this strange place.

A knock came promptly at my door as the sun gilded the mountains outside the window in my tower chambers. Thank the powers that be. I moved quickly to the other room and ran a hand over my winter-green skirts. Whispered voices hushed the moment I opened the door.

Ileana carried a covered tray and smiled at the young woman beside her. "This is Miss Anastasia. She is the…"

"The ward of Headmaster Moldoveanu, or, as I enjoy calling him, the Most Uncharming Man in the history of Romania." She waved her hand around and walked into my chambers. Her accent was slightly different from Ileana's but retained a similar essence. "Honestly, he's not as bad as all that. He's simply…how do you say…"

"Crotchety?" I supplied. Anastasia laughed, but didn't comment.

Ileana smiled. "I'll set this here."

I followed her over to the little settee and table while Anastasia inspected my shelves. She was plain but pretty, with wheat-colored hair and bright blue eyes.

She certainly knew how to use her assets to her advantage, especially when she flashed an infectious grin.

"Are you searching for something in particular?" I asked, noticing the methodical way her focus swept over the spines.

"I'm so pleased you're here. The boys are...*fără maniere.*" She lifted a shoulder, noting the confusion that must have shown on my face. "Most aren't very pleasant or polite. Perhaps it's the lack of oxygen. Or females. The Italian brothers are the biggest disappointment. Their noses stay stuck within their books at all times. They do not even glance in my direction! Not even when I show off my most prized attributes."

She grabbed a book from the shelf and pressed it, open, against her face, walking about in exaggerated fashion, giggling. Ileana dropped her attention to the floor, her smile wide.

"I was hoping for a gothic novel to pass the time when you're in your classes," she said, tossing the book aside. "Of course Uncle Moldoveanu wouldn't keep any such frivolity here. Did you bring any gothic novels, perchance?"

I shook my head. "Will you be taking classes as well?"

"Of course not. Uncle believes it's unbecoming for a girl of my station." Anastasia rolled her eyes and plopped onto the settee with a huff. "Though I don't care. I will be sitting in on some classes, if only to spite him. He cannot be everywhere at once."

"Has everyone else arrived?"

"All the ones who are from important families have, I believe. It's a small group this time. Uncle is said to be... out for *sânge,* they say."

"Why would they believe he's out for blood?" I asked. Ileana lifted the lid of the tray, revealing pastries and meat pies, her attention now glued to them. I politely took a bite of a savory meat-filled piece of bread and then tried not to devour it whole. Whatever these were, they were delicious.

"Castle gossip I've learned while bored to near-death. So far everyone who's in this course is either nobility or peasants with rumored links to nobility. Bastard-borns. No one knows what the point of all the royalty is, if there even is one. Don't even ask about the Italian brothers. They have not spoken to anyone but each other. I have no idea what their history is."

Anastasia popped a bit of bread into her mouth and groaned in pleasure.

"Though some believe it's part of your test," she continued. "Uncle enjoys games and intrigue. Finding common factors that may be beneficial when tracking murderers is a skill he believes all forensic students must possess." She gave me an appraising look. "You're obviously highborn. What is your family name?"

"Wadsworth. My father is a—"

"No ties to Romania?"

I blinked. "Not that I'm aware of. My mother was partly of Indian ancestry, and my father is English."

"Interesting. Perhaps not everyone is descended from this region." Anastasia bit into another piece of bread. "I heard you arrived at midnight with a young man. Are you betrothed?"

I nearly choked on my next bite of breakfast. "We're... friends. And work partners."

Anastasia grinned. "I heard he was quite handsome. Perhaps I shall marry him if you're only *work partners*." I'm not sure what she saw on my face, but she quickly added, "I'm teasing. I've got my heart set on another, though he pretends I don't exist. How was your trip here?"

A vision of the impaled body crossed my mind. I set down my meat pie, suddenly not very hungry. "Dreadful, actually." I gave a clinical account of the man on the train and the injuries he'd sustained. Ileana's bronze face had gone pale as a specter's. "I didn't get a chance to see exactly what had been shoved into his mouth. However, it was organic in nature and was a whitish color. The smell was... pungent yet familiar, though."

"*Usturoi,*" Anastasia whispered, eyes wide.

"What is that?"

"Garlic. I've read it's placed in the mouths of those believed to be... the English call them vampires."

"That's actually from a gothic novel." Ileana snorted. "*Strigoi* are disposed of differently here."

I thought back to the organic substance. It definitely fit the description of garlic, and it explained the scent. "My friend said *strigoi* are burned," I said carefully. "And all those affected drink the ashes."

"How vile." Anastasia sat forward, ravenous for more information. She reminded me of my cousin, except where Liza was obsessed with danger dashed with romance, Anastasia seemed excited solely by the danger part. "Do peasants still do such things here? In Hungary, some villagers are stuck in the old ways. Very superstitious."

"You're Hungarian?" I asked. Anastasia nodded. "But you also speak Romanian?"

"Of course. We're taught it along with our own language. I also know Italian quite well. Not that I get to use it with your classmates." She shifted her focus to Ileana. I watched the way the maid twisted her napkin in her lap, doing her best to avoid noticing Anastasia's intent gaze. "How do villagers identify *strigoi* in town? Or is it like a secret society? Like that of the dragonists?"

My attention snapped back to Anastasia. I could have sworn the illustration was burning a hole in my skirt pocket. For a moment, I felt the need to protect this drawing, keep it hidden from everyone until I discovered its origins. Which made absolutely no sense.

I withdrew the parchment and set it on the table. "Someone left this in my train compartment after the murder. Do you know what it means, if anything?"

Anastasia stared at the drawing. I had a hard time reading the expression she was guarding. A moment passed.

"Have you ever heard of the Order of the Dragon?" she asked. I shook my head. "Well, they're—"

"It's late." Ileana jumped to her feet and indicated the clock on the mantel. "Moldoveanu will toss me out if I don't get to work." She quickly gathered up our breakfast napkins and shoved the lid back on the tray with a clank that set my teeth on edge. "You both should go to the *sală de mese*. Moldoveanu will be watching."

"You mean the headmaster doesn't lock the dining hall doors after a certain time?"

Ileana gave me a pitying look. "He makes threats but doesn't follow through."

Without uttering another word, Ileana hurried from the room. Anastasia shook her head and stood. "Peasants are so superstitious. Even the mention of supernatural things makes them jumpy. Come"—she linked her arm through my own—"let's introduce you to your esteemed peers."

"Sounds as if a small herd of elephants are charging about the dining hall," I said to Anastasia as we loitered outside the doors. Feet stomped and lids clattered, the sound of carefree conversation droning over the din.

"They certainly act like a bunch of animals."

Anxiety twisted its way through the corridors of my innards. I peered inside the great oak doors. A few young men sat at tables, and others lined up to gather breakfast trays along the broad back wall, but Thomas wasn't among them. I had no idea how so few men could make that much noise in such a large space. The dining hall was grand enough—with the all-white cathedral ceilings and walls trimmed with dark wood that composed the rest of the castle's interior.

My thoughts turned to fairy tales and folklore. I could see how a castle like this would be inspiring to writers such as the Brothers Grimm. It was certainly dark enough to invoke a macabre atmosphere. I tried not to think about Father and Mother. How they'd read those stories to me and Nathaniel before bed. I needed to write to Father soon; I hoped he was feeling better. His recovery had been slow, but steady.

Suddenly I was bounced against the wall, startled from my reverie and shocked someone had not only bumped into me but also chuckled as if it weren't an affront to a young woman.

Anastasia sighed. "Miss Wadsworth, allow me to introduce you to Professor Radu. He'll be teaching you local *folclor* to round out your assessment course."

"Oh, dear. I didn't see you there." Professor Radu fussed with a napkin and inadvertently dropped a piece of bread off his tray. I bent to retrieve it the same time he did, and our heads knocked together. He didn't even blink. His skull must have been made of granite. I massaged the lump on my own head that was already forming, wincing with the throbbing. *"Îmi pare rău.* I do apologize, Miss Wadsworth. Hope I didn't spill my porridge on that lovely dress."

I glanced down at myself, relieved there was no offending porridge on my skirts. With one hand I held out the fallen bread and cautiously prodded the bruise forming under my hairline again with the other. I hoped it had knocked more sense into me than out. It certainly ached enough to make me wonder, though.

"Please don't trouble yourself, Professor," I said. "The only thing that's harmed is your bread, I'm afraid. And perhaps your head, thanks to mine."

"I'm not sure it was ever all right to begin with," Anastasia whispered.

"Er... what was that?" Radu asked, focus darting from the bread to Anastasia.

"I said I'm sure it's still delicious," she lied.

Plucking the dirt-speckled bread from my fingers as one might snatch a grape from the vine, he took a bite. I hoped my lip wasn't curling the way Anastasia's was; I didn't want to reveal the disgust roiling in my stomach.

"*Langoși cu brânză,*" he said around the mouthful of bread, bushy brows raised appreciatively. "Fried dough with feta cheese. You must try some—here."

Before I could politely decline, he pressed a piece of the bread into my hands, squishing it when he squeezed my fingers excitedly. I did my best to smile, though a bit of grease soaked into my gloves. "Thank you, Professor. If you'll excuse us, we're going to meet the other students."

Professor Radu pushed his glasses up his nose, leaving a cloudy grease smudge on one lens. "Didn't the headmaster tell you?" He eyed us closely, then clucked. "Everyone's clearing out now. Some will visit Brașov, if you'd care to join them. Don't want to walk down the mountain alone, now, do you? The woods are filled with creatures that snatch children from the path and gnaw the flesh from their bones." He sucked grease from his fingers in a show of medieval manners. "Wolves, mostly. Amongst other things."

"Wolves are eating students?" Anastasia asked, her tone implying she didn't believe it for an instant. "And to think Uncle didn't warn me at all!"

"Oh! *Pricolici!* That will be the first myth to discuss in class," he said. "So many delightful folklore rumors and legends to denounce and argue over."

The mention of child-snatching wolves chilled my

blood a few degrees. Perhaps I *had* seen signs of them while on the train, and then again in the woods close by. "What is a *prico*—"

"*Pricolici* are the spirits of murderers who come back as giant, undead wolves. Though some also believe they *are* wolves and they become *strigoi* when killed. I do hope you enjoy the lesson. Now, remember, stick to the path and don't venture into the woods, no matter what you may see. Many, many glorious dangers there!"

He tottered off, humming a buoyant tune to himself. For a brief moment I wondered what it might be like, being so utterly lost in daydreams and fiction. Then I recalled the fantastical visions my mind had produced over the last few weeks and chided myself. "Why are they teaching folklore and mythology when the course is only four weeks long?"

"All part of the mystery you're to unravel, I suppose." Anastasia lifted a shoulder. "Though Uncle believes science explains most legends."

A statement I very much concurred with, no matter how I despised agreeing with anything Moldoveanu said. I watched the professor drop his breakfast again. "I cannot believe he ate that piece of bread," I said. "I'm certain a dead bug was stuck to it."

"He didn't seem to mind," Anastasia said. "Perhaps he enjoys a bit of added protein."

I cringed as the professor bumped into another student—a bulky, dark-blond-haired young man with a jaw too square for him to be considered handsome.

"Ai grijă, bătrâne," the behemoth hissed at Radu before shouldering his way into the dining hall, knocking a smaller student aside without apology. Nasty brute. My Romanian was decent enough that I knew he'd told the old man to watch out.

"That charming specimen is Romanian nobility," Anastasia said as the blond boy disappeared into the dining hall. "His friends are slightly better."

"I can't wait to meet them," I said dryly. I deposited the oil-soaked bit of bread into a rubbish bin and blotted at the stain on my gloves. I'd need to fetch another pair before I left. "Why do you think students are traveling into the village?"

"I don't know, nor do I care." Anastasia lifted her nose in a faux-regal manner. "You won't catch me going out in this snowy weather. I doubt the others will venture far from their chambers either. Oh! I'd meant to ask Radu if I could sit in on his lessons." She bit her lip. "Would you mind if I caught up with you in a while? Will you be staying in?"

"If we're not forced to go, then I don't see why I'd leave. I'd rather explore the castle. I saw a taxidermy room I'd love to inspect."

"Extraordinar!" Anastasia exclaimed, kissing my cheeks. "I'll see you soon, then."

Raucous laughter echoed inside the room as I watched Anastasia hurry after our professor. No matter how much I wished to not do this alone, it was time to greet my fears and introduce myself to my classmates. Gradually. For now I'd show my face and take it slowly from there. Plus, it wasn't as if I didn't know anyone. Thomas would surely show up soon enough.

With my head held high, I marched into the dining hall. Five rows of long tables held curious students who grew quiet as I made my way to the opposite end of the room. One table held three young men, one being the rude, bulky boy from the hallway.

Another table had two brown-haired boys who didn't bother glancing up from their books, presumably the Italians. Their skin was a rich bronze, as if they hailed from a place near the ocean. One of them was the smaller student that the brute had bumped into without apology.

A wiry young man with dark yellow-brown skin sat across from a boy who wore spectacles and had thick ginger curls. They tucked into their meals but lifted their eyes to gawk at my arrival.

My cheeks warmed as the sound of my skirts swishing together rose above their scattered whispers. At least I had Thomas. Even if we needed to battle for spots in the academy, we could fight together. And commiserating with Anastasia was also something to look forward to.

One of the boys at Bulky's table snickered quite loudly, then whistled as if I were a common dog to be summoned. Of all the...I stopped walking and leveled a severe glare at him, cutting off his smirk with precision.

"Something amusing?" I asked, noticing the silence that descended on them as if they were soldiers who'd been called to war. When he didn't respond, I said it once more, in my best Romanian, my voice ringing out loudly in the sudden quiet.

The young man's lips twitched ever so slightly while I studied him. His hair was a shade darker than Thomas's, and his eyes were a deeper hue of brown. His deep olive complexion was alluring in the way most enjoyed in a dark hero. He was rugged, though I assumed he held a rank of sorts, based on what Anastasia had mentioned.

Bulky snickered from the dark-haired boy's side, upper lip curled. I had a feeling it was his normal expression thanks to genetics, and not one I should be offended by. How unfortunate for his parents.

I waited for the dark-haired boy to break away from

my gaze, but he fixed his eyes stubbornly on mine. A challenge to gauge how easily I could break, or something more flirtatious, I didn't care. I'd not tolerate being harassed because of my sex.

We were all here to learn. He was the one who had a problem, not I. Perhaps it was time for fathers to teach their sons how to behave around young women. They were not born superior, no matter how society falsely conditioned them. We were all equals here.

"Well?"

"I'm deciding, *domnişoară*." He lazily dragged his gaze down each inch of my body, inspecting me closely, then coughed into his hand, no doubt whispering something unseemly as Bulky burst into laughter.

A slimmer, slightly paler young man sat on his other side, shifting his eyes from the dark-haired boy, to me, then to his hands, his mouth drawing into a frown. There was something in their bone structure that made me think they were related. However, his countenance was vastly different. He flicked his attention around as if it were a fly landing on different spots, then buzzing off just out of reach. He seemed so familiar...

I gasped as recognition set in.

"You. I know you." He'd been on the train with Thomas and me. I was certain of it. He'd been the nervous passenger I'd wanted to question. He shifted in his seat, staring at the grain of the wood, ignoring me all together. His skin seemed to darken before my gaze.

I'd all but forgotten about the annoying dark-haired boy, and almost missed the fire that lit his eyes, as I gathered my skirts and headed for a table of my own.

EIGHT
VILLAIN WITH A HERO'S FACE

DINING HALL
SALĂ DE MESE
BRAN CASTLE
2 DECEMBER 1888

"You do make the best entrances, Wadsworth. Half the young men at that table want to marry you now. I'll have to work twice as hard on my fencing skills to defend your honor."

I loosed a breath as Thomas folded himself into the seat across from me, plate piled high with savories from different regions, likely intended to accommodate students from across Europe. And sweets. Mrs. Harvey had been right about his affinity for desserts. I'd been so distracted by the boy I was certain was on board the train, I hadn't noticed Thomas near the buffet.

"I hardly believe that's true. I just made enemies, is what I did." I stole a scone from his plate after he'd slathered clotted cream on it. "Anyway, I dislike *all* of the young men at that table, Cresswell. No need to turn in your scalpel for a foil just yet."

"Careful, now. You've voiced the same charming sentiments about me. I get jealous rather easily. I want to have a duel, not raze the academy or burn it to the ground. Though it might improve Moldoveanu's attitude, actually. Promise you'll visit me in my cell?"

I smiled despite the topic and inspected my friend. "You know no one could ever annoy me as much as you, Cresswell. Hopefully they'll think twice before mocking me again."

"I'm quite certain it won't be the last time you're teased." Thomas grinned while he covered another scone with cream. "Men enjoy the hunt. You have now proven you aren't easily won, which makes you an interesting challenge. Why do you think so many heads are mounted on walls? Displaying trophies of our accomplishments is like saying 'I'm strong and virile. Just look at that stag head in the study. I not only hunted it, I set the trap and coaxed it into my lair. Here's some brandy, let's pound our chests and shoot something.'"

"You're saying you'd like to trap me and hang my severed head above the mantle, then? That's so utterly romantic. Do tell me more."

"Ahem." Someone cleared their throat, interrupting us. "Would you mind if I sat here? *Vă rog?*"

Even while sitting, Thomas somehow managed to stare down his nose at the dark-haired boy who'd rudely laughed at me earlier and was now standing beside our table. There was nothing lighthearted in Thomas's expression now.

"If you promise you'll be nice." Thomas slowly pushed his chair back, the limbs screeching against the floor in protest. He'd not moved far enough to allow the young man to come between us. I was reminded of how tall and long-limbed he was, and how he could use it as another weapon in his arsenal. "I'd hate to see Miss Wadsworth embarrass you. Again."

Tension pooled from him in thick waves—so dark and turbulent I was nearly pulled under. I'd never known Thomas to show such strong emotions before and thought there might be something else going on besides his annoyance on my behalf. Perhaps Thomas had already encountered the dark-haired boy and it hadn't gone very positively.

It didn't take much to deduce that this wouldn't end well. The last thing either of us needed to contend with was Thomas being expelled for—whatever he was about to unleash. Right now he was every bit the villain with a hero's face.

"How may we help you, Mr....?" I allowed the question to hang in the air.

As if Hell wasn't unfolding around him, the young

man angled himself toward me in an intimate way, and I reconsidered who was in danger of being thrown out of the academy: Thomas might very well be the one holding *me* back from landing a well-deserved slap.

"I apologize for my earlier behavior, *domnişoară*," he said, accent soft and lilting. "I also beg forgiveness for my companions. Andrei"—he pointed to the brute, who nodded curtly in response—"and Wilhelm, my cousin."

My attention drifted back over to the sickly young man from the train. Wilhelm's color was even darker than before. Such an odd shade. It appeared as if he'd gotten smudges of reddish dirt on his face. I'd never seen a rash quite so horrible before. Beads of sweat dotted his brow line.

"Your cousin seems unwell," Thomas said. "Perhaps you should tend to him instead."

We watched as Wilhelm hoisted a large black cloak around his shoulders and hunched toward the door. I needed to speak with him, find out what he might know about the victim from the train.

The dark-haired boy moved into my line of sight. *"Permite-mi să mă prezint.* Er . . . allow me to introduce myself properly."

He offered a shy smile, but it faded a bit while I kept my expression neutral. If he thought turning his charm on exceedingly high would endear him to me, he was quite mistaken. He sat taller, and an air of station dropped across him as if it were a velvet cloak settling into place.

"My name is Nicolae Alexandru Vladimir Aldea. Prince of Romania."

Thomas snorted, but the young prince kept his gaze locked onto mine. I inhaled sharply, but made sure surprise didn't show in my features, assuming he'd dropped his title in hopes of seeing the reaction he'd gotten from some other young men and women.

My suspicion was confirmed when his smile faltered, then vanished altogether the longer I went without reacting. I'd not allow myself to be treated so poorly, then swoon in the next breath. His title could likely buy much, but it couldn't purchase my affections.

The entire room went silent as a church service while they waited for me to speak. Or bow. I was probably breaking all manner of protocol by not standing immediately and dropping into a curtsy. I smiled sweetly and leaned in.

"I'd say it was pleasant meeting you, Your Highness, but I was raised to not utter untruths."

To keep from being entirely improper, I offered a slight incline of my head and stood. The expression on Prince Nicolae's face was exceptional. As if I'd discarded my glove and slapped him with it in front of all these witnesses. I almost felt sorry for him—it was probably the first time anyone had offended him so ruthlessly. Whatever was he to do with someone who wouldn't hang on his every princely word?

"Mr. Cresswell," I nodded toward my friend, "I'll meet you outside."

The boy with the red curls, sitting nearby, shook his head as I gathered my skirts. I couldn't tell if he was impressed or disgusted by my audacity. Without looking back, I left the room. Clanking sounds of forks falling onto plates, mixed with Thomas's deep chuckle, accompanied me into the hall, where I allowed myself a small laugh of my own. Even the Italian brothers had lifted their attention from their studies, their eyes wide as petri dishes.

My satisfaction was cut short when I noticed Headmaster Moldoveanu standing there near the open doorway, vein pulsing in his forehead. He moved swiftly toward me, and I swore a great winged beast was prowling along behind, talons scraping the stone. I blinked. It was only his shadow, made enormous by the torchlight.

"Careful whom you make enemies of, Miss Wadsworth. I'd hate for more tragedy to befall your already fractured family. From my understanding, the Wadsworth name and lineage are nearly wiped from existence."

I flinched. Father had posted a rather vague obituary regarding my brother's death, though the headmaster sounded as if he suspected foul play. He inspected me closely, lip peeled back in what was either a smile or sneer.

"I wonder how strong your father would remain should something terrible happen to his last remaining child. Opium is an unpleasant habit. Rather hard to recover from completely. I'm sure you're aware of that, though. You seem to be mildly intelligent. For a girl. I hope I've made myself clear."

"How did you—"

"It is my duty to unearth every morsel about prospective students. And I do mean every crumb. Do not make the mistake of believing your secrets remain yours. I uncover them from both the dead and the living. I find truth pays quite well once discovered."

A coil of slick fear twisted in my intestines. He was threatening me, and there wasn't a thing I could do about it. He stared a beat longer, as if he could glare me from existence, then marched into the dining hall. I slumped only after he'd made it to the far side of the room.

"Breakfast is now over," he announced. "You may do as you wish for the remainder of the day."

I quickly ran to my room to fetch my winter coat and a new pair of gloves, anxious to be outside this wretched castle and its miserable inhabitants.

NINE
CROWN'S CITY

TRAIL THROUGH WOODS
POTECĂ
BRAŞOV
2 DECEMBER 1888

"Prince Pompous might not be your biggest admirer, Wadsworth." Thomas nudged me with his shoulder, doing a terrible job of hiding his pleasure at my new mortal enemy. "Once Moldoveanu left, he even broke a plate against the wall and cut his fingers. Blood splattered in the eggs. Very dramatic."

"You sound a bit jealous you didn't think to break glassware first."

I slipped over an icy paving stone, and Thomas steadied me, slowly dropping my arm and standing at an almost respectable distance. Excitement was present in each of his motions. He was practically skipping to

Braşov, also known as the Crown's City, according to his endless banter.

I'd watched Wilhelm scurry out of the castle, staggering a bit here and there, and rushed to grab Thomas. I wished to speak with the boy and ask what he'd seen on the train, though he seemed intent on evading me at all costs. His avoidance only made his guilt seem more likely.

Wilhelm's skin appeared a bit...I couldn't be sure. The olive tone looked as if it had been almost entirely replaced with dark patches. As if fever had brought on deep flushing. I could have sworn it was even worse than in the dining hall. I tried to think of any known infection that would cause two different rashes but failed to recollect even one. It certainly wasn't scarlet fever— I'd know those symptoms anywhere.

We trailed far enough behind Wilhelm that he either didn't notice us or assumed we were heading into the village for our own purposes. I wanted to study him, see where he was going first. Then perhaps we'd gain some extra insight. If we assaulted him with questions now, he'd likely change his course. I'd filled Thomas in on my suspicions, and he agreed it was the best action to take.

I kept my attention on the ground, noting the footprints Wilhelm left behind in the newly fallen snow and the even strides he'd made. The staggering seemed to have stopped, though a fresh patch of steaming vomit lay just off the trail. I did not inspect it closely and moved along as fast as I could. Maybe Wilhelm was simply on his way to see someone about a remedy for his ailment. Though why he would travel to the village and not inquire about a doctor in the castle was strange.

I stuck my hands in my pockets and nearly slipped again. I'd forgotten about the parchment with all the fuss in the dining hall. I glanced around, ensuring that Thomas and I were alone on the trail save for Wilhelm, who was too far ahead to pay us any mind. I stopped and dug around my pocket, realizing the paper was no longer there.

"Tell me I didn't quit my unseemly smoking habit only for you to pick it up."

"Pardon?" I patted down my skirt pockets, the interior pockets of my winter coat. Nothing. My heart thudded. If I hadn't shown it to Anastasia and Ileana this morning, I might be worried that I'd simply imagined the drawing. I turned my pockets out—they were empty.

"What are you looking for, Wadsworth?"

"My dragon," I said, trying to recall if I'd placed it back in my pocket before heading down to the dining hall. "I must have left it in my chambers."

Thomas stared at me for a moment with the strangest expression. "Where did you find this dragon? I'm sure all manner of scientists will want to speak with you and see the specimen. Small enough to fit in your pocket, too. Quite the discovery."

"It was a drawing in my train compartment," I said, letting out a deep sigh. "I found it after the guards came to take the body."

"Oh. I see." He suddenly turned and continued on toward the village, leaving me openmouthed in his wake.

I grabbed my skirts, mindful of not exposing any area above my boots, and hurried after him. "What was that about?"

Thomas nodded at the brush and brambles on the edge of the trail. I followed his gaze and noticed what appeared to be fresh paw prints from a large dog in the snow near the edge of the forest. They seemed to be following a trail of Wilhelm's vomit. I hoped to avoid both contracting whatever it was he was suffering from, and whatever animal was following him. I watched the boy stagger again along the path, nearly cresting the hill. I wanted to run after him and offer an arm—he truly wasn't looking well.

Thomas trekked through the snow, keeping his attention on our classmate.

"We don't want to get caught out here once the sun

goes down later," Thomas said. "It's winter, and food is scarce in the woods. Best not to tempt our fate by risking an encounter with the wolves."

For once, I was too annoyed to imagine the forest coming alive with beasts. I sped up, my focus set entirely on Thomas as I reached for him. "Are you going to pretend as if I didn't ask about that dragon?"

He stopped walking and lifted the hat from his head, dusting off a bit of snow that had fallen from branches above us before securing it again. "If you must know, I drew it."

"Oh." My shoulders slumped. I should have been happy there was nothing more sinister to the drawing, relieved a murderer hadn't sneaked into my compartment and left a taunting clue. And yet I couldn't deny my disappointment. "Why didn't you simply tell me that sooner?"

"Because I didn't intend for you to see it," he said with a sigh. "Seemed rather rude to just blurt out: 'Apologies. Please don't ask about the dragon. Very touchy subject matter at the moment.'"

"I was unaware you sketched so well."

Even as I said it, something nudged the edges of my memory. Thomas hunched over a corpse in Uncle's laboratory, drawing remarkably accurate images of each postmortem, hands smudged with both ink and charcoal he didn't bother cleaning away.

"Yes, well. It's a family trait."

"It was...lovely," I said. "Why a dragon?"

Thomas set his mouth in a grim line. I didn't expect him to answer, but he took a deep breath and replied softly, "My mother had a painting made of it. I recall staring at it while she lay dying."

Without uttering another word, he marched off through the snow. So that was it. We'd come much too close to an emotional fence he'd erected long ago. He never spoke of his family, and I longed to know more details of how he'd come to be. I collected myself and hurried after him, noticing with a jolt that Wilhelm was no longer in view. I moved as swiftly as I could, though part of me now worried there was nothing out of the ordinary about Wilhelm's train journey. It was simply another fantasy conjured up in my cursed imagination.

We were nearly to Braşov, and I was quite sick of sloshing through snow and ice. The hem of my skirts was soaked through and was as stiff as corpse fingers. Wearing close-fitting breeches and my riding habit would have been a better idea. Actually, staying inside the castle and studying the anatomy display cases and taxidermy chambers would have been the smartest idea yet. Not only were we wasting our time following a sick boy, we were miserably cold and wet. I was near convinced I could feel tendrils of my father's worry over catching an influenza wrap around my sensibilities.

"Ah. There it is." I caught glimpses of the buildings Thomas pointed out, his smile turning a bit more sincere. Nothing more than flashes of color through the evergreens, but excitement urged my feet to move faster. Then, as we started down another hill, I fully spied the gem that had been hidden between the craggy mountains.

We trudged along the snow-covered path, our attention fixed on the colorful village. Buildings stood crammed together as if they were pretty ladies in waiting, their exteriors painted salmon and butter and the palest ocean blue. There were other buildings, too, made of pale stone with terra-cotta colored roofs.

A church was the grandest sight of all, its Gothic spire pointing at the heavens. From where we stood, we could see its red-tiled roof spreading over a massive building made of light-colored stone with stained glass windows. My eyes stung before I blinked my awe away. Perhaps the trip hadn't been such a waste of time after all.

"*Biserica Neagră.*" Thomas grinned. "The Black Church. During the summer, people gather to hear organ music that pours from its cathedral. It also has well over one hundred Anatolian carpets. It's absolutely stunning."

"You know the strangest facts."

"Are you impressed? I didn't bother pointing out it had been renovated after a great fire, or that its blackened walls were how it received its name. Didn't want you to swoon too much. We do have a suspect to inquire after."

I smiled but remained silent, not wanting to share my fear of this being a fool's errand. Wilhelm had likely been just a passenger on the train and had already been ill. Sickness explained his jittery actions—he very well might have been feeling faint, and the stress of witnessing a murder proved too much.

We walked in silence, finally arriving in the old village. My feet were no longer numb but felt as if I'd been stomping about on bits of glass in my stockings. Liza would be enchanted by the way the snow dusted the rooftops, a sprinkling of sugar electrified by the rays of the sun. I would have to write to her later tonight.

I slowed to a halt, scanning the cobblestone streets for the black cloak belonging to Wilhelm. I saw a flutter of dark material disappear into a shop with a sign I couldn't read. I pointed it out to Thomas.

"I think he went in there."

"Lead the way, Wadsworth. I'm simply along for my brute strength and charm."

We entered a store that sold parchment and journals and all manner of things one needed to write or draw with. It wasn't an odd place for a student to visit. Wilhelm very well might be in need of supplies for class. I drifted down narrow aisles stacked with rolled paper.

It had a pleasing ink and paper smell that reminded me of sticking my nose in an old book. Antique pages were a scent that should be bottled up and sold to those who adored the aroma.

I smiled at the shop owner, a wrinkled old man with a generous grin. "We're looking for our classmate. I believe he came in a moment ago?"

The old man drew his brows together and responded rapidly in Romanian, his words too fast for me to process. Thomas stepped forward and spoke just as quickly. They continued back and forth for a few moments before Thomas turned to me and motioned toward the door. I'd finally gathered the gist of it, but Thomas translated anyway.

"He said his son just brought a new delivery in, and no one else has been in all morning."

I stared out the window at a line of shops. Their signs and windows made it clear what wares they were selling. Pastries and fabrics and hats and shoes. Wilhelm could have entered any of them. "We might as well split up and check each business."

We bid good-bye to the shop owner and exited. I walked down to the next shop and paused. A dress made for royalty hung proudly in the center of the bay window, stealing my breath. It had a pale yellow gem-encrusted bodice that gradually tapered into shades of butter, then winter white at the waist. The gown's skirts appeared as if clouds of white, cream, and pale yellow tulle swept over one another in the most magnificent gradient.

Its stitches were crafted by a deft hand, and I couldn't help but move closer for a better look. I all but pressed my face against the thick, wavy glass separating me from the garment. Gemstones were splattered across the low-cut bodice—stars set against the daylight.

"What exquisite artistry! It's...heaven. It's a daydream in wearable form. Or sunshine."

It was gorgeous enough that I forgot about our mission for a moment. When Thomas hadn't answered or even mocked me for getting distracted, I turned. He was watching me with deep amusement before snapping out of his own reverie. Straightening to his full height, he jerked his thumb at the next storefront.

"The neckline on that beauty would certainly cause an uproar. And quite a few...daydreams." He flashed a wolfish grin as I crossed my arms. "Not that you couldn't handle yourself when fighting off the hordes of gentleman suitors. I believe you could manage that just fine. Your father, however, *did* say to chaperone you everywhere and keep you out of trouble."

"If that's true, then he shouldn't have asked you to be my caretaker."

"Oh? And what would you ask of me? Should I forsake your father's wishes?"

The glint of an unexpected challenge lit his features. I hadn't seen such a serious expression since the last time he'd grasped me in his arms and allowed his lips the freedom of communicating his deepest desires without words. I found myself momentarily breathless as I recalled—in vivid detail—the sensation and rightness of our very wrong kiss.

"What do you want from me, Audrey Rose? What are your wishes?"

I took a step back, heart pounding. I wanted more than anything to tell him how afraid I was of my recent hauntings. I wanted him to reassure me that I would heal in time. That I would once again wield my blade without fear of the dead rising. I longed for him to promise me he'd never cage me were we to become betrothed. But how could I utter such things while he was being vulnerable? To admit that the fissure inside me kept growing and I'd no idea if it would ever truly be mended? That perhaps I might end up destroying him along with myself?

"Right now?" I stepped closer, watching the column of his throat tighten as he nodded. "I wish to know what Wilhelm saw on the train, if anything. I want to know why two people were murdered—staked through the heart—as if they were *strigoi*. And I want to find clues before we potentially have another Ripper case on our hands."

Thomas exhaled a bit too loudly for it to be casual. Part of me wished to take it back, to tell him I loved him and wanted everything I could see he was offering in his eyes. Perhaps I was the worst kind of fool. I kept my mouth shut. Better for him to be temporarily dismayed than permanently hurt by my wavering emotions.

"Let's go hunting, then"—he offered an arm— "shall we?"

I hesitated. For a moment I thought I saw a shadow angling toward us from around the building. My heart picked up speed as I waited for its owner to step forth. Thomas followed my gaze, a crinkle in his brow, before turning back to inspect me.

"I think it best if we split up and find Wilhelm, Cresswell."

"As the lady wishes."

Thomas stared at me a moment too long, then pressed a chaste kiss to my cheek before I knew what he was doing. He drew back slowly, mischief flickering in his eyes, as I quickly glanced around for witnesses to such untowardness. The shadow that I'd sworn was moving in our direction was gone.

Shaking off the feeling of being watched by things I couldn't see, I admitted to myself that I'd been bested by my imagination once again and entered the dress shop. Bolts of fabrics in rich colors spilled from rolls like they were silken blood freed from their host. I ran my hands over the satins and fine knits as I made my way toward the work desk near the back.

A short, rotund woman called hello. *"Buna."*

"Buna. Has anyone been in here? A young man? Very sick. Um...*foarte bolnav."*

The gray-haired woman didn't break her dimpled smile, and I hoped she understood my Romanian. Her gaze traveled over me swiftly, as if assessing whether I had any snakes hidden up my sleeves or other nasty tricks she should be wary of.

"No young men here today."

On the wall behind her, a sketch of a young woman caught my attention. There was a series of notes around the image, written in Romanian. Chills lingered on my skin. The woman's blond hair reminded me of Anastasia in a way. "What does that say?"

The shop owner brushed away strips of fabric and motioned at the calendar on her table, pointing her scissors to *Vineri.* Friday. "Missing since three nights ago. She was seen walking near woods. Then *nimic.* Nothing. *Pricolici.*"

"That's awful." My breathing stilled for a moment. This woman truly believed an undead werewolf prowled the area, hunting for victims. However, it was the thought of being lost in those dreadful woods that made my limbs go weak. I hoped for the girl's sake she'd made it somewhere safe. If snow and ice fell all that night, it would have made survival impossible.

I picked out new stockings and, after paying the shop owner, replaced my sodden ones with them. They were thick and warm and made my feet feel as if they were enveloped in soft clouds.

"Thank you... *mulțumesc.* I hope the girl is discovered soon."

A commotion outside drew my attention. I watched men and women run down the cobblestone street, their eyes wide and unblinking. The mild-looking shop owner drew an iron pipe from behind the counter, her mouth set in a sharp line.

"Get back, girl. This is no good. *Foarte rău.*"

Fear stitched itself into my veins, but I snipped it away. I would not succumb to such emotions here. I was in a new location and wouldn't fall into old habits. No matter if something was thought to be very bad. There was nothing to be afraid of other than our own worries. I was quite convinced no one was hunting people along these streets, especially during daylight hours.

"I'll be all right."

Without hesitation, I pushed the door open, gathered my skirts, and ran toward the small crowd that had sprung up near an alley at the end of the shopping district.

Chills invaded the cracks of my emotional armor, sliding their icy fingers along my skin. I gave in to their prodding and shivered in the waning morning light.

Another storm was approaching. Bits of ice and snow stumbled along in front of an angry gray cloud, a warning of worse things to follow. Much worse things.

TEN

MOST PECULIAR

VILLAGE STREETS
STRĂZILE DIN SAT
BRAȘOV
2 DECEMBER 1888

I dipped down, low enough to peer between people as they shifted around the scene. My first glimpse at what had caught their attention was of a foot that belonged to someone lying on the snow-covered ground.

Judging from the loafer, whoever the villagers were staring at was male. Panic seeped back in when I scanned the crowd.

I was searching for a distinctly tall young man. One with straight brows and a crooked tilt to his mouth. Thomas was nowhere to be found. He was *always* where trouble lurked. Something cold and heavy pooled in my core.

"No."

I lunged forward as if I were nothing more than a marionette on a string. If anything happened to Thomas...I couldn't finish the thought. Fear thrummed in my cells.

Using my smaller stature, I shoved my way through the young men, terror allotting me strength and a steely reserve as I wove my way through their limbs. I pushed one of them when he didn't move, and he stumbled into someone else. They began yelling in Romanian, and from what I interpreted, they weren't exchanging pleasantries. I knew I was being unforgivably rude, but if Thomas had been hurt, I would have plowed through the entire country if I had to, leaving bones and ash in my wake.

When the body finally came into view, I clamped my teeth together, biting down on shock. Lying in a motionless sprawl was Wilhelm. I closed my eyes, relieved it wasn't Thomas, and felt horrid for it. I was despicable, and it wasn't even the first time I'd experienced relief at someone else's expense.

Once that monstrous feeling passed, I turned my full attention to the boy. There was no discernible injury that I could see from where I stood. Judging from the absolute stillness, I knew Wilhelm was not breathing; no clouds of breath puffed into the frigid air. There did appear to be some slight discoloration and foaming around his mouth, though.

Aside from him lying in a heap, there was no disturbance in the snow around him. No one had attempted
to revive or even touch him. Not that I imagined they
would. Unless there was a physician close by, no one
would be trained. If anything, the villagers might be
too afraid to get close. Muscles in my abdomen twisted.
He was so young. I should have trusted my instincts
earlier when he was so clearly in distress.

I shifted closer, noticing a set of footprints a few feet
away leading down the alley. I narrowed my eyes, wondering if it was the path a murderer had taken. Perhaps
Wilhelm had died of natural causes, though young men
didn't usually keel over while walking through villages.
Sure, his skin had had a reddish tinge, but I did not
think he'd been sickly enough for sudden death.

I flipped through pages of medical theories and prog-
noses in my mind. An aneurysm wasn't entirely out of
the question, I supposed; that might explain the lack
of outward injury and slight foam at the mouth. But it
did not answer the mystery of his discoloration.

Someone would need to send for the headmaster.
One of his students was *dead*. And there was no better
place for forensic examination than our nearby academy. At least that was a positive glimmer amidst this
horror.

I bent down, doing my best to not touch Wilhelm
and risk contaminating the scene. Uncle's lessons barged

into my brain. If there were foul intentions involved, our murderer was likely present, watching. I scanned the crowd, but not one person stood out.

Men and women, all ages and sizes, stared. They whispered accusations in a foreign tongue, but I could read the distrust on their features. The way their eyes narrowed, the many times they crossed themselves or absently touched holy articles on their person, as if reassuring themselves of God's presence here.

Leaving the Lord out of the equation, I tried recalling any other sudden disease that might have taken my classmate. I doubted a myocardial infarction had killed him.

Unless he'd had a poor heart from childhood. As strong a possibility as any. My mother had suffered from such a condition; we were lucky she hadn't been torn from us sooner. Nathaniel had said it was her iron will that had kept her alive for so long.

I stared at the footprints again, stomach sinking. They were probably unrelated and Wilhelm had succumbed to whatever he'd been suffering from. The earlier murder that had occurred in this village was blatant—a man had been staked through the heart, not killed in some unidentifiable manner that resembled natural causes.

"Are you hard of hearing, Miss Wadsworth?"

At the sound of Moldoveanu's deep voice, I jerked

away from the corpse and stood. My cheeks burned when I realized he must have been addressing me for some time for him to inject that extra venom into his tone. The headmaster had certainly arrived on the scene quickly. His whole being was imposing, looming over both me and the body at my feet. Some innate mechanism urged me to step back. I glanced around, searching for Thomas. "No, Headmaster. I was thinking."

"Clearly that isn't your strong suit, Miss Wadsworth." Headmaster Moldoveanu's gaze sliced me in half. "Move along and let me do the real work."

Never in all my life had I had such a vicious urge to verbally attack someone before. He didn't even have to say what he was blatantly insinuating: that men could handle it better.

A woman near the body wiped tears from her child's face, screeching about something that set the crowd into another rush of arguing. Moldoveanu barked out orders in Romanian for everyone to stand back, forestalling the crowd from further agitation.

"Get on with moving out of my way before I freeze to death." He gritted his teeth and spoke English slowly, as if I were a complete dullard. "This isn't some excursion to the seamstress, though perhaps that's where you truly belong."

Heat flared across my cheeks once more. I took a small step to the side but refused to move to the outer ring of the crowd. I didn't care if he expelled me from the course for my insubordination. I would not be treated as if my mind were inferior because I'd been blessed with the ability to bear children. I mentally screamed at myself to let it pass, but I couldn't obey the simple command, consequences be damned.

I drew myself up. "I belong with a scalpel in my hands, sir. You've no right to—"

Out of the corner of my eye, I could have sworn the victim's finger twitched. My blood froze along with the harsh words I'd meant to say to the headmaster. Thoughts of deadly electrical machines, steam-powered hearts, and stolen organs flashed across my mind. Everything around me stilled into deafening silence—the tenor of murmured voices, Moldoveanu's taunt, sniffles and whispered prayers, the sound of sleet pelting against stones, all replaced by a vast nothing—while my memory tortured me with images of my mother's lifeless body struggling to come back from death.

I could still see her arms and torso lurching from that table. Still smell the acrid scent of burnt flesh and hair wafting throughout the laboratory. Sweet and revolting. That horrid, sinking feeling of both dread and hope as I groped for a pulse that had long since stopped.

A shutter came loose in a gust of wind, banging itself against the wall near a darkened window that faced the alleyway. Curtains fluttered inward, and I was almost certain I saw a cloaked figure vanish within their shadowy folds. I staggered back, ignoring the snide whispers from villagers that pierced my crumbling emotional wall, and ran.

It had been the same nearly each time I examined a corpse. I needed to breathe. I needed to lay these images to rest or else I'd truly become the failure Headmaster Moldoveanu thought me to be. I raced around the corner and stopped, panting as I stared at a brick wall. I wasn't religious, but I prayed I wouldn't be sick. Not here, possibly in front of the awful headmaster.

A tear squeezed its way out from under my eyelid. If I couldn't find a way to banish my hauntings, I'd never make it through this course and gain admittance to the academy.

Shadows thick as tar cut across my vision, and I knew who was there before he spoke. I held a hand up, stalling him. "If you say one thing about what happened back there, I will never speak to you again, Cresswell. Don't push me."

"Knowing I'm not the only gentleman you say such endearing things to is comforting, *Domnişoară* Wadsworth. Though not entirely shocking."

I swung around, surprised to find myself facing Prince Nicolae. A muscle twitched in his jaw as if he were chomping down on saying something ruder. His expression was a finely sharpened dagger, cutting every section of my face it landed on.

"I've heard rumors about your involvement with the Ripper murders. While I've yet to be impressed, I'm going to be watching you." He slowly circled me. "I saw you following my cousin; you cannot deny it. Then peering over his body as if it were a delicacy to be savored. Perhaps you slipped him something fatal. He told me you were on the train, traveling to Bucharest with him. An opportunity, yes?"

I blinked. Surely he didn't believe I would abandon the study of death to create it. "I—"

"You're *blestemat*," he all but snarled. "Cursed." A sob interrupted my thoughts as the prince angrily swiped at his eyes and turned away.

I shut my mouth. Whatever he was saying right now, the wrath and accusations—it was grief speaking. Lashing out. Searching for some sense amidst a part of life we had no control over. I knew that feeling all too well. I made to reach for him, then dropped my gloved hand. This was a pain I didn't wish to share with anyone. Not even a perceived enemy.

"I—I'm sorry for your loss. I know words are hollow, but I am truly sorry."

Prince Nicolae lifted his eyes to mine and clenched his fists. "Not as sorry as you will be."

He backed down the alley and left me shivering on

my own. If I wasn't cursed before, it certainly felt as if he'd set some darkness loose on me with that proclamation. Snow and ice began falling a bit more heavily, like the world was now mourning my eventual loss.

Thomas skidded around the corner the same moment the prince exited the alleyway, smashing his shoulder into my friend. Ignoring the slight, Thomas strode toward me, the corners of his mouth turned down at whatever he saw in my expression.

"Are you all right, Wadsworth? I was in a rather interesting argument with the...baker and came as fast as I could manage."

My breath fogged before me. I did not wish to know why he was fighting with a baker. Or if it was even true based on his slight hesitation. Though it was hard to retain any uneasy feelings with that ridiculous image barging into my mind. "Prince Nicolae believes I'm responsible for Wilhelm's death. Apparently he saw us following him, and I didn't appear appalled enough by the sight of his cousin's corpse."

Thomas was unusually silent a moment, studying my face with care. I fought the urge to fidget under his inspection. "How *did* you feel upon seeing the body?"

Snow seeped into my overcoat, coaxing an involuntary shiver. Thomas made to offer his warmer wool coat, but I shook my head, not caring for the undertone of his question. There was no way I could face this academy and its wretchedness if I knew Thomas doubted me as well.

"I felt as any student of forensics should. What are you truly asking, Cresswell? Do you think me incapable, as our headmaster believes?"

"Not at all." He motioned toward the end of the alley, where the crowd was growing by the moment. "However, grieving or being affected by something doesn't make you weak, Wadsworth. Sometimes strength is knowing when to tend to yourself for a bit."

"Is that what I should do?" I asked, my voice deadly quiet.

"If you want the truth? Yes." Thomas stood taller. "I believe it would be healing for you to acknowledge the fact it's only been a few weeks since your loss. You need time to grieve. I think we ought to return to London— we can apply to the academy again in the spring."

I stood there, mind churning. Surely Thomas and I were not actually having a conversation about what *he* deemed best for me. Before I could formulate a response, he plowed on.

"There's no reason we need to be here now, Wadsworth. Your uncle is an exceptional teacher, and we will continue learning under his tutelage until you're well." He took a deep breath as if gathering courage to continue. "I'll write to your father immediately and inform him of our change in plans. It's for the best."

Imaginary bars erupted around me, caging me in. This was precisely the reason for my trepidation regarding a betrothal. I could feel my autonomy slipping from my grasp each time Thomas offered advice on what I *ought* to do. Wasn't that how it happened? Basic rights and wants were slowly eroded by someone else's idea of how one should act.

I would never know what was best for myself with someone offering unsolicited advice at each step. Mistakes were a learning experience, not the end of the universe. So what if I were making one now, pushing myself forward instead of confronting ghosts of the past? The choice was mine to make, not anyone else's. I thought Thomas knew that much about me. And once upon a time he had, but somehow he was no longer thinking with his head. Somewhere along the line, Mr. Thomas Cresswell—or rather, the unfeeling automaton he'd been accused of being—had grown a tender human heart.

I could not bear for him to slip into an approved male role in society and treat me as if I were something to be protected and coddled. I respected and admired him and expected the same in return. I knew I needed to be harsh to jolt him back to himself, though I did not relish the task.

Hearts were beautifully fierce yet fragile things. And I did not wish to break Thomas's.

"If there is one thing you listen to, Mr. Cresswell," I said, my voice even and steady, "let it be this. Please do not make the mistake of telling me what's best for me, as if *you* are the sole authority on the subject. If you wish to return to London, you are free to do so, but I shall not be accompanying you. I hope that I've made myself perfectly clear."

I didn't wait for him to respond. I spun around and headed for the castle, leaving both Thomas and our fallen classmate behind as my own heart stuttered.

ELEVEN
SOMETHING WICKED

ANASTASIA'S CHAMBER
CAMERA ANASTASIEI
BRAN CASTLE
2 DECEMBER 1888

"Ileana said Prince Nicolae has done nothing but smash his room to bits since they brought Wilhelm's body back. Your class is to perform the autopsy tomorrow after Uncle inspects it."

Anastasia abruptly dismissed her lady's maid and stood before her looking glass, plucking pins from her golden braids and rearranging them in an intricate design about her crown. Her chambers were slightly larger than my own and were located on the floor above our classrooms. Moldoveanu made sure his ward didn't want for anything. It was an indication he was in possession of a heart after all.

My new friend prattled on about castle gossip regarding the prince, but I found my mind drifting away with thoughts of the building itself. While the academy was mostly empty for the Christmas holiday—save for our group of hopeful attendees and a skeleton castle staff—the corridors leading to these chambers were filled with nooks and alcoves that contained both scientific and religious sculptures. Tapestries depicting impalement and other morbid scenes hung between the nooks. Anastasia told me they were events from Vlad's reign, victories immortalized within these halls.

On one pedestal, a thorax sat encased in glass, lungs in another. One I dared not inspect too closely featured a serpent coiled around a cross. Parts of the corridor reminded me of Uncle's laboratory and his specimen collection. Other sections made my skin crawl. Though I'd prefer to be lost in thoughts of the dark castle rather than face the current conversation about Nicolae.

"Violent behavior is an indication of emotional instability, according to a journal I read last summer," she said, unfazed by the fact I wasn't chatting back. "It'll likely affect Prince Nicolae's place here. I doubt he'll regain his composure before your assessment course is over. Pity for him. Not so awful for the rest of you."

Gossiping about the prince while he was mourning the loss of his cousin set my stomach churning with guilt. I wanted to gain a permanent spot in the academy but didn't want my entry to be based upon impaired competition. Or lack of competition because of sudden death. I supposed I also felt a bit ill for the way I'd spoken to Thomas before leaving him in the alley. Wilhelm's lifeless corpse flashed across my mind. I also couldn't stop worrying about my reaction to the body. Each time I came near a cadaver, I saw reminders I wished to forget.

If I didn't deal with these terrors soon, I'd not survive the academy. A fact, I suspected, that would greatly please Headmaster Moldoveanu. I shifted on the large settee, running gloved hands over its wooden arms.

"Why does your uncle allow young women into the academy if he despises their presence?"

"He is technically not related to me." Anastasia reached for her journal. "Though he would have been had my aunt not been murdered."

"I'm sorry to hear that," I said, not wanting to intrude and inquire after potentially lurid details. "Losing a loved one is one of the most horrid things a person can endure."

"Thank you." She offered a sad smile. "My aunt was not interested in being a cosseted lady, locked away and dictated to by her husband. Moldoveanu respected her. Never pushed for her to remain by his side."

Anastasia tucked a golden strand behind her ear, and I was grateful for the slight break in the conversation. I was momentarily stunned. Moldoveanu's situation with his former betrothed was so similar to what I'd been upset with Thomas over. I did not forgive the headmaster for his reprehensible behavior, but I did understand him a bit more.

"After her body was discovered, he changed," Anastasia said. "I know it's hard to believe, but he's so cold because he thinks it might end up saving a life one day. It's also why I'm not allowed to actually become a student, though he permits me to sneak into classes sometimes."

Anastasia opened her journal, and I did not press for further information regarding her aunt's murder. I glanced around for a distraction of my own and noticed that a book of Latin phrases lay propped open on the table before me. We needed to be proficient in Latin in order to pass this course. Another thing I needed to improve on, though I had a decent, basic knowledge thanks to my uncle's lessons. Moments slowly dragged by in silence. I couldn't stop seeing the look of pain on Thomas's face.

I picked at the lace on my gloves. "I wonder what the cause of Wilhelm's death will turn out to be. He was so oddly colored." My own skin prickled, but I gripped my fears in a fist. "I don't recall ever seeing a body in such a state before."

"Awful." Anastasia scrunched her nose. "I forgot you inspected the body before Uncle forced you to return.

I've never read about symptoms like that before." She started speaking too quickly in Romanian for me to comprehend, then pressed her lips together. "I apologize. I forget you're not fluent yet. Would you like to visit the library? Perhaps you'll find something there that explains strange medical conditions."

"Maybe tomorrow. I'm tired." I stood and nodded toward the door. "I think I'm going to go soak in the tub. Perhaps we can go in the morning."

"*Măreț!* Soaking in the tub is a wonderful idea! I might do the same. I love a good bath."

"See you for breakfast?"

"Of course." Her lips turned down at the edges briefly before she offered a full smile. She dropped onto the settee with all the grace of a sack of potatoes and plucked up the Latin book. "Try to get some rest—it was a tragic day. Hopefully tomorrow will be brighter."

Torches in the corridor had been mostly extinguished when I crept from Anastasia's chambers. Midnight air was christened with arctic drafts, prompting gooseflesh to rise as I drifted down the vacant, dark hallway. Black shapes lurked around the sculptures, larger than the objects they stood guard over. I knew they were only shadows, but in the soft, flickering light, they seemed to be unearthly creatures stalking me. Watching.

I held fast to my skirts and moved as swiftly as I dared. It truly felt as if I were being monitored. By who or what, I didn't care to distinguish. Eyes tracked my movements; I sensed the force of them as I retreated. Which wasn't probable, I knew, and yet...I stumbled like a fawn on new limbs, aware that a predator pressed on, unseen. "It's not real," I whispered. "It's not—"

A small creak of the floorboards behind me spiked adrenaline in my veins. I glanced around, pulse thundering. Empty. The corridor was void of anything other than my nerves. Not one shadow moved. The castle seemed to hold its breath along with me, attuned to my every mood. I stood there, frozen, as seconds crept by. Nothing.

I exhaled. It was only a hall. No vampires or werewolves. Certainly no malevolent force stalked me to my rooms. Unless my wretched imagination could be counted. I hurried along, the swish of my skirts urging my heart into a trot despite my mind's attempt at soothing my fears.

I passed the boys' floor and continued up the stairs to my tower chambers, not pausing again until I heard the soft click of my door shutting. I pressed my back against the wood and closed my eyes.

A sharp snap had them flying open again, scanning. My focus landed on the fireplace, at the twigs glowing near-white and orangey red. The mystery sound was nothing more than firewood crackling in the hearth. A normal sound that should be pleasant on a blustery evening. I sighed, moving toward my sleeping chamber. Perhaps if I crawled into bed and left this day behind, things would truly be better in the morning, just as Anastasia had said.

When I entered my room I perceived something was amiss. My bed was undisturbed, armoire and trunk closed. But on my nightstand an envelope stood propped against an oil lamp, my name written in script I recognized as readily as my own. I'd watched him scrawl out medical notes during autopsies with Uncle all this past autumn. My heart raced for an entirely new reason once I read it.

Meet me in my chambers at midnight.

Ever yours,
Cresswell

Heat sizzled under my skin, pooling in my core. Going into Thomas's rooms this late at night was… reckless and would most certainly ruin me. I was positive it'd also be grounds for expulsion. Not to mention the death of my reputation. No decent young man would ever want me for his wife, regardless of how innocent our visit was. Sneaking into his rooms was far more dangerous than any immortal ghost haunting this castle, and yet I feared it less. I wanted to see Thomas, to apologize for the way I'd overreacted earlier. He did not deserve the brunt of my anxiety.

I paced around my bedroom, letter clutched to my chest. I couldn't bear the thought of how Father might react to my soiled name, and yet an idea took root and didn't relinquish its hold. If I was so apprehensive of marriage, then perhaps being caught wouldn't truly be the death of me. It might very well be my rebirth.

I glanced at myself in the looking glass. My green eyes twinkled with hope. And excitement. It had been such a long time since I could recall seeing that spark of intrigue.

Without another thought, I left my chambers and found myself knocking on Thomas's door as the courtyard clock struck midnight. The door swung open before I'd had time to drop my hand. Thomas motioned me in, his attention sweeping the hallway behind me as if he were expecting someone else to be wandering down the corridor so late at night.

Perhaps he was as nervous as I was. I subtly inspected the room. His frock coat lay discarded on one of three oversize leather chairs. A tea service breathed steam on an end table set between two chairs. On a sideboard there were a few covered platters of food and a carafe of wine. Seemed Thomas was ready to feed a small army. I faced him, trying not to notice the button that had been undone at his throat, or the sliver of skin it revealed.

"Thomas...I must apologize—"

He held a hand up. "It's all right, you have nothing to be sorry about."

"Oh?" I asked, sinking with relief. "If you're not after an apology, what is so important that you dramatically summoned me down here? If you imply it's for a tryst, I swear I'll—I'll...I'm not sure. But it won't be pleasant."

"You need to work on your threats a bit more, Wadsworth. Though the way your cheeks flush while you say 'tryst' is amusing enough." He grinned rather broadly at my scowl. "All right. I asked you here because I wanted to discuss Wilhelm's death. Not too romantic, I hope."

I slumped back. Of course. "I've been trying to think of diseases with his symptoms, but haven't had any success."

Thomas nodded. "I didn't study him for long, but he appeared quite pale. I'd wager that it wasn't only because of his ailment. Though perhaps it's as simple as the frigid weather. His lips hadn't turned blue yet, however. Very odd indeed."

I cocked my head. "Are you suggesting something a bit more sinister, then?"

"I—" He laughed, the sound jarring me into standing straighter. "I actually don't know. I haven't felt quite myself since our arrival." Thomas paced along the perimeter of the room, hands tapping his sides. I wondered if that was the true reason he'd been ready to leave the academy so quickly. "Being unable to make connections to symptoms and facts sooner. I…it's unpleasant. How do people tolerate it—this inability to deduce the obvious?"

I managed to only roll my eyes once. "Somehow we manage to survive, Cresswell."

"It's dreadful."

Instead of indulging him further, I brought our conversation back to Wilhelm's strange death. "Do you believe we might have been able to assist him? I keep thinking if we hadn't lost him, we could have administered aid."

Thomas stopped pacing and faced me. "Audrey Rose, you mustn't—"

"Good evening, Thomas," a sultry voice purred from the doorway.

We turned to see a young woman with dark hair glide into the room. Her face was both angular and dainty. A contradiction that was not unpleasing to the eye. Everything from her perfectly coiffed hair to the enormous ruby in her choker screamed wealth and decadence. And the way she carried herself, shoulders back and neck arched, exuded the confidence of a queen. She turned her little pert nose up and smiled at her subjects.

I watched Thomas's face light up in a way I'd never witnessed before. I slunk back, feeling conflicted. It was obvious they were quite fond of each other, and yet it stirred something uncomfortable within me. Something I dared not think on too much.

Thomas stood there as if he were photographing each detail of this moment to revisit time and again during the frigid winter months. A bit of warmth to cling to when the snow froze his black little heart. Then, without warning, he burst from his daze.

"Daciana!"

Without a backward glance, Thomas bolted for the girl and lifted her in a swinging embrace, leaving me all but forgotten.

TWELVE
MIDNIGHT ENCOUNTERS

THOMAS'S CHAMBERS
CAMERA LUI THOMAS
BRAN CASTLE
3 DECEMBER 1888

As I watched Thomas and the dark-haired beauty lose themselves in whispered chatter, my own heart shriveled up within my jealous skin. He was allowed to court whomever he wanted. No promises had been made or agreed upon.

And yet... my stomach churned as I watched Thomas with someone else. He might be free to do whatever he liked, but that did not mean I wanted to witness it. Especially at midnight in his chambers.

I stood near a deep blue settee, trying to force myself to smile, but knew it appeared too brittle. It was hardly the girl's fault Thomas was paying her so much attention, and I refused to dislike her because of my own newfound insecurity. After what seemed like a year of slow torture, Thomas wrested himself from Daciana's grasp. He took two steps toward me, then halted, head tilting to one side as he surveyed me.

It took most of my effort to not cross my arms over my chest and glare. I watched as he drank in every blasted detail—each exclamation of emotion I failed to hide from his lengthy read of me.

"You do know that expression is my favorite." He smiled broadly, and I wished one hundred unpleasant things to befall him at once. "So delectable."

He stalked closer, a confident air in his gait, his gaze never leaving mine, practically pinning me to the ground as if I were a specimen in our old laboratory. Before I could stop him, he lifted my hand to his lips and pressed a long, chaste kiss to it. Warmth rose from my toes to my hairline, but I didn't pull my hand away.

"Daciana"—he smirked at the reaction he'd teased from me—"this is the enchanting young woman I've been writing about. My beloved Audrey Rose." He kept my hand tucked into his arm and nodded at the other girl. "And this is my sister, Wadsworth. I believe you saw her photograph in our family's flat on Piccadilly Street. I told you she was almost as lovely as I. If you look closely enough, you'll see those irresistible Cresswell genes."

A memory of seeing the picture flashed before me, and shame covered my tongue. It tasted bitter and foul. How very foolish of me! His sister. I shot him a miserable look as I removed my hand, and he laughed outright. He was enjoying this situation entirely too much. I realized he'd orchestrated the entire setup to gauge my reaction.

The fiend.

"It's so very nice to meet you," I said, doing a terrible job of keeping my voice steady. "Please forgive my surprise; Thomas kept your visit a secret. Will you be studying here, too?"

"Oh, heavens no." Daciana laughed. "I'm traveling through the Continent with friends on a Grand Tour." She squeezed her brother's arm in a loving manner. "Thomas deigned to send a letter and said I should visit if I found myself in the area. Lucky for him, I just happened to be in Bucharest."

"My cousin Liza will be ten shades of green once I write to her," I said. "She's been trying to convince my aunt to send her on a Grand Tour for ages. I swear she'd run off with the circus if it meant visiting new countries."

"Honestly, it's the best way of becoming cultured." Daciana looked me up and down, a sly smile matching her brother's lighting her features. "I'll write to your aunt and beg on your cousin's behalf. I'd love to have another traveling companion."

"That would be lovely," I said. "Though Aunt Amelia can be a bit…hard to persuade."

"Fortunately, I've had experience with difficult people." She glanced at her brother, who did his best to pretend as if he hadn't heard.

Thomas poured himself a cup of tea on the other side of the room, and I felt his attention on me as Daciana hugged me close. Her warmth filled the broken bits of myself with that brief contact. I hadn't been truly embraced in a long while.

"So…" she drawled, looping an arm through mine. "How was traveling with my brother and Mrs. Harvey? Did she sip from her traveling tonic the whole time?"

"She did." I laughed. "Thomas was…Thomas."

"He's a special sort." She gave me a knowing grin. "Honestly, I'm pleased he hasn't scared you off with his mystical 'powers of deduction.' He's really quite sweet once you move past that sour exterior."

"Oh, is he? I hadn't noticed this mythical sweet side."

"Aside from those walls he puts up for work, he's truly one of the best people in the world," Daciana said proudly. "Being his sister, I'm only partially biased, naturally."

I smiled. I knew he was still watching, his attention a soft caress from the moment his sister hugged me, but now I pretended not to notice. "I'm curious, what else did he say about me?" I finally glanced in his direction, but he was now studiously engaged in staring into his cup as if he could read the tea leaves and divine his future.

"Oh, *lots* of things."

"What do we have here?" Thomas interrupted, yanking the lid off one of the platters with a clang. "I had your favorite sent up, Daci. Who's hungry?"

Before Daciana could offer any more of his secrets, Thomas handed her a glass of wine and ushered us over to a little table.

Daciana took a long pull from her glass, her gaze carving into me in nearly the same fashion as Thomas's. I watched as she eyed the pear-shaped ring on my finger, one of my most precious possessions.

I fought the urge to hide my hands beneath the table, lest she take offense where none was intended. Her focus slid up to the heart-shaped locket on my neck—another token I was hardly ever without. I was not inclined to discuss my mother tonight nor allow my thoughts to stumble into those darkened alleyways of treacherous memory.

"Forgive me," she said, "but does your affection for forensic medicine have anything to do with the loss you've suffered?" She nodded toward the ring. "I assume that diamond belonged to your mother. And that necklace as well?"

"How—" I shot an accusing glare at Thomas as my hand inadvertently found the heart clasped near my throat.

"Easy now. It's a family trait, Wadsworth," he said, spooning food onto a plate for me. "However, I doubt you'll be as impressed by my sister. I'm much smarter. And handsomer. Obviously."

Daciana shot her brother an exasperated look. "I apologize, Audrey Rose. I simply noted that ring and its style and assumed your mother had passed on. I did not mean to offend."

"Your brother noticed the same thing a few months ago," I said, dropping my hand. "It took me by surprise, is all. He'd not mentioned you possessed the same... ability to read the obvious."

"Quite the obnoxious sibling trait." Daciana smiled. "Has he told you anything about it?"

I shook my head. "It's easier to pry information from the dead than get Thomas to open up about himself."

"True enough." Daciana tossed her head back and laughed. "It was a game we used to play as children. At dinner parties, we'd study the adults around us, guessing their secrets and earning coins to keep them to ourselves. Noblemen aren't keen on having their private affairs made public. Our mother used to host the most thrilling parties." She swirled the wine around in her glass. "Has Thomas ever told you—"

"That perhaps wine is not such a good idea on an empty stomach?" he supplied, clearly hoping to steer the conversation away from their mother.

It seemed fate was a fan of Thomas as a knock suddenly interrupted us. Ileana stepped in and dipped her head. "Your rooms are ready, *domnişoară*."

Daciana beamed.

"It was wonderful finally meeting you, Audrey Rose." She whispered something to Ileana in Romanian and flashed me another grin. "Oh, there may be a surprise waiting for you in your chambers. A little gift from me to you. Enjoy."

"Perhaps I should accompany Audrey Rose back to her rooms," Thomas offered innocently. "It would be prudent to make sure this surprise doesn't have fangs. Or claws."

"Nice try, sweet brother." Daciana patted his cheek lovingly. "Do try to maintain the appearance of being a gentleman."

I bid Thomas good night as I climbed the stairs alone to my tower. Once inside, the fragrance hit me straight away. I entered my bathing chamber and halted.

Flower petals so deeply red they appeared black floated on top of scented water, steam lifting itself in great huffs; someone had just filled the tub and sprinkled intoxicating essences in. Daciana's gift was scented petals—quite a luxury for a forensic student in the mountains.

I removed my gloves and gently stroked the surface of the water, enjoying the ripples left in my fingers' wake. My body screamed with desire. I couldn't wait to soak in the bath. It had been such a long day, and the corpse of Wilhelm had been awful...A bath would rinse it all away, cleansing and comforting.

I glanced at a clock above the mantel in this room. It was almost twelve-thirty. I could luxuriate in the water for half an hour and be in bed before it was too horridly late. Without further thought, I unbuttoned the front of my gown and let it hit the floor, thankful it was something I could do without assistance. My maid from home and I had purposely chosen simple dresses that I could manage on my own; I didn't think the academy would offer a personal attendant.

I stepped from my satin layers and into the hot water, the liquid enveloping me like molten lava as I pinned my hair to my crown and sank down to my shoulders. The water was so warm my skin prickled at first, unsure if the new sensation was good or bad.

It was most decidedly very good for my sore muscles. I groaned at how soothing it felt.

For a few relaxing breaths, my mind drifted in any direction of its choosing. For a scandalous moment, I imagined Thomas soaking in his own tub and wondered what the planes of his bare shoulders looked like as they met the steam. Would he give me a cocky grin like the one he wore in public, or would that rare glimpse of vulnerability be present on his sensuous mouth before he pressed it to my own?

Heart pounding, I splashed the perfumed water on my face. The scoundrel held power over my senses when he wasn't even around. I prayed he wouldn't be able to deduce my wanton daydreams in the morning.

As I pushed those thoughts from my mind, darker ones filled in the crevices. Each time I closed my eyes I saw the corpses of the slain prostitutes from the Ripper murders, their bodies torn savagely apart. Whenever I was alone, I'd revisit their crime scenes, wondering if there was something I could have done differently. Some other clue I'd overlooked that could have stopped him sooner. Regret wouldn't bring the dead back, this I knew, yet I couldn't stop myself from repeatedly reexamining my actions.

"What if" were the two most tragic words in existence when paired together. "If only" were no better when coupled off. If only I'd seen the signs sooner. Perhaps I could have...

Whirl-churn. Whirl-churn.

I lurched from the bath, water dripping noisily from my naked body into the tub. Each drop seemed to echo in the small chamber, spiking my adrenaline like mortuary needles. I held my breath and listened hard, waiting for that unmistakable sound to reveal itself once more. A few twigs cracked and popped in the fireplace, and I jumped, nearly slipping on the slick surface of the tub. I breathed in, then out, listening as blood pounded my ears.

Nothing. I'd heard nothing.

There was no steam-powered heart. No sinister laboratory. No flesh-covered machinery. Just my mind taunting me with images I wished to forget as I drifted between sleep and waking. I lifted a trembling hand to my head, noticing how my skin burned beneath my touch. Gooseflesh puckered along my arms and legs. I hoped I hadn't contracted whatever Wilhelm had been wrecked by.

I glanced around until I found my orchid-dyed dressing robe, hanging from a hook on the door. I slipped the cool silk on, fighting shivers as I exited the bathing chamber. I was thankful I hadn't gotten my hair wet. I pressed my hands to my center, willing my nerves to steady.

And that's when I heard it. A sound that was not

brought on by specters haunting my half-sleeping thoughts. Whispered voices came from the next room. I was sure of it. The room where the bodies were stored. I moved quietly to the bedroom wall and laid my ear against it. Someone was having a rather heated fight, though it was physical, not verbal, from what I could deduce.

Something smacked against the wall, and I drew back, pulse roaring. Was it a body?

Curiosity was a disease that plagued me, and I'd yet to find a cure. Deciding that I would learn nothing by staying where I was, I moved into the sitting room, plucked a poker from the fireplace, and slowly inched my door open. I could barely think with the chorus of anxiety singing through my veins. Thankfully, there was no telltale creaking as I drew the door wider; my heart might have burst if there was. I waited a beat, listening intently, before sticking my head into the hall, the poker gripped tightly in my damp hands.

Without further hesitation, I crept down the corridor, sticking to the shadows, and paused before a partially closed door. I heard the rustling of material, followed by a soft groan. I imagined some horror taking place. Which seemed to be a reality as the muffled sounds coming from the room intensified. Someone gasped, only to have the noise smothered from existence—a candle being snuffed in the night.

I found my own breath coming in sharp intakes. Had the murderer from the train followed us here? Perhaps the rustling noise was the sound of a homicide in progress. My rational mind told me to go back to bed, that my imagination was running mad once more, but I couldn't leave without knowing for sure.

I moved toward the noises, gripping my weapon, as my blood thrashed in my veins. I was almost at the door to the morgue, which was open a crack. I inched around to peer inside. One more step. My breathing hitched, but I refused to yield. I braced myself for something dreadful and craned my neck around the doorframe. Flashes of another time when I crept into a place I shouldn't have swept across my thoughts. I paused, allowing myself another breath. This was not the Ripper case. I was not about to uncover his depraved laboratory.

It seemed I would never learn my lesson and run for help before diving into turbulent waters. I steeled my nerves and pushed the door open a bit more. I swore my heart was running in the opposite direction.

I would scream as loudly as I could and wield my poker. Then I'd run.

I readied myself for the worst as I glanced inside. Two figures were locked together, in a darkened corner, hands drifting over each other everywhere as if they were...I gasped.

"I-I'm so sorry." I blinked, completely and utterly unprepared for the sight before me. "I thought—"

Daciana dabbed at her crimson mouth with her free hand, face flushing as she released the skirts bunched in her other fist. "I...I can explain."

THIRTEEN
CAUGHT IN THE ACT

BODY STORAGE, TOWER CHAMBERS
DEPOZIT DE CADAVRE, CAMERE DIN TURN
BRAN CASTLE
3 DECEMBER 1888

"I—I'm so very... I heard noises and, and I thought—I'm dreadfully sorry." I stuttered over an apology, my gaze traveling from Daciana's disheveled hair to the woman she'd been kissing, their hands still entwined and their skirts rumpled.

I tore my gaze from their wrinkled clothes, unsure where to look. I was fairly certain the mystery guest wasn't wearing anything beneath her shirt. Those stone-colored eyes blinked back at me...

"Ileana?"

Shock must have addled my brain for me not to have noticed it was her straightaway.

"I...I didn't mean to...intrude." I sank my teeth

into my lower lip so hard I nearly drew blood as Ileana cringed back. "I didn't see...anything."

Daciana opened her mouth, then shut it.

"I..." I searched for something to say—something to break the tension coiled around each of us, choking words away, but hardly knew where to start. Every attempt at apologizing seemed to put Ileana further on edge. I feared if I attempted another apology she might run from this chamber and never come back.

As if recovering from her own surprise at being discovered, Daciana suddenly drew herself up and lifted her chin. "I make no apologies, if that's what you're after. Do you take issue with our affection?"

"O-of course not." I blinked, horrified by her conclusion. "I would never."

I glanced at the two cadavers on nearby tables covered under white shrouds. It was a morbid place to steal kisses, though it should have been the least likely place to be discovered by nosy castle occupants. And it would have been perfect—if I hadn't shown up. My face burned.

I was frozen with indecision on how to exit the morgue. Both girls stared at me—then at each other— and I wished for the floor to transform into a giant mouth and swallow me whole. Blast that magic didn't truly exist when one needed a fast escape. My entire body was aflame with mortification after being caught spying.

"I...I hope to see you both tomorrow," I said, feeling as if I were the most awkward person alive. "Good night."

Without waiting for a scolding, I burst into the hallway and ran for my chambers. I shut the door and pressed my back against it, covering my burning face with my hands. If Daciana or Ileana wanted to remain acquainted with me now, it would be the closest thing to a miracle the world had ever known. Foolish. I was so ridiculously foolish to be pulled by the lure of curiosity! Of course no intruder was here, killing classmates. Jack the Ripper was dead. The murderer from the train had no interest in hunting academy students.

It was time for me to accept that and move forward with my life.

I worried my bottom lip between my teeth, trying to place myself in their situation. The scandal that would befall an unmarried woman being caught alone in the company of a man would ruin her reputation. Being caught romantically with another young woman—society, vicious beast that it was, would destroy them both and take pleasure in ripping them apart.

I paced the small rug in my room, torn between going back to apologize and locking myself away forever to perish in embarrassment and shame. Finally, I decided to crawl into bed. I did *not* want to chance interrupting them again if they had picked up from where I'd so rudely found them.

A new wave of fire flickered across my skin when I thought of their kiss. It was so passionate. They appeared to be lost within each other's souls. I couldn't help thinking of being in a similar position with Thomas.

Our kiss in the alleyway had been very nice, but danger had corralled us. What would it feel like to have my hair gently knotted in his fist, my back pressed against a wall, him tangled around me like vines wrapped around brick?

I still didn't know if I wanted forever—or that I would ever be the marrying kind—but certain feelings were becoming...clearer. Part of me longed to trail ungloved fingers across his face, learning each curve of his bone structure in an intimate way. I craved the pressure of his warmth as his cutaway coat dropped to the floor. I wanted to know what his body felt like as our friendship was doused in crude oil and set on fire. Which was *completely* indecent.

I banished that image from my mind and yanked the covers up.

Aunt Amelia would certainly force me to attend church services on her next visit, muttering never-ending prayers for my crumbling morals. As awful as I felt for being bested by curiosity, a smile slowly spread in the dark. It was one of the first nights in weeks that I was falling asleep to thoughts that didn't revolve around failed electrical contraptions, dead prostitutes, and disemboweled bodies.

Tonight I'd fall asleep to the image of gold-flecked eyes and a wicked mouth. And all the wonderful ways I might one day explore those lips in dark, empty rooms. Our passion burning brighter than all the stars in the sky.

Saints drag me to Hell.

FOURTEEN
MANDATORY MEETING

TOWER CHAMBERS
CAMERE DIN TURN
BRAN CASTLE
3 DECEMBER 1888

I'd been up before the sun deigned to rise, pacing in front of the fireplace in my chambers.

My velvet skirts were a deep blue to match my plummeting mood. I wasn't sure if Ileana would come for breakfast, and the idea of losing an acquaintance I'd only just made had me changing gloves a second time. I walked one way, then the next, my skirts rustling in their own annoyance. Last night I'd fallen asleep with a thousand ways to apologize for my intrusion when I saw them both again.

This morning none of them seemed right. I covered my face and made myself breathe. Liza would have known precisely what to do had she been in my place.

She had a gift for social situations—and for being a good friend. I forced myself to sit, trying not to flick my attention to the clock with each passing second that ticked away. Dawn would break soon. And with it judgment on my curiosity would be delivered. Perhaps now I'd finally be broken of that wretched affliction.

A confident knock came a few moments later, my heart clamoring in response as I raced across the room and flung the door wide.

I slumped back, heaving a sigh. "Oh, hello."

"Not necessarily the reaction I was hoping for, Wadsworth." Thomas glanced down at his dark jacket and trousers, both fitted in all the right ways. His striped waistcoat was also quite fashionable. "Perhaps I should have gone with the gray suit instead. I do look rather scrumptious in that."

I peered into the corridor, half hoping that Daciana would be lurking behind him, readying herself for a verbal attack regarding my curiosity. I sighed again. The hall was empty aside from Thomas. I finally dragged my attention back to him. "To what do I owe the honor of your presence this early in the morning?"

Without being invited, he swept into my chambers and nodded at the space. "Cozy. Much better than the image in my head of tower chambers and fair maidens in need of...well, you're not one in need of rescuing, but I'd say you could do with some entertainment."

HUNTING PRINCE DRACULA

He sat on the settee, crossing one long leg over the other.

"My sister informed me of the adventure you all had last night." He grinned as the color rushed to my face. "Don't worry. She'll be up in a moment. I didn't want to miss the fun this morning. I'm having Turkish coffee sent up."

"I've never felt more wretched in all my life. Does she hate me?"

Thomas had the audacity to chuckle. "On the contrary. She adores you. Said you'd turned nearly each shade of crimson and adopted a wonderful stutter." His light tone vanished, replaced by something fierce. Here was a role I'd not seen him in—protective brother. "Most would have looked at them as if they were wrong for acting on their love. False, naturally. Society at large is staggeringly obtuse. If one simply looks to others for their opinions, they lose the ability to think critically for themselves. Progress would never be made if everyone appeared and thought and loved in the same manner."

"Who are you, and where is the socially awkward Mr. Cresswell?" I'd never been more proud of my friend for his determination to verbally admonish society's faults.

"I do get rather passionate about such matters," Thomas said, a bit of levity back in his voice. "I suppose

I've grown weary of a select few governing all. Rules are restrictions given by other privileged men. I enjoy making up my own mind. Everyone ought to have the same human right. Plus"—he flashed a devilish grin at me—"it drives my father absolutely mad when I speak in that manner. Shakes up his rigid beliefs in a delightful way. He's yet to accept that the future will be run by those who believe as we do."

Another knock came at the door. Somehow I managed to open it without fainting from nerves. Daciana looked tentatively at me, then nodded to her brother. "*Bună dimineaţa*. How did everyone sleep? Anything exciting happen?"

She gave me a playful smile, and the tension knotted in my chest loosened.

"Truly, I cannot apologize enough," I said in a rush. "I'd heard noises and thought . . . I don't know, I worried someone was . . . under attack."

Thomas barked out a laugh. I raised a brow as he nearly fell off his seat. I'd never witnessed such a bout of emotion from him before. Daciana simply rolled her eyes. He was nearly hoarse by the time he composed himself enough to speak.

If his sincere laughter hadn't been so entrancing, I would have jabbed him with my finger. He was certainly lighter here, more relaxed with himself and less guarded, than he was in London. I couldn't deny being intrigued by this side of him.

"I wish I could capture the look on your face, Wadsworth. It's the most endearing shade of red I've ever seen." When I thought he'd collected himself, he chuckled again. "Under attack indeed. Seems you have a bit of work to do on your wooing, Daci."

"Oh, stuff it, Thomas." Daciana turned to me. "Ileana and I have known each other for quite some time. When she learned of Thomas attending the academy, she applied for a position. It was a convenient way for us to see each other. I'm sorry for having scared you. It must have been awful, thinking something sinister was occurring in the morgue. Especially after the Ripper murders."

A lovely expression lit her face, and I marveled at the pang of envy that it stirred within my cells. I wanted someone to have such a look of utter longing while thinking of me. I took a deep breath and composed myself. Not someone. Thomas. I wanted him. I dared not glance in his direction for fear of those wanton emotions showing.

"I suppose we got a *bit* carried away last night," Daciana said. "It's been a while since we've had an entire evening alone. It's just…I adore her in every possible way. Have you ever looked upon someone and felt a spark within your core? She makes me want to accomplish grand things. That's the beauty of love, though, isn't it? It brings out the very best within yourself."

I thought on that last part for a moment. While I fully agreed that she and Ileana were exquisite together, I also felt impressive feats could be accomplished if one chose to remain unattached. The proximity of a romantic partner should neither impede nor facilitate inner growth.

"I do agree that love is wonderful," I began slowly, not wanting to offend, "but there's also a certain magic in being perfectly content with one's own company. I believe greatness lies within. And is ours to harness or unleash at will."

Daciana's eyes glinted with approval. "Indeed."

"While we could chatter on endlessly about love," Thomas said in a faux huff, "your midnight tryst is making me quite jealous."

A third knock interrupted Thomas before he could say anything inappropriate. He stood, a serious countenance falling over him as if he'd flipped a cooling switch. Though his sister was here, it would still be frowned upon that we were without a chaperone.

I swallowed my fear down and called out, "Yes?"

"*Bună dimineaţa*, mis—Audrey," Ileana said, cheeks flushing slightly. "I—"

"Good morning to you, Ileana," Thomas said from

beside me. "I didn't know you worked here until my sister showed up, all doe-eyed and excited. I should have known she wasn't here to bless me with her sparkling personality."

To my utter amazement, Ileana cracked a genuine grin. "It's good to see you, too." The smile quickly faded. "You're both needed downstairs immediately. Mandatory meeting. Moldoveanu is in some sort of mood. You shouldn't be late."

"Hmm," Thomas said. "This ought to be interesting. I was under the impression that he's permanently in some sort of mood."

Daciana dropped onto the settee, propping her silk-covered feet up on the low table. "Sounds lovely. Do give my regards to him. If you need me, I'll be here, sprawled by the fire."

Thomas rolled his eyes. "You're like a house cat. Always napping in patches of sunshine or lounging before a fire." A mischievous slant to his lips had me shaking my head before he opened his mouth again. "Please refrain from relieving yourself on the furniture."

Thomas ushered me and Ileana out before Daciana could respond, and I tried hard to not laugh at all the foul things she was shouting in Romanian at the closed door.

By the time Thomas and I entered the dining hall, Anastasia had already wedged herself between Nicolae and the large brute, Andrei. I raised my brows at her choice of attending this meeting with her uncle. It was a bold maneuver. Clearly she wasn't going to permit Moldoveanu an opportunity to shut her out of the castle's intrigue. I imagined being stuck in her chambers every day would be unbearably boring.

As had been the case yesterday, the tables were filled with the same pairings. I realized I didn't know anyone else's name and resolved to introduce myself by the evening. The boy with red curls sat with the boy with the dark skin. The Italian brothers were hunched together, studying. And Thomas and I were momentarily unsure where to situate ourselves.

Undeterred by the sidelong glances Andrei slid her way, Anastasia excitedly motioned for us to come sit with them. Nicolae lifted his attention from his plate, glaring in our general direction halfheartedly. Thomas ignored him and focused on me. Sitting with the prince appeared as if it were the furthest thing from what he wanted to do, but he was leaving that decision up to me. It was a peace offering after his insistence yesterday that we return to London, and I appreciated the gesture.

While I didn't relish the idea of becoming best friends with Nicolae, I didn't want to remain enemies either. If Anastasia had the fortitude to incorporate herself into the group against her uncle's wishes, I could follow her lead.

Nicolae picked at a meat pastry, pulling it apart and pushing the pieces around his plate. He never once took a bite. A bit of me softened. Losing a loved one wasn't easy and often brought out qualities we weren't proud of.

Anger was a wall to hide grief behind. I knew that firsthand.

I marched directly to their table and sat. "Good morning."

"Bună dimineaţa," Anastasia said, cheerful voice echoing in the mostly empty room. Her dress was a bright crimson, another statement. One carefully crafted for maximum effect. She turned to Thomas, running her gaze over him swiftly. "You must be the handsome traveling companion."

Thomas slid into the chair beside me, expression bland. "With Audrey Rose, I like thinking of myself more along the lines of 'handsome life companion.'"

My face burned at his proprietary use of my Christian name, but no one else seemed to notice. Andrei snorted, then quickly chomped down on any more laughter as his gaze took in the empty seat next to Nicolae. While Anastasia chattered on with Thomas in Romanian, I subtly watched Andrei, wondering how close he'd been with Wilhelm. Dark circles marred his face, leaving me to imagine he'd taken the news as hard as the prince had. This could not be easy for them, sitting here when they'd rather mourn properly.

I hoped the headmaster was going to deliver news of delaying our coursework. Perhaps he'd cancel the winter term and invite us back next season. A small bit of me sank at the thought. Nicolae kept pinching his pastry into pieces, his gaze set somewhere inward and far away.

I wanted to reach over and say something comforting, something to maybe help heal myself as well, but Moldoveanu entered the dining hall and silence fell. Even Andrei shifted in his seat, a bead or two of perspiration dotting his broad brow.

Moldoveanu wasted little time on pleasantries. He began speaking in Romanian, slow enough for me to pick up much of what he was relaying. Classes were to begin immediately. We'd be taught in English, since it was a common language for all countries present, but lessons would also include sections in Romanian for those who weren't fluent yet.

"Your first lesson will be with Professor Radu," he continued in English. "Basic knowledge of folklore helps when investigating a scene in villages, where superstition may override logic and scientific sensibility." He glanced at each of us, and I was surprised to see that his disdain was directed at the entire group. As if we were all wasting his precious time. "Due to the unfortunate passing of your classmate, I've decided to invite another student in his place. He will be arriving today."

A clock chimed the hour, loud enough to force the headmaster to press his lips together. I stole a glance at Nicolae, his jaw clenched tight. I could not fathom being in his place, listening as the headmaster cast off his cousin's death so easily. It seemed highly callous to invite a new student so cavalierly, as if Wilhelm had simply run off and decided against trying out.

Once the chimes stopped, Moldoveanu met each of our gazes. "I suspect some of you may be...distracted by the events of yesterday, and I understand. Loss isn't taken lightly. We will have a vigil at sundown to honor Wilhelm. Professor Radu will provide more details. Immediately following his class, you are to report to your first postmortem laboratory. An anatomy lesson instructed by myself will follow that. You are dismissed."

Without offering another word, the headmaster exited the room, his shoes clapping against the floor and his footsteps fading away down the corridor.

Vlad Țepeș, c. 16th century.

FIFTEEN
VOIEVOD TRĂGĂTOR ÎN ŢEAPĂ

FOLKLORE CLASS
CURS DE FOLCLOR
BRAN CASTLE
4 DECEMBER 1888

"The woods surrounding the castle are filled with bones."

Professor Radu didn't notice half the students' chins were dropping to their chests while he flipped through pages in his oversize folklore book. He was reading to us as if we were babies with nursemaids instead of serious-minded students of medicine. Presently, it took a great amount of effort to keep myself from laughing while he regaled us with fantastical tales of creatures and immortal princes.

All I wanted was to skip ahead to the laboratory study next period. There was a cadaver waiting to be explored, and I couldn't wait to put my new scalpels to use. Only two weeks had passed since my last post-mortem with Uncle, yet it felt like two decades.

I needed to see if I could put my difficulties aside and study the dead as I used to. Or if the way I'd been forgetful and terrified of previous hauntings would plague me forever. I was not as anxious to attend Moldoveanu's lesson, though anatomy was a subject I excelled in.

Thomas shifted his long legs under his writing desk, drawing my attention. He tapped his inkwell so hard with the end of his quill I feared the ink would spill all over his parchment. Another quick rap had the bottle teetering precariously until he seized it and started tapping again. He'd been rather distant since he'd run off to speak with Radu before class, leaving both Anastasia and me puzzled at his swift departure as we exited the dining hall.

"Have any of you heard rumors of Vlad Țepeș living in these woods?" Professor Radu asked the class of half-sleeping pupils. I exhaled. Honestly, I was surprised anyone would truly believe such nonsense. Anastasia shot me a knowing grin from the seat beside me. At least I wasn't the only one in the classroom who thought this to be utter rubbish.

Thomas rolled his neck, dragging my focus to him once again. He was uncharacteristically subdued. We'd shared Uncle's class at the start of the Ripper murders, and no one could keep him quiet then. Normally his hand shot into the air so often I had the urge to shoo him from the classroom. I wondered if he was feeling ill.

I tried catching his eye, but he pretended not to notice. I tapped my quill against my inkwell, eyes narrowed. The day Thomas Cresswell failed to take note of anything, most especially my attention, was a troublesome day indeed. Unease slipped into my thoughts.

"No one's heard these rumors?" Radu tripped up one aisle and down the next, head swooping from side to side. "I find that rather hard to believe. Come, now. Don't be shy. We're here to learn!"

Andrei yawned obnoxiously in the front row, and the professor practically deflated before our eyes. If I hadn't been so horribly bored myself, I would have felt sorry for the older man. It had to be difficult teaching fiction and myth to a class more interested in science and fact.

"All right, then. I shall tell you a story almost too fantastical to believe."

Nicolae shifted in his seat. I could tell he was trying not to be too obvious about watching me, but he was failing considerably at his task. Wilhelm, as unfortunate as his death was, had likely died from a rare medical condition. Not murder. Certainly not mystical powers working to assassinate him on my behalf. I hoped the prince wouldn't spread rumors of my supposed curse; I had quite enough obstacles of my own to overcome.

"Villagers believe the bones found in the woods outside the castle are the remains of Vlad's victims. There are those who've claimed his grave is empty. And there are others who say it's been filled with animal skeletons. The royal family refuses to allow anyone to exhume the body or casket to be sure. Some say this is because they know precisely what will be found. Or rather—what *won't* be found. There are those who believe Vlad rose from the dead, his thirst for blood defying Death itself. Others claim it's simply blasphemous to desecrate the resting place of such an important man."

Professor Radu went on about the legend of the alleged immortal prince. How he'd made a deal with the Devil and, in exchange for eternal life, needed to steal the blood of the living and drink it fresh. It sounded like the gothic novel by John William Polidori, *The Vampyre*.

"*Voievod Trăgător în Ţeapă,* or, roughly translated to, the Impaler Lord, was thought to drink from the necks of his still-living victims. It was meant to inspire fear in those who sought to invade our country. But history says his preferred method was dipping bread into the blood of his enemies and ingesting it in that more… civilized manner."

"Oh, yes," I whispered to Thomas. "Dining on blood is more civil when one dunks their bread in it as if it were a hearty winter stew."

"As opposed to calling it a precursor to cannibalism. First one drinks blood, then they move on to sautéing up some organ meat," Thomas mumbled back. "Next comes the blood gravy."

"Scientifically improbable," Anastasia whispered.

"What's improbable? Blood gravy?" Thomas asked. "Not so. It's one of my favorites."

Anastasia seemed momentarily stunned before shaking her head. "Ingesting blood the way Radu's implying would lead to too much iron in one's system. I wonder if he bathed in it instead. That would be more logical."

"What sort of journals do you read?" I said quietly, flashing Anastasia a curious look.

She grinned. "There's a limited number of novels in this castle. I make do."

"Unfortunate for dear old Vlad," Thomas said in a loud whisper. "His flatulence must have been legendary."

I hid my smile behind my quill as the professor nearly tripped over his shoes again. Poor thing. His eyes lit up as if he'd been offered a shiny Thomas-shaped gift from God above. Too bad Thomas wasn't commenting pleasantly on the subject. There was only so much fantasy that he could withstand. If anything, I was impressed it had taken this long for him to speak up. At least Nicolae seemed to be slightly amused. It was far better than that awful glazed-over expression he'd worn since his cousin's death.

"Did someone say something?" Radu asked, caterpillar brows waggling skyward.

Thomas drummed his hands over his journal, pinching his lips as if he could keep his comments from spewing out. I sat straighter; things appeared to be getting interesting. Thomas was a geyser ready to burst.

"We were speaking of flatulence."

I snorted in the most unladylike manner, then coughed the giggle away when Radu turned on me, eyes blinking expectantly. *"Scuzele mele,"* I said. "So sorry, sir. We were saying perhaps Dracula bathed in the blood."

"I believe you're confusing Vlad Dracula with the Countess Elizabeth Báthory," Radu said. "She is sometimes called Countess Dracula and was said to bathe in the blood of servants she killed. Nearly seven hundred of them, if reports are accurate. Very, very messy business! Another good lesson, though."

"Sir?" The boy with red curls spoke with an Irish brogue. "Do you believe historical accounts of Vlad drinking blood have been confused with folklore?"

"Hmm? Ah, I nearly forgot!" Professor Radu paused beside Thomas's desk, chest puffed up with pride as he faced Nicolae. "We have an actual Ţepeş family member in our midst. Perhaps he may shed some light on these legends. Did the infamous Impaler Lord drink blood? Or has that myth sprung from the fanciful minds of peasants who were in need of a hero more fearsome than the invading Ottomans?"

The prince was now staring straight ahead, jaw clenched tightly. I doubted he wanted to offer up any Țepeș family secrets, especially if his ancestors were rumored to enjoy sanguine delights. I studied him closely, deciding that I wouldn't be shocked to discover he enjoyed drinking blood himself.

"What of the *Societas Draconistrarum?*" Anastasia interrupted, her focus drifting toward Nicolae. "I heard they combat such myths. Do you believe Vlad was indeed *strigoi?*"

"Oh, no, no, no, dear girl," Radu said, "I do not believe such rumors. Vlad was no vampire, no matter how compelling a tale it makes."

"But where did those rumors originally come from?" Anastasia pressed. "They had to be born of some fact."

Radu chewed on the inside of his cheek, seeming to consider his next words more carefully than before. It was a serious expression I hadn't yet seen on him and I was intrigued by the subtle shift. I hadn't thought him capable of being anything other than scattered.

"Once upon a time men needed explanations for such darkness and bloodshed during times of war. They were quick to blame anything other than their own greed for their troubles. And so they sat down and created vampires—sinister creatures that sprang forth from the twisted depths of their dark hearts, mirroring their own bloodlust. Monsters are only as real as the stories that grant them life. And they only live for as long as we tell those tales."

"And the dragonists started these legends?" she asked.

"No, no. I did not mean to imply that. I'm getting all tangled up in my myths. However, the Order of the Dragon is a story for another time." He addressed the handful of us in the class, seeming to come back to himself. "For those who may be unaware, they were a secret society made up of selected nobility. Often called *Societas Draconistrarum,* or, roughly translated, Society of the Dragonists. They fought to uphold certain values during times of war and invasion. Sigismund, king of Hungary, used the Crusaders as a model when he founded the group."

"How on earth does this relate, sir?" Nicolae asked, his accented drawl expressing his disdain.

"The Order believes this academy is teaching young men—and women, I haven't forgotten you, Miss Wadsworth—to be heretics! I've heard on many an occasion that village folk believe if Vlad were alive today, he'd be appalled by this school and its blasphemous teachings. His family were crusaders of Christianity, which is how they became involved with the Order. We all know how society looks upon the practice of cutting open the dead for study. The body being a temple and all. Complete heresy."

I swallowed hard. Society had recently turned on Uncle as well, despising him for the practice of post-mortem examinations. It did not understand the bodies he cracked open on his table, or the clues he could unearth about their demise. Radu took in my troubled expression, eyes going wide.

"Oh! Please don't worry, Miss Wadsworth. Mr. Cresswell informed me of the sensitive nature of the Ripper case and its disturbing effects on you. I certainly don't want to upset your fragile constitution, as Mr. Cresswell warned."

For an extended moment, a piercing noise sounded within my head. "My... *what?*"

Thomas closed his eyes, as if he could shut Radu's revelations out entirely. I was dully aware that my class-mates were now twisting in their seats, staring as if one of their favorite plays were being performed and the hero was about to fall.

"Oh, nothing to be ashamed of, Miss Wadsworth. Hysteria is a common affliction for young, unmarried women," Radu went on. "I'm sure if you refrain from mentally taxing yourself, you'll be emotionally suffi-cient again soon."

Some of the boys laughed outright, not bothering to

mask their delight. Inside, the cord that tethered me to Thomas vibrated with anger. This was my worst night-mare come to life, and there wasn't a thing I could do to wrench myself out of it.

"Audrey Rose..."

I could barely look at him, too afraid of bursting into tears, but I wanted him to see the void yawning within. He'd betrayed me. He'd told our professor that I'd been affected by a case. That my *constitution* had been damaged. It was my secret to keep. *Not* his to share. His loyalty to me obviously didn't mean a thing. I could not believe—after I'd told him to not interfere with my choices—that he'd go behind my back and share personal information.

A few more classmates snickered. Bulky Andrei even pretended to have fainted from shock and required assistance from the boy with the Irish accent. My face burned.

"Don't worry, class. I do not believe you are all damned because of the science that's performed here," Radu went on, completely unaware of what he'd unleashed. "It's hard to break villagers of their traditions, though. Be mindful if you go into Braşov alone. Oh...I suppose there's been a meeting about that—"

A clock chimed in the courtyard, signaling the blessed end to this torture. I tossed my journal and writing utensils into a small sack I'd taken to carrying.

I could not remove myself from this room fast enough. If I overheard one more snide remark about fainting couches or hysteria, I would truly snap.

"Students aren't permitted off grounds unsupervised!" Radu called over the clamor of seats being pushed from desks. "Don't want anyone being sacrificed as a heretic. That would be quite bad for our program! The vigil will be held at sundown, don't forget."

Nicolae shook his head at the professor and stepped around him into the aisle. Thomas paused by his desk, stopped from closing the distance between us by the fleeing students, his attention riveted on me. I didn't wait for him to get close. I turned my back and walked for the door as quickly as I could.

SIXTEEN
IMMORTAL PRINCE

FOLKLORE CLASS
CURS DE FOLCLOR
BRAN CASTLE
3 DECEMBER 1888

"Audrey Rose, please. Wait." Thomas reached for me in the corridor just outside the classroom, but I moved swiftly. He let his arm fall limp at his side. "I can explain. I thought—"

"Oh? You *thought?*" I snapped. "You thought it a fine idea to make me into a mockery in front of our peers? To undermine me? Did we not just have a similar conversation yesterday?"

"Please. I swear I never meant—"

"Exactly. You never *mean* anything!" Thomas staggered back as if I'd struck a blow. I ignored his air of injury, dropping my voice to a harsh whisper as Anastasia tiptoed around us and fled down the corridor. "You care only for yourself and prove that through your cursed actions daily. You keep your emotions and stories and history to yourself. Then you freely tell others *my* secrets. Do you have any idea how difficult it is for me? Most men do not take me seriously based on the skirts I wear, and then you go and prove them right! I am not inferior, Thomas. No person is."

"You mustn't—"

"I mustn't what? Tolerate you thinking you know what's best for me? You're right. I don't. I do not understand how you believe yourself entitled to speak for me. To warn others of my *fragile constitution*. You are supposed to be my friend, my equal. Not my keeper."

A few weeks earlier I'd worried that my father would take Thomas and forensic studies from me the same way my brother had been torn from my grasp. I wasn't able to bear the thought of being without him. I couldn't have known that Thomas would betray me under the guise of protecting my best interests. I never would have predicted that *he* would be the one who'd destroy our bond.

"I swear I *am* your friend, Audrey Rose," he said earnestly. "I see you're angry—"

"Another fine deduction made by the infallible Mr. Thomas Cresswell," I said, unable to keep the bite from my tone. "You said you loved me once, but your actions show a much different truth, sir. I require equal standing and will accept nothing less."

The future I hadn't been sure I'd ever wanted was made clear as fine crystal. I was correct in my assumptions. No matter how much Thomas pretended otherwise, he was still a man. A man who felt his duty and obligation would be to speak on my behalf and set rules, were I to marry him. I would always be undermined in some manner by his thoughtless "assistance."

"Audrey Rose—"

"I refuse to be governed by anything other than my own will, Cresswell. Allow me to make myself even more clear, since you obviously missed the point earlier: I would rather perish an old maid than subject myself to a life with you and your best intentions. Find another person to torment with your affections."

I heard Thomas calling my name as I rushed down the corridor and blindly ran down a twisting set of stairs. Torches nearly blew out as I rushed past them, but I dared not stop. I ran around and around as I descended the winding staircase, my heart shattering with each step I took away from him.

I'd never felt more alone or more foolish in all my life.

◦⟡◦

The stiff body lying on the examination table brought me more comfort than should have been proper. Instead of admonishing myself for unseemly behavior, I relished the feeling of absolute control over my emotions. Never was I more confident than when a scalpel was in my hands, and a corpse was waiting with its flesh cracked open like the spine of a crisp new book to be studied.

Or at least—I'd never been more confident in the past. This test was far more crucial to me now, especially after Thomas's meddling.

I focused on the cold body, kept decent by carefully placed bits of cloth. My heart fluttered a bit, but I commanded it to calm. I'd not break apart during this examination. If need be, I'd allow stubbornness and spite to hold me together.

"*Fii tare,*" someone whispered from a spot nearby in the surgical theater. "Be strong." I glanced up, searching for the source. It was likely mockery thanks to Radu's declaration of my *fragile constitution*. I would prove to myself, more than anyone else, that I was completely capable of performing this autopsy.

I gripped the scalpel, putting aside my emotions as I stared at the boy who'd been alive yesterday. Wilhelm was no longer my classmate. He was a specimen. And

I'd find the strength I needed to identify his cause of death. Give peace to his family. Perhaps this was how I might help Nicolae cope: I could offer him an answer as to why and how his cousin had died. My hands shook slightly as I lifted the blade.

Our professor, a young Englishman named Mr. Daniel Percy, had already shown us the proper way to make a postmortem incision, and he offered one of us the opportunity to assist in the investigation of Mr. Wilhelm Aldea's death.

Since I'd completed similar tasks, I was the first to volunteer to remove his organs. I suspected Thomas was as anxious as I was to inspect the body, but he hadn't challenged me when I'd raised my hand. Instead he'd sat back and sunk his teeth into his lower lip. I was much too annoyed with him to appreciate the peace offering. He knew I needed to do this. I needed to overcome my fears or pack my trunks. If I could not handle this postmortem, I would never survive the assessment course.

"Class, please note the tools needed for your postmortems. Before each procedure, it's important to have everything you might need ready." Percy pointed to a small table with a tray of familiar objects. "A bone saw, bread knife, enterotomy scissors for opening both the small and large intestines, toothed forceps, and a skull chisel. There's also a bottle of carbolic acid on hand. New studies favor the practice of sterilization. Now, then, Miss Wadsworth, you may continue."

Using a decent amount of pressure, I cracked the sternum open using a pair of rib cutters. Uncle had taught me his method last August, and I was grateful for the lesson as I stood in the surgical theater, surrounded by three concentric tiers of seats that rose at least thirty feet into the air, though my classmates were all smushed together in the lowest level. The room was mostly quiet, save for the occasional shuffle of feet.

From the corner of my vision, I noticed the prince cringe. Percy had offered him the choice of sitting this lesson out, but he'd refused. I had no idea why Moldoveanu wasn't inspecting the body himself or why he'd turned it over for our studies. But Nicolae sat there, stoic. He'd chosen not to abandon his cousin until his body was laid to rest. I admired his strength but could not fathom sitting through such a procedure for a loved one.

Now I couldn't help but sense his gaze on me, sharp as the tool in my hands, while I spilled secrets of his cousin's unexpected death.

During pre-laboratory attendance, I'd learned that the Italian brothers—Mr. Vincenzo and Mr. Giovanni Bianchi—were fraternal twins. They were no longer staring hungrily at their books but at the method in which I was conducting my postmortem. Their intensity was almost as unnerving as the manner in which they seemed to communicate silently with each other. I glanced at my other classmates briefly. Mr. Noah Hale and Mr. Cian Farrell were equally intrigued. My gaze started to slide in Thomas's direction before I stopped it. I did not care to look at him.

I clamped the rib cage open and forced my expression to remain unaffected as the scent of exposed viscera wafted into the air. A slight scent of garlic was present. I shut out images of slain prostitutes. This body had not been desecrated by a horrid murderer. His organs hadn't been ripped from him. Now wasn't the time for thoughts beyond the surgical table. Now was the time for science. I sliced through some muscle, revealing the sac around the heart.

"Very good, Miss Wadsworth."

Professor Percy walked around the surgical theater, dramatically raising his voice. He was every inch the performer, a maestro leading a symphony into a crescendo. The sound of his voice slapped at the outer reaches of the room like its bass was a wave crashing against the shore.

"What we have here is the pericardium, class. Please note the way it covers the heart. It has both an outer layer and an inner layer. The first is fibrous in nature while the other is a membrane."

I narrowed my eyes. The pericardium casing had dried out. I'd never seen such a thing before. Without being told to do so, I plucked a glass and metal syringe from the table and attempted to extract a sample of blood from the deceased's forearm.

Pulling the stopper back, I expected the thick consistency of coagulated blood—and came away empty. An audible gasp raced around the lower ring in the hall, echoing like a choir singing a soul into heaven as it reached the upper levels.

Percy pointed out tools and procedures, this time in Romanian.

I stepped back, my gaze traveling over the nearly nude body, too focused on the mystery to blush. And that's when I noticed it—the absence of postmortem lividity.

I ducked closer, trying to find a hint of that bluish-gray pooling of blood that should have been present. Whenever a person perished, his blood stained the lowest area of the body where it last lay. If he died while lying on his stomach and then was flipped over, discoloration would still be present on his stomach. I searched each of Wilhelm's sides and under his limbs for lividity. None could be found. His pallor was odd even for a corpse.

There was something very wrong with this body.

"It's all right," Percy said, taking up a larger syringe. "Sometimes it's a bit trickier to remove a sample from the deceased. Nothing to feel embarrassed about. If you don't mind."

"Probably her weak constitution," someone muttered loud enough for me to overhear, and pretend not to.

Stepping aside, I allowed Percy room to draw a sample of his own, ignoring the snickers of my classmates. I flicked the side of my syringe, wondering how on earth it had failed to remove even a bit of blood from Wilhelm. The size of the needle shouldn't matter. I wanted to glance at Thomas but didn't give in to the urge.

"Interesting."

Percy picked up the left arm and slowly sank the needle into the thin skin of the deceased's elbow. When he pulled the plunger toward him, no blood accompanied it. The professor drew his brows together and tried another spot. Again, the syringe came away empty. Unsurprisingly, no one mocked *his* inability to withdraw blood.

"Hmm." He murmured to himself, trying to take samples from each limb. Every single time, he failed to draw blood. He stepped back, hands on hips, and shook his head. A few locks of ginger hair fell across his brow the way freckles were tossed about his face.

"Our mystery death deepens, class. It appears this body is missing its blood."

I cursed myself for doing so, but I couldn't help but search out Thomas's reaction in the crowd this time. My gaze drifted from stunned face to stunned face, everyone talking amongst themselves in anxious tones. Andrei pointed at the cadaver of his fallen friend, terror slashed into his every movement. I wanted to tell him that fear would cloud his judgment, that it would only complicate and delay our search for the truth, but I said nothing.

It was a horrific discovery.

I spun in a slow circle, eyes tracking around the tower room, but Thomas had already gone. A flicker of sadness lit within before I could extinguish it. It was better this way. I would need to learn to eventually stop looking to him for comfort he wasn't equipped to give anyway.

The prince leaned over the railing, knuckles going bone white. "Are there *strigoi* marks on his neck?"

"What?" I asked, hearing but not understanding such an absurd question. I bent down and turned Wilhelm's head to the side. Two little holes were crusted with dried blood.

I ran a hand over my plaited hair, not thinking about the rib cage I'd just cracked open as I did so. There had to be some explanation that didn't point to a vampire attack. *Strigoi* and *pricolici* were stories; they weren't scientifically possible. No matter how much local folk-lore Professor Radu fed us.

I rolled my shoulders, granting myself permission to lock my emotions away. Now was the time to adopt Thomas's method of deduction. If a werewolf or vampire hadn't bitten Wilhelm, then what had? I flipped through pages of scenarios in my head—there had to be a reasonable explanation for the two points on his neck.

Young men didn't simply drop dead and lose their blood due to natural causes, and I wasn't aware of any living thing that could leave those—bite marks. I shook my head. Bite marks indeed. That was hysteria clawing its way into my mind. An animal couldn't have made that wound. It was too neat. Too clean. Teeth marks wouldn't have been so precise when entering flesh.

Animal attacks would be brutal, leaving many indications on the corpse: flesh torn, nails broken, scratches. Defensive wounds would have been present on the hands, as Uncle had pointed out in cases of a fight. Bruising.

Vampires were no more real than nightmares were. Then it hit me.

The marks could have been made with a mortuary apparatus. Though I wasn't sure about what method morticians used to extract blood.

"Are there *strigoi* marks on his neck?" Nicolae asked again, a demanding edge in his voice. I'd forgotten all about him. There was something else in his tone, too. Something tinged with dread. Possibly even fear. I wondered what he knew of the rumors being discussed by the villagers. That his vampiric ancestor had returned from the grave and was thirsty.

The headline from the newspaper revisited my thoughts. HAS THE IMMORTAL PRINCE RETURNED? Did villagers secretly hunger for their immortal prince? Had one of them gone to great lengths to stage this death, draining the body and leaving it for display? I did not envy Nicolae in this moment. Someone wanted people to believe Wilhelm had been murdered by a vampire. And not simply any vampire—possibly the most bloodthirsty of all time.

Without glancing up, I nodded in response to the prince's inquiry. It was barely a perceptible movement, but it was enough. I hadn't the slightest clue how to go about solving this riddle. How had a body been drained of blood without anyone noticing?

We'd been in the village for only an hour or so. That was scarcely enough time to accomplish such a task. And yet, was it possible for a skilled hand? I had no idea how long it took to drain a body of blood.

Whispers rushed throughout the surgical theater, and

several drifted over to my spot on the main floor. A few chills tingled my spine as I stood straighter.

It seemed the villagers were not alone in their superstitions; some of my classmates were also convinced Vlad Dracula lived after all.

Dearest Liza,

As you've pointed out—on several occasions now, not that I'm keeping track of such things—your expertise with matters of a more . . . delicate nature are superior to my own. Especially when it comes to the less fair sex. (I jest, naturally!)

To speak plainly, I fear I may have wounded Mr. Cresswell in a manner even his bravado would have trouble recovering from. It's simply . . . he drives me utterly mad! He's been a perfect gentleman, which is at once intriguing and maddening in itself. Some days I'm sure we would live as happily as the Queen had with her beloved Prince Albert. Other moments I swear I feel my autonomy being ripped from my fingertips as he insists on protecting me.

However, back to the matter at hand: I scolded Mr. Cresswell greatly. He'd informed one of our professors that my constitution was not quite sturdy. Which doesn't sound that outrageous, except it was the second time he'd tried to interfere with my independence. Such unmitigated gall! Our classmates were quite amused, though I was (and am) anything but. My angry response may have alienated Mr. Cresswell's affections. Before you ask for the lurid details, I explained—quite harshly—that I would rather die alone than accept his hand. Were he of any mind to offer it, that is.

Please assist me with any advice you may possess. I'm much better equipped to extract a heart than encourage one, it seems.

Your loving cousin,
Audrey Rose

P.S. How are you getting along in the country? Will you be heading to Town soon?

SEVENTEEN
SNOWY VIGIL

FRONT LAWNS
PELUZA DIN FAȚĂ
BRAN CASTLE
3 DECEMBER 1888

Moldoveanu stood in the center of our small group, both his black cloak and silver hair flapping against the biting wind snapping through the mountains as he recited a prayer in Romanian.

Snow and ice fell steadily but no one dared complain. Right before Moldoveanu began the vigil, Radu had whispered that if it rained at a funeral, it was a sign the deceased was sad. I was thankful this wasn't a funeral service, but didn't know what to make of the weather and what its miserable state indicated about Wilhelm's emotions in the afterlife.

My mind wandered—along with my eyes— as Moldoveanu continued his eulogy. Our newest classmate—and the replacement for Wilhelm—was a young man named Mr. Erik Petrov from Moscow. He appeared as if he'd been born of ice. He ignored the sleet coating his brow as we stood in a circle on the front lawns, our candles flickering behind cupped hands. Aside from the teachers, there were eight of us from the assessment course, plus Anastasia. Thomas hadn't bothered to come.

In fact, I hadn't seen him since he'd left Percy's class earlier. Due to the worsening weather, Moldoveanu had postponed our anatomy lesson until after the vigil, and I wondered if Thomas would trouble himself by attending that. I pushed him from my thoughts and nestled into my duster. Snow found its way under my collar regardless. I blinked flakes from my lashes, trying my best to keep my teeth from chattering. I did not believe in ghosts but felt it was prudent to not annoy Wilhelm if he were indeed watching us from the great beyond.

Anastasia shifted closer, nose bright red and shiny. "This weather is *groaznică*."

I nodded. It was most certainly awful, but so was the brutal manner in which Wilhelm had lost his life. A little snow and ice were nothing compared to the infinite cold his body now resided in. Nicolae stared at the woods, eyes glazed with unshed tears. According to Anastasia's endless supply of castle gossip, he'd not spoken to anyone since the discovery of Wilhelm's blood having been taken, though Andrei tried engaging with him often, unwilling to let his friend suffer alone.

It was surprising how tender Andrei could be when he'd been so horrid to Radu. Though I knew there were many sides to each person if one searched hard enough. No one was entirely good or evil, another fact I'd learned during the Ripper case.

Movement near the edge of the forest grabbed my attention. It was nothing more than a slight shift, as if something was slinking into the shadows. Images of bright golden eyes and black gums flashed through my mind. I chided myself internally. Werewolves weren't surrounding our group of mourners, waiting to unleash a calculated attack. Just as vampires weren't real.

Anastasia glanced at me, eyes wide. She'd seen it, too. "Maybe Radu was right. Maybe *pricolici* are lurking in the forest. Something's watching us. Do you feel it?"

Hair rose on the back of my neck. Strange that she'd thought of the wolves, too. "More likely someone."

"That is a terrifying thought." Anastasia shivered so hard her candle flickered out.

"In light of the recent discovery regarding Wilhelm's death," the headmaster said in accented English, moving swiftly from remembrance to business, "no one is permitted off academy grounds. At least not until we uncover the true cause of death. A curfew will also be enforced to ensure your safety."

Surprisingly, Andrei exchanged a glance with Anastasia.

"Has a threat been made against the academy?" Andrei's accent was thick, sturdy. It suited him well.

Our headmaster met each of our gazes; this time no sneer was present on his face. If Moldoveanu was being kind, then something worse than a threat was coming for us. "We are taking precautionary measures. No threat has been made. Directly."

Moldoveanu signaled for us to return to the castle. Giovanni and Vincenzo were the first to bound up the stone staircase and disappear inside, eager to find the best seats for anatomy class. I knew I should feel excited or nervous about the lesson, too. Those two permanent spots in the academy dangled before us all as if they were bones offered to starving mutts. And yet my thoughts kept straying toward the forest.

I turned around, watching the shadows move under the trees, as my classmates drifted up the stairs. I wondered who was out there, watching our small group, possibly hunting us like prey. Something sinister had happened to Wilhelm. My imagination, no matter how overactive of late, hadn't conjured a vampire to drain him dry.

Some living monster had done that to him. I aimed to discover how. And why.

⌒

"When I call your name, please identify the bone to which I'm pointing." Moldoveanu walked in front of the first row of the class, hands behind his back as if he were a military man. "I want to gauge your proficiency with the basics before moving on to more complex lessons. Understood?"

"Yes, Headmaster," we all responded. I noticed no one slouched or drifted off to sleep in this class. Everyone was perched on the edge of their seats, quills dripping ink ready to scratch across blank pages. Well, everyone except for Thomas. He was craning his neck around, trying to gain my attention. I pressed my lips together, ignoring him. He'd done enough damage during folklore. I did not wish for that situation to repeat itself in this lesson. Moldoveanu was not nearly as forgiving or scatterbrained as Radu.

"Audrey Rose," Thomas whispered when the headmaster stepped briefly into a supply closet. "Please, let me explain."

I flashed him my most warning glare, courtesy of Aunt Amelia. If he ruined my prospects of placing in this academy, I'd murder him. He sat back but did not remove his gaze from me. I kept my mouth shut tight, afraid of unleashing a litany of unpleasant curses at him. I stared straight ahead, ignoring him.

A large blackboard took up the wall behind Moldoveanu's desk, its dark surface clean of any marks. The headmaster rolled a skeleton out of the supply closet and placed it beside him. He picked up a point- ing stick and began indicating each part he wanted us to identify. I shifted in my seat, hoping I'd not miss something easy. Thomas fidgeted, his focus burning a hole in my concentration. I gripped my quill, knuckles going white.

"Mr. Farrell, please name this bone."

I fought to keep my eye roll internal.

"That's the cranium, sir." The Irish boy pulled his shoulders back, grinning as if he'd found a cure for some rare illness and not correctly pointed out that it was a skull.

"Mr. Hale? The next one, please."

"Clavicle, sir."

The lesson went on in much the same manner. Each student was given something ridiculous in its simplicity, and I wondered if I'd been wrong about the difficulty of this class. Then Moldoveanu abruptly dropped the pointer and went back to the closet. He returned with a tray of what appeared to be chicken bones in jars of clear liquid. I sniffed the air. It wasn't carbolic acid or formalin.

"Miss Wadsworth, come to the head of class, please."

I took a deep breath, stood, and forced myself into action. I halted next to the headmaster, attention fixed on the jars in his hands. He offered me one.

"Observe and report your findings."

I lifted the jar to my nose and inhaled. "It appears to be a chicken bone soaked in vinegar, sir."

Moldoveanu gave a curt nod. "And how does that substance affect the bone?"

I fought the urge to sink my teeth into my bottom lip. The classroom was suddenly so quiet my ears were ringing. Everyone's gaze was fixed on me, dissecting my every pause and movement. I mulled over the significance of vinegar, but my attention was sliced in half.

Andrei snorted. "Looks like she might be ill, sir. Think her constitution is damaged?"

My face burned as the class laughed at the jab. The headmaster didn't so much as blink in their direction, and he certainly didn't offer any assistance to me. Furious, I began to retort and was promptly cut off by Thomas, standing so quickly he knocked his chair over.

"Enough!" he demanded, voice colder than the storm raging outside. "Miss Wadsworth is more than capable. Do not mock her."

If I had been mortified before, it was nothing compared to the utter embarrassment I was drowning in now. Moldoveanu drew back, staring at Thomas as if a lizard had suddenly been granted the ability to speak.

"That will be all, Mr. Cresswell." He pointed to the overturned chair. "If you cannot sit there quietly, then you will be asked to leave. Miss Wadsworth, my patience is growing thin. What might happen to a bone in vinegar?"

Blood was still rushing about my head, but I was too angry to care. My thoughts suddenly cleared. Acid. Vinegar was an acid. "It will become weaker. Acid is known to erode calcium phosphate, which renders bone more flexible, too."

Moldoveanu's lips almost twitched into a smile. "Prince Nicolae, identify which joints correlate to which movements in our bodies."

I released my breath and returned to my seat, fuming that Thomas had once again made me into a spectacle in front of our peers. Intentionally or not, he was doing a fine job of hurting our chances in the assessment course. For the remainder of our lesson, I kept my eyes fixed on my notes, afraid of what other foolish thing Thomas might do next.

"My brother begged me to speak on his behalf."

Daciana dragged the writing chair out of my bedchamber and placed it before the settee. Anastasia would be joining us in an hour or so, but for now it was just Ileana, Daciana, and myself.

A tray of food sat untouched in front of us. I had all

but lost my appetite. I motioned for them to take the settee and plopped onto the chair opposite them. I did not want to comment on my frustration with Thomas, but Daciana wasn't about to accept my silence.

"He feels dreadful. I honestly don't believe he thought how his actions would come across. Thomas sees the world in equations. A problem for him has a solution. He doesn't figure in emotions, but he's trying. And willing to learn."

I did not bother pointing out that if he was so interested in learning, then he would have taken note the first time we'd had a conversation regarding his involvement with informing me of what I *ought* to do. And *then* he most certainly wouldn't have made such a scene in anatomy class. Instead of expressing my exasperation, I simply said, "I need some time."

"Understandable. I've never seen him so…affected before. All he's doing is pacing around his chambers. Do you want me to pass a message along to him before I leave?"

I shook my head. I truly appreciated Daciana's attempt at mending our friendship, but now wasn't the time. I would not allow outside issues to affect what I'd come here to do—improve my forensic skills and earn a place in the academy. Personal distractions would be dealt with *after* I'd secured my future with one of those spots; I would not sacrifice myself or my goals.

Not even for Thomas. It wasn't something I felt anyone should do—especially a woman. The right partner would be supportive and understand that, even if they longed for things to be right again.

At this moment, I needed to understand how our classmate had lost every last ounce of blood in his body. How it happened within an hour. And how his corpse had been dumped in the middle of the village without any clues or witnesses. Though I supposed the headmaster had probably already inquired about that while inspecting the scene.

I hated that Uncle wasn't part of this case. I'd have been right beside him while he spoke to investigators, not sent back to the academy to wait. Even Detective Inspector William Blackburn—and his many secrets— had included me during the Ripper crimes.

Ileana lay nestled in Daciana's lap, lids half shut while Daciana ran her fingers through her hair. They spoke about where Daciana was traveling to next, which family she'd be visiting. Their tones were soft, caring, if tinged with a bit of sadness at the prospect of not seeing each other for a while.

Their distraction allowed my mind to wander back over what I had observed in the village. The way Wilhelm had been left. The lack of disturbance in the snow around his body. It was as if he'd been tossed from a nearby window...

I jumped off the chair and paced before the fire, something was breaking apart and coalescing in my mind but I couldn't quite make sense of the merging pieces.

"Everything all right?" Daciana asked.

"I apologize," I said. "I'm just thinking."

She smiled and went back to quietly speaking with Ileana. I recalled the figure I thought I'd noticed in the window above what had become a crime scene. The shutter that had smacked against the wall, drawing my attention upward. Odd that the shutters would have been left open during the storm. Less odd if that were, in fact, the place from which his body had been thrown.

A knock came at the door, startling us all from our respective places. Ileana and Daciana quickly moved apart. Anastasia waltzed in, waving to Ileana and smiling widely at me before inspecting Daciana closely. I hadn't been expecting her for a while, though I was quickly learning that Anastasia danced to her own rhythm in life.

"Are you the handsome one's sister?"

Daciana narrowed her eyes. "If you're referring to Thomas, then yes. And you are?"

"I'm the girl hoping to steal him away for herself." Anastasia threw her head back and laughed. "I'm teasing! Your expression was marvelous." She motioned toward me. "No offense to you, Audrey Rose."

Daciana pursed her lips. I could only imagine what

she longed to say. I knew how taken aback I'd felt at Anastasia's bluntness at first. Anastasia knew what she wanted and wasn't shy in voicing it. An admirable trait for a young woman being raised by the strict headmaster.

"I think I worked out where Wilhelm was killed," I said, hoping to break the tension. I quickly told them about the shutter, the open window, and the shadowy figure. I left no detail out about the state of the body or the lone set of footprints that led down the adjacent alley. As if whoever had tossed him from the building had examined him before slinking away.

Anastasia had gone entirely still. Ileana touched a cross she'd pulled from beneath her embroidered shirt, and Daciana got up and poured herself a dash of wine from a decanter she'd sneaked in.

Once I finished filling them in, Daciana set her glass down, concern etched across her brow. "If he'd been tossed from a window, wouldn't some of his bones have fractured?"

I lifted a shoulder. "Possibly. It's something to investigate further, but I didn't see any early indications of broken bones or bruising. The fall wasn't that high, and if he was already deceased..." I didn't finish the statement. Ileana appeared as if she might be ill.

"Well, I believe someone needs to find out who owns that home," Daciana said. "Regardless of anything, it's a very intriguing lead. You ought to tell the headmaster."

Anastasia snorted. "She should do no such thing. We should inquire into it on our own. If my uncle is informed, then he will discover secrets and not share them." She clutched my hands in hers. "This might be your opportunity to show him how valuable you are. *Te rog.* Please don't tell him this theory. Let me assist you. Then he'll see young women are capable of such things. Please."

I swallowed my initial response. She very well might be correct. If we told Moldoveanu about this, he'd force us to stay behind while he investigated. Then what? He'd not share a thing with us. Not even acknowledge our role in assisting him with the case. Then there was the matter of not being permitted off academy grounds; he'd most certainly use that as an excuse for making us stay behind.

"For now we'll keep this information to ourselves," I said. "But we must plan to investigate in the village soon."

Daciana and Ileana exchanged worried glances, but I pretended not to notice. Both Anastasia and I needed this.

Anastasia kissed my cheeks, smiling triumphantly at Daciana. "You won't regret it!"

But as I bid good evening to my friends and wished Daciana well on the next stop on her Grand Tour, I couldn't help feeling as if Anastasia was dead wrong.

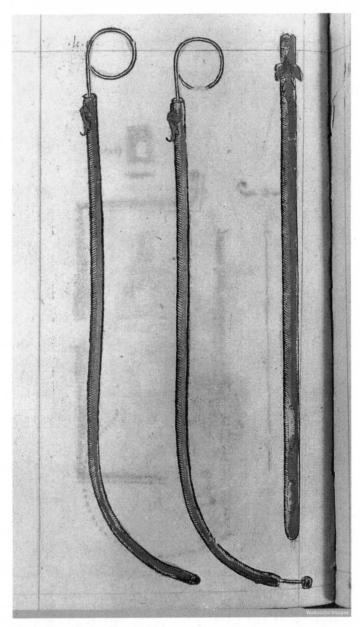

Cannula and sounds.

EIGHTEEN
BEST METHOD OF REMOVING BLOOD

TOWER CHAMBERS
CAMERE DIN TURN
BRAN CASTLE
4 DECEMBER 1888

Dragonlike flames roared against the cage of the fireplace in the small sitting room of my empty dormitory.

I watched them, half mesmerized, as my medical tome pressed into my legs, nearly making them prickle with numbness. Our part of Romania had dragons everywhere I looked. The sconces throughout the castle. Tapestries in the corridors. Sculptures in the village and insignias on carriages. I knew "Dracul" translated to *dragon* and assumed the designs were simply an homage to two fearsome leaders, Vlad II and Vlad III.

I made a mental note to ask Professor Radu if it also had anything to do with the mysterious Order of the Dragon. Perhaps the dragons held clues. To what

I wasn't sure, but it seemed a good lead to investigate. Maybe the Order was behind Wilhelm's death. Perhaps it was targeting members of nobility or families who no longer upheld their Christian values.

I sighed. That was quite a stretch. I didn't know if the Order was even still in existence. Maybe it was nothing more than peasant rumors and tales told to keep people behaving long after their beloved yet brutal prince had lost his head to the Turks.

I shifted my legs, hoping to regain some feeling in my toes. My mortuary-practices book was the size of a large house cat but was far less pleasant company. It neither purred nor issued a disdainful invitation to pet behind its ears. Instead it offered information and pictures I'd found disturbing.

Diagrams were done in black-and-white, showing exactly how to remove blood from the body as well as sew the mouth shut—requiring a ligature from the chin through the gums and septum—for funeral purposes. One sketch even advised the use of petroleum jelly to keep eyelids from opening.

Grieving family members would probably collapse at the sight of their loved ones' eyes or jaws snapping open as the priest delivered them from death to heaven. I wouldn't particularly care to witness such a thing myself. A dried-out tongue would be quite ghastly, a dark slug left sitting for hours in a desert sun. It was better left to the imagination.

I'd seen enough corpses in Uncle's laboratory to know well enough that most people would rather be spared such images, especially when it came to those they loved. I stopped lingering on thoughts of ones I'd lost, flipping to the next chapter of the book. The pages were thick and rough around the edges. It was a beautiful tome, despite its subject matter.

Unbidden, I imagined Thomas sitting with me, pointing out details most would never take note of as we studied these volumes. Though I'd permitted myself a few stolen glances, I had avoided him during both Radu's folklore lesson and Moldoveanu's anatomy exercise. He hadn't appeared well in either class. Shutting out that line of thought, I refocused on my book. I wasn't as familiar with mortuary practices as I was with postmortems, so I'd borrowed the volume from one of the libraries on my way up to my rooms after class.

According to undertakers, inserting a cannula—a long tube—into the carotid artery and then forcing liquids out by means of gravity was the best method of removing blood and other bodily fluids.

Morticians then moved fluids by massaging their way from the deceased's feet toward their unbeating hearts. Which seemed an awful lot of work for someone to have accomplished while people were walking about busy afternoon streets in Braşov. I wagered there would have been a great amount of disturbance in the snow around Wilhelm's body. Surely some fluids or blood would have splattered onto the ground. His body had to have been moved after the blood extraction. There was simply no other way for him to have gone through all that where he'd been found. I still very much believed that house with the unlatched shutter might hold clues.

I was becoming more convinced that a mortuary apparatus was the method used to drain his blood; however, it did not answer the question of how he died. If he'd been murdered, he'd have some sort of outward wound. Strangulation would have obvious signs—petechial hemorrhaging present in the whites of his eyes, discoloration around his neck. His body was free from all that. Except for the *supposed* bite marks, I couldn't recall any concrete evidence that showed he'd been killed.

I doubted he would have stood by idly and allowed someone to drain his blood without a fight, so the "bite marks" likely weren't the cause of his death. It didn't seem out of the question to believe he could have been slipped opiates. Perhaps that sort of toxin would have caused his rash.

As my mind wandered back over the strangeness of my classmate's bloodless body, my heart demanded that Thomas come and discuss this with me immediately. I told my heart to forget its plea. I would solve this mystery on my own. Even though I knew I was capable of accomplishing this task, I couldn't deny the emptiness that lingered in the space around me. Daciana was traveling around the Continent already, and Anastasia was unable to come to my rooms because of a book she was studying. She claimed it might help with Wilhelm's case. Ileana was busy with her tasks and I refused to put her position in jeopardy because I was lonely.

Where are you when I need you, Cousin?

I was still awaiting a return letter from Liza, hoping she might offer some much-needed advice on the matter between Thomas and myself. Romance was to her what forensics were to me, and I wished she could be here now to help me navigate this storm of emotion.

I despised being so distracted during a crucial time. No matter how often I commanded my brain to formulate scientific theories, it stubbornly pushed itself back to Thomas and the unrest I felt. I needed to resolve the situation, if only so I could concentrate. I sighed, knowing that wasn't the exact truth of why I wanted to address the issue. I missed him. Even when I longed to strangle him. I didn't care for this one bit, but it was far preferable to the other invasive thoughts I'd been having.

As if waiting to be summoned, memories of the Ripper's most heinous murder assaulted my senses. The way Miss Mary Jane Kelly's body had been torn apart... I stopped myself right there.

I closed the book and headed to my bed. Tomorrow I'd rise and begin fresh. Tomorrow I'd deal with the aftermath of our fight. For now, I'd tend to my own wounds. Thomas was correct about one thing: I needed to heal myself before I could address anything or anyone else.

I turned down the covers, about to slip into their warmth, when a knock sounded at my door. My breath caught. If Mr. Thomas Ridiculous Cresswell were calling at this indecent hour, *especially* after his reprehensible behavior...

Heart traitorously fluttering, I flung the door open, admonishments perishing on my tongue. "Oh! You're not at all who I thought you'd be."

Anastasia was dressed in solid black and there was a devilish slant upon her lips. "Who, pray tell, did you assume would be here at this hour?" She grabbed my hands and swung us around in a clumsy waltz. "Certainly not the dashing Mr. Cresswell... hmm? The intrigue! The scandal! I must admit, I'm envious of your secret life."

"Anastasia, be serious! It's nearly ten at night!" My accompanying smile did me no favors. "What on earth are you doing out of bed?" I took in her ensemble again, recalling a time when I, too, dressed in a mourning gown. "Actually, it seems I ought to be asking where you're planning on sneaking off to instead?"

"*We* are about to investigate the scene of Wilhelm's death." She skipped into my bedchamber and removed a few dark pieces of clothing from my trunk. "Hurry. The moon is full and the sky is mostly clear. We have to get to Braşov tonight. Uncle told me he's called for royal guards; they'll be arriving tomorrow and will make sneaking about difficult." She glanced at me over her shoulder. "You are still interested in searching that house, correct?"

"Of course I am." I nodded, trying not to consider the creatures in the woods. Monsters were only as real as our imaginations. And mine was intent on populating the world with the supernatural. "Shouldn't we wait until daylight? Wolves might be out hunting."

Anastasia snorted. "Professor Radu is simply filling your head with worries. However, if you're too afraid..." She allowed the taunt and challenge to hang between us. I shook my head, and her eyes lit with pride. *"Extraordinar!"* She tossed the dark clothing to me. "If we're lucky, perhaps we'll run into the immortal prince. A midnight stroll with the enchanting Dracula sounds delightful."

"Delightfully morbid, you mean." I slipped into my

black dress and fastened a matching fur-trimmed cloak about my shoulders. Before we left, I snatched a hat pin from my dresser and stuck it in my hair. Anastasia smiled at me, bemused, but didn't inquire about it. Which was good. I didn't wish to say so aloud, but I certainly hoped we would not run into anyone who thirsted for our blood.

In fact, I would prefer to never set eyes upon Prince Dracula.

Anastasia had been right; the sky was clear of both clouds and snow for once, and the moon was so bright that we didn't require a lamp or lantern. Moonlight glinted off the blanket of snow, glittery and shining in spots.

The temperature, however, was even colder than the laboratory in Uncle's basement where we inspected cadavers. We hurried along the well-worn path that connected the academy to the village below, our procession mostly quiet save for the occasional sounds of nature, our skirts swishing across the packed snow, and our breath steaming out between huffs. We were keeping up a brutal pace, hoping to move away from the castle as quickly as possible.

Shadows flickered above our heads as tree branches creaked and groaned. I tried ignoring the hair standing upright along my neck, and the feeling of being closely inspected. There were no wolves. No hunters keeping pace with us, immortal and feral. No one to delight in mauling our flesh and tearing us into unrecognizable shapes. Blood swooshed in my head.

For the second time that evening, a horrid image of Miss Mary Jane Kelly's corpse crossed my mind, as it often did when I imagined something truly brutal. Her body had been destroyed by Jack the Ripper until it barely resembled anything human.

I closed my eyes for a moment, willing myself to remain calm and steady, but the feeling of being watched persisted. The forest was charming during the daylight hours, but at night it was forbidding and treacherous. I vowed to never leave my rooms in the dark again.

Werewolves and vampires are not real. There is no one hunting you... Vlad Dracula is dead. Jack the Ripper is also deceased. There is no...

A branch snapped somewhere close by, thudding to the ground, and my entire body went numb. Anastasia and I sprang together, clutching each other as if we might be torn apart by a malevolent force. We listened in silence for a few beats, straining to hear any other sounds. All was still. Except for my heart. That was galloping through my chest as if being chased by supernatural creatures.

"The forest is as wicked as Dracula," Anastasia whispered. "I swear something is out there. Do you feel it?"

Thank goodness my mind wasn't the only one conjuring up starving beasts tracking us to the village. The skin on the back of my neck prickled as the wind picked up.

"I've read studies that claim human instincts are heightened in times of duress," I said. "We become attuned to the natural world in order to survive. I'm sure we're just being silly now, though Radu's lessons seem much more plausible under a cloak of darkness."

I noticed that my friend didn't comment further, but she also didn't relinquish her grip on me until we'd made it safely into Braşov. As I'd expected, the village was quiet—all its occupants fast asleep within their pastel-painted homes. A lone howl echoed in the distance, its mournful note finding another singer farther away. Soon a chorus of wolves disrupted the stillness of the night.

I pulled up the hood of my cloak and glanced at the castle standing guard above us, dark and brooding in the moon's silvery light. Something was out there, waiting. I could sense its presence. But what was hunting us? Man or beast? Before I could lose myself in worry, I led Anastasia to the place where Wilhelm's body had been discarded.

"There." I pointed to the house that bordered the murder scene and its window, whose shutter was now fastened tightly in place. "I swear the shutter was loose the last time I was here."

Anastasia pursed her lips and focused on the dark home. I felt ridiculous, standing there in the night, as reality struck. I couldn't be certain the shutter had ever truly been loose, or that I'd ever witnessed a silhouette watching the crowd from the window. For all I knew, it might have been another phantom dreamt up in my imagination. Hysteria, it seemed, was the trigger for each of my episodes.

"I apologize," I said, motioning toward the perfectly unremarkable building. "Seems I was mistaken after all. We traveled out here for nothing."

"We might as well be sure there's nothing to see," Anastasia said, tugging me toward the front door. "Describe what happened again. Perhaps there's something we might start with there."

An idea slowly took shape as I fixed my attention on the door, head tilted to one side. I removed the hat pin from my hair, knowing I was about to cross a moral line I'd never before considered crossing. But Anastasia was correct; we'd come all this way, risked the wrath of Moldoveanu, potentially jeopardized my place in the academy, and still had to make it back to our rooms in the castle while avoiding snarling wolves and headmasters.

No matter the consequences, I could not go back to the academy without knowing. My heart raced, not in fear now, but excitement. It was very troubling, indeed.

I stepped forward and gripped the doorknob in one hand, sticking the hat pin inside the lock and twisting the tumblers around until I heard a beautiful click.

"Audrey Rose! What are you doing?!" Anastasia said, focus darting all around us, voice scandalized. "People are likely asleep inside!"

"True. Or we may find it abandoned." I said a silent thank-you to my father. When he'd been consumed with laudanum last year, he'd often misplace keys, forcing me to learn the art of lock picking. Before tonight, I hadn't thought about using my hat pin for such purposes in a while. I replaced the pin in my hair and paused, waiting to be discovered, pulse roaring inside my veins.

One way or another, we were going to solve at least one mystery tonight. I had witnessed someone staring out that window, or I hadn't. Which meant there either were clues to be found, or there weren't.

Regardless, I could not continue running from shadows any longer. I took a deep breath, commanding my body to relax. It was time to embrace the darkness and become more fearsome than any vampire prince hunting the night. Even if that meant I had to sacrifice a bit of my soul and good morals to get there.

"There's only one way to be sure," I whispered before tiptoeing over the threshold and disappearing into the dark.

NINETEEN
A MOST CURIOUS DISCOVERY

UNKNOWN RESIDENCE
LOCUINŢĂ NECUNOSCUTĂ
BRAŞOV
4 DECEMBER 1888

Inside the tiny home, no fires burned and the air was nearly as frigid as the outdoors.

Frost crept up the windowpanes and my spine as I made my way toward the solitary shaft of moonlight streaming in. Even in the near complete darkness I could see that the living space was a wreck. A chair was upturned, papers scattered about, drawers turned out. It appeared as if someone or a few someones had ransacked the place.

Anastasia inhaled sharply behind me. "Look! Is that... *sânge?*"

I spun around and stared at the large rust-colored stain on the carpet. Chills slowly trailed down my body. I had an awful feeling we were standing in the very place where Wilhelm's blood had been forcibly removed. My heart beat double time, but I forced myself to investigate as if I were Thomas Cresswell, cool, detached, and able to read the pieces left behind.

"Is it?" Anastasia asked again. "I may be ill if it is blood."

Before I could answer her, my attention landed on a broken pitcher. I carefully picked up a piece of its glass, and stuck my finger in a dark crimson spot. I rubbed it between my fingers, noting the stickiness. My pulse throbbed throughout my body, but I tasted the dried liquid, fairly confident of what I would find. Anastasia's lip curled as I grinned up at her.

"It's juice of some sort," I wiped my hand down the front of my cloak, "not blood."

My friend was still staring at me as if I'd crossed some line too indecent to even comment on. I searched myself, finding that tingling thrill still lingering below the surface—an undercurrent of electricity making me feel more alive than I had in ages.

"What do you believe happened here?"

I glanced around the space again. "It's hard to surmise anything for certain until we find a lamp."

I pulled the curtains back on the window, allowing more moonlight to spill in. Anastasia crossed the room swiftly and plucked up an oil lamp that hadn't been destroyed in the chaos. With a quick hiss, yellow light filled the space, and a tragic story unfolded.

Bottles of spirits littered the floor in the tiny cooking area off the main room. Some were broken, and all were empty. Judging from the lack of odor in the air, none of the alcohol had sloshed out, which led me to deduce someone had been drinking quite heavily.

Upon second inspection, the room I'd thought was ransacked had likely just been turned over by whoever had indulged in all those spirits. Perhaps they'd been searching for another bottle to drink and had become enraged when they'd found the house bare. Anastasia located another lamp before setting off to inspect the other rooms.

I picked up a photograph, surprised to find one in a home such as this, then gasped. In the picture, the same young woman who'd been described as missing in the sketch in the dress shop smiled down at a baby. Her husband stood proudly behind them both. Could she have been the one drinking all these spirits? And if she'd been intoxicated and walking through the woods alone...

Anastasia returned, brandishing a book. The cross on its cover indicated it was a religious volume. "No one in the bedroom, but this appeared intriguing."

"You're not taking that, are you?" I glanced at the book while she flipped through the pages; it was likely a holy text of sorts. Anastasia's eyes widened as she shook her head. I set the photograph back down and motioned at the door.

"We should leave," I said. "It was wrong to sneak in here—I don't believe this place had anything to do with Wilhelm's death."

"Or perhaps it did." Anastasia held the book up again. "I've just remembered where I've seen this symbol before."

"Seems like heavy reading before bedtime."

I jolted up from the anatomy book I'd practically had my nose pressed into. An entire day had passed since my adventure with Anastasia, and not much had occurred. Thomas and I still hadn't spoken, Radu was as taken with vampire lore as ever, and Moldoveanu was intent on making my time in the castle as miserable as possible.

I smiled sheepishly as Ileana set down a covered tray, then perched on the edge of the settee. Whatever was under that platter smelled absolutely divine. My stomach grumbled its agreement as I placed my book on the table.

"I asked the cook to make something special. It's called *placintă cu carne şi ciuperci*. Like a meat pie with mushrooms only in flatbread."

She pulled the silver lid from the platter and made a sweeping gesture at the stack of palm-size pies. There were half a dozen of them, more than enough for the two of us. I glanced around for a fork and knife but noted only napkins and small plates. I made to grab for one of them, then paused, my hand hovering above it. "Do we..."

"Go ahead." Ileana mimed grabbing one and taking a bite. "Pick it up and eat it. Unless it's too unrefined. Eating with your hands must seem common. I wasn't thinking. Taking it back to the kitchens is no trouble if you'd prefer something else."

I laughed. "Not at all, actually. Growing up, we used to eat flatbreads and *raita* with our hands."

I took a bite, marveling at the savory tones of perfectly seasoned meat with diced mushrooms as they melted like butter on my tongue. The outer layer of the flatbread had charred bubbles that tasted of wood smoke. It took a great deal of my willpower to not roll my eyes or groan in sheer bliss.

"This is delicious."

"I thought you'd like it. I bring an entire basket of them when I visit Daciana. Her appetite is almost as hearty as her brother's." Ileana's smile faded a bit, turning more into a frown. I wagered she was sad Daciana was gone. "Don't let her delicate manners fool you. She's all steel. I've watched her finish the whole basket before a table of nobles. They were scandalized, but Daciana didn't care a bit."

The slight frown was gone, replaced by a look of great pride, and I couldn't stop myself from smiling. I wondered if she and Daciana had met at some nobleman's home Ileana had worked at, but I didn't want to intrude by asking. It was their story to tell when and if they chose.

"I could likely polish off the entire tray in front of the queen and not regret one delectable bite myself."

We ate in companionable silence, and I sipped tea that Ileana had also brought up. She explained that Romanians didn't often drink it, but she was being accommodating to my English preference for the beverage. I was grateful for the company.

Anastasia had sent a note saying she was staying in her rooms all evening, reading the mysterious religious book. She believed the symbol on its cover was one of the Order's, but I was skeptical that the missing woman from the village had been part of this ancient chivalric band.

I tore my third stuffed bread into pieces, thinking of how Nicolae had done the same thing a couple of days earlier. I wondered if he'd eaten at all or if he kept consuming grief. To stop those thoughts, I decided rather suddenly to ask Ileana for advice.

"I ... find myself uncertain whether I might consider a future with Thomas, given our recent disagreement," I said slowly. "Does it bother you ... knowing a future with Daciana might be impossible?"

"I cannot predict what the future will bring when tomorrow may not come. Any number of things may happen. God may decide He's had enough of us and wipe the slate clean." She swept the napkins from the tray, watching as they unceremoniously fell to the ground. "Yes?"

I took a sip of my tea, mulling over what she said as the bright herbal taste trickled down my throat. "Surely it's prudent to plan for different possibilities for the future. Shouldn't one have some sort of goal to work toward, even if the path they take is unknown?"

"You should follow your heart. Forget the rest." Ileana stood and gathered up the used plates and napkins. "Thomas is human and will make mistakes, and as long as he apologizes and it's something you can live with? It's worth loving him today. It's also worth forgiving him, too. You never know when he might be taken from you."

A tingle of fear worked its way down my spine. I did not want to contemplate such things. Thomas and I were temporarily at odds, and we'd live to resolve our differences. "You and I are quite the serious pair on a blustery night, Ileana. Between my mortuary book and this conversation, I can scarcely wait to see how the rest of the evening unfolds."

Ileana's grin was replaced by a more serious expression. "Wilhelm's family will be arriving in the morning to take their son home for burial. They are quite enraged about his body being...desecrated."

"How do you know?"

"Servants are to remain unheard and unseen while we take care of the castle and its occupants. But that doesn't mean we do not see or hear. Or gossip. The servants' hall is always buzzing with some new scandal. Come. I'll show you some secret passages. If you'd like, you may sneak about the empty corridors. It's my favorite part of this job."

I followed Ileana into the washing chamber, where she removed a key from her apron then pushed on a tall corner cupboard I'd previously paid little attention to. Inside was a door that opened onto a tiny hall that ended with circular stairs. I was intrigued by the thought of hidden hallways. Our own country estate, Thornbriar, had an entire maze contained within its walls, it seemed. If Bran Castle had even a fraction of those hidden spaces, I would be delighted. There was something magical about treading where most would never go, or think of finding anyone else.

After locking the door from the secret corridor,

Ileana drifted down the stairs with the ease of an apparition floating through the ether. I had a difficult time not sounding as if I were an elephant crashing through underbrush as I clunked down after her. I'd never thought of myself as loud, but Ileana's unusually silent tread put me to shame. We descended around and around until my thighs burned. Once we reached the main level, Ileana stalked straight over to a wide column.

I shook my head. I'd walked here several times earlier and had never noticed that what I'd assumed were only pillars ushering students into the main hall actually led to a narrow entrance on one side. Ileana never broke her sure stride as she disappeared into the dark corridor that ran behind the enormous tapestries lining the hall.

An eerie feeling settled in my center. When I'd sneaked through the halls the night I'd left Anastasia's rooms and ended up visiting Thomas, I'd sworn I'd been watched. I very well might have been. I shivered at the thought.

"Be as quiet as possible. We're not supposed to talk or make noise back here. Moldoveanu is unforgiving when it comes to breaking castle rules."

Silently, I bottled up every detail. There were more tapestries hanging on this side of the secret corridor, presumably extras stored here until needed.

We walked quickly enough that I had to gather up my skirts to keep from tripping over them as they wound around my limbs, but not fast enough for me to miss the scenes depicted on the tapestries. Persons being impaled, screaming in pain and terror, adorned one. On another was a forest of the dead, blood dripping from the victims' impaled mouths. Another showed a man feasting at a table, wine or blood spilled across its surface—it was hard to tell. I was reminded of Radu's mentioning that Vlad Dracula dipped his bread into the blood of his enemies.

Chills pierced my skin. Between the barely lit narrow hall and the artwork, I wasn't in the brightest mood. There was a heaviness around my chest, pushing me back. This sinister castle seemed to breathe in my fear with delight. My pulse accelerated.

Ileana came to a sudden stop, and had I not been forcing myself to stare straight ahead, I'd have sent both of us sprawling.

I drew my brows together, noticing the color drain from her face. She jerked her chin forward, hands occupied with the empty tray. "Moldoveanu."

"What—where?"

"Shhh. There." She pointed to a section of a tapestry where a patch of fabric had been carefully clipped away. I'd never have seen it if I didn't know to look. I assumed servants used it as a means of checking the public corridors before entering them. A slithering feeling snaked down my spine. I didn't care for the thought of the walls having eyes. "Through the tapestry."

I stepped closer, careful to not disturb the heavy fabric keeping us invisible to Moldoveanu. I prayed that the floorboards wouldn't sound the alarm and that he'd not hear the thundering beat of my heart.

The headmaster was having quite the heated discussion with someone, though he seemed to be the one doing most of the talking. He spoke in Romanian so quickly I had difficulty keeping up.

A cloudy looking glass hung on the far end of the public corridor, offering a hint to his expression. His long silver hair flashed like the sharp sweep of a guillotine blade as he jerked his head from side to side. I'd never witnessed such a severe man in every sense of the word.

Ileana quietly translated for me.

"I have my job to do and you have yours. Do not cross the line."

I strained to see around Moldoveanu, but he was thoroughly blocking the other person with his long black robes and his fists on his hips.

"We have reason to believe it will happen again. Here." His companion's gravelly male voice took me by surprise. There was an essence to it that was somehow familiar. "Members of the royal family received... messages. Threats."

"Of?"

"Drawings. Death. *Strigoi*."

Moldoveanu said something neither Ileana nor I could hear.

"The villagers are nervous." Again, the deep male voice. "They know the body was missing blood. They think the castle and the woods are cursed. The body from the train is also causing... alarm."

I covered my mouth, stifling the sound of surprise bubbling up. I no longer needed to see whom Moldoveanu was speaking to; I knew that voice even though I'd only heard it once before. I'd seen those sharp eyes that could cut a person in two.

Dăneşti, the royal guard from the train, stepped from behind the headmaster, brushing down the front of his crested uniform. His gaze paused on the spot where we hid, making my pulse still to a slow crawl. Ileana didn't so much as breathe until he refocused on the headmaster. He stood tall, all angles pointed at the older man in the most threatening of manners.

"Do not disappoint us, Headmaster. We need that book. If those chambers are not disarmed, the royal family will shut the academy down."

"As I've already informed His Majesty," Moldoveanu growled, "the book was stolen. Radu only has a few pages in his collection, and it's not enough. If you wish to tear the castle apart, be my guest. I guarantee you will not find what is no longer here."

"Then may God have mercy on your students."

TWENTY
A POOR DECISION

SERVANTS' CORRIDOR
CORIDORUL SERVITORILOR
BRAN CASTLE
5 DECEMBER 1888

Dăneşti spun on his heel and I started forward, but Ileana blocked my escape path while the headmaster swept down the hall—a shadow stalking the young guard.

"Don't," she whispered, holding an arm out. "Moldoveanu can't know we've overheard him."

"How can I pretend otherwise? They were talking about Wilhelm Aldea. Why else would the royal guard be here?" My mind raced with the bits of information I'd overheard. If members of the royal family had received threats, it would explain the fear Nicolae had shown after discovering his cousin's blood had been drained. Perhaps other members of the nobility had received similar threats. Which led me to wonder what else the prince might know or suspect. "If someone murdered Wilhelm, Prince Nicolae might be next."

"You don't know that. Maybe he was speaking about someone else." Ileana pinched her lips together as if she were stopping herself from saying the wrong thing. "The guard may simply be here because Moldoveanu is the official royal coroner."

"He is? How is he both the headmaster and working for the royal family?"

Ileana lifted a shoulder. "All I know is if Moldoveanu discovers we've been spying on him, it will end very badly. Either for both of us, or only me. I cannot afford to lose this position. I have a family to take care of. My brothers need me."

If there was an actual threat to the academy or students, the headmaster had no right concealing that information. Confronting him would be the right thing to do. Except... my focus slid to Ileana's pleading face. Worry etched itself into her flinty expression.

I sighed. "Fine. I won't tell anyone about what we heard." Ileana squeezed my hand once and began walking down the secret corridor. I waited a beat before following. "But that doesn't mean I won't try to discover why Dănești is here. And what book he was hinting at. Have you heard anything about those dangerous chambers he mentioned? Or of any chamber that might need to be disarmed?"

She whipped her head around. "You recognized the guard?"

"Thomas and I had the pleasure of meeting him on the train." I hesitated, peering through the tapestry and checking the public hallway to be sure both men had gone. "He removed the body of a man who had been murdered there. We offered help, but he was not in the market for our particular services. Well, Thomas had offered our assistance. He seemed rather annoyed, though."

Ileana stared at me for a moment, her expression stunned. "I am needed in the lower levels. The main morgue is also on that floor." A shiver wracked through her. "I'll try to meet you back in your common room for breakfast tomorrow." She jerked her chin toward the main hallway, tray clattering in her hands. "Check for anyone before entering the main hall. Oh"—she hesitated a moment—"if you choose to visit the morgue at this hour, you should be alone. No one goes there after dark. Perhaps you'll find some answers there."

Before I had time to respond, Ileana scurried down the secret corridor and turned a corner, disappearing from view. I rubbed my temples. These had been the strangest few days of my life. Two vastly different murders with the promise of more on the way, plus all the castle intrigue. I sincerely hoped the next few weeks would be calmer, though I doubted that would be the case while a murderer was likely prowling the grounds.

I chided myself. Dăneşti hadn't said that exactly.

I rechecked the hole in the tapestry before slipping into the main hall, mind spinning with new information and questions. What was the whole truth behind what Dăneşti and Moldoveanu were discussing? After my initial surge of adrenaline, I realized I'd assumed they were speaking of Wilhelm. They'd never actually mentioned the murder victim by name. Though I couldn't imagine another bloodless body having villagers worried. Then the strange murder on the train that resembled the one from the village...

I stopped abruptly, an idea lifting from the folds of my brain and taking shape. Had Dăneşti brought the train victim here to be studied? That would make sense—where else would the royal guard bring a corpse in need of forensic analysis? Surely to one of the most prestigious academies in all of Europe. One that was only a half a day's ride by carriage from the crime scene. And one where the official royal coroner worked.

If the guard was involved with this matter, there was a possibility of the victim being connected to the crown in some way, too. Perhaps that was why he hadn't left the body at the scene of the crime. I hadn't heard any rumors about the murder on the train, leaving me to believe the royal family had kept the individual's identity from the public.

Newspapers would have blasted that information

from their ink-spotted trumpets. Would that mean Wilhelm and the first victim had been traveling together? I supposed it was possible that while the method of killing was significantly different, there might be a common link between the two men after all.

My heart beat frantically against its cage of bone. I wasn't sure how it all connected, but I knew in my cells it did. Somehow. Three murders. Two unrelated methods. Or had the killing method evolved with practice from that first victim who made headlines?

Uncle had an uncanny way of placing himself in the mind of a murderer, and I tried to emulate his methodology. One victim was disposed of as if he *were* a vampire. The second as if he'd been slain *by* a vampire. Why?

If I could only examine the body from the train, perhaps I'd know more. Was that why Ileana told me where the morgue was? She knew secrets the castle held close, thanks to gossip—like who was waiting to be carved up and inspected for clues.

Ileana said the morgue would be empty, but if the headmaster or Dănești happened upon me, my prospects of finishing this course could be ruined. I should go straight back to my rooms and study for tomorrow's classes.

Indecision toyed with my emotions, tempting and teasing me to pick another path. I thought back to my earlier conversation with Ileana, about our tomorrows never being guaranteed. We truly didn't know what choices might drop into our moments. Which opportunities might come our way. I found myself walking steadily in a direction that wouldn't lead to my room.

Cadavers were kept in two places that I knew of in the castle: one in the morgue on the lower level, as Ileana had said, and the other in the tower next to my rooms. I'd take a quick look inside each mortuary drawer and see if I was right about the train victim being there. Then I'd decide what to do.

I walked swiftly, chin lifted, hoping I appeared as if I were on a mission approved of by the staff. I had a feeling that if I looked as guilty as I felt inside, my daring adventure would be over before it even took flight.

I could not, in good conscience, sit back and be a passive participant in my life. If a murderer was now prowling the halls of the Academy of Forensic Medicine and Science, I wouldn't wait until there was another cold body to inspect. If the murderer was stalking the Impaler's bloodline, Prince Nicolae might be next.

I stopped short, gasping. That had to be it. The irony of someone hunting the blood of a man rumored to drink it was astounding. But it made sense. I continued down the hall, mind running wild with too many thoughts to contain. I wished Thomas hadn't gone and complicated our friendship. I wanted to share my new theories with him, talk them out.

I paused again, considering my options. Perhaps I

should speak with Thomas now, apologize for my temper. Then we could sneak into the morgue together and…I grabbed my skirts and continued on. I would go to the morgue alone and then I'd share my findings with Thomas after. I needed to know that I could handle being around the dead without company.

A flicker of movement caught my attention and I swung around, an explanation already forming on my tongue, and was met with an empty corridor. Not a thing was out of place. I waited a beat, breath held, certain that if someone had sneaked into an alcove, they'd surely make some sort of sound to alert me to their presence. Nothing.

I inhaled deeply, then exhaled, but it didn't slow my rapid pulse. I was seeing things that didn't exist again. I cursed myself for the hauntings of my past, despising myself for having such difficulty sorting fantasy from reality. No one was stalking me. No scientific experiments were being performed on slaughtered women. This wasn't a gritty alley in Whitechapel filled with discordant music from nearby pubs. There was no cloaked figure gliding through the night.

If I kept repeating these assurances, I was bound to make them body memory. I heaved a great sigh. It had only been a few weeks since my world had shattered. I was still healing. I would make it through this. I simply needed time.

I turned around, half expecting to come face-to-face with whatever I had thought I'd seen, but the white corridor was still deadly silent, save for the sound of my own footsteps now hurrying along the wooden floors. I moved as swiftly as I dared, spurred on by the candelabra chandeliers, pointing fingers of light at me as if accusing me of wrongdoing.

I reached the end of the next hall and stood before a thick oak door marked with the sign MORGĂ. There was no window or other way for me to peek inside and see if the morgue was occupied. I would have to take my chances. My breath sped faster as I reached for the knob, then snatched my fingers back as if I'd been stung. Remembered whispers of steam-powered machines taunted me. But there was no whirling or churning coming from behind this door. I listened again anyway. I needed to be sure.

Silence was suffocating; not a sound could be heard. I breathed in through my nose, exhaled through my mouth, allowing my chest to rise and fall in a steady rhythm. I was a student here. Surely if someone were in the morgue I could come up with a valid reason for entering this room. It wasn't as if we'd been told we might enter only during the daytime accompanied by a professor.

With that thought, I drew myself up. This wasn't my father's house, where I'd had to tiptoe around forbidden rooms. It wasn't as if I were going to perform an autopsy this moment.

I clamped my hand over the doorknob, feeling the bite of cold iron beyond the protection of my thin gloves. The sooner I got this over with, the sooner I could seek out Thomas, I reminded myself. With that thought, I twisted the knob and then stumbled forward as the door jerked open from the opposite side. My heart nearly stopped. I glanced at the floor, forgetting to hide my cringe as I prepared for the wrath of Headmaster Moldoveanu.

"I was only going to catalogue—" I began, then looked up and saw a wide-eyed Ileana. The headmaster was thankfully nowhere around. The lie on my tongue disintegrated. "What—I thought you were heading to the kitchens?"

"I—I have to leave. We'll talk later?"

Without uttering another word, she ran down the hallway, not bothering to glance back. I stood there, hand against my chest, collecting myself. I hated Moldoveanu for forcing her to tend to a room full of cadavers when she was clearly uncomfortable with them. Ileana was raised in the village and likely grew up with their superstitions regarding the dead.

Pushing my anger at the headmaster away, I grabbed the knob again, refusing to leave after I'd come this far, and stepped inside.

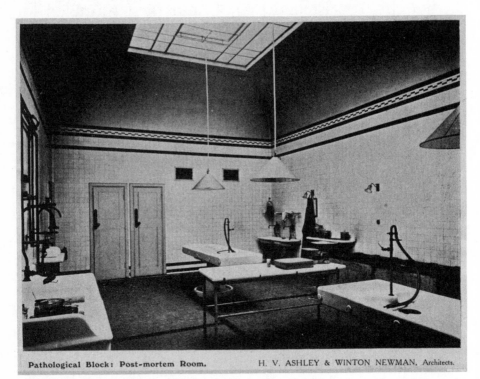

Pathological Block: Post-mortem Room.   H. V. ASHLEY & WINTON NEWMAN, Architects.

Royal Free Hospital, London: the interior of the post-mortem room in the pathological block. Process print, 1913.

TWENTY-ONE
REOPENING OLD WOUNDS

MORGUE
MORGĂ
BRAN CASTLE
5 DECEMBER 1888

I looked about carefully. A wall of metal mortuary drawers and three long tables greeted me. Gas-powered sconces quietly hissed at the intrusion, though one was unlit. An examination table held a body, covered from head to toe in a canvas shroud. I ignored the prickle of fear along my spine. I could ill afford to have another spell of anxiety interfere with my mission.

I exhaled, puffs of breath clouding in the freezing air, relieved to see the room was empty of the living. I moved as quickly as my skirts allowed toward the cadaver. I hoped it was the victim from the train. It would make things infinitely easier to have found him so quickly.

I stood over the shroud, suddenly hesitant to unmask whoever lay there. A familiar feeling of dread weighted both my thoughts and arms. I could have sworn the sheet moved. Just once. Barely perceptible, but movement all the same. A memory started breaking through the barrier I'd constructed around it, but I pushed back. Not here. Not when the clock was working against me.

Jack the Ripper's laboratory was destroyed. Corpses could not come back to life. One day my blasted mind would grasp that fact.

Without wasting another precious moment on nonsense, I yanked the cover away, and the world cracked beneath my slippered feet. My knees buckled as I took in the peaceful features. Long lashes reached toward defined cheekbones. Full lips lay slightly parted, void of their usual smirk.

Thomas lay still as an immovable statue.

"This isn't real."

I squeezed my eyes shut. This was *not* real. I wasn't sure what it was, a delusion brought on by severe hysteria, perhaps, but it was impossible that I was seeing the truth. I would count to five, then this corpse would be gone, replaced by the body of some other young man who'd lost his life too soon.

This was fantasy. Perhaps I truly *was* like one of Poe's unfortunate characters—driven to madness by months of loss and worry. This body only looked like

Thomas. When I opened my eyes I'd see who it truly was. And then I would rush to his chamber and fight with my best friend. I'd grab him by the lapels and press my lips against his, not caring an ounce about being untoward. I'd tell him over and over how much I adored him, even when I wished to strangle him.

As I counted, new images splayed their fingers across my mind.

I saw Thomas giving me a hundred different smiles. Each one a gift granted only to me. I saw all of our bickering. All of our flirtations that masked feelings neither one of us was quite ready to confront. A tear slid down my cheek, but I left it. There was a hollowness radiating from my core, growing more consuming with each breath that caught in its abyss.

"Please." I crumpled onto his chest as if my tears could pour my life force into him. "Please do not take him from me, too. Bring him back! I would do anything…" Anything at all—ethical or not—to fight with him again.

"Anything?"

My heart stopped. I drew away from the body, ready to lash out at the intruder when arms folded like expansive wings around me. I gasped, jerking back as bile seared up my throat. This couldn't be happening. The dead didn't come back—

Thomas twisted his mouth into that damnable grin,

259

and everything inside me went numb. The temperature seemed to drop several more degrees. I clamped my mouth shut to keep my teeth from chattering, though my body trembled violently.

"If I'd known the way to your heart was through dying, I'd have done this ages ago, Wadsworth."

I groped at my collar, fingers fumbling over the material as I tried tugging it away from my neck. If I could only take a deeper breath...

"You're...you're not..."

I staggered aside, hands clutching my center. The room spun in vicious circles. I squeezed my eyes shut for a moment, but that was worse; I kept seeing images I couldn't escape from. Thomas bolted upright, knocking the shroud off his perfectly intact body, his brow creased with concern. I watched him sweep his limbs across then over the examination table and stand.

He was fine. Not dead. Never dead. The room suddenly wasn't cold at all, but scalding. I swore that the ceiling was lowering, swore that the walls were herding me into the corner, where I was sure to suffocate in this damned tomb. I dragged in gulps of air, but it wasn't enough. I thought of all the bodies that were already in those closed drawers. All waiting for me to join them.

My chest heaved. Thomas was not dead. Not like my mother and brother. He had not come back as an undead monster. He was no *strigoi*. I bent, putting my head between my knees, cursing the air for being too thick to breathe properly, as blood throbbed. I kept my eyes shut, and those hauntings persisted against my will. My mind was trying to kill me. Vampires and immortal beings were myth, not reality.

No one could cross the boundary of death and return. Not even Mr. Thomas Cresswell.

"Audrey Rose, I'm so sorry." Thomas held his hands out toward me, placating, gentle. "It was a horrible ruse to get you to speak to me. Nothing more. I—I'm a rotten excuse for a friend. I never meant to—You need air. Let's go outside. Please. It's—I begged Ileana to somehow get you here so we could talk. Alone. Then I saw the table and thought—please let me help you get some air. I apologize. I didn't think..."

"You...you scoundrel!"

I stumbled into the corner, face blazing, tears leaking from my shut eyes. That void at my core was no longer empty, but filling with emotions too furious and too searing to be quelled. Thomas had been there that night—he'd witnessed it all. For him to lie there, playing dead, as if the mere *thought* of him crossing into death wouldn't be my final undoing. I clenched my fists. I realized there were quite possibly a hundred thousand things I could scream about. But only one I needed an answer to.

"How could you lie on that table and fake death?" I demanded. "You know. You *know* what happened in that laboratory. I cannot…"

I stood there, hands shaking, breathing loud enough to be heard. Thomas dropped his head into his hands and didn't utter a word. He scarcely moved. Enough seconds passed that my anger began writhing up again, searching for something to strike out at.

"Speak now, or do not ever seek me out again, Cresswell. How could you do that? Knowing that's what haunts me day and night. My mother lying on that table. That electricity."

I sobbed harder then, tears streaming down my face as I relived the horror of that night. This, *this* memory was what I could not get past. Could not stop seeing each time I stood over another body. My once beautiful and utterly broken mother. Marred by death. Tubes entering her partly decayed body. The twitch of her fingers, the same hands that had once held me, rotten and partially skeletal. Chunks of her long raven hair littered about the ground.

A new wave of sickness crashed through my system. It was something I would not, *could* not ever forget. And to have the added images of Thomas lying on an examination table now? My breath came out in shudders. I finally forced my gaze upward and stared at the young man who could so easily deduce the impossible, and yet miss the simple and obvious before him.

"I am so close to breaking, Thomas," I said, body trembling. "So close to losing myself. I don't even know if I can study forensic medicine anymore."

Thomas blinked as if I'd spoken so quickly and obscenely that his brain hadn't quite caught up to my words. He opened his mouth, then shut it, shaking his head. His gaze was as tender as his tone when he finally found the right words.

"You are grieving, Audrey Rose. Grief doesn't equate breaking. You are rebuilding after something...destructive. You're coming back stronger." He swallowed hard. "Is that what you believe? That you're irreparable?"

I wiped my face with the cuff of my dress. "Why did you lie on that table? I need the truth this time."

"I...I thought..." Thomas bit his lip. "I thought confronting your fear might be beneficial. Might... assist you so you're...performing at your best. We only have a few more weeks. Competition will become fierce. I thought you'd appreciate my effort."

"That is the stupidest thing I've ever heard come out of your mouth. Did you not think of what that might do to me?"

"I thought you'd be a little...annoyed, but mostly pleased. I imagined you...laughing, actually," he said.

"I didn't really think it entirely through, though. I see where I might have offered my assistance in a more... productive way. Perhaps this was a time for emotional support."

"Oh? You're only now deducing that it was a time for emotional support? How could you think I'd laugh over such a thing? To lose you—that would be the furthest thing from amusing I could ever imagine."

His gaze flashed with ill-timed mischief. "Are you finally admitting I'm irreplaceable in your heart, then? It's quite overdue, if you ask me."

"Pardon?" I stood there, nearly agape, blinking. He wasn't taking this seriously. I was going to murder him. I was going to shred him into a thousand pieces and feed him to the giant wolves prowling the woods. I lifted my face and could have sworn a growl ripped itself from my throat. Even though I didn't make a sound, my expression must have promised blood.

"It was a joke! Still not the time for levity, I see that now." Thomas stumbled back, shaking his head. "You've had quite a shock... my fault, naturally. But—"

I marched up to him, eyes narrowed as I brought my mouth close to his. Etiquette and decency and all of that damned polite society nonsense I was supposed to care about forgotten. I placed my hands flat against his chest and pushed him toward the wall, pinning him there. Though I hardly had to touch him to keep him in place—he seemed quite content with our current position.

"Please, Audrey Rose. I'm hopeless and cannot apologize enough." Thomas reached for my face, extending his hands until they were nearly on my skin, stopping when he registered the glare I leveled at him.

"Do not treat me as if *you* know what's best for me." I paused, trying to unravel my own feelings and determine why I'd reacted so strongly. "My father tried caging me, protecting me from the outside world, and this is my first true experience with freedom, Thomas. I'm finally making my own choices. Which is both terrifying and thrilling, but I need to know I'm capable of fighting some battles alone. If you truly want to help, then simply be there for me. That is all I require. No more experiments in helping me deal with my trauma. Or talking with professors about my emotional state or constitution. You undermine me when you do so. I will not tolerate such actions."

"I'm sorry about that, too, Wadsworth." The deep regret in his gaze told me he meant it. "You are, and have always been, my equal. I am so ashamed I've acted in a way that's made you feel otherwise." He inhaled deeply. "Would you . . . is it all right if I explain?"

"There's more to this idiocy?"

I stared, unblinking. Thomas had done plenty of ridiculous things before, but this was by far the worst. He had to have known it was not only reopening a fresh wound—it was tearing both it and my soul apart at once. I allowed ice to coat my entire being.

He released a shuddering breath, as if he could feel the coldness spreading out from me.

"In my mind, when I thought about how you'd feel if you were to find me here in such a way, I thought you'd...laugh. Feel relieved your worst fears had proven false. That the only thing you had to fear was my horrible attempts to assist you." His hand lifted to his forehead. "I'm losing my touch with deducing the obvious. Seems exactly what it is now: the worst idea known to mankind. I told you I have no formula for you. I also have no comprehension of women, it seems. Or perhaps it's people in general I don't understand. I can see how my brand of humor might not reflect the general populace."

Muscles in my cheeks wanted to twitch at the gross understatement, but I didn't have enough energy left to smile.

"It's just...sometimes when I'm afraid or lost, I try to find the humor. Break the tension. It always helps me to laugh, and I was hoping it might help you, too. I truly am sorry, Audrey Rose. I was completely in the wrong in discussing your emotional state with Radu."

"Yes, you were."

Thomas nodded. For a moment it appeared as if he might break down and fall to his knees, but he soldiered on. "My blunder had nothing to do with a lack of faith in you. I simply didn't trust *Radu* to not incessantly inquire about Jack the Ripper. I kept imagining him inadvertently hurting you, and I knew I'd want to murder him. I know you do not require protecting, yet I struggle with wanting to make you happy."

He took a deep breath; apparently there was more.

"In Radu's class…afterward I kept seeing your face. The light vanishing and that desolate nothingness snapping back. It felt like we were standing back in the laboratory the night he died. And the worst part? I knew it was something I could have prevented. If I'd tried harder. If I wasn't terrified of losing you." Thomas covered his face, breath ragged. This time, tears dripped over his chin. "I don't know how to fix this. But I promise to do better. I—"

"There was nothing you could have done that night," I said gently.

It was something I'd known myself for a while, but it didn't prevent my mind from returning to that scene and replaying it over and over, searching for a different ending to the story. I reached over and tenderly took Thomas's hand in my own. I was still upset with him, but my anger was tempered by perspective. He was still

267

alive. We could leave this behind and grow. Neither time nor death had stunted us yet.

He swallowed hard, throat bobbing, as he stared down at our joined hands. "Please forgive me."

"I—"

A floorboard creaked beneath us. I pushed myself away from him, testing the spot with my weight. It sounded as if it had hinges that were in need of a good oiling. I was fairly positive I saw the outline of a door. I prayed it wasn't another delusion. Thomas didn't seem to have noticed it; his focus was solely on me, expression guarded yet hopeful. I realized he was waiting for my response to his apology.

"If you swear to never, ever speak on my behalf without my consent, then I forgive you," I said, knowing full well I would have forgiven him regardless. He brightened, and it took everything in me not to wrap my arms around him. I cleared my throat and pointed to the floor. "I have a theory I'm trying to prove. And I believe the trapdoor we're standing on is our first clue."

Thomas stared at me a beat longer, then turned his attention to the floor. While standing back a few feet it was easier to make it out—there was most decidedly a hidden door within the morgue.

"I overheard Moldoveanu and Dăneşti talking about disarming chambers, though I'm not quite sure what they meant by it. They said they needed to find some book to locate them," I said. Excitement replaced my earlier dark emotions as I gazed at the trapdoor. "I believe we beat them to it."

"It's very possible." Thomas pulled his shoulders back. "Could be an old tunnel into the woods. Vlad used this castle as a fortress. I'm sure there were plenty of ways for him to make a strategic exit if he needed to. It's likely nothing but a spider's palace now. I'd prefer to not soil this suit."

I sniffed rather dramatically. "That reeks of excuses, Cresswell. Are you afraid of spiders?"

He tapped his fingers on his arms, expression thoughtful. "I feel no loss of dignity by admitting I loathe them."

I smiled. We were both going to be in trouble, then. I hoped we wouldn't encounter any eight-legged creatures. Curiosity's magnetic pull was much too great for me to resist. I felt around the wooden planks, searching for a release mechanism. The space below us was either old and filled with cobwebs, or it was regularly taken care of, leading me to believe someone knew about it.

And if someone knew about it, perhaps it was full of clues. If Dăneşti was seeking hidden chambers, I wanted to know why. I glanced up at Thomas.

"Aren't you going to help?" He gnawed on his lip and I nearly saw crimson again. "Honestly? You think this is a worse idea than the one where you played dead and scared the life out of me?"

"Point taken." He drummed his fingers against his lips, considering. "If I end up being devoured by ravenous spiders, at least I'll be memorable for something other than my good looks."

He grinned as I rolled my eyes, then walked over to the unlit sconce. I watched him study it briefly, then twist it to the side. Amazingly, the trapdoor swung inward, revealing a dank, musty stairwell. I lifted my eyes, incredulous, and Thomas beamed.

Of course. The broken sconce was glaringly obvious now.

"Shall I impress you with my powers of deduction? It was the only unlit sconce in the room, leading one to believe if there was indeed a secret—"

"Not now, Cresswell. Give me a hand. I want to see what Vlad Dracula was hiding down here. And what Dănești is after."

TWENTY-TWO
THOSE FEATHERLESS WINGS

SECRET PASSAGE
PASAJ SECRET
BRAN CASTLE
5 DECEMBER 1888

If the near-complete darkness wasn't enough of a warning to turn back, then the sickeningly sweet stench of decay that assaulted us should have been.

"Lovely." Thomas scrunched his nose. "There's nothing quite like the aroma of a bloated corpse to get one in the mood for adventure."

We stood on the threshold of the trapdoor, staring down into what was sure to be a dismal setting. Gray stones edged with cobwebs and other detritus yawned before us, opening their chipped teeth wide to allow entry into the bowels of the castle. I did my best to breathe through my mouth. "Think of it as if it were simply a ripe fruit ready to burst."

Thomas's gaze swept over me, brows lifted in appraisal. "You are morbidly enchanting."

"We need to hurry. I don't want to linger too long." I nodded at the trapdoor. "Should we close this?"

Thomas eyed the secret passage and then the main door, resignation settling on his features. He sighed. "I've a feeling we'll regret it, but yes. Go on down a few steps and I'll close us in with the dead body and spiders. In the dark."

I gathered my skirts, thankful that they weren't as bulky as normal, and descended one step at a time, cringing at what might be getting caught in my hemline. I was terrified of what was causing the stench and hoped it was only the carcass of an animal that had found its way into the castle. I wasn't keen on finding human remains.

Thomas huffed from behind me, his shoes finding every way imaginable to scrape over stone as he maneuvered the trapdoor into place. From previous experience, I knew he was more than capable of moving through the night with inhuman stealth. I gritted my teeth, ignoring the smack of his shoes as he stomped down the steps after me. Perhaps he was still shaken from his idiotic maneuver of playing dead.

A pebble bounced down the steps, sounding our arrival for all the world to hear. I stopped moving, my pulse a roaring wave crashing through my veins. We couldn't be positive we were alone down here, and I did not want to get expelled so quickly. Especially when there were so many unanswered questions about what, exactly, was happening at this academy.

Thomas muttered something too low for me to understand.

"Quiet, you." I tossed a glance over my shoulder, though it was too dark to make him out clearly. His silhouette was gilded by the gaslight filtering through a crack in the trapdoor. I fought the urge to shiver. There was always something about him that was—unsettling in an intriguing manner. Especially when we were secreted away in the dark.

"I can't wait to see if it's as pretty as it smells."

"Honestly? Is it impossible for you to hush?"

The strike of a match followed by a hiss was his only response. Thomas smirked at the candlestick he was flourishing, the light barely a flicker in the oppressive dark. I did not bother asking where he'd found the stub of wax. Perhaps he'd had it secured in his morning coat.

He leaned in, speaking quietly enough that I nearly missed his words. However, he did not miss the hitch in my breath as his lips grazed my neck, making my skin tingle with the contact. I felt him smile into my hair.

"You're the handsomest young man I've ever known," he said.

I squinted, trying to discern any bruising or imperfections on him. There wasn't anything out of the ordinary that I could see. Simply two golden-brown eyes staring back, amused. "You've hit your head, haven't you? Or did someone slip you a strange tonic?"

"You want my silence." Thomas grinned, then stepped around me after he leapt down the stairs. A perky hop to his step. "The phrase I just uttered is the code for when you want me to speak again. I promise I shall not utter one syllable until you unlock these lips with those words."

"If only I were so lucky."

Keeping his promise, he crept down the remaining stairs without so much as breathing too loudly. If I didn't already know Thomas was there with me, and couldn't see the slight flicker of light he held, I'd never have known he was only a few paces ahead. He certainly moved like a wraith when he chose to.

His silhouette dissolved into the shadows surrounding us. Taking care to use the same caution, I descended with a sharp focus, as the last thing I needed was to break a limb down here.

Wings flapped in the distance, the sound like leather striking leather in frantic succession. I ignored the way my heart longed to take flight and carry itself straight back up the stairs. I imagined those were the bats the headmaster had mentioned the night we arrived.

Foul-smelling corpses were one thing, but *bats*...
A shudder vibrated along my bones. Bats with their
rodent faces and membranous wings made my nerves
jangle.

Which was completely irrational. I tolerated rats well
enough. And birds were all right. But those feather-
less wings—and the veins that spread along them like
branches in the tree of life. Those I could do without.

As we reached the bottom of the stairs and entered
a corridor that appeared to have been hewn from the
rough stone of the mountain itself, I questioned my
need to discover secrets contained under the morgue in
a castle with such a forbidding past.

Condensation dripped from the stone, though no
one was here to wipe the sadness of this miserable tunnel away. At least no one we'd want to meet without a
weapon. Wind howled through the passageway, raising gooseflesh along my arms.

I cursed, forgetting to be quiet. Thomas turned,
his expression bemused, but I motioned for him to
keep walking. I'd need to look into having some sort
of scalpel belt made. Then I could strap it to my body
and wield it like the dangerous blade it was whenever I
needed to. I wondered if the dressmaker in town would
be able to manufacture such an accessory.

If one could create a belt, surely this could be done. I
was stalling again and knew it. I sincerely hoped no bats

assaulted us. There were a great many things I could withstand...but imagining their claws getting stuck in my curls as they screeched and tore strands of hair out...

I wiped my hands down the front of my skirts, wishing I'd had thought to bring a cloak. Though of course I hadn't planned on going anywhere other than the servant corridors. It was much colder this far beneath the castle's many fireplaces. As if he'd plucked the deduction from the darkness, Thomas abruptly faced me, offering his coat.

"Thank you. But you keep it for now." It was so long, I'd stumble over it.

He nodded and continued on. I hurried after him, managing to ignore the fluttering wings echoing in the dank passage ahead.

I tugged Thomas to a halt. At the far end of the very long stone tunnel we were in, a single torch flickered. While its light resembled a sun sinking into the horizon, there was absolutely no warmth to be found within its meager rays. If a torch was lit, someone was either down here now or had been fairly recently.

My breath clouded in front of me—ghosts of warning. Thomas signaled for me to lead the way. The walls seemed to draw closer now, the mountain crushing in on us from both sides. We passed a few doors, some of which were stained black, while others were dark oak, all almost indistinguishable from the cave walls until we came upon them.

I tried pushing one in, but it refused to budge. I carried on down the corridor, attention homed in on any flicker of movement. I wasn't sure what we'd do if we encountered someone sinister down here. Hopefully Thomas had a weapon hidden away wherever he'd secreted the candlestick.

A slight breeze gusted, and with it our candle blinked out. I longed to pull my hair free from its plaiting and cover my neck with it. The air near this end of the tunnel was more frigid than it had been by the stairs. Water no longer dripped but froze in a glistening sheet where it kissed the rock face.

Thomas caught up to where I'd paused and pointed toward the direction we'd come from. Looking back from this vantage point, I could see we'd steadily descended, though it hadn't felt that way while we were walking. We were also much farther from our entry point than I'd thought.

Darkness was playing tricks on my senses. I could have sworn that it felt us, watched every step we fumblingly took and delighted in our terror. Thomas swatted a spiderweb away before I could walk through it. Chivalrous, considering his fear. I thanked him and slowly continued down the passageway.

"Feels like a carnival with too many looking glasses. Doesn't it?" I asked.

A few beats passed. I twisted, expecting a sassy response, but Thomas simply nodded, grin spreading wickedly. Then I remembered his vow to remain silent.

"You know what?" I asked. He raised his brows. "I rather enjoy seeing you without hearing all the non-sense spewing out. You should be quiet more often." I allowed my gaze to inspect his chiseled features, pleased by the longing that lit in his eyes when my attention found his mouth. "In fact, I've never wanted to kiss you more."

I quickly moved down the passage, smiling to myself as his jaw swung open. A bit of levity was what I needed to hold my unease at bay. I did not want to consider what we were about to see. Death never smelled pleas-ant, and the overwhelming odor now made my eyes water. Hope of coming across an animal carcass was dwindling.

Unless it was a rather large, human-size animal.

I wiped wetness from the corners of my lashes. This was how bodies smelled when they weren't buried far enough below the earth. We hadn't dealt with advanced decomposition too often in Uncle's laboratory, but the few times we had had left memories that would be stitched within the seams of my brain for eternity.

Drawing closer to the lone torch, I distinguished two more tunnels forking off in opposite directions. At the point before they branched off, however, there was a thick oak door set to one side. Droplets of water seemed to leak from the porous wood. How very odd.

I took a few deep breaths, relishing the way the coldness now kept me alert. Here the passageway was wide enough for only one body to pass through at a time. My narrow shoulders nearly scraped against the walls as we inched our way toward that ominous door and whatever horror lay hidden behind it. Thomas twisted sideways to fit.

Glancing down, I was surprised to find rubbish. The scent of death was covering up most everything, but the greasy napkin at my feet appeared to be fresh enough. I swallowed, hoping whoever had deposited the garbage was long gone. It would be quite difficult to race out of this narrow passage without being caught.

I closed my eyes. I knew I was strong enough to handle whatever we were about to uncover. But the part of my brain still affected by the Ripper murders was filling my emotions with nonsense again. I only needed a minute. Then I would move.

Thomas tapped my shoulder, motioning that he wanted to pass by. I shook my head. In order for that to happen he'd have to squeeze past me. Before I could protest, he gently pressed me against the wall and slid over me, careful not to linger.

I reluctantly peeled myself off the wall, watching as he inspected the two tunnels. While he was busy calculating Lord only knew what, I focused on the door. He'd sufficiently distracted me from any growing fear, and he knew it. If I hadn't been grateful for the outcome, I would have slapped him with my glove for taking such bold liberties in our unchaperoned state.

I faced the door again. A cross with flames at each end had been burned into the wood—a long time ago, from the faded look of it. A Roman numeral seven was carved below the cross. I traced my fingers along the symbol, then drew my hands back at the surprising warmth.

Maybe I wasn't as free from my delusions as I'd thought. It would be best to open the door quickly, if it even would open. The suspense of who or what we'd find was only going to increase exponentially the longer I put it off.

Drawing in one more deep breath, I pushed with all my might, noticing again how hot the wood seemed for such a cold tunnel. That wasn't scientifically possible, so I ignored the warning chatter of my bones. To my astonishment, the door swung open. The creak I'd been expecting never came. Someone obviously had taken great care to grease the metal hinges.

I poked my head in, barely a few inches, confused by the tropical heat that blasted from within the shadowy space, and squinted. The room appeared to be no larger than a small bathing chamber, but there was a mound of black in the center of the floor, and similar mounds along the high walls.

Which didn't make sense—what could possibly be covering the walls? And how was it so disturbingly warm in here without a fire?

As if in answer to that very question, steam hissed from a crevice. There must be a source of heat somewhere close, perhaps a natural hot spring within the mountain or some sort of heating mechanism in the castle.

"Cresswell, hand me that torch, will you? I believe—" Something warm and furry smacked against my head. I reached up, but it was gone. Blood rushed in my ears, and every bit of reason left my mind as the mass of black lifted as one. "What in the name of—"

I jerked back, thrashing about as a hundred screeching bats swarmed and dived. Teeth scraped around the collar of my dress, then slid along the skin of my neck. It took every last rational thought I had to keep from screaming. If I broke now, someone would find us. I needed to be strong. I needed to not lose focus. I needed to—fight.

My hands connected with leathery wings. I swatted bodies from the sky and ignored the growing panic as blood dripped down my covered fingers, splattering on the floor.

We were under attack.

TWENTY-THREE
LILIECI VAMPIR (VAMPIRE BATS)

SECRET PASSAGE
PASAJ SECRET
BRAN CASTLE
5 DECEMBER 1888

Thomas was beside me a breath later, brandishing the torch from the wall as if it were a flaming sword.

He wasn't the only one capable of steady action in the face of danger. I catalogued every detail of the room and scene I could manage between assaults. The mound in the center of the room was a body lying facedown. Bats had been covering it entirely, likely feasting on it.

Skirts indicated the victim was female, her skin whiter than freshly fallen snow where it wasn't maimed by crimson bite marks. Her stillness left no doubt that she had perished. No one who still breathed could stay so motionless with that many creatures crawling over them. I ran to her side just to be sure.

"What are you doing?" Thomas yelled from the door. "She's gone! Hurry!"

"One...moment," I said, seeing blond hair beneath scarlet streaks. He could wield the torch, but I was determined to gather as much information as I could.

I tried to look for other details, but several bats dived on me at once, tearing through the lace of my gloves, drawn to the blood already leaking from my wounds. I hauled myself up, ran out of the room as fast as I could, and yanked the door shut. Thomas shoved the torch at the remaining assailants. His eyes were wild as they screeched and chittered, and dived for us once again.

After he'd chased the last bat off into the darkness, he plucked something from my shoulder and tossed it aside. "Are you all right, Wadsworth?"

We had just been attacked by a hellish nightmare turned reality. Warmth trickled down my neck. I had more cuts than I dared to think of at the moment. Instead of voicing all of that, I laughed. Surely this was something not even Poe could dream up.

Despite the horror, I felt flushed with the heat of excitement. Blood thrummed through my veins, amping up my heart, reminding me of how powerful I was. Of how wonderful it was to be alive.

"I thought you weren't supposed to speak again unless I said the magic phrase, Cresswell."

His shoulders slumped, dropping the tension he'd

been carrying along with them. "Being attacked by vampire bats is a good enough excuse to break my own rule." He frowned at the blood seeping through my gloves. "Plus, I already know I'm the most handsome young man in your life." A rogue bat dived for him, and I swatted it away. "Those bats aren't native to Romania."

"I had no idea you were also a chiropterologist," I said blandly. "Is this how you impress all the young ladies?"

He surveyed me with interest. "Well, *I* had no idea you knew the scientific term for bat study." He removed his long morning coat and offered it to me. It was warm and smelled of roasted coffee and fresh cologne. I resisted the urge to breathe in the comforting scent.

"Your brain is quite appealing. Even in the face of all this." He waved at the closed door, grin fading a bit. "By far my favorite asset of yours. But yes. I've studied them enough to recognize those as vampire bats. I haven't a clue who'd want to breed them."

Even snuggled within Thomas's coat, I loosed a shiver that had been teasing my flesh. This castle was more treacherous than I'd thought. "I wonder what other charming manner of wildlife we'll find down those tunnels."

My mind snagged on a detail from Moldoveanu's conversation with Dănești. I described the entire exchange to Thomas as fast as I could, words tumbling out.

"Why would the book Dăneşti was talking about have anything to do with these passages? Do you think it contains hints to where all of the doors and tunnels lead?"

"Perhaps." Thomas glanced from me to the two dark tunnels behind us. For once his expression was easy to read. We'd just found a body and were attacked by bats. Now wasn't the time to wander this far below the castle without first arming ourselves with knowledge and physical weapons. "We should do some research. Come. I know the perfect place."

We'd sneaked back to our rooms and scrubbed most of the blood from our faces. I had also returned Thomas's morning coat, not wanting to elicit any unwanted questions or attention should we run into anyone at this hour. Now, in a shadowy hallway in the castle's west wing, we stood before two oak doors that were carved in all manner of beasts, both mythical and all too familiar. Although no plaque had been erected in his honor, I imagined DRACULA'S BLOODY LIBRARY in bold Gothic letters all the same.

Torches set into wrought-iron urns stood proudly on each side, both inviting visitors and warning them to behave while in the library. I spotted a few flying bats within the door's design and tugged them open.

"If I never see another one of those ghastly creatures again, I'll die a happy girl."

Thomas chuckled softly beside me. "Yes, but the way you slapped away the one attacking me was so valiant. Shame I'll never get to witness such ferocity again. Perhaps we can go bat hunting at least once a year. But then we'll have to set them free, naturally. They're too adorable to harm."

I paused before crossing the threshold. "They tried to drink our blood, Cresswell. 'Adorable' is hardly the word I'd use."

I swept into the room, then halted, hand fluttering to my center. The ribbed vault of the cathedral ceilings made me think of stone spiders whose long legs crawled down the walls. Stone ogival archways housed aisles of books.

This was by far the grandest library in the castle; the one in which I'd found the book about mortuary practices was much smaller. Leather and parchment and the magical scent of ink on pages overwhelmed my senses. Wrought-iron chandeliers—made of the same design as the hallway urns—hung from the web of gray stone above them. It was foreboding and intriguing at once. Part of me wished to spend hours within its shadowy alcoves, and part of me longed to secure a weapon. Anyone or anything might be hidden within the gloomy nooks.

I closed my eyes for a moment. While addressing our cuts, Thomas and I had decided to delay notifying anyone about the body we'd discovered. It went against every fiber in my being to leave that poor girl's remains in that terrible place, but I did not trust Moldoveanu. He'd likely punish or expel us for exploring the castle's secrets. Thomas also argued that it might alert us to who else knew about the passages if her body was discovered. I'd reluctantly agreed under one condition: If her body wasn't found by the next afternoon, we'd leave an anonymous note.

Someone sneezed several aisles away, the sound echoing in the vast chamber. My body froze. We weren't doing anything wrong, yet I couldn't stop my pulse from accelerating at the thought of encountering anyone.

"This way," Thomas whispered, guiding me in the opposite direction. As if breaking from a trance, I moved forward, drinking in each aisle of books, shoving the vicious attack from my mind. They weren't simply regular rows either: There were shelves from floor to ceiling crammed with tomes of every shape and size.

Thick books, thin ones, leather-bound and soft-cover: they were stacked together like cells composing a body. I wanted to run down each aisle to see if there was any end to them.

We could spend the remainder of eternity and not read every book housed there. Though, on a normal day, it would have been magnificent to simply sit with a cup of tea and a warm blanket and pluck new scientific adventures from the shelves like inked petits fours to savor.

There were books written in French, Italian, Latin, Romanian, English.

"I haven't the slightest idea where to begin," Thomas said, startling me from my book Utopia. "They've got the sections labeled, at least. It's not much, but it's a start. Are—" He waved a hand in front of me, lips curving upward as I swatted it away. "Are you paying attention to a word I'm saying, Wadsworth?"

I paused at an aisle labeled ŞTIINŢĂ.

"Look at the science section alone, Thomas!"

I selected a medical journal from the nearest shelf, flipping through the pages and marveling at the anatomical drawings. An article by Friedrich Miescher caught my attention. His work with nuclein was fascinating. To think there were phosphorus proteins in our blood cells we'd yet to name!

"This is what they should be teaching us. Not vampire lore regarding a man who died centuries ago. Do you think it's medically possible to open my cranium and stuff the pages inside? Perhaps the ink will leach in and create some sort of compound reaction."

Thomas leaned against a shelf, arms crossed. "I'm strangely intrigued by that notion."

"You would be."

I shook my head but continued walking down the aisles. POEZIE. ANATOMIE. FOLCLOR. Poetry. Anatomy. Folklore. Plush leather armchairs were set up in nooks with little tables meant to either write notes on or hold more reading material. It took every ounce of my will to not get distracted by the overwhelming urge to simply curl up in one of them and read about medical practices until dawn dragged itself across the sky.

"I know what to gift you with this coming Christmas," Thomas said. I spun, skirts wrapping around my legs as if they were an ebony cocoon. His eyes glittered. "Medical journals and leather-bound tomes. Maybe I'll throw in a shiny new scalpel, too."

I smiled. "I've already got a few of those. I will gladly accept any and all books, however. A person can never have too much reading material. Especially on a fall or winter evening. If you're feeling extra generous, you may include tea. I love a unique blend. Really sets the atmosphere for medical study."

Thomas trailed his gaze up and down the length of my form, pausing until I finally cleared my throat. A bit of color rose around his collar. "Audrey Rosehips."

"Pardon?"

"I'll have a signature blend made for you. A bit of English rose, perhaps some bergamot. A hint of sweet. And definitely strong. It'll need petals, too." He smiled.

"I might have found my true calling. This is quite a moment. Should we commemorate it with a waltz?"

"Come on, tea connoisseur." I nodded toward the waiting aisles, heart fluttering pleasantly. "We've got a lot of investigating to do if we hope to find any books with the layout of the castle."

"And its many secret tunnels." Thomas swept his arms out. "After you, dear Wadsworth."

"Goodness! You scared me!"

Professor Radu emerged from the adjacent aisle, sending a shower of books to the floor. He swooped down to retrieve them as if he were a pigeon pecking at crumbs. "I've been searching for a particular tome on the *strigoi* for class tomorrow. Blasted library is too large to find your own nose in. I've been telling Moldoveanu for ages that we need to hire more than one librarian. That malingerer Pierre is never to be found!"

I was still steadying my nerves. Radu hadn't made a sound—an impressive feat for the clumsy professor. I retrieved a book titled *De Mineralibus* from the floor and handed it to him, noting its gnarled leather and old script. "Here, Professor."

"Ah. Albertus Magnus. One of our next lessons." He paused, large eyes blinking behind spectacles as he added the tome to his armful of books. "Have you seen Pierre, then? Perhaps you've sent him off for a book of your own. I did not mean to interrupt. Though this is precisely what I mean. More librarians, more knowledge. Why Moldoveanu insists on one is…"

Radu was so upset that he unthinkingly started to gesture with his arms, forgetting about the books currently occupying them. Thomas lurched forward and secured the stack before it collapsed on us.

"Blasted Pierre is never where you need him to be. Tell him I've found my own material, no thanks to him. Next I'll be doing both his job and my own."

Radu tottered off, mumbling to himself again about his lesson plan being in complete disarray and how he'd be speaking to the headmaster about multiple librarians.

"At least he didn't ask why we're out of our rooms unchaperoned at this hour," Thomas said. "Poor librarian, however. He's got his work cut out for him. Tending to an entire academy and Radu."

"He's fascinating." I watched our professor walk into a stone column and bounce off it, arms too full to gesticulate wildly at the inanimate object. "I wonder how on earth he managed to get a position here."

Thomas turned his attention back to me. "His family has always been involved with the castle. Generations back, from what I recall. The academy keeps him on because it's tradition and they believe the locals enjoy knowing one of their rank can climb the social rungs."

I knitted my brows. "But if that's true…then his

family has been doing this for hundreds of years. The academy hasn't been around that long."

"Ah. Let me amend. I believe his family has been involved with the *care* of the castle. His teaching position is new to their line. An honor and inspiration."

"Why wasn't he offered the position of headmaster? Surely that would send a more positive message than hiring him as a folklore professor."

Thomas lifted a shoulder. "Unfortunately for Radu, I'm sure the academy is wrong. I doubt most villagers in our generation care as much as those in the past. They likely think of him as they think of the rest of us here. Blasphemous evildoers who should be ashamed of turning this holy castle into a place of science. Ah, look."

Thomas pointed to a secluded section near a blazing fireplace. At first I thought he was being improper, suggesting a place where we would have privacy. But for once, he was focused on our mission. A sign in English hung proudly at the end of the aisle: BUILDING & GROUNDS.

"Today might be our day after all."

I set off for the massive aisle of books dedicated to the castle, hoping this was another of those times Thomas was right.

Tonga bat. Colored etching by S. Milne and Turvey.

TWENTY-FOUR
STRANGE ILLUSTRATIONS

TOWER CHAMBERS
CAMERE DIN TURN
BRAN CASTLE
5 DECEMBER 1888

Ileana stood on a rickety stool, dusting the crammed bookshelves in my sitting room when I finally made it upstairs shortly before midnight.

A pair of my boots—shining as if they'd been freshly polished—sat on the windowsill, but I didn't have the energy to ask why. Our grand foray into the master library to see what information we might glean about where the two tunnels possibly led had been fruitless. The only things we'd discovered were that Radu was even more clumsy than originally thought and that he enjoyed reading old German texts.

The Building and Grounds section had obviously not been well maintained—there were books of poetry and journals with silly tales regarding the castle and the surrounding area, but nothing useful. Not that I'd expected us to simply waltz into the library and walk off with a book neither the headmaster nor the royal guard could locate.

I closed the door behind me with a soft click. Without turning, Ileana paused, hand mid-swipe with the dust-coated rag, the wood creaking beneath her feet. The dirt on the bottom of her embroidered apron made it appear as if she'd been trudging through wet earth. I didn't want to think about what dank part of the castle she'd been forced to clean. If it were anything like the passage we'd been in, it was most decidedly wretched.

"I'm—I'm very sorry for earlier," Ileana burst out. "Thomas asked for help and I couldn't—I couldn't... I didn't want to say no to Daciana's brother. I told him it was an awful idea, but he was desperate. Love makes fools of the wisest. I can leave if you don't wish to speak with me."

"Please don't trouble yourself. I'm not upset with you. It's been a long day, is all."

Ileana nodded and went back to carefully wiping down the bookshelves. I flopped onto the settee and rubbed my temples, hoping for a bit of serenity to fall from the sky and splatter across my soul like a cleansing rain shower. If only I'd simply been upset by Thomas's attempt at reclaiming our friendship. His feigning of death felt as if it had occurred millennia ago. We had much bigger problems to contend with.

Though the bats were terrifying, I knew they weren't responsible for Wilhelm's blood loss. He certainly would have had discernible scratches on his person if they had been. Which made me all the more confident that his blood had been removed with a mortuary apparatus.

The bite wounds on my hands still burned. I wanted to soak in the tub and cleanse the lingering bat saliva and never think about those grubby little monsters again. Father would start abusing his laudanum once more if he ever found out about my exposure to such potentially disease-spreading creatures.

Of course someone would be breeding vampire bats in a castle whose most infamous occupant was rumored to have become a vampire. My initial impulse was to blame the headmaster, but being rash was the exact opposite of what Uncle would instruct me to do. Coming to a hasty conclusion about the identity of the culprit, and then manufacturing evidence to confirm that conclusion, wouldn't lead to truth and justice.

"You seem ... is everything all right?" asked Ileana.

Even though I'd promised Thomas to remain silent, I decided to share our discovery with her. Perhaps she had heard something about the passages from other servants or occupants.

"We found a rather... mutilated body in the morgue. Well, below the morgue. There was a trapdoor and..." Ileana went rigid. I hurried on, hoping to spare her too much talk of the dead. "Anyway, I wish we'd left well enough alone. It—was difficult to tell if there were similarities to any other case we've been involved with. Bats had been... feasting on the blood. I don't know what to make of it. You mustn't tell anyone. Not yet, at least."

"Bats were... drinking from a corpse?" At this Ileana turned, blinking. She appeared shaky enough to fall backwards in a stiff wind. "Was it a student? Did you tell anyone?"

An image of the moon-white body assaulted my mind, viciously taunting me with each vivid detail and the lacerations she must have sustained before taking her last, damned breath. I shook my head.

"It—it was hard to make out anything. I only know her sex by her clothing. We couldn't inspect the room with all the... bats swarming. We're going to send the headmaster an anonymous letter if she's not discovered by tomorrow afternoon. We thought the person responsible for the murder might happen to 'find' her body, and thought it best to wait a few hours."

I closed my eyes, trying to forget the sounds of wings beating against my head, the feel of claws digging into my soft flesh. Her death must have not come fast enough. I hated thinking of how long she'd lingered while they'd drunk deeply. Again and again. Razor-sharp teeth slicing and biting. How powerless she would have felt the more her life force was drained.

I focused on the fireplace, getting lost in the flames. If I allowed my imagination to run so freely, I was sure to be sick.

"Do you think the same person who's impaled those two others is responsible?" Ileana fiddled with the dust cloth. "Or is there another murderer in Braşov?"

I ticked off the facts I knew. "So far there are two bodies that have been impaled off grounds: one on the train, and the one reported in the newspapers. Then there's the bloodless body of Wilhelm Aldea. Now this young woman, who likely died from being a living host to the bats. Judging from the lack of rigor mortis, I'd say she…passed away at least seventy-two hours ago. It's hard to be certain, though."

I didn't mention the slight stiffness present in the limbs, or how the warm temperature of the room might have accelerated the process. Uncle had made me memorize different factors that contributed to the speeding up or delaying of the aftereffects of death last summer. Since the temperature had been moderate to warm in the room, and her body was decomposing, that meant a minimum of twenty-four hours had likely passed since she'd taken her last breath. Though I placed her time of death closer to three days earlier, maybe almost four. The stench had been horrid.

"Is it possible she was another victim of the Impaler?"

I peeled off my lace gloves, wincing at the tattered pieces as I unveiled scratches and bite marks. "I wish I knew. One pair of bodies are made to appear as if they *are* vampires. Another as being feasted on *by* vampires."

From outward appearances, these crimes weren't all committed by the same person. It seemed as if the woman and Wilhelm had been murdered in different ways than the other two, and than from each other.

I wasn't even sure someone had forced her into that room. Perhaps she'd gone wandering and had the misfortune of getting trapped. It was black as pitch in that chamber—she might have stumbled in, been attacked by starving bats, then fallen, unable to escape from her hell. Until her body could be inspected, there were too many unknown variables.

"Either someone is trying very hard to stage vampiric crimes," I said, disengaging from thoughts of her battered corpse, "or there are two murderers working— I don't know, almost working to outdo the other. One who imitates the methods of a vampire hunter, the other those of an actual vampire. I'm not sure what to believe. There are still too many missing pieces. If Wilhelm died because of bats, we would have seen multiple wounds on him. They were quite savage."

I held my hands up, showing the bites that had dried ruby red.

"The castle is old, as are the tunnels you found," Ileana said, tearing her attention away. "Maybe they've been breeding since Vlad's time."

"Maybe." A charming thought indeed. "I think *someone* is breeding them, all right. Thomas said they're called vampire bats, but they're usually found in the Americas. I cannot, for the life of me, figure out how it relates, unless it's simply misfortune."

"Perhaps the Impaler has a connection to the academy," Ileana said, her focus stuck on the allegedly risen immortal prince. "The first murder occurred in the village. Then Wilhelm's body was found there as well. If what Dăneşti said about threats being made against the royal family is accurate, then perhaps the Impaler was looking to create panic with the first two murders."

"Or perhaps he was practicing."

"Maybe he's collecting blood," she whispered.

My own blood chilled. The thought prodded the sensible part of my brain until other, more menacing ones sprouted to join it. It was certainly possible that a career murderer was living beneath this turreted roof, stealing blood for his own purposes.

Uncle's theory on murderers involving themselves in the crimes flitted through my head. In a school composed of students and professors, who had more to gain from the murders? Unless the motivation was simply the thrill of the hunt. That bloodthirsty compulsion always terrified me the most. I wished Uncle were here now to discuss this with me. He always saw beyond the obvious.

Ileana had gotten so quiet that I started when she shifted off the stool. "You believe the Impaler exists?"

"Not in the literal sense, no," I said. "I'm certain a very human person is re-creating methods of death made famous by Vlad Dracula. I do not believe—for one instant—he's risen from the grave and is hunting anyone. That's both preposterous and completely contrary to the laws of nature. Once someone is dead there is no way to reanimate them. No matter how much one wishes otherwise."

I would not divulge how painfully familiar I was with the truth of my last statement. Fingers twitched across my memory, and I shoved the image away.

"Some villagers would disagree," Ileana said quietly. "A few have gotten ill over the last couple of weeks. One girl has disappeared. They are certain a *strigoi* is to blame. Now Wilhelm's body is discovered, his blood missing. They are not unaware of what that might mean."

I began to comment on the village girl's disappearance and stopped myself. I was ashamed to admit to sneaking into her home. I believed her case was simply an unfortunate one, brought on by drinking too many spirits and getting lost in the woods. No vampires or werewolves snatched her from the path.

"Do you know of anyone who'd want to shut the academy down?" I asked.

Draping her cloth over a galvanized bucket, Ileana tapped the sides, creating a hollow, echoing sound that ricocheted in my skull. I narrowed my eyes as she glanced toward the door and then swallowed. I was about to ask what was wrong when she hurried over to the settee. She pulled a leather-bound book from a pocket on her apron, handing it to me as one might pass on a reeking bedpan. I reluctantly took it.

"I...I know it's wrong. But I found this journal. It was in Prince Nicolae's room." I lifted my gaze, but Ileana kept hers locked on the book and stammered on. "Remember when I told you servants are to be neither seen nor heard?" I nodded. "Well, it's very easy for some of the more highborn students to forget we exist. Some think their fires magically light themselves, and their chamber pots grow wings to empty their waste."

"I'm sorry people are so cruel."

Her eyes were shards of ice before she blinked the expression away. "I'm not proud of filching the journal, but I heard him mentioning something about drawings. When I peeked inside, I saw awful images. Here."

I flipped the leather journal open, scanning a few

diagrams. Hearts, intestines, a human brain, and…
bats. Skulls of bats with horrendous fangs. Bat wings
with notes and details of claws at their apex. Each page
proudly displayed a new section of a bat's anatomy. I
flicked my attention back to Ileana, whose gaze was
locked on her hands.

"He's got quite a few specimens in his chambers, too."

"Why did mention of his drawings trouble you?"

Ileana wrung her hands. "I recalled what Dăneşti
and Moldoveanu had said about the royal family receiving those threats. That they were drawings."

I sat straighter, as if the movement would make
what she'd said more palatable. Waves of nausea roiled
my stomach. "He couldn't possibly have sent those
himself…"

"That's why I looked. Then I saw the sketches
of bats and noticed all the skeletons he has in his
room…I don't know why I took his journal. I just"—
she shrugged—"I thought there might be more to see.
And then I saw this one near the back."

Reaching over, she turned the pages until she found
what she'd been searching for. My breath stilled along
with the rest of my body. A girl with onyx hair, eyes a
deep emerald green, and lips that were dripping blood
smiled boldly.

With my finger I traced the jawline up and around

to the catlike eyes, then touched my own face. "I don't—this cannot be me. He wouldn't have had time to—"

Ileana turned to the next page. On it, drawn with great care, was the image of a girl wearing an apron splattered with gore, an autopsy blade poised above stark white flesh. I tore my gaze away. The cadaver was male, and no cloth covered his nude form. Heat flashed over my cheeks.

I hardly knew what to make of the crude drawings.

"There's more." Ileana showed me image after image. Each featuring me as a beautiful creature delighting in blood and death. The way the prince had captured me, it was as if he'd turned me into an immortal being, a little too perfect to be human. A bit too cold and hard for this fragile world. The flames in the fireplace flickered wildly, its heat suddenly sweltering. I longed to fling my windows wide, letting the cold wind of the Carpathians cleanse this space.

One final image had me sucking in a gasp. It was hard to tell exactly who the male was—either Thomas or Nicolae—but he and another Audrey Rose stood side by side. The young man wore a suit made of bones, holding an ivory skull as if it were an oracle to divine from. My bodice hugged my frame. The illustration was gorgeous, despite the large anatomical heart and circulatory system that branched from my chest, then wound its way down my arms and ran fingers to my skirts.

The black gloves in the drawing caught my attention next. Lace and swirls covered my arms as if they'd been inked permanently onto my skin. Ileana watched closely before pointing to the design on my arms. "Prince Nicolae's arms are covered in ink. Not so delicate as these. But I've seen them when he rolls his sleeves back."

I raised my brows. How intriguing. I'd read that many aristocrats had gotten themselves tattooed over the previous several years. Once magazines had announced how fashionable it was, nearly one in five highborn ladies and gentlemen, it was estimated, had them secreted on their bodies. They were also growing in popularity in the royal courts. It made sense that the prince might dabble in something such as tattooing. It added to his mystique. I imagined many young women would be more than delighted to unwrap his layers for a peek at what he was hiding.

"What are his of?"

Ileana pushed herself up from the settee, then took back the journal and motioned toward the door. "It's late. I polished your boots and left them for Moş Nicolae. You should get some rest so he has time to deliver his winter gifts." She smiled at my confusion. "I believe your version of Moş Nicolae is called Father Christmas. It's a tradition for him to bring sweets. If he shakes his beard and snow falls, then winter may truly begin. Sleep now. Tonight is Magic Night. Maybe he'll leave you a trinket."

Sleeping was the furthest thing from my mind, especially when someone else named Nicolae might be prowling about the castle, delivering "gifts," but I bid her good night. I pressed my fingers against my eyes until flashes of white streaked across them like stars shooting against the sky. In one day, I'd thought Thomas was dead, found a secret passage, been attacked by blood-leeching bats, discovered another body, and now had become acquainted with Nicolae's disturbing illustrations. The dark prince very well might be the person we were searching for. He had the opportunity to send illustrated threats to family members.

Perhaps it was an attempt to secure the throne for himself.

I couldn't help but wonder if Nicolae might also be responsible for his cousin's death and, if I continued to unearth his secrets, that something worse than a threat might befall me soon. Thinking what morning would bring was enough to weight my lids against their better judgment. I removed my layers and slipped beneath chilly covers. The last image I remembered before falling into darkness was of an unearthly young woman with tattoos swirling over her arms, her lips twisted into a feral grin as her incisors sank into her own blood-soaked lips. If Prince Nicolae truly thought I was cursed, perhaps he'd crafted that illustration as propaganda. He'd certainly turned me into Princess Dracula.

I hoped no one would seek to stake me through the heart.

Audrey Rose,

If you're reading this, then you likely came by my chambers. I apologize for leaving without saying good-bye. I found a connection between the Order and the murders—I told you I recognized that book! Trust no one. I swear I will return in one week with more information. I believe that young woman staged the scene in her home.

I did some investigating in the village and discovered her husband was the victim the newspapers first reported on! (Unfortunately, her child had passed away a few months prior.)

Uncle Moldoveanu believes I've rushed to Hungary to assist with an urgent personal matter. Please don't say otherwise; I do not wish to alarm him or be punished unjustly.

Do not travel into the village again. It's not safe. Eyes are everywhere.

—Anastasia

P.S. Please burn this letter. I suspect the servants have a habit of acquainting themselves with personal belongings.

TWENTY-FIVE
GARDEN OF ASH

WALLED COURTYARD
CURTE INGRĂDITĂ
BRAN CASTLE
13 DECEMBER 1888

The afternoon after our discovery of the tunnels, Thomas and I had sent Moldoveanu an anonymous letter with directions on where to find the corpse. We hadn't heard a thing regarding it for days. I'd no idea if he'd sent someone to check, and I hadn't had an opportunity to sneak down there myself. More and more guards seemed to be filtering into the nearly empty academy, intent on keeping us locked in tight.

Frustrated, I sent another note. I sincerely hoped the headmaster had taken it seriously. I hated thinking of the body being left to rot. Any potential clues would be lost forever. Not to mention the thought of leaving a person in that state...If I didn't hear anything by this evening, I swore to myself, I would drag the headmaster down into the tunnels single-handedly.

I quietly popped a piece of hard candy into my mouth, thanking whoever had played the part of Moş Nicolae in the castle for the treats. They—along with Ileana's company between tending to her duties—had been the most pleasant part of a very long week. Anastasia still hadn't returned from wherever she'd traveled to. Something about the rushed nature of her letter hadn't sat well with me. What had she discovered about the Order of the Dragon? Ileana hadn't thought Anastasia's exit from the castle was suspicious, and I was loath to worry her by voicing my fears.

Midweek, Radu had successfully lulled Vincenzo to sleep while stuffing us to capacity with local folklore about bodies being burned to ash, then ingested. Then we'd all taken turns in Percy's surgical theater, removing organs and learning the intricacies of death, trying to outshine our peers and secure our place in the assessment course.

During Percy's lessons, we all feasted on the knowledge being served to us. The subtle details of murder and its many markings. How to read a body's language for definitive proof of cause of death. I loved those lessons, and gradually felt myself becoming stronger around bodies. Though the nightmares of the Ripper murders were still lurking near the surface of my mind.

Moldoveanu's lessons were always conducted with precision, and though I didn't enjoy his company, he was exceptionally gifted at both anatomy and forensics. I noticed no one dared speak out of turn for fear of being expelled on the spot.

No one had spoken of Wilhelm or uttered a mention of his untimely demise after his family collected his body. It was as if time had heaved itself up from falling to its knees, and carried on as if it weren't scraped and bruised.

Thomas and I had tried sneaking back into the tunnels at odd hours, but had been thwarted by a contingent of royal guards. Moldoveanu took our new curfew seriously, and had more guards posted throughout the halls than I imagined were at the royal court of Romania.

By the end of the week, a letter arrived for me, postmarked London. A new chambermaid had brought it to me along with news that Ileana would be tending to other duties for a while. I was sad to lose companionship at night, but the letter warmed me. I knew precisely who the sender was and couldn't wait to tear into it after class. Radu chattered on and on about this being some unholy night. The prince cracked his knuckles, Andrei's head drooped, yet the twins and even the brooding Cian were wholly engrossed by this particular tale. I shifted in my seat, praying for the courtyard clock to toll the hour.

"It's rumored to have its base in Roman culture," Radu continued. "A sacrifice is made. Then animals speak to us. Whether it's through our language, or through theirs, no one is sure." He shoved his glasses further up his nose and peered at the classroom. "Blasted Mr. Hale. Where is he? Did he leave class early?"

Noah fidgeted uncomfortably and raised a hand. Radu walked right past him, attention torn between the other students and his notes.

"Mr. Hale is sitting right there, Professor," Nicolae drawled. "Perhaps that veil between worlds has already thinned enough for you to misplace reality."

Radu snapped his attention to the prince, gaze hard. "You'd all do best to stay locked in your chambers tonight. The dead will rise and seek out those foolish enough to wander outside. Spirits will inhabit those they do not feast on. Even princes are hunted."

The remainder of class went on in much the same manner until the tolling clock finally released us from Radu's folklore grasp. I lingered in the hallway outside our classroom, but Thomas was engaged in a mild dispute with Radu about the origin of the holiday, and it was as entertaining as waiting for a blade of grass to erupt from the ground over several days. The letter in my pocket nearly burned a hole through my skirts. I needed to read it or I'd surely combust on the spot. Thomas nodded in acknowledgment as I motioned toward the corridor.

I managed to slip outside and nestle into a corner of the castle's walled courtyard; I had a bit of time before our next lesson began. It was the one place where I was free from the prying eyes of students, professors, and an unwanted army of men. Guards patrolled the turreted roof above but didn't bother walking in the courtyard below.

From the comfort of my spot, I released the tension I'd wrapped myself in, one twist of my shoulders at a time.

A wishing well sat proudly in the center of the tiered cobblestone levels. It was another bit of beauty in the harsh winter world. If one were to cut a Corinthian column at its capital, it would come close to the decorative acanthus leaves embellishing the well's outer wall. I tugged the hood of my cloak up, doing my best to retain as much body heat as I could while flurries splattered themselves across the stone. I'd taken to carrying my cloak to classes, unsure of when Moldoveanu or Radu might want to spring an outdoor lesson upon us.

I touched the envelope and smiled. From previous correspondences, I knew that Aunt Amelia and Liza were visiting my father, readying the house for the upcoming holiday. With the excitement of the murder on the train, classes, the trip to the missing woman's house, and the mysterious deaths of Wilhelm and the young woman below the morgue, I'd nearly forgotten all about Christmas.

Thomas and I had decided that we were going to stay in Bucharest during our short two-day break—his family kept a house there—but the thought of not seeing my family was proving difficult to overcome. I'd never missed a holiday with Father. As the days had worn on, I wondered what I should do. A trip to London would be refreshing, though it'd be impossible to make one and not miss any classes. I could ill afford to fall behind, especially if I hoped to beat out my classmates for a place in the academy. Still, a wild part of me longed to forget about the academy and return home for good. My stomach churned at that idea—my peers were exceptionally gifted, and I couldn't stop worrying about who might win those two open spots. I shoved that fear away, focusing on reading my cousin's note once more.

Liza had mentioned previously that she and Aunt Amelia would likely stay throughout the winter, keeping Father company in the big, empty house in Belgrave Square. My heart clenched. Father struggled with all that had happened and felt immense guilt over one of the Ripper killings. In the midst of the murder spree, he had been found by the police in an East

End opium den and firmly encouraged to rest at our country estate. He had only recently returned to London when he'd come across Miss Kelly during a search for laudanum. She'd claimed to know someone who might provide it to him, and Father willingly followed her to that doomed house on Miller's Court.

He'd left Miss Mary Jane Kelly alive, and had no idea he'd been stalked that evening. Jack the Ripper had followed him, watching, waiting to strike.

Perhaps Thomas had been right; going back home to London wouldn't be a terrible idea. We could keep a close watch on Father, and Uncle would be only too pleased to have us back. And yet… to leave the academy would be a failure and I'd worked too hard to run away now. I despised the headmaster, but I wanted to earn my place here. I couldn't fathom what I'd do if neither Thomas nor myself made it in.

A new thought had my heart racing. At the end of the four weeks, what if only one of us was accepted to the academy? The mere thought of saying good-bye to Thomas stole my breath.

Without wasting another moment on sad thoughts, I tore open my cousin's letter, eager to gobble up every morsel of her message.

"Would you mind terribly if I sat out here, too?"

I glanced up at the American accent, surprised that one of my classmates was engaging me in conversation. They

Dearest Cousin,

Allow me to be quite frank. Since I've read every novel by the immeasurably talented Jane Austen, and because I am three months older than you, I obviously have a vast amount more romantic knowledge. I don't fancy myself a poet, but I have been flirting (quite shamelessly, I daresay) with an intriguing young magician—and escape artist—who performs with a traveling circus, and, well . . . I shall tell you all about that another time.

Anyway, we were discussing romance one afternoon near the pond, and he spoke of love being akin to a garden. Do not roll your eyes, Cousin. It's not becoming. (You know I adore you!)

His advice was this: Flowers need plenty of water and sunshine to grow. Love, too, needs attention and affection, or else it slowly withers away from neglect. Once love's gone, it's as brittle as a dried-out leaf. You pick it up, only to discover that it's turned to ash beneath your once-careful touch, gone on a swift wind forever.

Do not turn your back on a love that could jump the barrier between life and death, Cousin. Like Dante's valiant journey into darkness, Mr. Thomas Cresswell would descend into each circle of Hell if you needed him to. You are the beating heart inside his rib cage. It's a rather macabre way of saying you complement each other—though that's not to say you aren't whole on your own.

Unlike my mother, I believe all women should stand on their own without needing anyone to hold them up. Surely a wife worth having is one who is secure in who she is? That is a discussion for another time, I'm sure. Back to your dearest Mr. Cresswell...

There's something powerful in that kind of love, something that deserves to be kindled and tended to, even when its embers are flickering dangerously close to darkness. I implore you to talk with him. Then write and tell me each delicious detail. You know how much I adore a grand romance!

Do not allow your bountiful garden to turn to ash, Cousin. No one wants to stroll in the aftermath of neglect when they could be dazzled by a lush garden full of roses.

Yours,

Liza

P.S. Have you reconsidered returning to London for the holiday? It's positively boring without you here. I swear that if Victoria or Regina attempts to boss us around during one more tea party, I will toss myself from the Tower of London. At least then Mother won't cluck at me to practice, practice, practice for my coming-out ball. As if society would condemn me for stepping right instead of left during the waltz!

If my future husband would be appalled by such trivial matters, then he wouldn't be worth having. He'd be the sort of dullard I should like avoiding at all costs. Imagine if I told Mother that? I shall wait until you're home so we may have the pleasure of watching her flush devil red together. Something to look forward to.

Kisses and hugs. — L.

mostly spoke in groups and—after Thomas's poor attempt at helping me by speaking to Radu of my constitution— accepted my role in the assessment course only when absolutely necessary. To them, I was not a threat and was hardly worthy of their notice.

Noah smiled. His features appeared as if they'd been carved from the most alluring ebony, deep and rich and beautiful. I shook my head. "Not at all. The courtyard is certainly large enough for the two of us."

His brown eyes twinkled. "That it is." He studied the snow that was coming down a bit more heavily, blanketing the exposed stones and statues. I watched his gaze drift up to the castle. Muscles in his back tensed as Moldoveanu appeared briefly in one of the windows, striding down the corridor. "Am I mistaken, or is the headmaster a miserable fellow?"

I laughed outright. "I daresay he's awful in general."

"He's pretty good with a surgical blade, though. Guess we can't have it all, right?" He yanked the collar of his overcoat up and swatted at the bits of ice now mingling with the flurries. They pinged and skittered against the ground, the sound an almost lulling accompaniment to the gray skies. "I'm Mr. Noah Hale, by the way. Though you already know that from class. Thought it was time I properly introduced myself."

I nodded. "You're from America?"

"I am. Grew up in Chicago. Have you ever been?"

"No, but I hope to travel there one day."

"What did you think about Radu's lesson?" Noah asked, abruptly changing topics. "About the rituals supposedly taking place tonight? Do you believe all the villagers will make a sacrifice and are convinced animals speak our language this one night?"

I lifted a shoulder, choosing my words with care. "I'm not sure this lesson was any stranger than the folktales regarding vampires and werewolves."

Noah glanced at me sidelong. "How did a young woman such as yourself get involved in all this"—he motioned vaguely at the castle—"business of cadavers?"

"It was either that or embroidery and gossip," I said, allowing humor to creep into my tone. "Honestly, I imagine the same way anyone else who came to study such subject matter did. I want to understand death and disease. I want to offer families peace during difficult times. I believe we all have a special gift to offer the world. Mine happens to be reading the dead."

"You're not too bad, Miss Wadsworth. No matter what anyone else says." Noah was blunt, but I didn't mind his straightforwardness. I found it as refreshing as the mountain air.

A clock tolled the hour, a somber reminder that this bit of levity was over. I stood, stuffing Liza's letter into my skirt pockets, and brushed snow from my bodice where my cloak had fallen open. "Are you excited about class? We're in the dissection room today."

"It's the good stuff." Noah stood and rubbed his leather clad hands together. "We're all getting a specimen today. Some of the boys have placed wagers on their performance."

"Is that so?" I raised a brow. "Well, then I apologize in advance for earning the top spot."

"You can certainly *try* for that top place," Noah said. "But you'll have to fight me for it."

"May the best person win."

"I love a good challenge." Noah took my gloved hand in his and shook it. I found that the action of a young man grabbing my hand didn't offend me one bit. It was a sign of respect, a sign that Noah now thought of me as an equal. I beamed as we made our way inside.

This was precisely what I lived for: the exploration of the dead.

The interior of a dissecting room: five students and/or teachers dissect a cadaver, c. 1900.

TWENTY-SIX
A MOST INTRIGUING CASE

DISSECTION ROOM
CAMERĂ DE DISECŢIE
BRAN CASTLE
13 DECEMBER 1888

"What is the purpose of inspecting the bodies of those who die from no outward sign of trauma?"

Professor Percy stood beside the exposed brain of the specimen before him, his apron stained in rust-colored blood. His reddish hair and matching whiskers were neatly styled—so at odds with the fluids marring his wholesome features. I imagined it was how Uncle appeared when he was a young professor. The thought warmed me despite the crispness of the dissection-room air.

"Why carve them open when we can plainly see they've died of 'natural' causes?" he asked. "Hmm?"

Eager hands shot into the air like fireworks, exploding with the need to answer and prove themselves, ready to outshine their peers. The prince glanced around the room, sizing up the competition. There was an edge to him today. It was one of the first times I'd seen him show more than a passing spark of interest. Percy ignored them all, turning his attention on the one student who was distracted.

"Mr. Cresswell? Do you have any thoughts on the matter?"

Thomas, unsurprisingly, was a hand space away from being face-first in his cadaver, ignoring everyone and everything except for his scalpel and the cadaver. I watched the line of skin part under his blade as if it were a wave pulling back from the shore. He snatched up toothed forceps from his tray, inspected them, then went about the task of exposing the viscera, humming quietly. The tune was rather upbeat and jaunty given what he was doing. I raised a brow. Perhaps he had a bit too much passion for his work. Percy didn't bother interrupting. He'd learned rather quickly that Thomas was a force unto himself while in the laboratory.

"Prince Nicolae?"

I forced my gaze to land back on Nicolae. He chewed his bottom lip, attention transfixed by the specimen before him. "We need to prove if they've died naturally. Unless we inspect them, there's no other way of knowing for certain."

"Partly true. Anyone else?"

Andrei swung his scalpel as if it were a sword and he the most inept defender the kingdom had ever known. Noah, distracted by Andrei's antics, ducked away from the fool. The Bianchi twins were no better than Thomas—their gazes were wholly fixed on the bodies before them, their scalpels already making precise incisions. Cian and Erik both raised their hands, staring each other down in the process. One boy was like fire and the other ice—neither pleasant for anyone exposed to them for an extended period of time.

"So we can understand disease and its effects on the body?" Erik said.

"Sometimes. Should we always open up specimens for no good reason, then?" Percy asked.

Cian nearly tumbled from his seat in his haste to answer. "No, sir. Postmortems aren't necessary for all. Only those who die under suspicious circumstances."

"Thank you, Mr. Farrell. Mr. Branković, kindly put your scalpel down. It's not a weapon. You're going to hurt or maim someone. Most likely yourself. Anyone else have something more to offer?"

I raised my hand. Percy nodded at me, his gaze steady. "Go on, Miss Wadsworth."

"Because, sir, as in the case of the deceased before me, who clearly died in water, one might think he simply drowned or died of hypothermia. Conducting a postmortem is the only way to be sure of his cause of death."

"Good. Very good. And what will studying his innards tell us?"

"It will alert us as to *why* he may have fallen in the water. There may be a preexisting condition—perhaps he had a heart attack. Or an aneurysm."

"Or perhaps he'd had one too many spirits because it's so bloody cold," Nicolae added, coaxing nervous laughter from Noah and Erik. When the prince's attention shifted to me, an uncomfortable chill trickled down my spine. It was hard to forget the drawings he'd done of me. Or the illustrated threats that had been made to the royal family. *His* family.

"Prince Nicolae, keep the jesting outside the dissecting chamber. It's in poor taste. Miss Wadsworth, very good. Foul play might also be a factor. That's precisely why it's important to inspect each body thoroughly. One may never know what secrets we'll uncover when we dare to plunge into less…pleasant places."

Thomas leaned close and whispered. "He's a bit odd, that one."

"Says the young man who missed his name being called out because he was too taken with his cadaver,"

I whispered back. "Percy's no stranger than you or I or Uncle. You're only envious that I'm his favorite."

Thomas flicked his attention to me, but before he could dazzle me with a retort, I plunged my blade into my cadaver's icy flesh, ignoring the deep blue discoloring and protruding eyes as I carved down to the rib cage. I fought with everything I had to see the corpse as it was, and not something staring coolly back at me, inconvenienced by the blade in my grasp.

Its torso was bloated, along with the rest of the body, making it rather difficult to find identifying features. I swallowed a bit of revulsion down, unwilling to cower when this cadaver needed respect.

I closed my eyes briefly and then inspected his heart, noting that all appeared normal before walking around to his head and pulling an eyelid back. There was no sign of petechial hemorrhaging in the whites of his eyes. This man had not been smothered or strangled before falling into the water, then. He likely had lost his life to the harsh mountain elements and hypothermia, not to some sinister cause. It was not the best way to go. Certainly not the most pleasant way either. I hoped he hadn't suffered long—though I still had much to learn regarding hypothermia and its characteristics.

Glancing around the room, I noticed my specimen wasn't the most foul to be seen. Nicolae had a rather ripe cadaver, its torso bloated and stretched beyond capacity. Little wormlike grayish-black lines crawled over its skin. That wasn't a good sign. I watched the prince set his face blank as stone, then slice into the body. But his cut was too deep and swift...

Maggots shot from the intestinal area along with a terrible gaseous odor. Nicolae stepped back and swiped the larvae from his brow, hands shaking ever so slightly. His chest expanded and contracted as if he could contain the disgust with a few measured breaths.

Silence descended like a curse. It was an extremely undignified position for a member of royalty to be in, and yet he maintained that air of superiority even with maggots slung over his face. Erik paused, finally glancing up from his own cadaver. He slowly took in the scene, blinking as if it were all a terrible dream, then shrieked, tossing his apron toward the sullied prince.

Though it was hardly funny, I nearly choked on the laughter I swallowed down. Andrei was unable to contain himself even for a moment. He doubled over, laughing so hard he started wheezing. Erik clapped his back as Andrei coughed and sputtered.

Nicolae's face flushed as Noah and Cian and even the Bianchi twins chuckled. Whether because of the horror of seeing those maggots, or the uncontrollable levity the scene brought, a small giggle of my own finally broke free. The prince stared coolly at me. But instead of lashing out with some obnoxious comment, he wiped the mess from his face and laughed. It was quick and restrained, but still. The action seemed to shatter the tension he'd been carrying since Wilhelm's death.

Thomas lifted his eyes from the table beside mine, a smile spreading even though he tried taming it. "I'm utterly disgusted, yet can't turn away."

Percy strode over to the scene of the maggot attack, his mouth a grim slash of annoyance. "That's quite enough, class. This is a forensic hall, not a bawdy house. Prince Nicolae, go wash up. Erik…" The professor handed him a new apron, then pointed toward his own teaching table as he addressed us all. "Please sit quietly and observe. If this is too much for your constitution, you may be excused. Class? Do not laugh during a serious scientific exercise. Have some respect for the dead. If this is something none of you are capable of controlling, then I will recommend that none of you make it through this course. Here at the academy, we take our duty seriously and execute it with great dignity. One more outburst and you will all be dismissed. Understood?"

"Yes, Professor," we all uttered in unison.

We followed Percy to a table holding a specimen covered in a shroud. The fear of being tossed from the assessment course was enough to erase any lingering giggles. Without ceremony, Percy yanked the cloth back, revealing a body that was vaguely familiar. A bit of decomposition made it difficult to place at first and then—

I inhaled sharply, bumping into Erik, who had the nerve to sneer at my reaction as if he hadn't just screeched at the maggots.

"Apologies." I stared at the blond woman on the table, bite marks splattered across her flesh, dried blood indicating each wound. I could have sworn the sound of leathery wings echoed in the dissecting chamber. A cloth still covered her face for reasons I dared not ask about.

Thomas went rigid from his place near the corpse's head, his gaze finding mine and holding it. I prayed our reactions would be thought of as the result of seeing a brutalized woman and not of having recognized her from the tunnels. Something uncomfortable prickled between my shoulder blades, tempting me to turn around and swat it away. I squeezed my eyes shut. If this was another figment of my imagination...

I subtly shifted and glanced behind me. Headmaster Moldoveanu entered the room and tapped a finger against his arm, focus drifting from the body on the table to my pinched expression. Deep in my bones I knew with certainty that he'd read the recognition on my face.

I pretended not to notice and wondered if Thomas

was doing the same. I stole a glance at him, but he was watching the prince closely. I assumed he was trying to discern if Nicolae had already been acquainted with this cadaver.

Thomas finally noticed Moldoveanu just as the headmaster turned on his heel and left. He made no sound and yet it felt as if gongs were banging in my ears at his departure.

"This unidentified woman was discovered in the morgue before class, in one of the cadaver drawers," Percy said. "The body has been drained of most of its blood. Bite marks are present over much of her person. Seems as if someone moved her there to keep her cold and to slow decomposition. We have a most intriguing case to crack, class."

Percy had no idea how correct he was.

TWENTY-SEVEN
BLACK LEATHER WINGS

TOWER CHAMBERS
CAMERE DIN TURN
BRAN CASTLE
14 DECEMBER 1888

I bolted upright, blinking away the fang-toothed images my subconscious had created from darkness.

Moonlight streaked down the curtains in rivulets and pooled on the floor like a silver waterfall. A chill lay tangled in the sheets around me, but the cold wasn't what had roused me from sleep. Sweat coated my skin in dewy patches—somehow my nightgown had untied itself, exposing more of my collarbone than was decent.

Still panting from my nightmare of winged creatures swarming and biting, I gently prodded my neck, half fearing my fingers would come away wet with blood. Nothing. I was completely unsullied. No *strigoi*, or bats, or bloodthirsty demons had feasted while

I'd tossed and turned. I felt only smooth, hot flesh, unharmed by anything other than frigid winter air or the scandal its exposure would cause.

I squinted toward the shadows, pulse racing on high alert. The fire in my bedchamber had died out, not long ago, judging from the winking embers. I sank back, but only marginally. My mind was groggy with strange nightmares, but I could have sworn I'd heard voices. They couldn't *all* be the product of disturbed dreams. I'd been visited less often by my hauntings recently, or so I'd thought. I gripped my blankets, quieting my frantic heart as I took in the unmoving silhouettes of my dresser and nightstand.

I waited for it. For shadows to peel away from the wall and take the shape of the immortal prince, his serpent wings stretched wide enough to stop my heart entirely. But all was wretchedly silent. So much for spirits visiting the human realm on this supposedly wicked night. It had to be the high altitude of the Carpathians. The thinning oxygen was clearly affecting my brain.

"Foolish." I flopped back onto my side, drawing the covers up to my chin. Long pieces of unbound hair tickled my back, raising gooseflesh. I sank lower until my head was practically covered from the world outside my blankets. Nightmares were for children.

Silly Radu and his folklore nonsense. Of course there

was no such thing as a winter night that could call forth the dead. A scientific explanation could always be found. I closed my eyes, focusing on how cozy I was in my little cocoon of warmth. My breathing slowed, my lids suddenly heavy enough that I didn't try opening them again. I felt myself fading into an exquisite dream. One where Thomas and I were on our way to Bucharest for the holiday, I was dressed in a beautiful gown I'd wear to a ball, far from the murders—

Thump.

Adrenaline erupted through my body in the form of action.

In the space of two breaths, I swung myself off my mattress, stuffed my feet into slippers, and was halfway across my bedchamber, ears ringing with the strain of listening so hard. There was no mistaking the sound of someone or something moving in the hallway outside my rooms.

I collected my fear and shoved it into the deepest pocket of my mind, ignoring the way it kicked and scratched on the way down.

Forgoing a dressing gown in favor of stealth, I slowly cracked open my bedchamber door. I peered into the sitting room; the fire's embers were nearly out there as well. For some reason, my new maid must not have stoked them before bed. The deep orange glow wasn't enough to see by, which also offered an opportunity to not be seen by anyone who might be lurking about. Clouds of cold breath slipped out in uneven intervals.

Thump-thump. I halted, straddling the threshold between my bedchamber and the sitting room. All was still as the grave.

And then . . . a harshly whispered "Quiet" in Romanian. *"Liniște."*

Thump.

After having spent time wrangling bodies in Uncle's laboratory, I knew the sound that limbs weighted by death made when connecting with the ground. Images of corpse robbers whipped through my thoughts. I didn't know why I pictured them as skeletal figures with claw-tipped hands, fangs dripping blood, and leathery wings when they had to be robust enough to hoist dead weight. And certainly human.

I held my breath, terrified that even the smallest inhalation would echo like a bell tolling my fate. Whoever they were, I did not want them turning their sinister attention on me. Humans were the true monsters and villains. More real than any novel or fantasy could invent.

Moments passed and the whispers continued. I eased my frozen joints into motion, moving as quickly and silently across the small room as I dared. I'd never been more thankful for the sparse furnishings as I was in that moment as I headed for the door to the corridor.

I ghosted across the room, hesitating once I reached the door. Perhaps Radu's silly tales had been correct. This was a night fit for haunting after all. Except I would be the specter, running about unseen.

Pressing my ear against the wall next to the door, I listened, willing myself to remain cold and still as marble. Hushed voices rumbled too low for me to make out. It was hard to tell if they were both male or if a female was also involved. I leaned against the wall until my face ached with the force, but still couldn't understand what the late-night prowlers were whispering. It almost sounded as if it were a chant...

I drew back, confusion tugging me away. Why on earth people would be chanting unpleasant hymns in the dead of night was beyond logic at this hour. Maybe the thudding was only the result of a clandestine affair. Hadn't I already learned this lesson with Daciana and Ileana? I turned, ready to march myself back into bed, then paused.

Whispers grew louder, cresting like waves before crashing back to near-silence. This was no romantic tryst in the tower. As the voices let the fervor of their cryptic song distract them, I was able to recognize every few words, chanted in Romanian.

"Bone... Blood... Here... something... dead... wings of black... heart of... enter... woods alone... he'll mark... tracks... Hunt... down... then..."

Thud. The chanting stopped as if a guillotine had severed the tongues from whoever dared speak such blasphemous words on this hallowed winter's eve. I didn't want to give any credence to Radu's superstitions, but perhaps there was something *other* about this night.

Light flickered beneath the doorframe, gilding the floor and lapping at my slippered toes. I dared not move. I sucked in a quiet breath, watching as the light faded down the corridor, accompanied by the sounds of something being dragged behind going with it. At least two sets of boots marched rhythmically down the stairs, their stolen cargo dully thumping after. Curiosity reached inside my mind, making thinking logically difficult. If I didn't follow them soon, I'd lose them in the maze of castle corridors.

Going alone seemed an awful idea, and yet what else was I to do? I couldn't very well pretend nothing untoward was happening. There wasn't enough time to rush down to Thomas's sleeping chamber and wake him. Plus, he shared the floor with other male students. I could not imagine the scandal I would cause by dragging him from his bed this late at night. We would both lose our place in the academy. And rumors of clandestine affairs would surely reach those in London who seemed to gain power through gossip and trade it as if it were currency. I wished Anastasia had returned— she would surely have assisted with this dilemma.

I bit my lip. I didn't think our murderer was behind this midnight theft—I couldn't imagine why he'd steal a body. He enjoyed murdering, not corpse robbing. Indecision continued to toy with the rational section of my brain. The part that said I should wake the headmaster and let him deal with the thieves. I could imagine the twisted curve of his mouth when I relayed what I'd heard. His sneer sharp enough to pierce skin and draw blood. That decided it, then.

I rushed across the room and fetched my cloak and a scalpel, hands shaking so powerfully I almost dropped my weapon. At least I was armed with some measure of defense. If I ran to Moldoveanu, he would snap at the late-night intrusion and think me a liar. I might even end up as one of the bones he picked his teeth with. I'd rather take my chances with the body snatchers and their wicked-sounding chants.

I dashed into the corridor and ran down the stairs, catching the last flicker of movement before they entered the lower levels, and halted, my breath catching.

Apparently, we were going subterranean with the stolen corpse.

TWENTY-EIGHT
CORPSE THIEVES

CORRIDORS
CORIDOARE
BRAN CASTLE
14 DECEMBER 1888

Black hoods were drawn over the corpse thieves' heads, obscuring their identity in the shadow-laden corridors as they picked their way from the tower to the lower levels. My own cloak was deep charcoal—reminiscent of hazy half-moon nights and foggy alleys—and was perfect for slinking through unlit spaces. I was grateful I'd left the scarlet cape in London. I held fast to my scalpel, ready to wield it like a sword, as Andrei had done earlier.

The thieves moved with the steady caution of those who had done this many times in the past. Pausing and listening before slipping down the next hallway. As they made their way to the lowest level, their procession was silent save for the scraping sounds of the body they pulled behind them. It didn't take long to understand that we were trudging toward the basement morgue. I pressed myself against a wall and allowed an entire litany of doubts to wriggle through my mind. Maybe these *supposed* thieves were simply servants moving the body between morgues on orders of the professors.

After all, someone had to transport the corpses from one place to the next. I'd never witnessed them being carted around during waking hours. The chanting, however—well, that was a bit odd. But not damning evidence of guilt. Actually, as I stood there, contemplating, I wasn't entirely sure they even were chanting. Perhaps they were singing a tune to distract themselves from their job. If they had anything close to Ileana's skittish temperament, they likely didn't relish being among corpses. Most didn't.

I kicked at the threadbare carpet, worn from the countless feet that had passed by over the past several hundred years. I could not believe I'd gotten out of bed for this. A pair of corpse thieves indeed. It seemed I'd never let my romantic notions go.

Not everything that thumped and thudded in the night was a monster. I'd clearly heard one too many tales of vampires and werewolves since arriving here. It was all my cursed imagination. Somewhere, deep down, I wanted those strange and deadly tales to be true.

Though I was loath to admit it even to myself, there was something terribly appealing about the idea of immortal beings. Perhaps it was the monster inside of me that wished for others, especially those found only in stories.

Dragging their shrouded package as best they could, the two figures rounded a corner, disappearing from sight. I decided to linger a bit longer. Might as well confirm they were depositing this specimen in the lower morgue before climbing those abysmal tower stairs again so soon. I eyed the giant fern on the opposite side of the hall, wondering if I should simply curl up behind it and sleep until morning.

A door clicked shut, and I rounded the corner, situating myself in an alcove hidden by a massive tapestry. Shouldn't be long now. I squatted down, covering my nightgown with my cloak to avoid any pale fabric catching unwanted attention. No need for the castle servants to be aware of my late-night escapades. I buffed my scalpel with the edge of my cloak, recalling one of my favorite Shakespeare quotes: *The instruments of darkness tell us truths.*

Needles pricked my toes, warning them they'd be fully numb in moments. I shifted, hoping to ease some life back into my feet. Surely it didn't take this long to place a body on a table or in a mortuary drawer. Unease wound itself around me until I could barely breathe.

I closed my eyes. "Of course. Of course this is the sort of night I'm having."

I'd not allowed the thought of them entering the secret tunnels to cross my mind. I would not, *could* not willingly go down into that cursed place alone. The mere thought of following those unknown people into tunnels brimming with bats and other loathsome creatures was enough to make me consider going straight back to my rooms, weapon or not.

I counted the increasing beats of my heart, knowing what I should do. I had no real weapon. No light source. And no one knew I was out of bed. Should something happen, I'd quite possibly never be found. Moldoveanu certainly wouldn't send anyone out searching for me.

That thought brought me upright. My sleep-addled brain wasn't quite as sharp as it should be. Where were the royal guards? They'd been posted in the halls and outside the morgue each day this week. It was odd I hadn't encountered any of them already. Though perhaps they only patrolled the main exits and entrances during these late hours. Students were long since tucked away in their beds, dreaming of viscera and science. And the inhabitants of the morgue needn't be watched over. No one but me saw illusions of them rising.

I clutched my cloak, wrapping it around my body like armor, and left the sanctuary of my hidden space.

I peeked around the corner and released a slow breath. No one in sight. Thrusting my shoulders back, I crept down the hall. Before I could talk myself out of it, I twisted the knob and slipped into the morgue. It was empty and still. Not a thing was disturbed or out of place.

Except for the trapdoor. That was slightly propped open—an alluring trail of morbid bread crumbs I could not resist following. The same foul scent of rotten meat assaulted my senses as I tiptoed down the broken stone stairs, watchful for signs of traps.

I prayed no bats were stalking the tunnels tonight. Or spiders. I could do without their long, spindly legs and reflective eyes. Corpses and thieves and foul odors were one thing to contend with in dark, wretched places. Bats and spiders were where I drew the line.

Once in the tunnel, I oriented myself to the heavy darkness. I blinked a few times, adjusting to the lack of light, and watched the darker shapes of the pair move swiftly, no longer afraid of making noise or rousing students or professors. How many times had they done this? It certainly seemed as if it were a familiar routine.

I ran a few feet, then paused, waiting for the light of their lantern to fade but not vanish entirely as I scurried from shadow to shadow, remaining far enough behind them to avoid detection.

They paused at an intersection, holding their lantern to the wall, and traced something there with their fingertips. I made a rough estimate of how high on the wall this object was, hoping to feel what had caught their attention after they'd moved on.

Continuing down the tunnel—one of the ones Thomas and I had decided against investigating the night we'd discovered the woman's body—I waited for the shadows to embrace me again. Once I could no longer be seen, I bolted to the corner, groping around the rough stone wall. Cool wind brushed the hemline of my nightgown.

For a horrifying moment, I imagined spiders crawling up my stockings, and my blood prickled. *Breathe,* I commanded myself. I could ill afford to have an episode down here, alone. My fingers brushed against sticky webs and things I preferred not to put a name to before slipping into deep-set carvings.

XI

I felt around, one eye trained on the tunnel that was nearly black now that the thieves were at its opposite end. XI. That was all there was to the carving. No other letters. Tucking that information away, I sprinted down the next corridor, witnessing the hooded figures do the same thing before continuing on. Each new fork in the tunnel system brought a new set of carvings and a new wave of fear.

XXIII
VIII

I silently repeated the Roman numerals, hoping to be able to retrieve them from my memory for further inspection once I returned to my chambers. Their significance now was a mystery, one I'd have to unravel another time.

Wings flapped anxiously, drawing my attention up toward the gray ceiling separating me from the upper levels of the castle and ultimately from fresh air and starry skies. I sucked in a few short breaths and focused on the ground, forcing myself to remain calm as the sound intensified. I knew too well what was making that awful flapping. Without waiting to become a meal, I hurried along, placing one foot in front of the other, filling my thoughts with anything other than the creatures flying above me, or the sound of my pulse pounding in my head.

Moments bled together until I was uncertain if it was night or day, yet the haunting whisper of aerial pursuit persisted. I hated thinking of them swarming out of sight, waiting for an opportunity to attack. I was tempted to find a torch, consequences of being caught be damned. There was only so much terror my body could endure; I feared my heart might stop altogether from overuse.

"Hurry, hurry," I urged the figures ahead, praying we would arrive wherever we were headed without being bitten. It seemed as if we'd never leave these cursed corridors. We continued down so many loops and circuits, I worried I'd never find my way back. I heard something scuttle behind me and froze. Praying it wasn't a newly risen corpse hunting down a warm meal, I grabbed my skirts and hurtled forward, gaze trained on the thieves and the body.

Finally we came upon a wide expanse where four tunnels met. One of the figures wandered ahead, his light flickering like fireflies in the dank cave as he spun in a slow circle. Darkness loomed from every corner, waiting to swallow us whole.

I watched the person with the lantern move ahead, growing smaller the farther he walked. The center chamber dipped in the middle, creating a small indent where a silver sheet of water had collected. Light from the lantern reflected as if a small sun were setting on a mirrored horizon. It was strangely lovely for such a terrifying place.

Too bad the soft flames couldn't take the chill out of the air or the burning acid out of my intestines. I had a feeling I wasn't going to breathe normally until

I was safely free from bats again. Rubbing my arms, I fought a full-body shiver that tangled its way under my unbound hair.

It wasn't simply the temperature that was chilling. These tunnels, like the castle, felt alive somehow, haunted with spirits and otherworldly beings. I imagined a million eyes staring at me from gloomy recesses. Animal or human; I wasn't sure which was more frightening.

Blessedly, the figures moved with a new fervor. After briskly traveling through a few more dank tunnels, silver light edged the walls and ceilings of the last one, indicating an exit was near. An owl hooted in the distance, its eerie call answered by another. I remained in the corner of a tunnel set farther back, waiting for the cloaked thieves to steal into the night. The air here was fresh and smelled of pine. I wanted to drop to my knees and worship the frigid outdoors, but kept back, waiting for the corpse robbers to continue.

It didn't take long for the thieves to exit into the moonlight, their prize dragging behind. I watched each step I took, mindful of any leaves or twigs that might have blown in and would crack beneath my weight. I scarcely breathed until I'd made it to the barrier between the castle and the outdoors, my fingertips trailing against the rough stone walls.

Peering from the mouth of the tunnel, I scanned

the frozen world. Tree branches twisted and creaked, annoyed by the intrusion when the human world should have been still. Keeping my eyes locked onto the retreating forms, I crept down the earthen path, my nightgown pale as the snow-dusted ground beneath my cloak.

Flurries fell from the sky, light and silent. Shivers gnawed at my bones through the thick cotton, but I kept my gaze fixed on the shadows before me, who were lurching through the woods with their mysterious bundle slumped between them. There was no way I'd turn back now, no matter if the winter night bit through my clothing and punctured my skin.

I heard the heavy tread of boots stomping frozen earth and fell back a few steps. A shadow flickered across the sky, dragging my attention away from the hooded thieves. The moon cracked a half-smile, its expression mocking those who dared leave their warm beds to trespass in Vlad the Impaler's forest of bones. I wrapped my cloak even tighter around myself.

Stopping abruptly at the edge of a fork in the path, the figures appeared to be arguing over which direction to take as they carefully put down the shrouded body. I squinted. There was something strange about its shape. It was lumpy and smelled of... it couldn't be garlic. Memories of the victim from the train came to the forefront of my mind. It very well could be garlic, though the amount they'd have to had stuffed the corpse with would be extraordinary if I could detect it from this distance. My senses were good, but I was no immortal being.

I watched them pick the corpse back up and amble down the path. If the body had been stuffed with garlic, perhaps one of the thieves was the Impaler. Maybe he was working with someone else. Like Wilhelm's bloodless body, this very well might be another staged *strigoi* attack.

I hesitated. Following corpse thieves into the woods was one thing; blindly pursuing someone who might have impaled two people was quite another. The scalpel I carried would be no match against the two men.

A twig snapped behind me.

I slowly turned around, pulse roaring in my ears.

Moldoveanu crossed his arms, staring down at me as if I'd gone and made his evening.

"Curfew has been imposed for all students. Yet here you are, marching into the forest as if it were your birthright, Miss Wadsworth." I had half a mind to shush him, but I kept my jaw locked. Moldoveanu jerked his chin toward a shadow that withdrew itself from the massive trees near the castle's exterior. My earlier nightmare sprung to life in the form of an arrogant royal guard. "Escort her inside. I'll deal with her disciplinary action in the morning."

Dăneşti stepped forward, his glare powerful enough to make me wilt. A rough hand was around my arm an instant later, yanking me away from the forest line. I stared at Dăneşti as he pulled me forward, wondering how on earth he'd been tasked with curfew watch. Perhaps he'd been demoted for being so unpleasant.

"Wait!" I cried, squirming from his grasp. I thrashed around until I faced the headmaster. "A body was stolen from the tower morgue. Two thieves in hoods dragged it through here just moments ago. That's the only reason I left my chambers." A muscle in Moldoveanu's jaw twitched. "See for yourself. They were right ahead of me. I think one of them might be the Impaler. The body smelled of garlic. They are—"

I blinked at the forest, eerily quiet as if it were holding its breath, waiting for Moldoveanu's verdict. The owls didn't even dare to hoot. I stared ahead at the undisturbed trail where the thieves had just been; no footprints were visible as snow fell with more abandon.

No sign of the figures I knew I'd seen or the body they'd taken. It was as if the forest were cleansing itself of wrongdoing, concealing a crime I was sure had taken place.

"Tell me. Does your imagination always run so... colorfully? Perhaps these 'thieves' you speak of were nothing more than kitchen staff, preparing for the morning meal. The excess food stores are located down that path, Miss Wadsworth."

"But…I swear…" I hardly knew anymore. I glanced to where Dăneşti had been hiding, but he wouldn't have seen them from the corner of the castle. And if the excess food stores were down there, then he might not have paid much attention to servants doing their jobs.

The headmaster didn't even bother looking in the direction I'd pointed out. "Until further notice, you are on academic probation, Miss Wadsworth. This sort of erratic behavior might be acceptable in London, but you'll find we take things a bit more seriously here. One more word from you, and I will lose my remaining patience and send you from this castle at once."

Dear Liza,

After reading your last correspondence, I took a great deal of time thinking it over. I believe you're right, though I know you likely didn't doubt that. I realized that I was hurt and angry. Thomas's misguided actions arose not from a lack of affection on his part but from a misunderstanding of how he might offer the correct support. (Which clearly does not include warning professors of my emotional state.)

I have other worries, though. Ones that I'm frightened to even put a name to. Please burn this letter once you've read it, and tell no one of its contents. I can't shake the feeling of being watched. One student was found dead and an unidentified body was discovered here in a matter of weeks. One showed no outward signs of murder, and the other had perished from . . . more horrendous measures. Yet both of their bodies had been drained completely of blood. Ghastly to speak of; I do apologize. I also haven't heard from a friend here in nearly a week and I'm worried for her.

I won't be able to travel home for the Christmas holiday due to severe weather and lack of time off, but I will write often to make up for it. Thomas's family keeps a house in Bucharest and his sister has invited us to a ball there, and I haven't a clue what I'll wear to such an event. I left my most cherished dresses at home. Silly to speak of such frivolity when there are many worse things happening.

Has Aunt Amelia given any more thought to you touring the Continent? Thomas's sister, Miss Daciana Cresswell, has promised to write her on your behalf. Perhaps you might ask your mother to reconsider and grant you permission as a holiday gift. Or maybe she would agree to us traveling to America? I should love to spend time there and visit Grandmama. We might be able to persuade my grandmother to speak on our behalf as well. You know how convincing Grandmama can be.

Apologies for not sending along a more detailed

note. I must dash off to bed. Anatomy lesson is first thing in the morning. It's by far my favorite class (even though the headmaster is an awful brute). How surprising, I'm sure.

Your loving cousin,
AR

P.S. How is my father? Please give him a hug from me and tell him I shall write soon. I miss him terribly and worry he'll fall under the spell of his laudanum in my absence. Be wary of him locking himself in his study. No good ever comes of that.

TWENTY-NINE
GLIMPSES OF BLACK RIBBON

TOWER CHAMBERS
CAMERE DIN TURN
BRAN CASTLE
14 DECEMBER 1888

Unease of my letter to Liza falling into anyone else's hands had me delivering it to the castle's outgoing post first thing in the morning. After I returned, I watched from the doorway of my tower rooms as an uninvited guest tiptoed across the sitting area and made his way toward my bedroom as if he had every right to it. Truly, it was remarkable how confident he could be while doing something wrong in every possible manner.

I hadn't the slightest notion what he was up to, but the scoundrel would likely have an interesting excuse. Since I'd been escorted to my rooms, I hadn't yet had the opportunity of discussing the events of the previous evening with him. Ileana still hadn't been available to attend to me, so I'd sent a note via the new chambermaid, and had told him to meet me after class.

In the master *library*.

We were supposed to have met ten minutes ago, but even though I hadn't been permitted to attend Moldoveanu's class, I was running shamefully behind. Prior to writing and delivering my letter, I'd spent much of the morning reading anything I could about the castle and had lost track of time. I cleared my throat, satisfied when he flipped around, brows practically touching his hairline.

"Oh, hello. I thought you were in the library? It's impolite to lie to your friends, Wadsworth."

"Do I even dare ask why you're sneaking about my private chambers, Cresswell?" His gaze darted to my open bedchamber door, calculating Lord only knew what. He was only a few paces from it, less if he used his long-limbed advantage. "Or shall we pretend as if you weren't being the indecent scoundrel I know you to be?"

"Why weren't you in class?" Thomas shifted from one foot to the other. There was a rather large package partially hidden behind his back. I moved into the sitting room, peering around him, but he danced back a step. "Uh-uh-uh," he sang. "This is called a surprise, Wadsworth. Go on about your business and leave me to it. You know I wouldn't scorn you for entering *my* bedroom. Being as I'm such a scoundrel."

I moved closer to where he stood, eyes narrowed. "You broke into my chambers. Now you want me to leave you alone to do whatever manner of mischief you're up to? Doesn't seem very logical."

"Hmm. I do see your point."

Thomas slowly backed into my bedroom, foot hooking around the threshold with utter control. I would have focused on his intent more if I hadn't been trying to see the tantalizing package he was hiding. Glimpses of black ribbon tied in a ridiculously oversize bow had me fully intrigued.

"When you put it that way, of course I don't want you to leave me alone," he went on. "We could have so much more fun together."

His gaze purposely flicked to the single bed, lingering there to clarify his intentions. I'd completely forgotten my next question, as Thomas shifted I could now see brown paper covering the entire box. It was large enough to store a body. I inched closer, curiosity spinning wildly through my mind. What on earth could it be? I kept my focus on it, hoping to glean a clue.

"Though," he added slowly, "I would prefer to roll around on something a bit more...accommodating to my size."

I stopped moving. Nearly ceased breathing as his words batted my curiosity about the package away. I could not imagine what it would be like: lying in bed together, kissing without restraint...and—

Thomas smirked, as if he knew precisely the direction my wanton thoughts had taken and was pleased I hadn't tossed him from the window. Yet.

Face burning, I pointed to the chamber behind me. "Get out of my bedroom, Cresswell. You may leave the box on the settee."

He tsked. "Apologies, my sweet. But you really should act immediately when you read my body language. I saw you take in my foot. A decent job of collecting details, I must admit. Too bad you let those scandalous thoughts distract you. Though I can hardly blame you."

"Take in your...Thomas!" Before I could charge at him, he swept the door closed with his blasted foot. I tried the knob, but he'd already twisted the key, locking himself in. I was going to murder him.

"For such a modest young woman," Thomas called from beyond the door, "you certainly have an intriguing number of lacy unmentionables. I'm going to be imagining all sorts of improper things while you're sawing up the next body in Percy's class. Do you believe that makes me some sort of deviant? Perhaps I should be worried. Actually, maybe it's you who should be afraid."

"Cresswell! You've made your point, now kindly leave. If the headmaster discovers this impropriety while I'm on academic probation, I'll be expelled!"

I pounded the door, jumping back a step when it creaked open. All humor was wiped from his expression as he cocked his head, staring down at me. "Did you say academic probation? What manner of mischief have I missed out on and what, exactly, does probation entail?"

I slumped against the wall, suddenly exhausted from the previous night. I'd barely slept, tossing and turning as if that might help sort out what I thought I'd seen. Were there really two people chanting in the corridor? Did they truly steal a body, or was that bundle they were carrying simply excess food stores, as Moldoveanu suggested? I no longer trusted myself.

Thomas mimicked my position by leaning against the doorjamb and I relayed each detail I could recall, knowing he'd find meaning in anything I might have missed, as he often saw things in a unique manner. I spoke of my adventure with Anastasia in the village, and the discovery of the missing young woman's possible involvement with the Order of the Dragon. I even told him about my suspicions regarding Nicolae's illustrations and how that might possibly tie in with his cousin's death. I didn't inform him that I'd also been featured in the prince's journal, though. That I didn't want to share for several reasons. When I finished, Thomas gnawed his bottom lip until it seemed it might bruise.

"I wouldn't be surprised if Nicolae was responsible for sending those threats," he said. "But the *why* is a bit buried. I'll have to watch him in class. Pick up on any tics or hints."

"Regardless," I said, "I have a theory someone is hunting Vlad's bloodline. Making a statement. To what purpose, I'm not sure. In two of the murders it appears as if there's a vampire hunter. The other murder definitely has the marks of a vampire attack. I think Prince Nicolae might be in danger. Unless he *is* the one who's sending out the threats. What is the common bond amongst the victims? And how does the woman from the tunnels figure into it all?"

"Nicolae's technically not one of Vlad's descendants." Thomas stared directly into my eyes, but I could see he was on another continent. "He's part of the Dănești line. The Dănești and Drăculești families were rivals for many years. I'd say someone is targeting the House of Basarab—both branches of the family. Or perhaps one family line is being portrayed as vampires, and the other as the hunters."

"So Dăneşti the guard is related to Prince Nicolae?" I asked. "I'm a bit afraid to ask how you're so well versed on a medieval family."

"There's something I've been meaning to tell you." He inhaled deeply. "I'm Dracula's heir."

I was grateful I was already leaning against the wall for support. I stared at him, trying to unravel the confusion surrounding such a simple statement. I couldn't possibly have heard him correctly. He waited, not uttering another word, tensed for my response.

"But... you're English."

"And Romanian, remember? On my mother's side." He offered a tentative smile. "My mother was a *cel Rău,* a descendant of Vlad's son Mihnea."

I rolled that information around my mind, choosing my next words with care. "Why haven't you mentioned Dracula's lineage before? It's quite an intriguing topic."

" 'Cel Rău' means *the Evil One.* I wasn't keen on exposing that. In fact, your friend Anastasia cornered me the other week and accused me of bringing this blood curse to the academy. She said Dracula's last remaining male heir should not have come to this castle, unless I harbored a grandiose scheme of taking it over, or some other such nonsense."

He dropped his gaze to the carpet, shoulders curving inward. My heart sped up. I realized Thomas

365

believed that foolish moniker. Worse, he believed *I'd* think that of him, too. All because of which family he'd been born into. I had no idea how Anastasia discovered the truth of his lineage and didn't care at the moment. I touched his elbow, gently encouraging him to look at me.

"Are you sure it doesn't translate to *the Foolish One*?" He didn't so much as crack a smile. Something in my core twisted. "If you're an evil one, I'm equally so. If not worse. We both carve the dead, Thomas. That doesn't make us damned. Is that why you didn't tell me sooner? Or were you afraid your princely title would change my...feelings?"

He slowly lifted his gaze; for once he didn't hide his emotions. Before he responded I saw the depth of his fear sketched across his face. All posturing and arrogance gone. In their place stood a young man who appeared as if the world might be breaking around him and there wasn't a thing he could do to save himself. He'd fallen over a cliff so high all hope of survival had perished before he'd hit the ground.

"Who would blame you for not speaking to me again? The unfeeling monster who's descended from the Devil himself. Everyone in London would love it. An actual reason for my reprehensible social behavior." Thomas ran a hand through his hair. "Most people find me hard to be near under the best of circumstances. I was, if I were being honest, terrified you'd see what everyone else does. It's not that I don't trust you. I am selfish and don't want to lose you. I am heir to a dynasty drenched in blood. What could I possibly offer you?"

There were a thousand things we needed to focus on. The possibility of the impostor Impaler being close to the academy. The growing number of murders. Our suspicious classmate...And yet, when I stared into Thomas's eyes and saw the agony behind them, I could think of only one thing. I moved closer, heart racing with each step I took toward him.

"I don't see a monster, Thomas." I paused with a few inches between us. "I see only my best friend. I see kindness. And compassion. I see a young man who's determined to use his mind to help others, even when he fails miserably at emotional matters."

His lips twitched, but I still saw the underlying worry in his countenance. "Perhaps we can stick with all the ways in which I'm wonderful..."

"What I mean to say is, I see you, Thomas Cresswell." I placed a gloved hand to his face in the barest hint of touch. "And I think you are truly incredible. Sometimes."

He remained perfectly still for a few, taut moments, his focus sliding over my features, gauging my sincerity. I kept my expression open, allowing the truth to reveal itself.

"Well, I *am* charming." Thomas ran his hands down the front of his waistcoat, his tension ebbing with the movement. "And a prince. You were bound to swoon. Though Prince Dracula is the very gothic opposite of Prince Charming. A minor detail, really."

I laughed full and rich. "Aren't you technically from a displaced family? You're a prince without a throne."

"Deposed Prince Charming doesn't have quite the same ring to it, Wadsworth," he said, huffing faux exasperation, though I could see the twinkle now gleaming in his eyes.

"I'm charmed all the same."

A different sort of light sparked in his gaze as it slowly traveled to my mouth. Very carefully, he stepped forward and tilted my chin up. I realized—even through ups and downs and mistakes—it wouldn't be a terrible way to go through life, having him by my side while the world went mad around us. My eyes fluttered shut, ready for a second kiss...that didn't come. Thomas's hands were suddenly gone and my skin instantly missed his warmth.

"How inconvenient." He stood straighter, nodding at the door, and stepped away. "We have a guest."

The maid I'd sent out with Thomas's note earlier flushed so deeply I could see the dark hue from where I stood as she entered my chambers. It was not the first time I wished for Ileana to return. I had the urge to melt into the floor, positive she'd read the tension between Thomas and me, even though we were now a respectable distance apart. She lifted the wooden buckets she was carrying in response.

She mumbled apologies half in Romanian, half in English, but I understood.

"No, no, it's quite all right. You weren't interrupting anything," I said, moving toward the now-open door. I did not want her making the wrong assumption. Or the right one. The scandal of Thomas standing in my chaperone-free rooms was already enough to ruin me were news of it to get out. Would this quiet girl ever do such a thing? The way she lingered at the perimeter of the chambers, not quite able to meet my gaze, was enough to incite panic. I did my best to speak in as much Romanian as possible: "We were on our way to the library. Please tell Ileana I'd love to speak with her later."

The young maid kept her head down, nodding. "*Da, domnişoară.* I'll be sure to tell her if I see her."

I felt Thomas's attention drifting toward the new maid but didn't want to draw any more attention to our inappropriate position. I smiled at the girl, then walked with Thomas as swiftly as I dared to the library. We had a case to solve. Now armed with the knowledge of Thomas's lineage, I feared Nicolae might not be the only one in danger, if my suspicion of Vlad's bloodline being targeted was correct. Then again, perhaps Thomas was even more in danger since he was Dracula's heir.

If one branch of the family tree was being impaled and the other drained of blood, neither was safe.

THIRTY

A CLOSER LOOK

LIBRARY
BIBLIOTECĂ
BRAN CASTLE
14 DECEMBER 1888

"Couldn't stay away from me, now, could you?" Noah beamed at me from behind a large tome standing upright on a small desk. "Why weren't you in anatomy class?"

I exhaled. "Our mutual friend may have caught me outside after curfew."

Noah shook his head and chuckled. "I hope whatever lured you outside was worth it. That man is more terrifying than any vampire haunting the academy." Seriousness quickly replaced the levity in his tone. "You're lucky Moldoveanu found you last night. That maid wasn't as fortunate. Something got her."

Thomas and I blinked at each other, and dread pooled in my veins. I hadn't seen Ileana all morning. In fact, I hadn't seen her in nearly two days.

"What maid?" I asked, stomach twisting. "What was her name?"

"One of the girls who was assigned to Prince Nicolae's and Andrei's chambers. Moldoveanu and that guard are questioning them both right now. Canceled both Percy's and Radu's classes this afternoon and everything. We're supposed to be back in our rooms by three." Noah eyed us. "I'd consider listening to the headmaster today. Erik, Cian, and I are locking ourselves in to study. That maid's body was drained of blood. I'd like to keep mine."

"You don't truly believe a vampire attacked her, do you?"

Noah shrugged. "Does it matter if it was a real vampire or a fake one? Either way, she's dead and her blood is gone."

I couldn't corral my thoughts fast enough. If now both this maid and the girl from the tunnels had been murdered, perhaps I'd been wrong in my assumption that only members of the royal family were being targeted. The village girl didn't have any apparent royal ties, and I still didn't believe she was a member of the Order, regardless of Anastasia's cryptic note.

"How do you know the blood is missing?" Thomas folded his arms neatly against his chest. "Did anyone see the body? Where was it discovered?"

"After anatomy class, the twins found her in the corridor outside the science wing. Apparently they were hurrying back to their rooms for lunch. That's when they found her body. Said she was paler than Wilhelm. No postmortem lividity present." Noah swallowed hard. "She also had no outward signs of trauma. No obvious wounds besides two punctures in her neck. *Strigois* might be myth, but whoever's killing these people doesn't seem to know or care."

"I believe the murderer is using a mortuary apparatus," I said. "Does the headmaster take inventory of the academy's equipment?"

"Don't know. If he does, I'm sure he's already investigated, though." Noah closed the book he'd been reading and eyed the librarian, who'd come in and taken a seat behind a large desk. He slid his gaze over each of us, smiling politely. Noah dropped his voice and leaned in. "Though I doubt he'd tell us if one was missing. Moldoveanu isn't really the sharing type. If someone sneaked into the academy and stole a device that's being used in murders..." He lifted a shoulder. "That wouldn't be a popular thing for people to know. The academy would be ruined."

As we all considered the new information, the librarian caught my eye again and smiled.

"*Bonjour,*" he said. "*Je m'appelle* Pierre. May I help you find anything?"

"No, thank you," Noah said, shouldering his satchel. "I'll see you both in class. Whenever that is. This assessment course might get canceled. At least that's the rumor." He shook his head, disappointment etched into the movement. "I traveled a long way to get here, and pretend vampire or not, I'm not giving up on earning one of those spots yet. Like I said, Erik, Cian, and I are studying later—you're both welcome to join."

"Thank you." I smiled. It was a sweet offer, but there was no way I'd be permitted to stay in a room full of young men for an entire night, no matter how innocent the reason. I could see Aunt Amelia crossing herself at the mere thought of my sullied reputation.

Thomas bid Noah good-bye and inspected the librarian with microscopic precision. He was a slender man with curly brown hair and wore an oversize jumper. "Where might we find a book on the Order of the Dragon, marked with Roman numerals in any way?"

Pierre steepled his fingers, gaze calculating before he stood. "This way, please."

~∙⟨⚬⟩∙~

A stack of books sprawled over nearly each inch of the aisle Pierre had instructed us to search. The librarian reminded me of a hermit crab, reluctant to come too far out of his shell before retreating into its depths. I had a suspicion that he hid from Radu whenever he heard him coming.

Thomas flipped another tattered text shut, sneezing at the handful of dust motes shooting into the air. Undeterred, he selected another. We'd been doing the same thing for hours. Sitting quietly, sneezing, and scanning each old journal. There must have been hundreds at my feet alone. We were more determined than ever to tie some of these seemingly random clues together. Someone was quite gifted with peppering the trail with false leads.

"Let's pretend as if we're in Uncle's laboratory, Cresswell."

Thomas glanced up, bemused. "Shall I don spectacles and mutter to myself, then?"

"Be serious. I'll offer my thoughts and theories regarding the murderer first, all right?"

Thomas nodded, though I could see he wished to be the one to act out Uncle's role. If given an opportunity, he would have rushed to his rooms and donned a tweed jacket.

"I believe our killer has a very good grasp of forensic

practices and how to cast suspicion elsewhere," I said. "The manner in which the crimes have been carried out suggests meticulous planning, or more than one killer. Which then leads us back to the Order of the Dragon and their potential involvement. But why them? Why would they stage vampire crimes?"

Thomas shook his head. "They've been around for centuries, and from what little I know, they have had lots of assassination practice passed down through their ranks."

"Perhaps they murdered the missing girl from the village to use her home for its proximity to the castle. Or maybe her death was ritualistic in nature."

Thomas considered that for a moment. "But why would the Order of the Dragon want to hunt students at the academy? If they were created to protect the royal line, why destroy members of it?"

"I can think of one reasonable explanation," I said. "What if they're loyalists who want to put Dracula's heir back on the throne? Maybe they are slowly working their way through anyone with a claim to the throne, distant or otherwise."

Thomas blanched. "It's a good theory, Wadsworth. Let's see what else we uncover about them, though."

We went back to pulling books we could find off the shelves—the Order's association made obvious by their multiple insignias and crosses. Their sigil was a dragon coiled around itself, and a recurring theme was a cross with flames. There was something familiar about that, but I hadn't a clue where I'd have seen it before.

I kept thinking about the latest death. If my science-minded classmates were beginning to fear vampires, I couldn't imagine what the superstitious villagers would think once they discovered that another bloodless body had been found. In Vlad Dracula's castle, no less.

"This is an impossible task." I stood, brushing down the front of my plain dress. "How are we supposed to find out who's in the Order now?"

"Roman numerals weren't built in a day, Wadsworth."

I sighed so deeply I practically needed a fainting couch. "Did you honestly just utter that abysmal pun?"

I didn't wait for his response, fearing it would be as stellar as the last one. I drifted toward the aisle labeled POETRY across the way.

"Perhaps we should investigate the food stores tonight."

I jumped, scowling at Thomas, who'd sneaked up behind me.

"Then we could prove if Moldoveanu was lying," he continued.

"Oh, yes. Let's sneak about outdoors. I'm sure

the headmaster would be quite kind if he caught me again, doing the very thing he warned me against. If the vampiric murderer or rogue chivalric group wandering the halls of this castle don't get to us first, that is," I said. Thomas snorted, but I ignored his dismissal. "Do you believe our headmaster knows precisely who's murdering students and staff? That he's possibly responsible? I don't want to risk expulsion if we're wrong."

"I believe he's too obvious," Thomas said. "But I'm not as convinced that he's completely ignorant of the strange occurrences in the castle. I wonder if he's sympathetic to the Order. Though I do not believe he's a member. He doesn't have the birth rank. In fact, I believe we've both been distracted by other truths."

"Are you suggesting the Order isn't involved at all, then?" My mind churned with several new ideas as I removed the Order of the Dragon from the equation. "It very well might be someone *pretending* to be them. Perhaps that's why we're unable to discover a true connection to the Order. What if they in fact are playing no part in this case?"

"They might simply be an elaborate distraction created by the murderer."

"It would explain how you haven't managed to deduce

or concoct a theory in that magical way of yours." I narrowed my eyes. "You haven't read scuff marks on boots and sacrificed something to the math gods to solve the case, have you?"

"This may be hard to believe," Thomas said, voice suddenly grave. "But I have yet to tap into my psychic powers. I do, however, have questions and suspicions I cannot ignore."

"You've intrigued me. Do go on."

Thomas took a deep breath, steadying himself. "Where has Anastasia been? I'm afraid we've both been ignoring facts. Ones that have been blinding in their obviousness."

My blood prickled. Thomas was being overly cautious. It wouldn't be the first time he'd told me to suspect those closest to us, and yet part of me knew Anastasia had secrets. In fact, if I were being truly honest with myself, I knew Ileana had them, too. I had known someone else who'd harbored secrets. . . .

I shut my emotions off, not allowing devastation to cloud any more of my judgment. I would neither be willfully blind to the truth nor keep my suspicions to myself from this point forward, no matter the cost to my heart.

"I also haven't seen Ileana in two days. Which was

the evening before the body was taken from the tower morgue."

Thomas nodded. "And? What else? What else doesn't quite add together?"

I thought back on all the times we'd spoken about *strigoi*. About how she'd change the subject before Anastasia could ask more questions. How superstitious she'd been about the bodies. "Ileana's from Braşov. The village where the first murder occurred."

"She's also aware that Vlad Dracula's blood runs through my sister's veins."

I knew it wasn't medically possible, but I swore I felt my heart stop beating. At least for a moment. I stared at Thomas, knowing our thoughts were straying to the same horrid conclusion.

"Do you know where Daciana is now?" I asked, pulse racing. "Which city she was visiting next?" Thomas slowly shook his head. A darker feeling tugged at my core. "Are you certain she left the castle? What about the invitation to the ball?"

"Daci is a bit of a planner; she'd probably have written it out ahead of time. The invitation could have been sent through the post by anyone." Silver lined the edges of Thomas's eyes, but he quickly blinked the liquid away. "I never saw her off in her carriage. She slipped away with Ileana. I didn't want to intrude. I thought they wanted a bit more time alone."

The body stolen from the tower morgue—was it Daciana's? I could barely breathe. Thomas had already lost his mother; losing a sibling was as close to a mortal wound as one could withstand. I forced my brain to move through its grief and connect any dots or clues. What did we know about Daciana's last days or hours at the castle? Then it struck me.

"I know precisely where we need to go." I made to grab his hand, then paused. Even behind castle walls, the impropriety of my action would not go unnoticed. As if my fears had summoned him, the librarian walked past, arms filled with books. "Come," I said. "I have an idea."

We exited the library and scanned the wide corridors. No maids or servants or guards. Not that we would have noticed the maids straightaway—they could be hidden away behind the tapestries in the makeshift corridor. I motioned for Thomas to follow me into the secret hallway, and we moved swiftly and alertly. Focus primed for any movements or sounds.

The air was particularly cold—hallway fires had burned down to nothing, and torches weren't lit. It was as if the castle were closing off its own emotions, descending into that icy calm. I hoped a storm wasn't about to break around us.

Some nooks now seemed even more sinister—they were places that might shelter anyone who wished to do harm. I kept one eye out for any flash of movement there. We passed a pedestal with a serpent, and I shivered. Anyone might be ducking behind it, waiting to pounce.

Ileana was small enough to disappear among the displayed artifacts. Thomas followed my gaze but kept his expression neutral. I wanted to know if it was the first time he'd been in the servants' passages but didn't risk speaking aloud. Not yet.

Scuffled boots tramped along the carpets in the main corridor. We froze, backs pressed against one of the large tapestries. I didn't dare glance at which scene of torture we'd hidden against. Judging from the heavy tread, I guessed there were at least four guards. They didn't speak. The only sounds of their arrival and departure were the *clunk, clunk, clunk* of their rhythmic steps.

I barely breathed until the thump of their boots faded. Even then, Thomas and I remained motionless for a few beats more. I peeled myself away from the wall and checked both ways. We'd exit the secret corridor soon.

Thankfully, we managed to find our way toward Anastasia's chambers undetected. Seemed everyone heeded the headmaster's warning and were tightly locked away in their rooms.

I pressed my ear against Anastasia's chamber door, listening for a moment before opening it. The fires hadn't been lit, but the sunlight streamed in through the open curtains. Everything was just as I remembered it the last time Anastasia had been here.

"Why are we in this chamber, Wadsworth?"

I scanned the room. The book Anastasia had taken from the missing woman's house had appeared to bear one of the Order's symbols. And if that were the case, perhaps...

"Look." I crossed the room and lifted the book from the table. It was titled in Romanian: *Poezii Despre Moarte,* "Poems of Death." I'd been so distracted by the idea of the missing girl being lost and frozen in the woods that I hadn't bothered reading the title earlier.

"When Anastasia and I entered that house, she claimed there was a connection between this book and the Order." I held the book up for him to see. A cross was burned into the cover, each of its sides ablaze with crude flames. "At first I thought she'd been mistaken, there was no logical reason for the missing woman from the village to be connected to a chivalric order made up of nobles. A mistake on my part, clearly."

"Everyone makes mistakes, Wadsworth. There's no shame in that. It's how you go about mending them that truly counts." Thomas flipped through the book quickly. "Hmm. I believe—"

"That it is time for you to go to your own chambers. You have no reason to be in these rooms." Thomas and I both tensed at the intrusion and the gravelly voice. Dănești stood in the doorframe, his mass taking up the entire space. Seemed like this castle was full of people who could move about without a sound. "All activity within the castle has been canceled until the morning. Moldoveanu's orders. The headmaster has decided to hold classes tomorrow under one condition: everyone will be escorted to class and then back to your chambers."

Thomas had somehow hidden *Poezii Despre Moarte,* and he held his hands up. "Very well. After you."

I didn't dare search too hard for the now hidden book. I didn't want Dănești to snatch it from us, especially if it turned out to be the very volume he'd been hunting. After depositing Thomas at his rooms, the guard watched me enter my chambers and then tugged the door shut behind me. Keys jangled and before I knew what he'd done, I was locked in my tower chambers. I raced into the bathing chamber and checked the door to the secret stairwell. It was bolted from the other side.

I did not sleep well that night, pacing as if I were an animal plotting its escape. Caged until someone set me free.

Carbolic steam spray, Paris, France, 1872–1887.

THIRTY-ONE
AUTOPSY INTRIGUE

Prince Nicolae appeared paler than the corpse Percy was carving into as he handed the professor toothed forceps and coughed, turning away from the incision. It was odd behavior for the normally fearless prince. Perhaps he was coming down with an influenza.

Certainly it couldn't be the nearly unrecognizable body from the tunnels making him ill. Though Percy had unveiled the body during our lesson two days earlier, Moldoveanu had recollected it before any of us could better inspect it and had released it to class only that afternoon.

Our headmaster had been oddly quiet and contemplative during our previous lesson, his mind seemingly stuck somewhere else. I wondered if the royal family was pressuring him to forensically solve or link the murders, or lose his position as both royal coroner and headmaster. It was also possible that his distress was completely unrelated to the body. Perhaps he was worried about Anastasia's true whereabouts. He had to have concluded she was not in Hungary by now. I could not imagine what else might cause him such worry.

Percy placed his blade down on a tray, leaving the *Y* incision incomplete. Most of the girl's features had been ruined by hungry bats, so her face was covered with a small shroud—a kindness for either her or us. Though I didn't believe Percy would shy away from exposing us to the brutality of our chosen profession. Death didn't always come peacefully, and we'd need to prepare ourselves for when it waged war.

"The carbolic steam spray, if you please."

Percy waited for Nicolae to fumigate the surgical theater. Our professor took the same pains Uncle did to avoid contaminating a scene, though other scholars still claimed such measures unnecessary while studying corpses. I'd never seen a device like the carbolic steam spray before and couldn't wait to tell Uncle all about it. He'd surely order one for his own laboratory.

Nicolae took aim, spraying the room down in a fine mist. Wisps of gray fog drifted through the air, smelling of sharp antiseptic that tickled my nose.

"We've gotten permission from the family to perform this autopsy..."

Something about Percy's statement troubled me, but my mind drifted back to Ileana while the professor continued with our lesson. I couldn't figure out what her motive would be in any of the murders, but that didn't mean she hadn't been involved. In fact, I no longer believed she'd been working alone. Anastasia hadn't returned to the academy when she'd said she would. I wondered if she had somehow played a part in the crimes, too. Despite their difference in station she and Ileana were friends. They'd both gone missing within a week of each other. I'd initially believed Anastasia's note about investigating the scene at the house in the village. Now I wasn't so sure.

Maybe I'd come too close to uncovering their secrets and they'd fled. I'd learned that trusting those who appeared innocent only led to heartbreak and devastation. Monsters could wear the smiles of friends while secreting away the rotten soul of the Devil in the darkest crevices of themselves. I thought back to the times we were all together in my rooms, and a new idea elbowed its way into my mind. If Anastasia and Ileana were working together, then perhaps each encounter and action had been a well-crafted act. They might have scripted their reactions, leading me purposely down the wrong path.

"Miss Wadsworth, are you with us today?"

I snapped into the present, face burning as I glanced around the theater. The Bianchi twins, Noah, Andrei, Erik—all had their attention fixed upon me, even Thomas.

"Apologies, Professor. I—"

Moldoveanu strode into the surgical theater, hands clenched at his sides. I had no idea he'd sneaked into the room. His robes were the exact color of his silver sheet of hair and hung as severely as the look he leveled at me.

"I require a private word with you. Now."

Andrei snickered and said something under his breath. Erik also chuckled as I walked past them. The thought of stepping on his foot with my heel was enough to distract me from actually doing it. Cian caught my eye, offering a hesitant smile. It was quite the show of support, as the Irish boy had barely acknowledged my existence in the past. Noah must have put in a good word for me.

I picked my way down the stairs, hugging the walls of the surgical theater, and exited into the hallway where the headmaster was waiting, foot stomping the seconds away as if they were roaches he was exterminating.

"When is the last time you spoke with the maid Ileana?"

My heart pounded. Seemed Thomas and I weren't the only ones who thought her behavior suspect. "I believe it was two days ago, the evening of the thirteenth, sir."

"You believe so. Is attention to detail not critical to being a student of forensics? What other things might you miss that would be detrimental to a case? I ought to strike you from the course now and save us both time and energy."

I bristled at the bite in his tone. It was harsh even for him. "I was being polite, sir. The last I saw her was the thirteenth. I'm certain of it. I've had a new chambermaid since then. She's informed me Ileana's on duty elsewhere in the castle, though I no longer believe that to be true. Perhaps you ought to speak with her and see what she might be hiding about Ileana's whereabouts."

Moldoveanu inspected me with the squinty-eyed look of someone staring at a specimen under a microscope. I pressed my lips together, no longer trusting myself not to snap at him for taking so long to speak again. "And what, exactly, do you believe to be true about Ileana now?"

"I believe she knows something about the murder of Mr. Wilhelm Aldea, sir." I hesitated before voicing my next concern, worried that if Anastasia returned unharmed, she would murder me when she learned I'd betrayed her trust. "I—I also wonder if she knows where Anastasia is. Anastasia left a note for me…begging not to tell you where she'd gone, but never offered any further details."

Moldoveanu's hand flexed at his side, the only outward sign of how furious he was. "Yet you didn't bother to inform me of your suspicions. Do you recall anything out of the ordinary over the last few days? Anything substantial to confirm your claims?"

There was the matter of the two people I was certain I'd seen dragging a corpse through the woods. I'd already told him about that, and he'd sneered. I wasn't about to subject myself to further scrutiny. "No, sir. Just a feeling."

"A feeling. Otherwise known as a nonscientific finding. How unsurprising for a young woman to be ruled by her emotions instead of rational thought."

I slowly inhaled, letting the action calm the flames of my own annoyance. "I believe it's important to incorporate both science and instinct, sir."

The headmaster curled his lip away from his pointy incisors. It was truly remarkable that a man could be in possession of such animalistic teeth. I was beginning to wonder if it wasn't a medical condition he ought to have checked out when he finally clicked his tongue against those instruments of impalement.

"We've already spoken with your new chambermaid. She's been dismissed from her duties. I suggest you stay away from Ileana if you do see her again. You may return to class, Miss Wadsworth."

"Why? Do you believe she has something to do with Anastasia's disappearance? Have you searched the tunnels?" The expression the headmaster offered was nothing short of terror-inducing. If I'd thought his teeth were intimidating, it was nothing compared to the depthless loathing in his icy gaze.

"If you were a wise girl, you'd stay out of those tunnels and any chambers located in them. Heed my warning, Miss Wadsworth." He glanced into the surgical theater, gaze landing on the corpse. I could have sworn there was a flash of sadness before he turned back to me, eyes full of rage. "Or you might find yourself under Percy's blade next."

With that, he pivoted on his heel and marched off, leather soles slapping the floor. Snakes seemed to slither through my intestines. Somehow I made my way back into the surgical theater and sank into my seat. I went through the motions of taking notes, but my mind was torn in half.

I needed to know how the girl on Percy's dissection table had perished, if not solely from the bats' depredations. But I needed to sort out the mystery of both Ileana's and Anastasia's whereabouts as well. Thomas watched me over his shoulder every few moments, lips pressed in concern.

Percy's next words pierced my racing thoughts. "Clearly Miss Anastasia Nádasdy succumbed to the wounds she sustained."

All thoughts were tossed from my head as if a washbasin had been thrown out. I stared at Percy, blinking disbelief away. He couldn't mean—My gaze traveled from my teacher to the corpse laid out before him. He tugged the shroud from her face. Little gears clicked and turned, hissing as this new information fitted into place. The young woman who'd been attacked in the tunnel chamber by vampire bats was *Anastasia?*

The earth seemed to rumble beneath my seat. Flames rose from my core, then turned icy. I blinked tears away, unable to prevent a few from sliding down my cheeks. I didn't actually care if anyone in the class mocked my show of emotion. I stared unseeing at the body, trying to force the image to make sense. Anastasia. It couldn't be. I sat there, heart thudding dully, looking at the lifeless form. I took in the blond hair but couldn't bear to inspect her decaying face too closely.

My friend was dead. This could not be happening again. My chest felt as if it were caving in from the weight now pressing on it. How could I have thought her guilty of the murders? When did I become so untrusting? I longed to run from the room and never study another body for as long as I lived. Thomas wasn't the cursed one,

I was. Every person I grew close to died. Nicolae had said as much in the alleyway. He was correct.

Through tears, I glanced at our classmates. All were stricken. Gone were the fiercely competitive students, thirsting for knowledge and battling for those two precious spots in the academy. Science needed coldness for exploratory advancements, but we were still human. Our minds might be made of steel when needed, but our hearts beat with compassion. We still cared deeply for people and mourned.

Thomas swiveled in his seat, attention landing on Nicolae and then on me. My friend appeared rattled but was focused enough to seek out suspicious behavior. I'd almost forgotten about the prince's illustrations and what part they might have played in all this. Andrei clamped his jaws together, tossing a murderous glare at his friend, though his throat bobbed with tears he was obviously holding back. How very peculiar.

"The bite marks are consistent with those of small mammals," Percy said quietly. "Does anyone want to hazard a guess as to what might have attacked this young woman?"

I held my breath along with the rest of the surgical theater. Neither Thomas nor I dared to respond—or even glance at each other—though we had seen exactly how Anastasia had died. The question was, who else in this classroom would know? If anyone else was collaborating with Ileana, they'd be privy to the source of death.

Percy trailed his gaze over each student, waiting for someone to break the heavy silence.

"Snakes?" Vincenzo and Giovanni finally asked in unison.

"Venomous spiders?" Cian added.

"Good guesses, but no," Percy said, his expression becoming less hopeful. "Does anyone else wish to share an idea?"

Nicolae barely glanced at the body, attention fixed on the carbolic steam spray still in his hands. He rolled it from side to side, then pressed the release button, startling us all with a burst of antiseptic spray. Its mist was as foreboding as the tone he used.

"Bats," he mumbled. "Those wounds are characteristic of a type of bat rumored to infest this castle."

Percy clapped once, the sound jolting us all in our seats. "Excellent, Prince Nicolae! Notice the spaces between the teeth marks. These indicate rather large specimens, too. I imagine they must have fed on her for quite some time, though she likely lost consciousness at some point."

I swallowed hard, stomach churning with the image. If I didn't keep my emotions locked away tightly, I'd break apart piece by piece. I focused on breathing. If I thought about my friend, how vibrant she was in life,

I'd be of no use to her in death. Still, even with having had some practice in controlling my feelings, bits of my heart shattered. I was through with loss. So very tired of constantly saying good-bye to those I wished to adventure with through life. I swiped at the wetness on my cheeks and sniffled.

Erik and Cian cursed. I knew they weren't capable of being the Impaler or working with Ileana. There was kindness and compassion fusing their cells together. I'd watched Erik help Nicolae when he'd tossed him an apron, willing to help someone out when they needed a friend.

But the prince and his obsession with bats, well, that seemed too much of a coincidence to ignore.

"All right," Percy said, "who would like to make the next incision?"

Cian and Noah eyed each other and slowly raised their hands. I admired their ability to push beyond the horror, but I couldn't bring myself to use my blade on my friend's body. I didn't care if it cost me my place in the academy; even thinking of the stupid competition felt horribly cold, though I knew Anastasia would chide me for feeling defeated. She'd expect me to push forward.

With that thought fortifying me, I sat straight as an arrow in the first row of Percy's surgical theater, knowing there was absolutely nothing I could offer Anastasia, aside from my will to avenge her death. Thomas leaned forward in his seat but did not raise his hand.

"Mr. Hale," Percy said. "Please come take your place."

Noah adjusted his apron and took the scalpel from Percy, doing a fine job of rinsing it with carbolic acid before placing it against unmoving flesh. Uncle would have been proud. I forced myself to watch the *Y* incision he made on Anastasia's lifeless chest. I kept my breathing steady, not allowing my pulse to spike. We needed to find out for certain if the bats were truly her cause of death, or if something more sinister had ended her life first.

My gaze trailed down to her hands. There weren't many defensive wounds. I found it hard to believe someone as feisty as Anastasia would simply lie back and give in to Death without battling it with everything she had. She fought to be treated equally, fought to prove her worth to her uncle. A fighter like her wouldn't give up during the ultimate battle. The thought bolstered my own spirits, encouraging me to carry on.

"Note the way in which Mr. Hale is separating the ribs. Very clean cuts."

Professor Percy handed our classmate the rib cutters and took the scalpel again. I cringed a bit at the exposed viscera but reminded myself this was no longer Anastasia—this was a victim who needed us. A slight garlic scent wafted through the theater as Percy paced around the operating floor. I narrowed my eyes. Before I could call out my question, Noah pried the jaws open. Nothing unusual was there. Thomas chanced a look in my direction, his expression hard to read.

Noah moved down the cadaver, inspecting the abdominal cavity. He drew close enough to smell the organs and stifled a small gag. "A garlic odor is present in body tissues and mouth, sir, though there are no signs of the substance on her. Inspecting the contents of her stomach might reveal more."

Percy stopped pacing and bent to examine the body himself. He inhaled in small intervals as he moved from the mouth to the stomach. He shook his head and addressed the class.

"In the case of ingesting toxic substances, you'll note a stronger scent in stomach tissues. Which is precisely what I've noticed here. The garlic odor is overwhelming near the victim's stomach. Does anyone know any other signs associated with intentional or accidental poisoning?"

Vincenzo raised his hand so violently he nearly knocked himself over the railing. His brother latched on to his arm, steadying him.

"Yes, Mr. Bianchi?"

"More...er...mucus will be evident," he said, Italian

accent strong as he searched for the English words. "As the body's natural defense against...a...foreign attack."

"Excellent," Percy said, gathering up toothed forceps and passing them to Noah. "Where else might one find indications of poison?"

Cian cleared his throat. "The liver is another good place to check."

"Indeed." Percy motioned for Noah to remove the organ in question and handed him a specimen tray. I knew what it felt like, sticking one's hands deep within the abdominal cavity and coming away with a liver that squished ever so slightly between one's fingers. The weight of it was difficult to manage with only forceps. Noah showed no emotion, though his hands weren't as controlled. The liver slid onto the tray, smearing it with rusty liquid. I swallowed revulsion down.

Percy held the tray up, then walked slowly down the line of students, allowing each of us an opportunity to inspect the organ from our first-row seats. "Note the color. Yellow is commonly found after exposure to..."

My heart sped up with my thoughts. "Arsenic."

Percy beamed, tray of liver proudly displayed before him as if he were serving us tea in fine china. "Very good, Miss Wadsworth! Both the garlic odor and presence of yellow liver tissues are indicative of potential arsenic poisoning. Now, before anyone jumps to conclusions, it would behoove you to note the following: arsenic is found in most everyday items. Our drinking water contains trace amounts. Ladies used to mix it with their powders to remain youthful in appearance."

I gripped my hands together, mind churning with this new information as I thought back to the first victim we'd encountered in Romania—the man on the train. His mouth had been stuffed with garlic, but the smell was too overwhelming to have resulted from such a small amount of the organic substance. I should have investigated that further. The murderer clearly used real garlic to mask the telltale scent of arsenic.

I focused on breathing correctly. *Inhale. Exhale.* The steady flow of oxygen fed my brain. I thought of Wilhelm's symptoms. How quickly he'd gone from a healthy seventeen-year-old to a cadaver lying beneath my blade in the laboratory. Highly unnatural.

No cause of death had been noted in Wilhelm's case. The missing blood served as a distraction. And it was a good one, too. I'd been so preoccupied by the thought of scientifically proving vampires impossible, I'd never checked his liver. Percy, too, had let the obvious drag his attention away from inspecting other organs.

I thought of other symptoms of arsenic poisoning. Discoloration or rashes on the skin. Vomiting. It had all been there, present and waiting for someone to add up the symptoms. A simple math equation, nothing more.

Whoever had planned these murders had done so brilliantly. Even Thomas hadn't found the thread binding it all together. The culprit likely knew Thomas would not be as sharp as he normally was, the fear of his lineage being exposed hindering him in a way he was unused to. My head spun. This murderer was more cunning than Jack the Ripper.

We hadn't examined the maid's body, yet apparently she'd also shown no outward signs of murder, according to the Bianchi twins. It wasn't hard to deduce that she'd also been poisoned.

Anastasia. Wilhelm. The man from the train. The maid. All seemingly unrelated because of the outwardly different causes of death—impalement and blood loss. Those were both simply provocative distractions, created either postmortem or close to death to inflame emotions in a highly superstitious community.

We did not have more than one murderer. We had someone blessed with a knowledge of poison and the opportunity to offer it to each victim. I swallowed hard. Whoever had done this was smart and patient. They'd been waiting a long time to execute their plan. But why now . . .

"Miss Wadsworth?"

I jolted into the present, cheeks burning. "Yes, Professor?"

Percy studied me closely while threading a large Hagedorn needle. "Your stitches the other day were exemplary. Would you like to assist with closing up the cadaver?"

The class didn't so much as breathe. It was a far cry from the sneers and snickers of earlier days. We were now bound together through loss and determination.

For now.

I glanced down at the girl who'd been my friend and stood. "Yes, sir."

THIRTY-TWO
POTIONS AND POISONS

FOLKLORE CLASS
CURS DE FOLCLOR
BRAN CASTLE
17 DECEMBER 1888

Guards stood outside the classroom, eyes fixed on nothing and yet alert enough to strike at any moment, though Radu paid them no notice. He continued with his folklore lesson as if the castle weren't being overrun by royal guards and missing or murdered students. Either he was extraordinarily talented at appearing unaffected, or he truly was lost within his own imagination, trapped somewhere between myth and reality.

Two days had passed since the discovery that Anastasia was the victim from the tunnels, and the headmaster practically had the castle swarming with guards. I couldn't tell if their presence comforted or frightened me more.

"In light of recent findings, our next lesson is on Albertus Magnus, philosopher and scientist. Legend says he was the finest alchemist who ever lived. Some believe he possessed magic. *Magie.*" Radu flipped through pages in the old book he'd taken from the library days earlier, *De Mineralibus.* "He studied Aristotle's work. Fine, fine man he was. He's said to have discovered arsenic." Noah bravely raised his hand, and Radu hopped in delight. "Yes, Mr. Hale? Do you have anything to offer on the subject and legend of Mr. Magnus?"

"I understand discussing arsenic because of the murders, sir, but how, exactly, does this relate to Romanian folklore?"

Radu blinked several times, mouth opening and shutting. "Well...it's foundational to understanding certain legends involving the subject of today's lesson: the Order of the Dragon. During its prime, the Order did quite well in places such as Germany and Italy. Some believe the rise in their nobility ranks was due to the secret practice of using arsenic to slowly poison their targets."

I raised a brow, intrigued. Arsenic was known as "inheritance powder" in England, so called for its use by noblemen who wanted to attain a title faster than natural death allowed.

"Are you suggesting the Order were a group of noble alchemist assassins?" Cian asked. "I thought they were supposed to fight perceived enemies of Christianity."

"My, my, my. Someone has been doing some research! I am impressed, Mr. Farrell. Very good." Radu puffed his chest out and walked up and down the aisles. "After Sigismund of Hungary died, the Order became vastly important in this country and its neighbors. Less so in western regions of Europe. The Ottomans were invading, threatening the boyars...er, yes, Mr. Farrell?"

"What exactly are the boyars, sir?"

"Oh! The boyars were the highest-ranking members of the aristocracy under the Wallachian princes. They were feuding over whom to name as the prince, and our ruling system was hopelessly corrupt."

"Shouldn't the title of prince be passed along to the next in the family line?" I asked.

Andrei snorted, a bit halfheartedly by his usual standards, but I ignored him. He might know the particular rules of his country, but I didn't and felt no shame in inquiring.

Radu shook his head. "That wasn't the way things were done here during medieval times. Those born illegitimately were able to claim the title of prince. In fact, most everyone who'd been born of either Dănești or Drăculești seed was legitimized when the boyars appointed them to the throne. They did not need to be pure-blooded to rule; they simply needed the might of a fierce army. Much different than what you're used to in London. It often led to a lot of relatives murdering each other for the right to rule."

Not so different from England in that sense, I thought.

"Those who were opposed to the in-feuding and corruption swelled the ranks of the Order," Erik said, Russian accent prominent. "I assume they were afraid of losing their culture to invading forces."

"*Ai dreptate.* You're correct. The Order, though they've never called themselves by any name as part of their secrecy, banded together, fighting for their freedom and rights. Legend says they were fierce, taking it upon themselves to eradicate threats from both inside the kingdom and out. In fact, there are stories that suggest they wanted to unify the country by eliminating the infighting within the two royal lines."

Thomas and I glanced at each other. My senses perked up at this revelation. It was precisely what I had worried about. I raised my hand.

"Oh! Yes, Miss Wadsworth? What do you have to add to this discussion? I cannot tell you how pleased I am by everyone's interest in today's lesson. Much more lively than our lesson on *strigoi*."

"When you say 'royal family,' in this instance you're

referring to the House of Basarab, correct? Not the current royal family of the court?"

"Another fine detail. The current royal family—the Hohenzollern-Sigmaringen dynasty—is not related to the House of Basarab in any way. For our purposes, when I say 'royal family,' I'm discussing the lineage of Vlad Dracula and his ancestors. I enjoy keeping our lessons focused on legends surrounding our illustrious castle's medieval history. We mostly deal with the Drăculești line. Vlad Dracula's descendants last ruled in the 1600s. People have been led to believe his direct descendants are all gone." His focus slid in Thomas's direction. "There are still those in Romania who recall the truth, however."

"Is the Order functioning today?" Cian asked, leaning forward on his elbows. "Are there new members?"

"There—" Radu paused mid-answer and scratched his head. "Not for quite some time. I believe they died out around the same time the Basarab family lost their seat as prince. Though there is one family who claims to hail from that line—they are actually boyars here today. Now, now. Before we get too far ahead of ourselves, I do have some old poems that show the craft and cunning of the Order. Arsenic wasn't the only trick they used in disposing of their enemies."

He passed two pieces of parchment to each of us. Scribbled on them were poems in Romanian, which he promptly translated into English.

"Oh! I just love this one. I recall the first time my parents had introduced me ... bother all that. Ahem.

LORDS WEEP, LADIES CRY. DOWN THE
ROAD, SAY GOOD-BYE.
LAND SHIFTS AND CAVES DWELL. DEEP IN
EARTH, WARM AS HELL.
WATER SEEPS COLD, DEEP, AND FAST.
WITHIN ITS WALLS YOU WILL NOT LAST.

Blood frosted inside my veins. The words weren't exactly the same, but they were strikingly similar to the chanting I'd heard snippets of outside my chambers. Thomas narrowed his eyes, ever in tune with my shifting emotions, and leaned back in his seat.

"Pardon, Professor," he said. "What is the title of this poem?"

Radu blinked several times, bushy brows raising with the movement. "We will get to that in a moment, Mr. Cresswell. This is copied from a most special and sacred text, known as 'Poems of Death.' *Poezii Despre Moarte.* The original text has gone missing. Very strange and unfortunate indeed."

I felt Thomas's attention on me, but I didn't dare meet his gaze. We *were* in possession of the very book Dănești had been searching for. How the missing woman from the village had had it in her custody was yet another mystery to add to our ever-growing list.

The Bianchi brothers scratched notes into their journals. This lesson apparently had just become more intriguing to them with the mention of death. I could hardly contain my own excitement. Radu's incessant rambling might be worthwhile after all.

"And this text was sacred to the Order?" I asked.

"Yes. Its contents were used by the Order of the Dragon as a sort of...well...it was used to rid the castle of perceived enemies during medieval times. Is it something you recall, Mr. Cresswell? As one of the remaining—and almost secret, I believe—members of that household, your family would have known more about this text, I imagine. Your education must have been exceptional."

It was subtle, but I did not miss the slight flicker of tightness in Thomas's spine. Our classmates shifted uncomfortably in their seats, the revelation unnerving even to those who studied the deceased. No wonder Thomas wasn't keen on sharing his ancestry. Hiding his ties to Vlad Dracula spared him from unwarranted scorn.

Radu apparently had done some research on Thomas's matriarchal lineage. How intriguing. My body thrummed with alert. Radu was much less clueless than he appeared.

Thomas lifted a shoulder, taking on the air of someone who couldn't care less about the topic of conversation or the tension now tugging at the room. He transformed himself into an emotionless automaton, putting on an armor against judgment. Nicolae glared at his sheet of parchment, not deigning to look at his many-times-removed cousin. I imagined that he'd known who Thomas was and hadn't shared it with anyone.

"Can't say the poem sounds the least bit familiar," Thomas said. "Or particularly interesting. Though I do believe if used on one's enemies, it might very well kill them over time. One more line from that book and I might collapse from boredom myself."

"No, no, no. That would be most unfortunate! Moldoveanu wouldn't be pleased if I caused the death of his students." Radu clapped a hand over his mouth, eyes protruding. "Poorly timed use of words, though. After poor Wilhelm, Anastasia, and now Mariana."

"Who is Mariana?" Thomas asked.

"The maid who was discovered the other morning," Radu said.

He sealed his lips together, watching the Bianchi twins squirm in their seats. I'd forgotten that our classmates had discovered her body. Studying death and coming across corpses outside the laboratory weren't the same, and the latter was hard to simply get past. I knew all too well the lingering effects of such a discovery.

"Perhaps that's enough for today's lesson."

I scanned the second page of poetry, sucking in a breath sharp enough to pierce. I needed a few more answers before class ended. "Professor, the poem you read is called 'XI.' None of the poems appear to have titles other than Roman numerals. Why is that?"

Radu glanced from the page to the class, chewing his lip. After a moment, he shoved his spectacles up his nose. "From what I've gathered, the Order used this as a code. Legend has it they marked secret passages beneath this very castle. Behind doors marked with a certain numeral there would be... well—there'd be all manner of unpleasant devices or traps by which their foes would perish."

"Can you give us examples?" Erik asked, first in Russian and then in English.

"Of course! They would appear to have died of natural causes, though the way in which they'd come to their end was hardly natural. It's rumored that Vlad— a member of the Order, just like his father—would send a noble down beneath the castle with the promise that he would find treasure there. Other times he'd send corrupt boyars to these chambers to hide, saying an army was outside the castle walls and they should take shelter. They'd follow his instructions, enter the marked chambers, and meet their deaths. He could then pass their demises off as an unfortunate accident to other boyars, though I'm sure they suspected otherwise. He had quite the reputation for razing corruption from this country in sweeping ways."

Thomas's eyes narrowed, focus now latched on to Radu as if he were a starving mutt with a bone. I knew precisely what that expression meant.

"What of the poetry, though?" I asked. "What did it signify to members of the Order?"

Radu pointed to the parchment with stubby fingers, careful to not smudge the ink. "Take this one here." He translated the text from Romanian to English once again:

XXIII
WHITE, RED, EVIL, GREEN. WHAT HAUNTS
THESE WOODS STAYS UNSEEN.
DRAGONS ROAM AND TAKE TO AIR. CUT
DOWN THOSE WHO NEAR HIS LAIR.
EAT YOUR MEAT AND DRINK YOUR BLOOD.
LEAVE REMAINS IN THE TUB.
BONE WHITE, BLOOD RED. ALONG THIS
PATH YOU'LL SOON BE DEAD.

"Some believe this poem refers to a secret meeting place of the Order. One in the woods, where they hold death rites for other members. Others believe it refers to a crypt beneath the castle: a crypt only because once unsuspecting guests traveled inside, they were locked in by the Order until they rotted away. I've heard villagers claim their bones were turned into a holy site."

"What sort of holy site?"

"Oh, one where sacrifices are made to the Immortal Prince. But not everything you hear is to be trusted. The dragons-taking-to-air bit is metaphorical. Translated plainly, this means the Order moves about stealthily, stalking and protecting what is theirs. Their land. Their God-chosen rulers. Their way of life. They are transformed into ferocious creatures who eat you whole and leave your bones. Meaning, they murder you and the only thing left is your remains."

"Do you suspect the Order of the Dragon maintains the tunnels to this day?" I asked.

"Goodness. I don't believe so," Radu said, laughing a bit too loudly. "Though I suppose I cannot say for sure. As mentioned earlier, the Order first fashioned themselves after Crusaders. In fact, Sigismund, king of Hungary, later became Holy Roman Emperor."

Before Radu could go off about the Crusaders, I blurted out another question. "Exactly what methods of death did the tunnels contain?"

"Oh, let's see, Miss Wadsworth. Some passages

contained bats. Some were overrun with arachnids. Wolves are said to have hunted in other passages. Legend claims the only way to escape the water chamber is to offer a dragon a bit of blood." He smiled ruefully at the thought. "I don't believe the creatures would be able to live underground without a source of food or care. If the passages exist today, they are likely harmless, though I'd not suggest searching for anything this book contains. Most superstitions have some basis in fact. Hmm? Yes? Take *strigoi,* for instance—there must be some truth behind these rumors."

I wanted to point out that the legends regarding *strigoi* were likely the result of not burying bodies far enough underground during winter. Bodies became bloated with gases and pushed out of their graves; nail beds receded, making hands look like claws—ghastly and vampiric in appearance but not practice. To the uneducated, it would most certainly seem that their loved ones were trying to climb out of their graves. However, science proved that was simply myth.

The clock outside tolled the end of our class. Guards wasted no time making their presence once again known. I collected the pieces of parchment Radu had given us and tucked them into my pocket.

"Thank you, Professor," I said, watching him closely. "I rather enjoyed this lesson."

Radu clucked. "My pleasure. I thank you. I now have—is it really three o'clock? I was hoping to get to the kitchens before retiring to my chambers. They're making my favorite sticky buns. Off I go!" He grabbed an armful of journals from his desk and vanished out the door.

I had turned to Thomas, ready to talk through everything we'd learned and discuss Radu's possible involvement, when Dănești waved from the doorway. He grinned at Thomas, taunting my friend in a way I knew he wouldn't resist.

"*Să mergem*. We do not have all day."

Thomas inhaled deeply. There was only so much goading he could withstand. Before I had time to react, he opened that cursed mouth of his.

"Lapdogs do as they're told. They have nothing to do but sit and wait and beg for their master's next orders."

"They also bite when provoked."

"Do not pretend escorting me to and fro isn't the highlight of your miserable day. Shame you didn't do the same for that poor maid. Though I am much prettier to stare at," Thomas said, running a hand through his dark locks. "At least I know I'm in no danger of being whisked away by a vampire—you're too busy admiring me. Quite the compliment. Thank you."

Dănești's grin turned absolutely lethal. "Ah. I have

417

been waiting for this." He called out in Romanian, and four more guards piled into our now-empty folklore classroom. "Escort Mr. Cresswell to the dungeon for the next few hours. He needs to be shown Romanian *ospitalitate.*"

Dear Wadsworth,

I have finally been sprung from
the dank hellscape they dignify with
the name "dungeon." Now I'm sat in
my chambers, contemplating scaling
the castle walls for amusement. I
overheard the guards speaking, and it
seems tonight might be our best chance
of sneaking out to search the woods for
whoever was dragged out through the
tunnels that night.

Unlike our esteemed headmaster,
I do not believe you invented that
scenario, and I worry we may have
been wrong about Ileana being involved,
criminally. She may very well be
another victim, but there's only one
way we can be sure.

If you do not hear any more from
me, it's because I am sneaking through
corridors, en route to your chambers.

Ever yours,
Cresswell

THIRTY-THREE
DANK HELLSCAPE

TOWER CHAMBERS
CAMERE DIN TURN
BRAN CASTLE
17 DECEMBER 1888

Such a dramatic young man. If Thomas was already in his rooms writing a note to me, that meant he'd spent only a short time in the dungeon. I finished drafting my response and folded it up, adding a bit of red wax and pressing it with my namesake rose seal.

"Please take this to Thomas Cresswell." The new chambermaid stared. I tried again, hoping my Romanian was accurate. My mind was in several places at once. "*Vă rog... dați-i... asta lui* Thomas Cresswell."

"*Da, domnișoară.*"

"Thank you. *Mulțumesc.*"

"Do you require assistance with getting ready for bed?"

I glanced at my simple dress and shook my head. "No, thank you. I can manage."

The maid nodded, swiping the note up and sticking it under the lid of a tray she was carrying. She exited my chambers, and I prayed she'd deliver it without the guards noticing what she was up to.

I paced along the carpet in my main chamber, mind stumbling and running over every last detail of the day. I scarcely knew where to start with untangling this new thread. Either Radu or Ileana might be the murderer. Radu for his knowledge of poisons. Ileana for her ability to slip them into meals.

But, with little education, did she have the understanding of how to administer such a thing as arsenic? And did Radu have an opportunity to feed it to students? And yet Thomas believed Ileana might be a victim—which left Radu as a prime suspect. Something niggled in my core. I still had a feeling that Ileana was involved somehow. I couldn't explain it.

I'd taken my riding habit and breeches out of my trunk and didn't miss the bulk of my skirts as I continued pacing around the room in my new outfit.

Who else besides Ileana would know Thomas would be distracted by the shame of his lineage, though? How did anyone here know him well enough to use that against him and thwart his normally stellar method of deductions? Ileana might have gleaned some information from

Daciana; perhaps she'd been using her this entire time. I stopped pacing. That didn't quite feel right either; a love so powerful could not be easily faked. Which brought me back to our professor.

No amount of research Radu could have done would unearth the secrets of Thomas's personality. Or perhaps that was simply a spot of good luck, a serendipitous gift. An even better idea: the murderer might be someone we hadn't interacted with at all. A shiver glided down my spine. Imagining a faceless murderer who was not only skilled but also blessed with luck was especially frightening.

Half an hour scraped by, and still no sign of Thomas. I sat at my writing desk and plucked a pen from its inkwell. I'd promised Father I'd write to him and had yet to send a proper note. I stared at the blank piece of parchment, unsure of what to disclose.

I couldn't very well discuss the murders. Father's blessing and encouragement for pursuing my career in forensic medicine went only so far. If he'd known about the body we'd found on the train, he'd have brought me back to London immediately.

A faint scuffling noise dragged my attention toward the window. It sounded as if an animal had scuttled across the roof. My blood prickled all over.

I bolted from my chair and stared out at the snowy world, trapped in darkness. Heart thundering, I expected to see a ghastly face staring back at me, milky eyes unblinking. No such thing happened. It was likely a chunk of snow or ice falling from the roof. Or a bird seeking shelter from the storm. I sighed and sat back down at my desk. I'd never stop creating villains out of shadows.

I rolled the pen between my fingers, trying to think of anything other than ghouls and vampires and people adept with poison. I'd nearly forgotten it was the Christmas season again. The time for joy and love and family. It was hard to remember life existed outside of death and fear and chaos.

I gazed at the photograph of Father and Mother, allowing warm memories to thaw the colder, scientific parts of me. I recalled the way Father would have our cook pack a hamper full of treats, then play hide and seek with us in the maze at Thornbriar.

He'd laughed freely and often back then—I'd never realized how much I'd miss that part of him once it perished along with Mother. He was slowly emerging from that desolate nothingness that follows losing a piece of your soul, but I worried he'd fall into old patterns now that he was alone. From this point forward I vowed to write to him often, to keep him engaged with the living. We were both surrounded by enough death.

I took my brother's old advice and forgot about murder and death for a few moments, allowing myself to remember that life was beautiful even during the

Dear Father,

The Kingdom of Romania is truly enchanting.
One of my first thoughts upon seeing Bran Castle
and its spires was of those children's stories you
and Mother would read to us before bed. The tiles
on the towers are cut in a way that reminds me of
dragon scales. I half expect a knight to come riding
in on his steed at any moment. (Though we both
know I'd likely borrow his horse on my own to seek
out a dragon to slay. If he's truly a knight and a
gentleman, I'm sure he wouldn't mind.)

The Carpathian Mountains are some of the
grandest in all the world, at least what I've seen of
them. I cannot wait to admire this land during the
spring. I imagine the ice-capped mountains must
burst with greenery. I believe you would enjoy taking
a holiday here.

They have these divine meat pastries—filled with
savory mushrooms and all manner of wonderful

juices and spices. I have eaten them nearly every day so far! In fact, my stomach is grumbling at the mere mention of them. I must bring some back when I visit.

I hope you're doing well in London. I miss you terribly and have a photograph of you I often say good night to. Before you inquire, I will say that Mr. Cresswell has been a most perfect gentleman. He has taken his duty seriously and is quite the troublesome chaperone. You would be proud.

His sister, Miss Daciana Cresswell, has invited us to a Christmas ball in Bucharest. If the weather permits, it shall be a lovely time. I do wish I could come home for the new year and visit. Please give my love to Aunt Amelia and Liza. And do take care of them and yourself.

I shall write again soon. I am learning much here at the academy and cannot thank you enough for allowing me to study abroad.

Your loving daughter,
Audrey Rose

P.S. How is Uncle faring? I do hope you've
continued to see him and invite him over for supper.
It may be forward of me to say, but I daresay
you need each other, especially during this trying
season. Merry Christmas, Father. And many happy
tidings for the new year. 1889! I cannot believe
it's almost upon us. There is something fresh and
wonderful about the start of a whole new year. I
hope it ushers in the promise of new beginnings for
us all. It shall

darkest hours. I thought about the magnificence of this country, the history behind its architecture and its rulers. The gorgeous language of its people, the food and the love that went into making it.

Thump. Thump.

Ink splattered across the last words on the page, my careful script ruined. I shoved away from the desk so quickly my chair knocked over. Something was on the roof. Even though I knew it was madness, I imagined a humanlike creature, just risen from the grave, the scent of freshly turned earth enveloping my senses, as its fangs shot out, ready to drain my body of blood.

I sucked in a quick breath and darted over to my trunk of postmortem supplies, snatching up the largest bone saw I could find and holding it before me. What in the name of the queen—

Scraaaaaaaaaatch. It sounded as if that same something were clawing its way down the red-tiled roof. Again, an image of a *strigoi* assaulted my sensibilities. A humanoid creature with dead, gray flesh and black claws dripping the blood of its last meal, scraping its way to my chambers to gorge once more. Part of me wanted to dash into the corridor and scream for the guards.

Thump. Thump. Thump. My heart pounded double its normal beat. It was the sound of heavy treading. Whatever or whoever was on the roof was wearing thick-soled boots. Images of vampires and werewolves gave way to the more disturbing thoughts of depraved humans. Ones who had successfully murdered at least five victims.

I backed toward my nightstand, never taking my gaze from the window, and lowered my saw to turn the dial on my oil lamp. Darkness fell, hopefully rendering me invisible to whoever was still slowly crawling down the roof.

I waited, breath caught in terror's grasp, and watched. At first all I saw were heavier drifts of snow falling past my window. The sounds of scraping and the heavy tread were replaced by a sort of slipping noise.

Then it happened at once.

A shadow blacker than coal eclipsed the snowy world outside. It shook my windowsill with tremendous force, the tiny latch barely staying in place. Fear paralyzed my limbs. Whoever was out there was seconds away from either shattering the glass or the flimsy latch.

I hefted the saw and took a small step forward. Then another. The reverberations of the assault on the windowpane amplified my racing pulse. I came ever closer to the window, hearing the phantom picking and prodding and—cursing.

A gloved hand pounded against the pane. I tossed the saw and moved swiftly, unlatching the window, and grabbed him as if both of our lives depended on it.

THIRTY-FOUR
NIGHT MISADVENTURE

TOWER CHAMBERS
CAMERE DIN TURN
BRAN CASTLE
17 DECEMBER 1888

"Have you completely lost your senses?"

Thomas's long legs wildly kicked for the edge of the roof while I gripped his overcoat with more strength than I knew I possessed. "Stop thrashing about, you're going to lose your grip and take me with you."

He huffed a laugh. "What, exactly, do you suggest, Wadsworth?"

"Pull yourself forward while I tug."

"How...silly...of...me to panic. While dangling... inches away...from certain death."

It took some maneuvering, but I managed to hook my hands underneath his arms, then used my entire body weight to fall backward, pulling him through the windowsill toward me. We crashed to the floor, causing all sorts of noise as we knocked limbs and heads.

Snow gusted into my chambers, swirling and angry. Thomas rolled off me and lay flat on the ground, staring at the ceiling, hand clutched over his torso, panting. His black overcoat was nearly soaked through. I pushed myself up, arms shaking uncontrollably from both the adrenaline and terror still coursing through my body in wicked torrents, and shut the window.

"What in the name of the queen were you thinking? Climbing a stone roof…during a blizzard. I…" I gripped my hands in fists to keep them from trembling in the cold. "You almost fell off the roof, Thomas."

"I told you I was getting ready to scale the castle." A damp lock of hair fell across his brow as he craned his neck up. "Maybe a bit of coddling or congratulations is in order. It was rather heroic of me, setting out against all odds to break into your rooms. I needn't be chided."

"'Heroic' is not the term I'd use." I sighed. "And don't be cross. It's unbecoming."

Thomas sat up, that damnable crooked grin set upon his mouth. "Daci and I used to sneak out of our rooms and climb the roof when we were children. It would drive our mother absolutely mad. She'd be hosting some boring dinner in Father's absence, and we'd spy on the nobles in attendance." He heaved himself up from the floor, dusting his overcoat off with a few flicks of his gloved fingers. "I don't recall any of our outings involving a blizzard, though. Minor oversight."

"Indeed." I inhaled deeply. Only Thomas could do something so maddening—like practically falling to his death before my eyes—and then offer up a bit of his past to soothe my ire. "Did your mother often host events while your father was away?"

The lightness faded from his expression. "Father hardly ever traveled with us to Bucharest. He did not believe in celebrating our accursed ancestry." Thomas strode over to my armoire and rifled through my things. He handed me my cloak. "We ought to hurry. The storm is only beginning."

I was grateful for the thick stockings tucked into my boots as we trudged through the snow. It was heavy and wet, and clung to the bottom of my cloak with everything it had. In the past I had loved wintry nights. The silence that encapsulated the earth, the glittering sparkle of ice glinting in the moon's glow. But that was while safely tucked inside my London home with a mug of tea and roaring fire, a book nestled in my lap.

"This is where you saw them take the body, correct?"

Thomas pointed toward the break in the woods, the slight trail at the rear of the castle's grounds where we'd exited. I nodded, teeth clattering as snow mixed with sleet. It was a miserable night for an outdoor adventure, but we no longer had the luxury of waiting for better circumstances. If Daciana or Ileana had been taken, perhaps we'd find a clue out here—a swift check of the morgues had yielded nothing. Though how we'd find anything in the dark, with snow covering it, was seeming like an unachievable task.

We paused near the entrance to the forest, the moonlight throwing the long, thin shadows of the trees in our direction. Talons, claws—the imagery unsettled me.

Thomas inspected the ground on either side of the trail, his body slightly shaking as the wind picked up. "Seems undisturbed. We should be able to go in a little ways—see if we come across anything at all. Maybe look for the food stores Moldoveanu claims are out here. Then we'll return to the castle and reenter the way we came, through the kitchens."

Wind whipped strands of hair from my braids, but I was too cold to untuck my hands from beneath my cloak. I was fairly certain this was the coldest night ever known to the world. When I didn't respond, Thomas turned. He took in the tears slipping down my cheeks, the wind smacking my face with my own hair, and slowly approached. Without any innuendos or flirtation, he tucked the hair behind my ears with trembling fingers.

"I'm sorry it's so miserable out, Wadsworth. Let's hurry and get back indoors."

He made to assist me back toward the castle, but I dug my frozen heels in. "N-no. No. Let's s-see what's o-out there."

"I'm not sure—" He held his hands up in surrender as I flashed a look of determination. "If you're positive..."

I took in his own shivers and the redness of his nose. "Are you able to stay out here a bit more?"

He nodded, though hesitation was there. I gathered my strength and headed into the woods, Thomas following in my wake. Boughs of snow-covered spruce hung low, doing strange things to the sound around us. It was as if someone was holding their mittens over my ears, though it also seemed as if I could hear for miles in either direction. I focused on the crunch of Thomas's boots as he sped up to keep pace with me. Bits of snow fell in clumps, hitting the ground with a splat.

No animal noises. Thank goodness for small favors. It was likely too cold for even the wolves to be prowling these grounds. The trail went on for what felt like miles, though it was only a few hundred feet before we came upon a fork. The path to the right appeared wider, as if someone had taken great care in chopping down saplings and brush. I imagined that was where we'd find the food stores.

The pathway to the left, however, was overgrown with prickly-looking shrubbery. Thorns and sharp leaves posed a warning to anyone considering taking it. I choked down the urge to flee in the opposite direction. That familiar feeling of being watched by someone ancient and menacing pierced the area between my shoulder blades.

I knew Dracula wasn't real, but his ghost certainly felt as if it were haunting these woods. The skin on the back of my neck prickled as images of *strigoi*, creeping through the forest, waiting to strike, emerged. I took a moment to steady my nerves. I did not have any desire to explore a passage Nature was so intent on keeping to itself. Especially at night, during a blizzard, while a real murderer was nearby. It might be cowardly, but at least we'd live to hunt another day. I motioned toward the more well-worn path, snow falling ever faster.

"We'll check the other way during daylight. Let's see if the food stores are down here." The only response was silence, punctuated by a few drifts of falling snow. I spun around, cloak whirling about me like a ballerina's skirts. "Thomas?"

Nothing. Everything around me remained eerily silent, save for my ringing ears. I rushed toward the path on the right, noting the single set of footprints leading down it. Blasted Cresswell. Splitting up during a blizzard in the middle of the forest was yet another winning idea of his. I quietly cursed him the entire time it took for me to kick through the snow. After a few more strides I came upon a small stone structure that sat nestled between two larger boulders. It was no more than a hut, really.

Thomas's footprints disappeared within. I swore I was going to give him a piece of my—

Suddenly, he came crashing out of the building, nearly breaking its door as he slammed it shut. Before I could ask what on earth was happening, a loud snarl ripped through the quiet snowfall. A long, mournful howl followed.

Goosebumps rose across the entire length of me as several other cries tore through the night. "Cresswell!"

Thomas flipped around, hands still clutching the doorknob. Scratches and huffs frantically pawed at the wood, the sound terrifying in the otherwise still night. "Wadsworth—on the count of three, run!"

There was no time to argue. Thomas counted down too quickly for me to protest. Before he called out "Three," I was off. I had never been more thankful for leaving my skirts behind in favor of breeches as I hurtled over embankments of snow and branches.

Thomas crashed through the woods behind me, yelling at me to not turn back, to keep running. I ignored the answering howls, though I could now hear other creatures bounding through the snow behind us. I didn't slow. Didn't think about how the frosted air burned my lungs as I gulped it down. I didn't focus on the cold sweat coating my skin or the seemingly endless trail back to the castle. I most *especially* did not imagine wolves the size of elephants crashing through the forest behind us, ready to tear our limbs off and scatter them about.

I wished that Moldoveanu and Dăneşti were monitoring the woods again, but we weren't that lucky. We broke from the forest, running as fast as the elements and our bodies allowed.

Thomas grabbed my hand, a lifeline in the storm of terror. Barks and snarls crashed from the brush, the wolves now mere feet behind. I thought my heart might seize up any moment. We were going to be attacked. There was no way we'd outrun them. We were—

A gunshot exploded from the wood line.

Thomas threw me to the ground, sheltering me with his body. I lifted my head over his shoulder, watching as two large wolves retreated into the woods. Every bit of me was frozen, but all I could concentrate on was the thrashing of my adrenaline. Someone had shot at the wolves. Were we next?

Clumps of snow dotted my hair and my clothing. Thomas pushed himself off me, slowly scanning the area. I noticed the rapid rise and fall of his chest and the way he tensed for any further attack. He took my hand and helped me up. "Hurry. I don't see anyone, but someone's definitely out there."

I searched for a shadow or silhouette of the gunman. There was nothing but lingering smoke and the acrid scent of gunpowder. This time when I shivered, it had nothing to do with the ice sliding down my spine. We ran toward the yellow light of the kitchens, not looking back until we were safely inside and Thomas had kicked the door shut. I collapsed against a long wooden table, barely missing a few mounds of rising dough.

"Who do you—"

The door banged open and a rather husky figure stomped snow from his boots, musket slung over his back. Thomas and I both grabbed for knives from the counter. The figure moved forward, oblivious to the cutlery now aimed at him. With a swift movement, his hood was tossed back. Radu blinked at us.

"Mr. Cresswell. Miss Wadsworth." He removed the musket from his shoulder and leaned it against a trestle table. On it sat a bowl of stew, steam still rising from its center, and a hunk of bread torn into a few pieces. "I warned you about the woods. Hmm?" Radu pulled a stool out and sat, tucking into his late-night meal. "Run along back to your chambers. If Moldoveanu discovers you've left the castle, you'll wish the wolves had gotten to you first. Dangerous. Very dangerous what you did. *Pricolici* everywhere."

Thomas and I didn't so much as exchange a glance as we apologized and ran for the door.

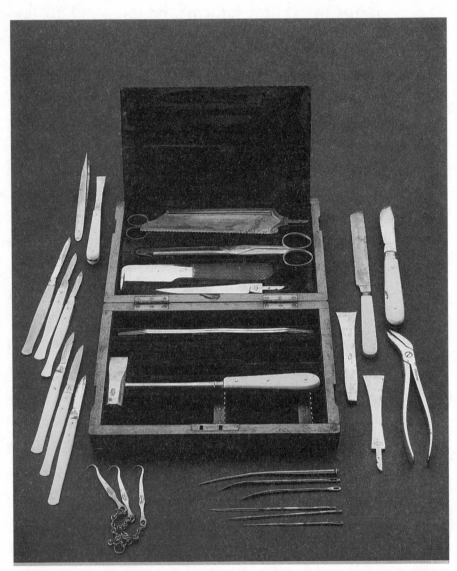

Post-mortem kit, c. 1800s.

THIRTY-FIVE
BLOODLESS

PERCY'S SURGICAL THEATER
AMFITEATRUL DE CHIRURGIE AL LUI PERCY
BRAN CASTLE
21 DECEMBER 1888

"I will be leading today's lesson in place of Professor Percy." Moldoveanu pointed up at the Bianchi twins. "If you'd still like to perform this task, I suggest you come to the operating table."

Without further prompting, the twins rushed down to the surgical stage and took their places. Even though our academy was seemingly under attack, there was still the matter of the assessment course and those two, tantalizing seats we were all fighting for.

Giovanni did an exceptional job creating a taut surface for his blade to slide across. His twin handed him a forensic breadknife after he'd opened up the body of the slain maid, Mariana. He carefully removed her liver, noting the same discoloration that had been present in Anastasia's corpse. Giovanni used the long knife to shear off a sample and placed it on a slide. It seemed an awful thing for a medical tool to be called a breadknife when its purpose was to carve into specimens and not baked goods.

Cian had offered to conduct this postmortem, but the twins insisted on doing it. Since they'd discovered the maid's body, they'd felt a duty to assist her in death. An uneasy feeling was present in the theater with us; it was difficult to study the bloodless bodies. Having Moldoveanu lead this lesson didn't help the heavy atmosphere. His expression was harder than usual, an added shield he wore since the discovery of his ward's remains. I had wanted to offer condolences before class, but the threat in his gaze stayed my tongue.

"Excellent technique." Moldoveanu adjusted his apron. "Like the other cadavers, this one is also missing its blood, as I'm sure you all can see. Why, if you were to hazard a guess, do you believe the murderer is taking the blood?"

Noah's hand was the first in the air. "Local papers are saying the Impaler Lord has returned. Villagers are panicking. It's someone who enjoys the fear, I think. Death and murder aren't the satisfying part. It's the hysteria surrounding them."

"Interesting theory. Where do you suppose they're disposing of the blood once it's been taken, then?"

Noah's brow furrowed. "There's a river close to the village. Maybe they dump it there."

"Perhaps." Moldoveanu lifted a shoulder. "Let's see who's read ahead in their anatomy texts. How many quarts of blood are in the human body? Anyone?"

"Five…maybe…a little more…depending on the size of the person," Erik said.

"Correct. Which is around one gallon." Moldoveanu walked around the body, attention landing on each of us. "That is quite a decent amount of blood to transport through the village. Though not impossible, yes?"

"Could be too risky, though," Noah added. "Even if it was carried in a wooden bucket, the possibility of it sloshing over the sides would exist. Plus, if anyone noticed it, the villagers might sound the alert."

"Indeed. Though a seemingly excellent depository for the blood, the river poses too great a threat to this particular murderer. He strikes me as the sort of person who does not wish to be stopped. He is careful. He has likely been plotting this for quite some time. I believe he has a history of violent acts, beginning in childhood. Though others will claim this to be of no consequence, I find it a useful tool to consider the history of the perpetrator."

Moldoveanu motioned for the twins to continue with the postmortem. Giovanni removed a bit of the stomach. Its contents would be examined for signs of arsenic, though a familiar garlic odor already hung in the air. I glanced around the room; each student was carefully scribbling notes, their focus more intense under the watchful gaze of the headmaster.

I tried thinking back on my conversations with Anastasia, convinced there had to be some indication of what she'd discovered about the scene in the missing woman's house. I hated thinking of her traveling into the village alone and meeting her doom. But I didn't even know if she'd made it that far. For all I knew, she never made it past the tunnels in which her body had been found. Was the murderer someone in this room, and if so, who would have been able to dispose of that much blood so quickly?

I surreptitiously inspected Andrei and Nicolae, who quietly spoke to each other in Romanian. They could be working together, though I cautioned myself to not focus entirely on them and miss other clues.

My attention strayed to the Bianchi twins. I recalled Anastasia remarking on how they ignored her attempts at chatting. Was one of them the person she'd been intrigued by? If disposing of the blood was too much of a risk for a single individual to handle, did that point to the two of them working together? They were very good at forensics and likely had ample knowledge of poisons. Perhaps it also wasn't a coincidence that they'd discovered the maid's body.

I glanced toward Thomas. He was already watching me, head cocked to one side as if he were reading my thoughts. We hadn't known what to make of Radu the other night, and we couldn't talk afterward due to the guards patrolling the corridors. We had been fortunate to make it to our chambers without being caught.

I still couldn't believe that Radu had saved us from predatory wolves in the dead of night, then returned to his stew as if nothing at all had occurred. His behavior was predictable in its unpredictability. Though I still had a difficult time imagining him murdering students or anyone else.

"I'm afraid that's all the time we have for today's lesson. In light of recent events, I have decided that this is your final class before Christmas break," Moldoveanu said as the clock tolled the hour. "Classes begin again on the twenty-sixth. Do not test my patience; I'm not keen on late arrivals."

THIRTY-SIX
HOUSE OF BASARAB

FOYER
FOAIER
BRAN CASTLE
22 DECEMBER 1888

The next morning Thomas and I met in the castle's receiving chamber, ready to embark on our journey to Bucharest. Noah and Cian had bid us good-bye before disappearing into the dining hall, and I was now lost in thought, dreading that Daciana wouldn't be there to greet us upon our arrival. Thomas had written her immediately after our initial suspicions regarding Ileana, but Daciana hadn't replied. If she was hurt, or worse . . . I could not allow myself to think this way.

Thomas shifted every other moment, his attention riveted on the small window beside the door. Our carriage was due to arrive any moment. I closed my eyes, doing my best to ignore the memory of Anastasia's corpse.

There were so many scratches and bite marks, it had been hard to recognize her. The memory of those bats covering her body—a sudden burst of heat overwhelmed my senses. I needed to get out into the cold before I was sick.

I rushed past Thomas and wrenched the door open, gasping in huge gulps of icy air. Outside, the scent of pine mixed with that of the fires roaring inside. The cloud-covered sun had barely stretched its arms across the horizon, and the temperature was cold enough to create icicles that looked like fangs surrounding the main doorway. Snow fell in a consistent rhythm.

The cold steadied my body temperature, allowing the bout of sickness to pass.

"Are you all right?" Thomas stood beside me, brow crinkled in concern.

I nodded. "The air is helping."

Thomas turned his attention to the cobbled path, though it appeared as if he were lost inside his mind. We were both bundled up in our warmest cloaks, tucked into layers upon layers of heavy material fighting the winter storm. Thomas's cloak was black as tar, with matching fur around the collar. He stared out at nothing, jaws locked tight. I could not imagine the thoughts running through his head.

I stuffed my hands into the muff hanging from my neck. "No matter what we discover, we'll make it through this. We're a team, Cresswell."

Thomas stomped his feet and blew warmth into his leather-clad hands, steam rising like London fog around him. "I know."

A familiar coldness settled into his features. This was the Thomas Cresswell I'd first met in London. The young man who didn't permit anything or anyone too close. The one who felt much too deeply, I realized. Liza had been right all those months ago, more than even she'd guessed. Thomas used distance as a barrier against being hurt. He wasn't cold and cruel—not even close to the relatives he feared being compared to. He was breakable and knew precisely where his weakest points lay. To help those he loved, he'd tear apart the world.

"Thomas. I—"

A sleek black carriage pulled up before us, horses as tall and proud as the driver who opened the door with an exaggerated flourish. Thomas offered his hand and helped me into the coach before seating himself across from me. I tried to ignore the sense of wrongness that sitting in such a small space unchaperoned stirred within me, as he nudged the hot brick at my feet.

"You were saying, Wadsworth?"

I smiled. "Nothing. It can wait."

"What are you sorting out over there? Some deep-seated fear or..." His powers of perception clicked in at once. A lazy grin stretched across his face, replacing the intensity of his previous expression. He sat back, then patted the small space beside him on the seat. "Bucharest is several hours away. Let's not talk about serious matters yet."

I inspected my friend but said nothing. My thoughts returned to my discomfort. It was quite scandalous to be traveling without a chaperone, but Mrs. Harvey had already left Braşov and we needed to confirm that Daciana was safe in Bucharest. Decorum and even our reputations needed to be set aside for the greater good. Though Father might not view it the same way were he to find out. I leaned back and forced those worries away.

We rumbled off, leaving the gothic castle in its commanding perch among the mountains. I watched as it slowly disappeared behind swirls of snow. I imagined the fortress's icy glare had reached into our carriage, trying in vain to drag us back. I could not get over how much a building made of stone could take on human qualities. Monstrous qualities, actually.

I dropped my hands in my lap, smile fading with the action. "I did some research on the House of Basarab last night."

Thomas angled his face away, studying me from the corner of his eye, which prevented me from fully reading his reaction. "Sounds dreadfully boring. Mother hired a governess for Daciana and me, and part of her glorious teachings included memorizing our Basarab family tree. More branches and thorny offshoots than an entire forest of brambles, with Daci and I being the sole blooms. Are you certain you'd rather not cuddle? It'd be a vast improvement over this topic. I should very much like to not think of anything related to Uncle Dracula."

He fidgeted in his seat, an indication I'd come to recognize that there were secrets he wasn't divulging. His tics and quirks were subtle, but I'd been a studious pupil. I sat forward, heart pounding with intrigue.

"Bear with me. As you said, long ago the House of Basarab broke off into two sparring families. One line was the Dăneşti, and the other was the Drăculeşti. Your family and Prince Nicolae's are from the two different off-shoots. He is of Dăneşti blood, and you are of Drăculeşti. Technically Wilhelm Aldea and the royal guard are also of royal blood, all related to Nicolae. Correct?"

Thomas twitched the curtains apart, mouth stubbornly shut. A few moments came and went as we crawled over a snowy pass. When he sat back and exhaled, I knew he'd decided to answer my questions.

"Yes. We are both descended from the House of Basarab. Though that was many, many generations ago. I'm not sure where the guard Dăneşti sits on the family tree, but I assume he's related to Nicolae and Wilhelm in some manner. I am technically related to Vlad Dracula, and Nicolae is not."

"Do you think that works in your favor? And... Daciana's?"

Thomas let the velvet slip back into place, the window covered except for one tiny sliver. Light filtered in through it, gilding one edge of his jawline. "Are you suggesting my sister might not be dead?"

"I'm not sure what I think." I nibbled my lip, unsure how to proceed. "Is it odd that Ileana—a likely uneducated peasant from the village—would know the historical line of a deposed house? It's all so convoluted. *You* are descended from it and it's difficult for even you to work out. Would she understand the intricacies of medieval families, even if they are so infamous?"

"What are you suggesting?"

"What if someone is using Ileana...what if the Order of the Dragon somehow forced her into their scheme? How would we uncover who's a member? Who would be well versed in the bloodlines? Why are they murdering only members from the Dănești clan, yet also killing the lower class?" I inhaled deeply, forcing myself to voice my biggest worry. "So far not one member from your line has been murdered. Daciana may very well be in Bucharest, unharmed. Or...what if...what if she's not missing at all? At least not missing through foul measures. Who are the Order, Thomas? What do they ultimately want? Are they protecting your sister, your line? How does the current royal family fit in with all of this; was Radu mistaken? Are they at all related to your family?"

"The current royal family is of no relation to either side of the House of Basarab." He sat forward, eyes earnest. "Do you believe they are—"

The carriage came to an abrupt halt, the coach jerking forward before rocking back. Our driver called to someone in Romanian, his tone not quite as cheerful as his expression had been moments before. I pressed my face against the frigid window, but couldn't see whom the driver was talking to. Sleet practically poured from the sky in frozen sheets.

Thomas's gaze wasn't on the window when I turned around; it was fastened on the handle of the door. The handle slowly twisting to one side. Chills slid down my bodice. Our driver shouted something that sounded like a curse in Romanian. Without conscious thought, I sprang across the seat and clutched the handle, but I didn't have enough weight to stop the door from being wrenched open.

A twisted face popped into our coach, brows white with snow and cheeks flushed crimson from the whipping wind.

Dăneşti flashed a delighted smile that didn't reach his eyes. "No one leaves the grounds, on the orders of the royal family."

Thomas subtly shifted his limbs in front of me, creating a slight barrier between me and the guard. "You cannot hold us here. The headmaster has already given permission for us to leave."

"Prince Nicolae was not in his chambers when we went to escort him home. Until he is recovered, we hold everyone." Without uttering another word, Dăneşti slammed the door shut. I watched in silence as guards on horses flanked our carriage. We were guided back toward the academy, the ruthless forest swaying with excitement the closer we traveled to the grounds.

My mind churned with this newest revelation. Nicolae wasn't related to the current king and queen, so why was the court panicking about his disappearance? If the prince were truly missing, then he couldn't possibly be working with Ileana or be a member of the Order. Which meant someone else with ample knowledge of the bloodlines was. I couldn't stop my suspicions from rising. Was Daciana the one we were truly hunting? Had we been blinded once again?

Perhaps she was neither being held against her will nor being protected. Perhaps she was the one orchestrating this entire thing. If aristocratic families were members of the secret society, as Radu had claimed of the Order's origins, then she very well might be involved. Though would they allow a young woman into their ranks?

Wind howled as if in pain, the sound raising the fine hairs on my arms and neck. I couldn't help but imagine we were being escorted back to our doom. Vlad Dracula's castle was alive with a malevolent anticipation as we pulled in front of the fortress.

It felt as if the academy couldn't wait to sink its teeth into us.

THIRTY-SEVEN
A ROOM FULL OF SUSPECTS

DINING HALL
SALĂ DE MESE
BRAN CASTLE
22 DECEMBER 1888

Candles flickered nervously in the chandeliers strung up over our heads as we waited in taut silence for an update on our forced sequestering.

In the kitchens, someone was baking with cinnamon, the scent wafting through the grates, far too pleasant for the storm that was raging literally outside and figuratively inside the castle walls. Headmaster Moldoveanu stood near the door of the dining hall, cloaked in shadows and whispering with Dăneşti, Percy, and Radu. Our folklore professor kept sniffing, no doubt distracted by the aroma of his beloved sticky buns. Moldoveanu snapped his fingers, his expression near-lethal, as Radu muttered an apology.

I searched around the room for the librarian, but Pierre was noticeably absent. Odd, since we'd been told everyone in the castle was to attend this meeting. Everyone was now suspect, in my eyes.

I trailed my gaze along each table, inspecting my peers. Vincenzo and Giovanni no longer had medical journals open before them. They sat together, not uttering a word, shoulders tense. Erik, Cian, and Noah were quietly speculating on Nicolae's disappearance, their attention flicking back to the headmaster. No one knew what to make of the situation.

I ignored the dead weight in my center, that heavy sense of loss, that I felt when I spied Anastasia's empty chair. I still couldn't believe my friend was gone forever. That someone had destroyed such a bright light. I had no doubt that had she lived, she would have ruled the world.

And she'd been murdered for what? Her bloodline was unrelated to Dracula or the House of Basarab. I still had no idea if she'd ever made it to wherever she'd planned on going, or if she'd been slain before investigating her new lead, and the unknowing was driving me mad.

I wished I'd been able to speak with her before she left. I had no idea what she could have known about the Order that would equal a death sentence.

Anger slowly seeped in like oil, replacing that empty well of sadness as I encouraged the fire to ignite action within. I despised murder and all it took from both its victims and the people left in its wake. I would not allow another person to die in this castle. No more students or friends would be taken and extinguished as if they were nothing. I'd been blinded before and wouldn't permit myself to falsely identify the person responsible. I shut off all emotions except for one: determination.

If not Ileana, or Daciana, or Nicolae, then who?

I glanced around the room, uncertain if the murderer was among us, donning his mask of concern and hiding his internal glee.

Professor Radu caught my attention once again. He dabbed at the sweat beading his brow, nodding a bit too enthusiastically at whatever the headmaster was saying. Were his rantings and active imagination regarding folklore more than just an interest in history? He knew details about both royal lines of the House of Basarab, and the Order of the Dragon. Perhaps he'd grown bored with simply relaying stories of *strigoi* and supernatural beings hunting the woods. Had his love and admiration of Vlad Dracula set him on his own dark path? Anything was possible.

Then there was Dăneşti. He was fond of his role of

doling out punishments. Was that the mark of a person who'd descended from disciplinarian to murderer? I couldn't be sure.

I searched for other oddities, no longer accepting anyone at face value. Andrei sat alone at the end of one long table, focus fixed on a knot in the grain he was picking at. Gone was the cocky curve of his lips and the squared-shouldered stance I'd come to know him by. He now sat folded in on himself, as if he could no longer find the energy to sit up.

I nudged Thomas with my foot, then leaned in, my lips nearly brushing his ear. I noted the slight shiver it elicited from him and ignored the answering stutter in my pulse.

"What do you make of that?" I said, indicating Andrei. "Is it all for Nicolae?"

"Hmm." Thomas studied him for a few moments, sharp gaze taking stock of each movement or lack thereof. He drummed his fingers along the edge of our table. "His worry doesn't appear to be entirely related to Nicolae. Note the chain around his collar and the pendant hanging from it. I wager it's a lock of hair. He's been preoccupied since Miss Anastasia Nádasdy's appearance in our laboratory. I believe he's mourning both, but is broken by her death in particular. He might have longed to secure a union with her."

"She'd mentioned admiring someone. She thought he hadn't noticed her affections, though. Do you believe he might be involved with her death? Everyone around him is either dead or missing. Is it a coincidence?"

Thomas considered that. "A definite possibility. Though it seems Andrei is the sort of dog that growls loudly and bites rarely. I've a feeling whoever took Nicolae has deeper motives. If he's been taken at all."

"You believe he's not missing, then?"

"For all we know, he could be in hiding. Ileana very well might be the one *he's* captured and done horrid things to. We still don't know why he created those illustrations. Or how he knew the injuries on Anastasia were made by bats. He barely even glanced at her. Quite impressive that he identified those wounds so effortlessly."

An idea sparked like flint striking stone. "If you were guilty and wanted to hide, where might you go first?"

"Depends on what I'm guilty of. Dirty thoughts or wanton follies, I'd send myself straight to your quarters to be punished."

"Honestly," I chided, subtly checking over my shoulder to make sure his remark hadn't been overheard by Percy or Radu. "We need to find a way to get back into the tunnels. I guarantee that's where we'll find the missing prince."

Guards flooded the dining hall, swords clacking

together as if they were the talons of dragons. Headmaster Moldoveanu marched to the front of the hall, long silver hair flowing behind, a general's cape of sorts.

"You are all required to stay here until we locate Prince Nicolae. To maintain a sense of normality, you will continue with classes. Everyone will be escorted to and from the classrooms. Meals will be sent directly to your private quarters. No one is to leave their chambers or this castle until the royal family has declared otherwise. Anyone caught disobeying will face serious charges." He glared down the tables at us, his gaze pausing on me for emphasis as he strode to the door and shoved it open. "You are all dismissed. Guards will escort you out now."

The Bianchi twins slowly pushed back from their seats, followed by Andrei, Erik, Cian, and Noah, the wooden benches scratching against the floor in grave protest. It made absolutely no sense for the royal family to keep us locked away in the academy when a murderer might be somewhere within its walls. Unless they wanted to keep news of Nicolae's disappearance contained.

Especially if they knew something about him we were still unaware of.

If he were the Impaler alluded to in the newspapers, then perhaps they were trying to keep him from the rest of the kingdom. To protect their citizens at the cost of losing a few. Or maybe they were preventing him from turning his attention to their throne.

Dăneşti and several other guards barked out orders for us to move quickly, their hands lingering near their weapons. None of us so much as uttered a word as we filed out of the room and into the corridors. It seemed as if Thomas and I would have to find another way to communicate. I prayed he'd not attempt scaling the castle again.

After being escorted to my rooms as if I were a common prisoner, the first thing I noticed was an envelope pinned by a dagger to my bathing room doors. My guard hadn't been tasked with searching my chambers and had left promptly after depositing me in the tower.

I yanked the paper from the door, noticing that the dagger resembled something that I couldn't quite place. The hilt was a serpent with emeralds for eyes. Where had I seen this design before?

I flipped through my memories of arriving in Romania and halted. On the train. The victim outside my room had been in possession of a similar jeweled cane. How that related to this case was one more mystery to solve later. The parchment and whatever it contained was my first concern. I hesitated for only a breath before ripping the message from its envelope. Inside the message was simple—a Roman numeral scratched in blood.

XI

My knees buckled. At first, my rational thoughts were washed away by the flood of emotions threatening to undo me. Whoever had left this note had tried imitating the letters Jack the Ripper had written in blood. I slumped to the floor near the tub, pulse racing, as I collected myself. It was a shot aimed directly at my weakest parts, but I was not the same young woman I had been weeks ago.

I was emotionally stronger now. Capable of so much more than I'd ever known. This strike would not force me into compliance; it would propel me into an offensive position. I was no longer prey, but the hunter. I pushed myself up and grabbed the note. I did a quick check of the hidden door located in the cabinet and found it was still locked from the outside. Either the person who delivered this note had the key or was unaware of the secret staircase.

A plan of action was already forming as I entered my sleeping chamber and undressed. Whoever had sent the message thought or hoped I'd come after them. I wouldn't disappoint. I'd overcome death, and destruction, and heartache, and would not let any of those dark times define me. I was the rose with thorns my mother knew me to be.

My breeches were still drying from our adventure

last night, so a simple skirt was the next best thing. I stepped into it, grateful to be rid of my bustle and corset, and buttoned up my bodice. It felt magnificent to move about with ease. I wanted no hindrances while I stole about the castle tonight.

I was going to hunt down the Order and whoever was pretending that Dracula lived.

I strode over to my looking glass and pinned my hair up, taking pains to secure it tightly to my head. A headache teased my temples, but I fought it away with sheer will. Once I'd taken care of my outfit, I wrote a note to Thomas.

"Will you take this to Mr. Cresswell for me?" I asked the maid when she'd come to deliver my luncheon. She gulped and glanced at the letter as if it had teeth ready to bite her. *"Este urgent."*

"Foarte bine, domnişoară." She reluctantly placed it on her tray. "Is there anything else you need?"

I shook my head, feeling terrible about involving her in my scheme but seeing no other way to pass the message along.

I paced and planned the remainder of daylight away, which was an enormous test of will. Afternoon certainly took its time slipping into its evening attire, but once it pulled its cloak of night on, I'd never been more pleased to see the inky black sky. As I marched around the sitting room, I became fearful that Thomas might

Cresswell,

I have an urgent request. I need to see the Poezii Despre Moarte. Bring it to my chambers after supper. I have a bit of an adventurous evening planned for us.

Yours,
AR

P.S. Please do not clamber about the castle walls this time. I'm sure you will think of some creative way to sneak about without ending up in the dungeon again, or splattered on the academy's lawn.

not come after all. Perhaps the maid hadn't delivered my letter. Or maybe he had been caught by a guard and was once again in the dungeon.

Of all the scenarios I'd envisioned, I hadn't thought of carrying out my plan alone. When I'd convinced myself he wasn't coming and it was time to move on to the next course of action, a soft knock came at my door. Thomas slipped inside before I had moved two paces, his gaze alight with interest.

"I have a feeling you haven't invited me here for kissing. Though it never hurts to ask." He grinned at my ensemble and rubbed his hands together, mischief sparking like fireworks around him. "You're dressed for sneaking about Dracula's castle. Be still my thawing, dark heart. You certainly know how to make a young man feel alive, Wadsworth."

THIRTY-EIGHT
THE HUNT BEGINS

TOWER CHAMBERS
CAMERE DIN TURN
BRAN CASTLE
22 DECEMBER 1888

"Did you bring it?" I asked, ready to search Thomas's pockets myself if he didn't move faster.

"Hello, nice to see you as well, Wadsworth." He stepped away from the door, stopping within reach as he brandished the *Poezii Despre Moarte*. Without preamble, I snatched it from him, flipping to the poem "XI" as I informed him about the note I'd found on my bathing chamber door.

XI

LORDS WEEP, LADIES CRY. DOWN THE
ROAD, SAY GOOD-BYE.

LAND SHIFTS AND CAVES DWELL. DEEP IN
EARTH, WARM AS HELL.
WATER SEEPS COLD, DEEP, AND FAST.
WITHIN ITS WALLS ~~YOU~~ SHE WILL NOT
LAST.

"Look at this," I said. Someone had taken a quill
and struck the *you* out, replacing it with *she*. I swallowed down the anxiety swirling in my system. "Do
you believe this is in reference to your sister?"

Thomas read the poem again. I watched the trans-
formation as his warmth and flirtatiousness were
replaced by the clinical expression he wore for most
everyone else. Tension was still present in his shoulders, though, the only sign that he was ill at ease.

"I believe it's referring either to her or possibly Ileana.
Maybe even Anastasia." Thomas continued staring at
the poem. "It's extraordinary, really. Whoever plotted
this out..." He squared his shoulders. "This has all
been a morbid game and we're just now realizing that
we're players."

I shuddered. Anastasia had once mentioned that
Moldoveanu enjoyed adding gamelike elements to
the assessment courses. Though I didn't believe that
included murdering hopeful students or his beloved
ward. No matter if castle gossip led one to believe he
was out for blood during this trial. I'd seen Moldovea-

nu's expression of true devastation after Anastasia's body had been recovered.

Thomas sighed. "I don't suppose you'll be satisfied with staying in and playing a round of chess until the royal guards run this lead down, will you?" I slowly shook my head. "Very well, then. What do you have in mind?"

I left a note on my settee addressed to the headmaster, fearing it might be the very thing that prevented us from obtaining those two prized spots. I ignored the tinge of regret. For all I knew, if we stopped this murderer, we might all be granted admission to the academy. One thing I was certain of: If we didn't make it back tonight, I wanted to make sure Moldoveanu would know where to find us. Before expelling us for good.

I motioned for Thomas to be quiet. "We're going vampire hunting, Cresswell."

We crept down the tower stairs and managed to make it all the way to the servants' corridor before spotting a patrol. They marched down the main hall, noisily making their way toward us, creaking leather and weapons loud enough to alert the dead of their presence. I yanked Thomas into an alcove hidden by a tapestry. As long as they didn't shine a lantern or glance too hard behind the artwork, we'd be fine. I hoped.

I shifted in the small nook, realizing just how small a space it was for one person, let alone two. The warmth of Thomas's body was distracting in ways I hadn't imagined possible, especially while hunting the Impaler or the Order or whoever was truly behind these deaths.

Part of me wished to leave this mission to the royal guard and take advantage of the position we were in. Similar thoughts appeared to be running through Thomas's mind; the column of his throat bobbed a bit more than usual as he pressed closer to me. Footsteps grew louder in the corridor, the tread as heavy as the charge building between us.

Thomas angled his face toward mine, our breath coming in quiet bursts. In fear or longing, I couldn't discern. Perhaps he was fabricating an excuse for us to be in the hallway if we were discovered. Or perhaps he wished to close the remaining distance as much as I wanted to.

His eyes fluttered shut, and the desire I'd seen in them was enough to undo me right there. I lifted my face, allowing the slightest, briefest contact between our lips. It was nothing more than a shadow of a kiss, but it ignited a fire throughout my body. Thomas's breath hitched loud enough to still my heart, his entire body going rigid, when the guards' footsteps abruptly halted.

The guards paused not far from where we were nestled together, their quiet chatter ceasing. Without making a sound, Thomas closed the distance between our bodies. Every inch of him touched me as he hid my form with his, sheltering me from view.

We stayed like that, caught between the wall and the guards, barely breathing. I could scarcely think straight. Logic took a holiday and didn't bother returning. I fought every irrational urge I had and kept my hands pinned to my sides rather than sliding over him.

After a decade seemingly passed, the guards continued down the corridor. Neither Thomas nor I moved. Heat radiated from us in ways that made me think the most indecent thoughts I'd ever considered before. Gone was the girl who'd blushed at the mere thought of expressing her passion.

Lord help me, I wanted this case to be over soon. If I didn't kiss Thomas, I might very well combust to ashes. Aunt Amelia would have been appalled by my sinful actions, but I didn't rightly care. If romance wasn't a distraction we could ill afford, I'd live in the rush of this moment for all eternity. Even with those rational thoughts swirling about my head, I still experienced great difficulty breaking our contact.

Finally, Thomas moved enough to whisper into my ear, his lips trailing along my jawline. "You are most certainly going to be the death of my dignity, Wadsworth."

I smiled sweetly, allowing myself a moment to collect my breath. "That perished a long while ago, my friend. Come, we've got to move quickly before they double back." And before I decided against forensics and sleuthing and spent the rest of the evening kissing him in a deserted hallway while a murderer was prowling about. An amused grin lit Thomas's face, and I realized he'd been whispering. "What?"

"What on earth were you just thinking about? I said, dear Wadsworth, that you appear as if someone had laid a tray of sweets before you. Perhaps"—he dipped his mouth tantalizingly close to my own—"I might offer you a treat before we leave?"

"Tempting." I ducked beneath his arms and shot a look over my shoulder, thoroughly enjoying the way his gaze tracked each of my movements. "Unfortunately I must decline for now. We have a clandestine meeting in the secret tunnels."

Thomas sighed. "I rather enjoyed my suggestion more."

If one had believed in forces greater than those on earth, then it was possible someone from a better place had been watching out for us. We didn't encounter any other guards and slipped into the basement morgue without a hitch. I ran to a cabinet and rummaged through it until I found a few supplies. A lantern, scalpel, and cranium hammer.

"I've been thinking," I whispered as Thomas lifted the trapdoor leading to the tunnels.

He paused, arms stretched above his head, and inspected me. A smile toyed with the edges of his mouth, though he was clearly trying to quell it. "Always a dangerous pastime for you, Wadsworth."

"Hilarious, as always," I said. "However, I believe maybe Prince Nicolae is whom we're hunting. Ileana just doesn't... I don't know—it doesn't sit right. I cannot imagine her impaling anyone or draining their blood with a mortuary apparatus. Besides, I saw the way she looked at your sister. There's no hiding that sort of love. Nicolae, however." I lifted a shoulder. "He was in possession of those drawings, including those of bats. He had the opportunity to send threats to the royal family. And... I've been meaning to share something else he's done."

"Will I wish to kill him?" Thomas raised a brow. "Nicolae didn't profess his undying love, did he? Although," he continued slowly, dropping the trapdoor back in place, "a healthy bit of competition never hurt anyone, I suppose."

"There were...illustrations of me in his journal. He'd made me into something terrifying. Almost as if he thought of me as a vampire."

"Why is this the first time you're mentioning this?" Thomas's voice was a bit too quiet, his tone no longer laced with his earlier levity. "If you don't confide in me, Wadsworth, how am I supposed to assist? We're partners." He paced around the room, hands tapping wildly at his sides. "I told you, I cannot help deduce when facts are obscured from me. I'm not a magician." He stopped moving and took a few deep breaths before meeting my gaze. "What else?"

I inhaled deeply. "Prince Nicolae knows forensics and had access to each victim—plus the threat just left in my chambers mentioning a *she*. I do not believe it refers to me."

Thomas hefted the door open again and motioned me toward the stairs. "Are you suggesting we're about to find my sister and her lover impaled in these tunnels?"

Though his tone was carefully composed and his comment brash, I heard the underlying worry. No matter how cold and clinical he could be in the laboratory, relaying the devastating news of Daciana's death to his family would be an unbearable task for him. I stepped closer and squeezed his arm gently.

"I'm saying to prepare yourself for the worst. I might be wrong."

As I took up the lantern and cautiously picked my way down the stairs, I thought I heard him mutter, "I fear you may be right."

ARANEA.

The Fasciata, or Barbary Spider.

A large barbary spider with her young in her web.

THIRTY-NINE
LYCOSA SINGORIENSIS

SECRET PASSAGE
PASAJ SECRET
BRAN CASTLE
22 DECEMBER 1888

"To be clear. When you'd invited me on 'an adventurous evening,' this wasn't how I imagined it going, Wadsworth."

Thomas plucked a cobweb off his frock coat, mouth puckered at the stickiness clinging to his fingers. We'd made wonderful time, traversing quickly through the tunnels we'd already been in. Now we were standing before the first clue. Or at least I believed that's what it was. Thomas fidgeted beside me.

"If we're all being hunted by some highly creative murderer, we might as well enjoy our last moments alive," he continued. "Might I offer a few alternatives to spiders and dingy tunnels? Perhaps drinking too much wine. A warm fire. Inappropriate flirtations."

I held the lantern away from my body, gaze gliding across the darkness as I spun in place. Shadows shifted obediently around the beam of light.

"Amazing," I said.

"I thought so as well. Though it's nice to hear you agree with some of my suggestions for once."

"I meant this. There's a door here." I squinted at the black letters on it, chipped with age. I was certain we were on the path to discovering where the Impaler or Order was dwelling. "There's... is that Latin burned into the wood?"

"It is. A cross was burned into the other chamber. Seems we're on the right path, then." Drifting forward, Thomas nibbled his bottom lip as he read the words on the door. *"Lycosa singoriensis.* That sounds... familiar."

A soft crunch of pebbles nearby made us tense for battle. I held on to the scalpel, and Thomas was armed with the hammer used to crack open craniums. It was the best we could do.

"Did you hear that?" Thomas whispered, shifting so that he was beside me.

I twisted the knob on the lantern, the hiss of gas spluttering out at the same time the flame did. I blinked, though that hardly made a difference. Without the light, the tunnel was practically a solid wall of black pressing down on us. Something twisted in my chest, nearly choking the breath from me. I pretended it was the blue-velvet night sky and I was cushioned on a cloud. Otherwise I'd start imagining being buried beneath the stone and I'd perish on the spot. The sound grew louder and was coming from the tunnel we'd just vacated.

We'd decided to leave the trapdoor in the morgue open, hoping a guard would come across it if something terrible happened to us. I hoped they hadn't already started pursuing us. Thomas brushed against my arm in the dark, a gentle reminder he was there beside me.

"We probably disturbed a nest of rats, Cresswell. No need to get your drawers in a bunch."

I heard the smile in his voice before he answered. "When that's the most comforting thought you can come up with, things aren't going very well. Though I'm pleased you're thinking of my underthings."

Before I could respond, the distinct sound of footsteps broke through my thoughts. The tread thumped loud enough for me to determine that there were at least two people pursuing us. Or whatever secret we might be about to unearth. They were getting closer. Suddenly, the possibility of Moldoveanu and Dănești coming upon us wasn't the most fearsome thought. We had no idea who the Order was or how many people might be involved.

"Whoever is heading toward us probably isn't the kind of person we'd want to meet in an abandoned place, far away from where people can hear our screams, Cresswell."

I could hear Thomas fumbling in the dark, and imagined his hands flying around the wall. Steps echoed behind us. Long shadows folded themselves around the corner, pointing out those who did not belong to their masters. If we did not find a hiding place now...

A quiet groan followed by an exhale of stale decay indicated Thomas had wrestled the door open. I prayed our pursuers hadn't heard it. "Ah. That did it. Let's hurry, shall we?"

Remembering the door that housed vampire bats sent gooseflesh skittering over my skin. I was not keen on experiencing that delight again but saw no way out of it. If the Impaler or the Order was hunting us, I'd much prefer the bats. Light bounced from torches or lanterns, and hushed voices curled into this tunnel. It was time to move.

We slipped inside the black chamber and closed the door, blind to what might be watching us. An acrid scent hung in the space, as if something there had rotted away a long time before. An eternity might have passed while we waited in the unlit room for our uninvited intruders to move along. Thomas must have reached out, his fingers getting caught in my hair.

"Honestly?" I whispered harshly. "Must you paw at me now?"

"While I've thought a great deal about groping you in this delightfully macabre setting, Wadsworth, I doubt my mind has the ability to will it into fruition."

"Do you swear?"

"On the potentially empty grave of Great-Great-Great-Uncle Dracula, yes."

"Then who is, Cresswell?"

Instead of answering, I felt Thomas step before me, his hands—invisible in the dark—slowly drifting from my bodice to my cheeks before he moved away. If they weren't tangled in my hair, then who—or what—was? My heart thudded in a frantic pace. Swallowing my rising panic, I slowly eased the lantern on. The small glow filled the enormous space as if it were molten gold spilling across the ground. It took a moment for my eyes to adjust, and when they finally did, an illuminated, hideous face grinned wide before me.

I inhaled sharply, almost dropping the lantern and forgetting about what might have touched my hair.

My limbs went weak once I'd put together what I was staring at: a smattering of stalactites twisted in a half-circle along with some shadows cast by protruding rocks, which offered the odd impression of a demon giving us a sharp-toothed grimace. Beyond the hanging stones, I could see that the tunnel continued on for quite some distance.

"I have a…I'm not sure. I think it's a feeling. I must be coming down with something." Thomas's stance was as rigid as his clamped jaws, his joke an obvious attempt at lightening our situation. "It's as if a bunch of snakes inhabited my body at once. Most unpleasant."

"Ah yes. But you're experiencing feelings, Cresswell. That's a vast improvement."

Continuing to play the light around the area, I noticed pale, silvery threads hanging between the stalactites. I broke away from Thomas, hoping to better inspect the sinister formation. A shadow twitched away from the ceiling and dropped to eye level.

A spider almost as big as my fist peered at me through reflective eyes. Covered in thick black bristles, it boasted fangs almost as long as my thumbnail. Ice ran in rivulets down my neck. If the threat of being murdered or expelled hadn't been so great, I'd have screamed until my lungs gave out.

A drop of thin crimson liquid dripped from the tips of its fangs; whether blood or venom, I couldn't tell. Deep inside, that scream was battling to emerge. Thomas held his hand up, taking a cautious step toward me.

"Focus on how handsome I am. How much you want to press your lips against mine. And definitely do not panic, Wadsworth. If you scream, I'm going to join you, and then we're both in trouble."

Everything inside me threatened to go dark. When someone warned a person against something, it usually meant that was precisely what they should be doing. Against my best judgment, I held the lantern up, arm shaking slightly, and spotted two more spiders dangling above our heads.

"I wonder how often they get fed. Not much activity happening in these tunnels." Thomas turned around and cursed. My attention slid behind him, focusing on the door we'd come through. It was practically a living organism, there were so many arachnids on it.

"Thomas…" I nodded at the door, though he was already transfixed by it. "There have to be over a thousand of them. Every bit of its surface is alive with movement."

"Lycosa singoriensis…" Thomas muttered the Latin to himself, his focus more intense each time he repeated

the words. His emotions had been discarded as one would remove gloves, replaced by that cool mechanical mask he sometimes wore. "It's a Romanian tarantula."

"Wonderful. Are they venomous?"

"I...I'm actually not sure." Thomas swallowed hard, the only indication of how scared he now was. "I don't believe so. At least not this breed."

"Are they all tarantulas?" I asked.

He slowly shook his head, methodically inspecting each bit of movement. Of course they weren't all tarantulas. Why would a castle filled with so many nasty ways to perish house only *harmless* spiders? My heart thrummed a panicked beat.

We needed an escape plan, but a quick survey proved there weren't many options. We couldn't go back the way we'd come—too many spiders blocked our path. Arachnid eyes glinted from several hundred points in the near-darkness, obscuring any alternate exit.

I took another hasty step back and tripped over a large rock. I cursed, then directed my light to the ground and saw I was wrong again. It wasn't a rock.

What I'd stumbled over was a milky white skull.

"Oh, my goodness." I nearly collapsed, terror pressing in from all angles. If there was a skeleton here, that didn't bode well for our chances of escaping. "Thomas, we should..."

Eight long legs slowly curled from the skull's eye sockets while another eight crawled from open jawbones. Both impossibly large spiders stalked toward me, their movements as disjointed as an undead monster lurching toward its next meal. If the villagers told these types of stories to their children—tales of man-eating spiders lurking below the earth and then produced their carcasses—then no wonder they believed vampires existed, too. Why denounce one monster when there was proof of another?

My vision swam with undulating black, and it wasn't from the lack of oxygen making it to my brain. Spiders were pouring in from cracks and crevices, demons being called from their nether realms. We needed to move. Immediately.

I handed Thomas the lantern and gathered both my skirts and wits. Something fell onto my shoulder and brushed my throat. I reached up and felt a spider tangling itself in my hair. I could handle removing organs from corpses, and rooting around inside the gelatinous innards of most deceased things. I was not above admitting that a spider burrowing into my hair was too much. Its legs scuttled down the exposed flesh on my neck. I screamed.

Reason left me. I flung myself over, shaking my hair wildly, trying not to scream again as the spider crawled along my neck, darting away from my batting hands.

Before I dislodged it, a sharp pinch pierced the skin near my collar. Panic swept over me in sickening waves. "It bit me!"

Thomas dropped the lantern and was on me in an instant. "Let me see."

I was about to pull my collar aside when another spider fell before us. All I saw was Thomas's mouth form an *O* of surprise before I yanked my skirts up to my knees and ran, forgetting all about being quiet. Let whoever was in the tunnels brave the tarantulas on their own.

Muscles in my limbs shook so hard I could barely keep moving, but I ran as if the rumors about Vlad Dracula being a *strigoi* were true. At this point, I was willing to believe anything.

I lost momentum for a fraction of a breath, tripping over my ruined skirts. Something sharp pierced my calf, and I staggered to the side. Pain shot up my leg as if someone had pricked me with several mortuary needles at once. "Ouch!"

I choked on another yelp. It was impossible to tell if another spider had bitten me or if I'd sliced my leg on debris that likely consisted of more human bones. Stopping to check was an option I could ill afford. Thomas swept a mass of spiders off the doorknob, then pulled us through the door, the light swinging and causing the world around us to tilt. This was a circus house that had lost its magical illusions. We sprinted as if our very lives depended on our escape. I hoped we weren't leaving behind one horror for the next.

Several minutes later, we emerged from the dark tunnel into another quiet space, bent over and wheezing. Thomas collected himself and held the lantern up; the dim light showed it to be an enormous stone room. I wanted to scan our surroundings, but couldn't swallow enough air to steady myself.

Before fully catching his own breath, Thomas placed the lantern next to me and sat on his heels, examining my wounds. His hands were cool and precise as they peeled my ruined stockings down. A crease of worry worked its way between his brows.

"You've only been bitten by one spider—of the nonvenomous variety, from the look of it, no swelling or leeching to indicate venom—and cut your leg on a sharp rock." He gently tapped the wounded area on my leg. "This needs to be rinsed. And a plaster would be rather nice."

"I left my medical supplies in my other dress. How inconvenient."

Thomas's lips twitched, the first sign he was warming from that cold, isolated part of himself. He dug in his trousers and brandished a small roll of gauzy material. "Lucky for you, I remembered mine."

Without wasting more time, he cleaned my wound as best he could and wrapped it with mechanical efficiency. Once he had addressed that matter to his satisfaction, he stood and scanned the cavernous room. Several passages marked by numbers spread out before us. None of them correlated to the poems we'd read in class.

"I don't think we've been followed, or else we surely would have heard sounds of pursuit by now," he said, holding the lantern up. "Which nasty little passage should we try first?"

"I'm not—" A thought struck and I couldn't stop myself from exhaling. I pointed to the narrowest tunnel. Above its arched entrance were the Roman numerals VIII. "It's almost a clue within a clue, Thomas."

He raised a brow. "Perhaps it's the dankness or the spiders, but I'm not exactly following the relation."

"The Roman numeral eight very well might be code for Vlad the Impaler. V Three. Vlad the Third. Prince Dracula."

"Impressive, Wadsworth," Thomas said, turning his gaze to me. "If we weren't about to face another terrible passageway filled with life-threatening danger, I'd take you in my arms this instant."

FORTY
FLOOD OF INFORMATION

SECRET TUNNELS
TUNELE SECRETE
BRAN CASTLE
22 DECEMBER 1888

Once inside the passageway, I grabbed the lantern from Thomas and played the light around the space, spinning slowly.

Words were hard to come by as I studied the walls. Instead of another forgotten tunnel far beneath the castle halls, this passage ended in a perfectly square stone room. The walls, floor, and ceiling were covered in carved cross patterns a bit smaller than my hand. Jewels and tiles glinted in the lamplight.

There were more riches in the glimmering mosaic than I'd ever seen. It reminded me of ancient temples where magnificent painters had spent a lifetime capturing each detail. What purpose such a chamber served here in Vlad Dracula's former fortress was beyond me. Perhaps this was a secret meeting place of the Order of the Dragon. It certainly had a Crusader aura about it. I did not think it was another chamber of death.

I walked toward the nearest wall and traced the outer ridge of stone. Each and every cross was identical. I scanned the chamber, surprised to see algae growing in patches along the top and bottom corners of the room.

"This is... incredible."

"Incredibly suspect. Look there." Thomas pointed to another carved Roman numeral, XI. "Will you read that poem?"

"Yes, give me a moment to find it."

Thomas slowly rotated in place, taking in as much of the damp stone chamber as possible. I opened *Poezii Despre Moarte* and scanned the poem correlating to the passage we were now in. I had no idea how to decipher it the way Radu had done, nor any clue what doom might be waiting for us here.

"Well?" he asked. "Is there anything more to it?"

"No. It's the same verse from earlier," I said. " 'Lords weep, ladies cry / Down the road, say good-bye. / Land shifts and caves dwell. / Deep in earth, warm as Hell. / Water seeps cold, deep, and fast. / Within its walls you will not last.' "

In the exact center of the room, a stone table stood about four feet high and was covered in more of the same cross carvings. A pang of anxiety struck as if it were a chime in my chest, but I breathed through the nerves. The table was likely an altar used for sacrifices.

Knowing to whom the castle had belonged conjured ghastly images of torture. How many people had been brutalized in the name of war here? How many boyars tortured and maimed for the sake of creating a peaceful nation? There were no winners during times of war. All suffered.

"I'm almost certain there's a tapestry in the servants' corridor that depicts a chamber like this one," I said, cringing at how loudly my voice echoed. "The walls in that image seemed as if they were covered in blood, though."

Thomas glanced in my direction. An expression that could almost be interpreted as fear crossed his face before he blinked it away. "Covered in blood, or filled with it?"

I conjured up a mental image of the artwork, the downward drips.

"Raining with blood, actually." My lip involuntarily curled at the distinction. "I didn't study it too closely."

He moved across the room and pried an egg-size ruby from the wall, tilting it one way and then the next. It reminded me of a giant drop of crystallized blood.

"You should put that ba—"

A series of clicks and groans erupted as if a monstrous clock gear had been brought to life. Confusion, then panic, flickered across Thomas's face. He tried shoving the ruby back in place, but the walls were now shaking and rumbling like giants waking from a long slumber. Bits of rock crumbled around the area he'd taken the precious stone from, ensuring the piece would no longer fit as it once had.

I slowly backed away from the altar, barely missing a round stone that popped as if it were a cork from the wall next to me. Another cylindrical rock burst from the wall, then another.

"Perhaps now would be a fine time for us to leave, Wadsworth. No need to stand around while the ceiling caves in."

I glared at my friend. "Brilliant deduction, Cresswell."

Without waiting for a response, I turned and was running for the passage, Thomas on my heels, when he grabbed me about the waist and yanked me back toward him. A steel door dropped from the ceiling like a guillotine, severing us from the world, sealing us in with a loud, reverberating crash. It nearly sliced my body in half. I shook so hard Thomas's arms trembled.

"Oh…we cannot get buried alive, Thomas!" I charged the door, first pounding it with my fists and then running my fingers along the smooth surface, searching for any latch to free us. Nothing. There was no handle or lock. No mechanism to release it. Nothing but a solid piece of steel that didn't dent from the kicks I now assaulted it with.

"Thomas! Help!" I attempted to push it back up, but it was stuck firmly in the ground. Thomas tried shouldering it open while I continued kicking. It didn't so much as ripple. Rubbing his arm, he took a few steps away to survey our situation.

"Well, at least this is the worst of our problems at the moment. Could be filled with snakes and spiders."

"Why? Why would you utter those—"

A faint hissing started in the far corner. The noise grew louder, as if the chamber wall had been the only defense standing between us and whatever was on its way.

"What in the name of the queen is that?" I quickly drew away from the door. The alarm in my voice pulled Thomas to me in a heartbeat. He subtly shifted his body close to mine, ready to protect me from the menacing sound. I latched on to his arm, knowing we'd face whatever was coming together. And then I saw it.

The trickle streaming down the wall.

I ran over to be sure of what I was seeing. "Water. Water is pouring in—"

More hissing erupted from holes in the floor, walls, and ceiling as liquid came gushing in on us. A hundred tiny cascading waterfalls poured white foamy water into the room. Within seconds, our ankles were covered. I stared, unblinking, at the floor. This couldn't be happening.

"Look for a trapdoor!" I shouted over the noise of the downpour. "There's got to be a lever or some way out of this chamber."

I pulled my skirts up, then stooped low to the ground, hoping to locate an exit. But of course there wasn't one. There were only more crosses chiseled into the floor. A mockery of whoever was unlucky enough to find themselves in this chamber of death. Or perhaps it was a merciful way of saying we'd be seeing God soon enough. If one believed in that sort of thing.

This chamber cleansed those of their sins.

My mind went utterly blank for a moment. This was the worst fate I could imagine.

"Check the walls, Wadsworth." Thomas shoved himself onto the table and ran his hands along the ceiling, searching for any kind of escape.

I sprang back into action. "I'm trying!"

Ice-cold water inched up to my knees. This was truly happening. We were not being buried alive, we were being drowned. My fear was nearly as cold as the water soaking my underskirts and almost as heavy to push through. If we were about to die, I'd not go easily.

Running back to the door, I searched a second time for a hidden latch, running my hands frantically over every possible surface. My skirts were weights dragging me down, but I couldn't get out of them by myself.

Water reached past my thighs, making it difficult to move at all. Thomas jumped down into the rising pool, reaching me in seconds.

"Here, Audrey Rose. Stand on the altar." Thomas took my hand, but I slipped out of his grasp. There had to be a way to unlock the door.

"I refuse to stand on a table and wait for a miracle— or, more likely, imminent death, Cresswell. Either help me remove my skirts, or stand back."

"We're about to die and this is your shameless request?"

"We most certainly are not going to perish here, Thomas."

His eyes glistened with emotion. He truly thought there was no way out of this. My heart sank faster than my skirts as the water lapped at my waist. He was the master at seeing the impossible. If he were giving up, then we were...

"Thomas—" A memory of Professor Radu's lecture slammed into my chest at the same time uncontrollable shudders took over our bodies. "Feed the dragon!" I shouted, dodging a stream of water as another spigot opened above us. Water was rushing in so fast it was now covering the altar. "That's got to be the key!"

"Where is this mysterious dragon we need to feed, Wadsworth?"

"I-I—"

Thomas didn't wait for a response. He scooped me into his arms and deposited me on the altar, dragging himself up a moment later. More frigid water rained down on us as if we'd landed on an abandoned island in the middle of a monsoon. At best, we had minutes before the water reached the ceiling. My vision threatened to go black at the edges. Being buried alive was always a scary thought; dying in a watery grave was something I never knew to fear. Emotions rolled through me, crashing against my thoughts. Hypothermia was close, its effects already clouding my mind.

Thomas's lips were already turning a slight blue as he trembled beside me. If the water didn't kill us, the cold certainly would. Where was the dragon? It had seemed like an inspired idea moments before…

Thomas pulled me toward him, lifting me up as the water reached my chin.

"S-stay w-with me, Wadsworth."

He stood a good head taller than me and was using his height to offer me extra time before I gulped water. I wanted to cry, bury my face in his neck, and tell him how sorry I was that I had dragged him here, to this horrid tunnel on this ridiculous adventure. Who cared if we were the ones to find the Impaler or the Order?

I should have brought my theories to the headmaster. The royal guards should have been scouring these tunnels, not us.

"Thomas…" I spat water out, suddenly eager to unleash all my secrets. "L-listen, C-Cresswell," I said between chattering teeth, "there's something I-I have to tell you. I—"

"S-stop, Wadsworth. No l-last-minute confessions a-allowed. We're going to get out of this." Water slid down my cheeks and I shook my head. Thomas cupped my chin and looked fiercely into my eyes, his hands frozen. "F-focus. Don't give up. Use that alluring brain of yours to find Radu's dragon and get us out of here. You can do this, Audrey Rose."

"There are no such things as dragons!" I screamed, dropping my face onto his shoulder.

I was so cold I wanted to curl up and float away. I wanted the pain in my limbs to recede. I wanted to give up. I stared at the altar under our feet, eyes blurring with unshed tears as the shape beneath us swam into focus. We were standing on the solution.

A dragon nearly the entire size of the altar was carved onto its top. Its mouth was wide open, showing off teeth made of stone that appeared sharp enough to slice through skin.

"I found it!"

"H-how…f-fascinating," Thomas said, his body and

voice both wracked with shudders. "W-we have a table like this in our home in Bucharest. Except our dragon is less…s-sneering. I n-named him H-Henri."

I cut a sharp glance in his direction. He was near convulsions. I needed to move quickly. I wrestled out of his iron grip and tilted my head back as far as it would go, then took a deep breath and submerged myself. I kicked toward the carving, not having to work too hard as my clothing acted as an anchor. I shoved my finger into the dragon's mouth and dragged it across the stone tooth, wincing as blood blossomed in the water.

My heart tapped out an anxious rhythm. Something gave way a little, the dragon's teeth receding ever so slightly. A trapdoor cracked open in the stone floor, allowing some water to escape, but not enough. I tugged again but the teeth refused to give further. Of course it couldn't be that easy. Nothing ever was.

I needed to breathe. I tried kicking my way back to the surface, but my layers proved too heavy. Panic seeped in as I flailed underwater, air bubbles streaming out around me. I wanted to scream for help but couldn't risk losing more air.

When I thought I'd come to the last of my breath, Thomas yanked me up, wiping soggy strands of hair from my face as I gasped and nearly vomited. He made sure I was all right before swimming down to the trapdoor, trying to wrench it open. I took a deep breath and followed, hoping our combined might would work. We twisted and tugged to no avail.

Thomas clutched my shaking hand in his own, and we kicked up toward the remaining air. As we broke its surface water rained down on us—now sloshing past our chins—and I caught the exact moment Thomas resigned himself to our doom.

He drew in a ragged breath, one that might have arisen from hypothermia setting in or from the realization that we were staring down our final moments. I had never seen him without a plan before. He fixed me with the kind of stare that seemed to memorize my every feature. His thumbs caressed the apples of my cheeks. Water covered my mouth and I lifted my face higher. I knew this was it. These were the last moments of my life. Regret filled me with immeasurable sorrow. There was so much I hadn't done, so much I'd left unsaid.

"Audrey Rose, I—" Panic raged behind his normally measured gaze. I could barely make out the garble of his words as the water rushed over my ears.

Straining to lift my face above the water, I gasped in a final gulp of air.

"Audrey Rose!"

Thomas's plea was forgotten the second the room quaked. A sharp crack echoed off the chamber walls as the ground beneath us split wide open. He grabbed for me, shouting something I couldn't hear over the deafening noise. As quickly as the water burst out from the walls and ceiling, it tunneled down even faster in a giant whirlpool, yanking us along with it.

I reached for Thomas's outstretched hand, screaming as water ripped us apart.

We were sucked into a hole that swept both our words and our bodies away.

FORTY-ONE
BONE WHITE

CRYPT
CRIPTĂ
BRAN CASTLE
22 DECEMBER 1888

I struggled to keep my nose and mouth above water as we slid down what I assumed was an ancient pipe covered in slippery algae, heading toward Lord knew where.

I kept my hands tucked against my body, which helped prevent sludge from covering them. If I had known we weren't about to be spat into a worse chamber—or that my scalpel and Thomas's hammer weren't about to cause grave injury—I might have enjoyed the giant underground water shoot. However, I didn't believe Vlad Dracula or the Order of the Dragon had designed this for amusement. My muscles clenched in anticipation of where we might land.

I shuddered against more than the icy water as I slipped down the seemingly endless pipe. I couldn't imagine how far underground we must have been— the dark was so complete I couldn't see my hands in front of me.

The pipe twisted and turned, and after several rotations of my body, it eventually flattened out. Seconds later, I was dumped into a shallow pool. I refused to consider what might be bobbing across the surface as I splashed about; at least the smell wasn't too foul. As I pushed myself up, Thomas came flying out and landed on me, knocking us both down, our knees and foreheads smacking together in a clumsy backward dance.

Somehow he'd managed to cup my head so I avoided smashing my skull into the stone below us. I imagined his knuckles hadn't been as lucky.

"That...was...terrifying...and incredible," he said, losing himself in a fit of laughter. I wanted to agree, but all I could think about was his hands wrapped around me. We'd been so close to death. As if it were a star shooting across the night expanse, our lantern sailed into the water, floating on the surface and offering a bit of light.

Thomas glanced down at me, then stopped chuckling. His expression was now serious and measured. I stared, noting that his lashes were long and dark like the nighttime sky. His eyes were my favorite constellations to gaze at; each fleck of gold surrounding his pupils were new galaxies begging to be discovered. I'd never been fascinated by astronomy before, but now found myself an eager student.

"You saved me once again." Thomas leaned on his elbows, grinning at my dazed expression. He reached over and plucked sludge from my hair. "You're beautiful, Wadsworth."

"Oh, yes. Covered in grime and whatever that foul-smelling bit of…"

"You truly do not wish to know."

I suppressed a gag and gingerly moved each limb, testing myself for broken bones and fractures. All seemed to be in working order, though it was hard to tell without standing.

"How was that for adventure?" I asked, shivering in place. "Closer to what you'd had in mind?"

The tiniest smile curved his lips, erasing the awkwardness. "Clearly, you're in need of sleep. I'm not sure we should be friends any longer, Wadsworth. You are too wild for me."

I winced as he shifted his weight. Lying on the stone floor of the pool, soaking wet, was too horrid to ignore, no matter how much the devious part of me enjoyed being that close to Thomas. Concern flashed in his features.

"What is it? Are you injured?"

"Perhaps we should get back to our task of locating the Impaler. And if you wouldn't mind moving off me so I might breathe properly... You're worse than a corset."

He blinked as if coming out of a dream, then hopped up and offered me a hand. "Apologies, fair lady." He scooped the lantern out of the water and wiped off its sides. "Which chamber of doom is next on the menu?"

"I'm not sure. Do you still have *Poezii Despre Moarte?*"

"Right here." Thomas patted his front pocket. "Though the cranium hammer has gone missing."

"My scalpel, too." I glanced around the chamber, noticing a ledge on either side of the pool of water we were standing in, and indicated we should head there. "Let's see about drying off a bit."

We picked our way up the ledge and wrung our clothes and hair out as best we could. My skirts stuck to my limbs, making each movement more difficult than the last. I was surprised to see steam rising from a few crevices in the rock face, taking most of the biting chill out of the air. I held out trembling hands, and Thomas quickly did the same.

"Must be hot springs in one of these mountains," he said, removing his frock coat and hanging it over the steam. I stared at his chest, defined and on full display thanks to the water soaking his shirt. He was finely sculpted, his body recalling ancient sculptures of half-clad heroes or gods.

I tore my gaze away, holding my skirts as close to the steam as possible. Now was not the time to be distracted by improper desires. I turned around, hoping to dry the back of my bodice, and spotted another tunnel entrance, marked with the numeral XII. Chills wracked my body for an entirely new reason.

"Let me see the book, Cresswell."

Thomas spied the entrance I'd pointed out and handed over the old vellum tome. I flipped through it, marveling at how the pages had survived the waters. Whoever had created it must have planned for it to withstand these dangers. I found what I'd been searching for and stopped. It took a moment to work out the Romanian in my head, but I sorted it out.

XII
BONE WHITE, BLOOD RED. HERE LIES
SOMETHING LONG DEAD.
TREE OF DEATH AND HEART OF STONE.
NEVER ENTER THE CRYPT ALONE.
IF YOU DO, HE'LL MARK YOUR TRACKS,
HUNT YOU DOWN, AND THEN ATTACK.
BONE WHITE, BLOOD RED. THERE LIE
THOSE WHO SHOULD HAVE FLED.

I read it out loud for Thomas, my thoughts entirely set on our mission once again. He pushed strands of dark hair off his forehead and sighed. "I don't recall Radu mentioning anything about battling *strigoi*, do you?"

"Unfortunately, no." I shook my head. Our lessons on vampires hadn't offered any hints on how we might survive a chamber dedicated to them. "Come on," I said, lifting my partially dry skirts and nodded toward the entryway, "staying here won't get us out of these tunnels any faster."

"No," Thomas agreed, following slowly, "but I'd much rather be covered in sludge than see what other delights are awaiting us."

The tunnel wasn't very long and spat us into another chamber, as if we'd walked from one grand room in the castle to another. "Like this. How charming."

I tore my attention from the stone walls and inspected where we were, immediately regretting it. This chamber was an enormous old crypt split into two sections by an elaborate archway. Someone had recently been down here lighting torches, and my blood chilled at the thought. There had to be a way to get here other than the hellish route we had found. I found myself torn between pushing forward and running in the opposite direction.

Thomas and I stopped under the archway, unwilling to cross into the space beyond. He glanced at me and lifted a finger to his lips. We needed to move as quickly and quietly as possible.

I inspected the arch, trying to control the gooseflesh erupting down my body. It was made entirely of antlers. I couldn't begin to comprehend how many stags must have died to fashion such a horrid thing, but my attention was quickly drawn elsewhere. The rest of the chamber was even more horrific.

The dead did not rest peacefully in this crypt. Their remains had been disturbed, manipulated into a nightmarish scene straight from the pages of gothic horrors. Everything was created from cold, white bone. Grave markers. Ornate crosses. The walls. Ceiling. Fencing. Everything, *everything* was made of parts of skeletons, both human and animal, at first glance. I swallowed down my revulsion.

Radu had been wrong about the woods being filled with bones. The space below the mountain was.

From here, we could see a fenced-in mausoleum, standing like a small, unholy chapel within a vast burial ground. Instead of having stone flooring, the graveyard had packed earth, making me wonder if we'd finally reached the true bottom of the mountain. The fence was constructed of upright bones that had been stuck into the soil. A crude, partially open gate sat at its center. My body hummed with anticipation and dread. I did not wish to cross into that section of Hell.

Huge columns of entwined bone stood tall along the four sides of the mausoleum, which was also made entirely from remains. In the center of what could best be described as a sprawling graveyard of half-unearthed skeletons, there was a large tree whose branches nearly reached the high ceiling. Like everything else in this horrid chamber, the tree limbs were composed entirely of bones. The monstrosity had to be at least twenty feet tall.

We walked on, pausing outside the fence. Thomas had gone as silent as the cemetery we were standing near, attention sweeping from one outrageous sight to the next. Upturned earth and mildew tickled my nose, but I dared not sneeze. Any number of things could be lurking in the tangle of horror surrounding us.

Thomas shifted his focus to the macabre scene directly on our path. "I believe we've found the Tree of Death mentioned in *Poezii Despre Moarte*," he whispered, still glancing around.

"At least it's aptly named. It certainly wouldn't be confused with the Tree of Life."

"It's so...appalling. Yet I'm oddly enchanted." Thomas rattled off each new bone he identified in the tree situated within the fence. "Humerus, radius"—he sucked in a breath, pointing to another bit of ivory—"and that's an admirable ulna. Must have come from a near-giant. Tibia, fibula, patella…"

"Thank you for the anatomy lesson, Cresswell. I can see what they are," I said quietly, nodding toward the gated entrance and its unearthed bones. "Where should we begin?"

"With the tree, naturally. And we need to hurry. I have a feeling whoever lit the torches will return soon enough." Thomas handed the lantern to me. "After you, my dear."

A vast part of myself did not wish to enter this devil's acre—it seemed an annihilation of the sanctity of death—but we'd come too far to let trepidation rule my senses. If Daciana or Ileana or Nicolae was in trouble, we needed to keep moving forward. No matter that my instincts were screaming for me to grab Thomas's hand and run in the opposite direction.

I breathed deeply, hoping neither my imagination nor my body would fail me now. If ever there were a time for clear thoughts and a steady pulse, this would be it.

Without letting fear sink its claws into me, I lifted my chin and tiptoed toward the fence of long-picked-over cadavers. However, I couldn't stop my sharp intake of breath when I entered the graveyard containing what the *Poezii Despre Moarte* called the Tree of Death.

I could very much imagine Vlad Dracula rising from this spot, coming to greet his last male heir.

FORTY-TWO
BLOOD RED

TREE OF DEATH
COPACUL MORȚII
BRAN CASTLE
22 DECEMBER 1888

The tree was even worse than I'd thought from several yards away. Hand bones, skulls with hollow eye sockets, and broken rib cages created the frightening masterpiece. I marveled at how they fit together without any string or binding—they'd simply been woven together.

Femurs were bunched together, making up the center of the trunk. Rib cages faced each other, caging the leg bones as if they were bark. Eyeing the area around the base of the tree, I noticed stacks of bones lying in heaps, perhaps waiting to be assembled. Some of them still had bits of flesh and sinew attached. Not all of these skeletons were old. A chilling thought.

I realized I was holding my breath, terrified of making too much noise. I wanted to hurry, and yet this place made it impossible to not pause and gape at each new horror. Like the one before us now.

Sitting beside the pile of bones was a large claw-foot tub. It was filled to the brim with dark red blood, the scent of copper stinging my nose. It was likely a trick of my senses, but I swore something bubbled from within its sanguine depths. Thomas stilled, his attention latched on to the bathtub as he held an arm out, stalling our movements. I dared not wander close to it, the fear of what my mind would conjure too great. Thomas continued staring at it, shoulders tensed. We'd found the missing blood of the Impaler's victims—the ones we knew of and God knew who else. The murderer was close. Too close. My whole body tingled with anticipation.

It felt as if we'd traversed deep into Dante's Inferno, unaware.

"'Abandon all hope ye who enter here.' It's so disturbing," I whispered. "I cannot fathom how anyone would fashion an entire crypt from bones. Or that tub...poor Wilhelm and Mariana." I shivered, knowing my damp clothing was only partly to blame. "The Order is quite gifted with psychological war games."

"It is a literal bloodbath." Thomas tore his gaze from the tub, expression grim. "Someone has a very dark and very twisted sense of humor."

I closed my eyes, demanding that the rapid pounding of my heart slow down. We needed to find Daciana and Ileana. I kept repeating that thought until fear released me.

We quietly moved away from the tub of blood, but the horror of it clung to us. I felt it behind me, waiting, as if it were beckoning me with its nightmarish essence. I would not even consider what we'd do if another clue was located within that bloodbath monstrosity. If the villagers were superstitious about desecrating the dead, I could only imagine their reaction should they ever stumble upon this blasphemous burial site.

"There must be over two hundred human bodies that went into making this morbid sculpture." Thomas held the lantern toward the top branch. A cluster of phalanges were strung together as if they were white leaves. "Perhaps the rumors of Vlad Dracula being immortal are true."

I ripped my gaze from the bone tree, inspecting my friend for any signs of trauma. He shot me a crooked grin. "You're most delightful when you stare at me like that, Wadsworth. However, I'm only teasing. Judging from the bath of blood, I do believe whoever's amended that nasty little poem for you visited this spot. Maybe we'll find a clue regarding Daci."

"Do you see any Roman numerals carved into the tree?" I focused on the graveyard and mausoleum; I couldn't stop myself from being intrigued by our surroundings. Flesh-free skulls lined the walls. Actually, the skulls *were* the walls. They were stacked on top of one another, packed so tightly I doubted I could stick my fingers between them.

Thomas shook his head. "No, but according to that sign, one must climb the tree to pluck its fruit."

I stared at the plaque nailed to the bone gate. It was etched in Romanian, the letters rough as the tool that had been used to mark it. I stepped closer, reading it to myself.

Smulge fructe din copac pentru a dobândi cunoştinţe

Thomas was correct; it basically stated that one needed to pluck fruit from the tree to gain knowledge. I trailed my gaze over the tree limbs, searching for any sign of this so-called fruit. Bird skulls of all sizes were strung in intervals, their beaks facing this way and that. I pointed them out. "Perhaps those skulls? In some sickening way, they almost resemble pears."

Something faint bubbled from behind. I spun around, searching, my heart near-ready to gallop from my body. The blood was undisturbed, the surface dark as crimson-tinted oil.

"Did you hear that?"

Thomas took a deep breath, his attention methodically scanning the room and the chamber behind us. "Tell me again why we aren't using this time more wisely. We could be wrapped 'round one another instead of"— he motioned in front of us—"all this."

"We need to hurry, Cresswell. I have a horrible feeling."

Without saying another word, Thomas faced the tree and reached forward, placing his weight on a rib cage as he slowly scaled the ivory-colored bones. He put his left foot on another rib, testing it nimbly before transferring his entire weight.

He repeated the movement twice more, barely making it a few feet off the ground, when a horrible crack rent the air, echoing like a switch that had been slapped across knuckles. I lurched forward to catch him, but he gracefully leapt down unassisted.

"Seems I won't be harvesting any ripe fruit from this tree after all." He wiped his hands off on his trousers, mouth pressed into an annoyed line. A few drops of blood appeared like rubies on his fingertips before he sucked them away. "Read the poems once more for me, please? One of them has to be relevant to this situation. There aren't that many to choose from."

I pulled the worn old book from my pocket and handed it to him. I didn't care to speak the dreadful words aloud any more than was necessary.

While Thomas read the poems to himself, I quickly

unfastened my overskirts. Time was slipping from our grasp. One way or another, we had to pluck whatever knowledge we could from this dreadful tree before heading back to the academy. By this time, Moldoveanu and Dăneşti were probably aware we were missing. We might as well come back with something useful if we were about to be expelled. Plus, I did not want to be caught here by the murderer.

The buttons on my bodice popped off with ease. Their tiny tinkling struck the ground as my heart struck my rib cage with vigor. Thank the heavens I'd changed out of my more complicated dress earlier that evening. I had no bustle or corset to wrestle out of. Before I could change my mind or find reason to be embarrassed, I stepped out from my underskirts, feeling exposed in my chemise and smallclothes, though they covered past my knees and had several inches of Bedfordshire Maltese lace. They were not so different from my breeches, I reasoned. Though my breeches were less . . . frilly and delicate.

Thomas dropped *Poezii Despre Moarte* along with his jaw, it seemed.

"Not one word, Cresswell." I pointed toward the top of the tree of bones. "I'm lighter than you and should be able to scale the tree. I think I see something in that skull up there. See it? Looks like a piece of parchment."

Thomas kept his attention fixed on my face, his own reddening each time it slipped to my chin. I half wanted to roll my eyes. Not one part of me was uncovered aside from the scandal of my arms and a few inches of leg not covered by smallclothes or stockings. I had evening gowns that showed more décolletage.

"Catch me if I fall, all right?"

A smile curved his lips in a most delightful manner. "I've already fallen hard, Wadsworth. Perhaps you should have warned me sooner."

Devilish flirt. I turned my focus to the tree and scanned the route I'd take. Without dwelling on what I was about to touch, I hoisted myself up, placing one hand after the other, thinking only of the task. The cut on my calf stretched uncomfortably and the warmth of fresh blood trickled down my limb, but I ignored the discomfort in favor of moving quickly.

I refused to glance down. With each new limb I climbed up, the parchment grew closer. I was halfway to the top when a clavicle snapped beneath my feet. I hung, suspended in the air, swinging from side to side as if I were a living pendulum.

"You've got it, Wadsworth!" My fingers shook with the effort of maintaining my grip. "And if you don't... I've got you. I believe."

"Not comforting, Cresswell!"

Using the momentum of my body to my advantage, I swung over to a sturdy-looking rib cage and shifted my weight. My muscles quaked with both surging adrenaline and pride. I'd done it! I mastered my emotions and... The bone at my fingertips creaked in warning. Celebrating victories could wait. I moved steadily but cautiously, climbing with slow precision.

Testing and moving. Testing and moving.

Once at the top, I paused to catch my breath and glanced down at Thomas, immediately regretting the action. He appeared much smaller from this vantage point. I was at least twenty feet from the ground, and the fall wouldn't be pleasant.

Not wanting to picture all the vivid ways in which I could become part of the artwork of skeletons myself, I inched my way up the last few bones and reached the parchment. I extracted it from the skull it had been fastened to. Someone had used a dagger—whose hilt was encrusted in gold and emeralds—to stab the parchment through the eye socket of the deceased.

"It says 'XXIII,'" I whisper-shouted down, mindful of not swinging around and losing my footing. The last thing I wanted to do was impale myself while hunting down the murderer known for using the same deadly method.

Thomas found the correct poem and read it aloud.

I cringed at how strong and powerful his voice was in this morbid space.

XXIII
WHITE, RED, EVIL, GREEN. WHAT HAUNTS THESE WOODS STAYS UNSEEN. DRAGONS ROAM AND TAKE TO AIR. CUT DOWN THOSE WHO NEAR HIS LAIR. EAT YOUR MEAT AND DRINK YOUR BLOOD. LEAVE REMAINS IN THE TUB. BONE WHITE, BLOOD RED. ALONG THIS PATH, YOU'LL SOON BE DEAD.

"Oh, goodness," I muttered. That poem…it was one that Radu had read to us in class. The meeting place of the Order. And the place where it sacrificed people to Prince Dracula.

We needed to get out of this crypt at once. I knew, deep within my bones, that we were about to encounter something more horrendous than we could fathom. Another sheet of parchment caught my attention as I began my descent. I carefully moved toward it, then read it aloud for Thomas: *"Fă o plecăciune în faţa contesei."*

Bow to the countess.

"What was that?" he called.

"One moment." An illustration accompanied the

sentence. I blinked, reading it over again. I certainly hoped this was a remnant from the Crusades, though the slick sensation in my innards told me otherwise.

We were wrong again about the Order of the Dragon's involvement. This appeared to be the work of Prince Nicolae Aldea.

And the countess in this drawing was entirely covered in blood.

FORTY-THREE
HUNTING PRINCE DRACULA

CRYPT
CRIPTĂ
BRAN CASTLE
22 DECEMBER 1888

I tucked the second clue into my underclothes and climbed down as quickly as I dared. I didn't want to shout for fear of calling even more attention to ourselves.

Dread made my hands tremble as I reached for a femur and missed. I concentrated on my breaths. I would treat this as if it were a body in need of study—precision was key. I swung over to the next bone, fingers sliding off its smooth surface. If I didn't collect myself and make it back down to Thomas...I didn't want to consider what might happen. Prince Nicolae was close; I sensed his presence as each cell of my being warned me to flee.

We needed to leave the crypt at once or else we'd go

from being the hunters to the hunted. When I reached the halfway point on the macabre tree, a strange shape caught my eye from the far side of the bone gate. At first I thought it was some peculiar, cave-dwelling animal.

Then it stood, stumbling forward a bit.

"Thomas…"

My breath caught. The heap had risen from the bones, revealing a robed figure who was no reanimated corpse or *strigoi*. I wagered he was human; there was absolutely nothing fantastical about him aside from his taste in theatrics.

A cloak covered his head, drawn over his features as if it were a hood, and a large cross hung from around his neck. The cloak vaguely reminded me of those worn by the men who'd vanished into the woods with that corpse a few nights before. The cross was larger than two fists and was made of gold. Very ornate and medieval, it appeared as if it would make a fine weapon itself.

"Thomas… *run!*"

Thomas cocked his head, unaware of the new threat. "I can't hear you, Wadsworth."

Clinging to the tree and unable to point, I watched as the figure staggered closer. He looked injured, but it could be an act to lure us into a false sense of security.

"Behind you!" I shouted, but it was too late. The

figure fell against the gate, slamming it shut as he stumbled backward.

Three-quarters of the way down, the rib I'd been gripping snapped, and I dropped like a felled tree in this forest of corpses. Moving faster than I could blink, Thomas dove into my path, breaking my fall. It was not a glamorous rescue, but his effort was valiant.

He hissed as he smacked the ground, then issued another grunt when my forehead slammed into the back of his head. I hurried off him, spinning in place, searching for the figure who'd been stalking toward us, but saw nothing. We had moments to run. Thomas turned over, and blood gushed from his nose.

"Where are your plasters?"

He held his nose. "Lost them in the water chamber."

I ripped off a piece of my thin chemise and offered it to my bleeding hero. He might be able to use it to staunch the flow of blood, or perhaps he could strangle our attacker with it while I distracted him.

"Hurry, Cresswell. We've got to move—"

Out of nowhere, the figure reappeared, falling toward us from behind the Tree of Death, the promise of violence clearly visible in his stance.

"Get. Out," he said through gritted teeth, then clutched at his torso. His breathing was labored, accented voice strained. "Hurry."

Fear released its grip on my logic. I leaned forward, squinting to see the face I knew matched the voice. "Prince Nicolae? You're—are you—who did this to you?"

The prince shook the hood back from his face. It was splotchy with dark patches, and his cheeks were gaunt. "If you don't hurry...she'll—"

He collapsed to the ground, chest heaving with effort. The prince wasn't pretending to be injured—he was near death. I dropped to my knees, lifting his head into my lap. His eyes were glassy, unfocused. I would've wagered anything he'd been given arsenic. We needed to get him out of these tunnels and to a doctor immediately. "Thomas...lift him by the..."

Then, as if a nightmare was given permission to be born of this world, a figure rose from the blood-filled bath. I blinked, barely understanding the absurdity of the ruined drinking straw that fell to the ground, so horrific was the sight before us. Blood so dark it was nearly black coated every inch of its face and body. Hair dripped crimson back into the tub, slender fingers covered in it. I could scarcely breathe. Thomas held his arm out, as if he might be able to keep this monster from seeing both Nicolae and me.

Its eyes opened wide, the whites a stark contrast to the crimson surrounding them. Everything came to a crashing halt within my mind. I could not tell who it was from here, but it was most certainly a woman.

We'd been correct after all, but was it Ileana? Or could it possibly be...Daciana?

The blood-soaked nightmare kicked one leg from the tub, making a grand show of stepping out of the bath. Blood splashed onto the ground and splattered against the bones nearby.

Whoever she was, she wore a gossamer gown, its dripping red length trailing behind her like a sodden wedding-day curse as she moved toward us. As she bent down near a heap of bones, I considered running. I longed to grab Thomas and flee this crypt and never glance back. But there was no way out and we couldn't leave the prince. The living nightmare stood and pointed a small ladies' revolver at us.

She drifted forward, the countess of blood, a grisly smile exposing the white of her teeth.

"*Extraordinar!* I'm so glad you both made it. I was worried you'd not arrive on time. Or that you'd bring Uncle and that annoying guard."

I stared at the girl before us, blinking disbelief away. It could not be, and yet...her voice was unmistakable, her Hungarian accent slightly different from the Romanian one.

"*Anastasia?* How...this cannot be real," I said, unable to accept this truth. "You died. We saw you in that room—those bats." I shook my head. "Percy inspected your body. We *autopsied* you!"

"Are you certain? I expected you to catch on, *prietena mea*." Anastasia smiled again, those teeth shining too pleasantly against the blood. "When you mentioned the shutter in the village, I nearly fainted. I had to run back and stage the room before we investigated that night. *Nervii mei!* My nerves were a wreck."

I could not fathom how this could be real. I forced my mind past the panic threatening to drop me to my knees. We needed to keep Anastasia talking. Perhaps we'd come up with a plan on how to maneuver out of this. "Why did you allow me to live?"

"I considered killing you that very night, but I thought he," she nodded toward Thomas, "might leave before I was ready to strike. Come, now, my friend. I know you're smarter than those boys. Tell me how I did it. Uh, uh, uh!" She waved the gun at Thomas. "Not a word from you, handsome. It's impolite to interrupt a lady."

I wanted to vomit, but I forced my mind into action. *Anastasia* wished to be rewarded for the brilliance of her game. That need for recognition might be her very undoing. I swallowed hard, ignoring the revolver now pointed at my chest. Little oddities suddenly clicked into place.

"The missing girl." I closed my eyes. Of course. It all made sense. It was brilliant in the most horrible way. "You used her body to stand in for your own.

Planted her in the tunnels to coincide with your disappearance. You knew her face would be too marred to be identified. Her hair and body measurements were similar enough. Facial features, too. I'd even thought she looked like you when I saw her in that sketch. The resemblance was striking enough to fool the class and our professors." I paused as the full horror set in. "Even your uncle believed it to be you—one of the best forensic academics in the world."

"*Excelent.*" Anastasia grinned, her teeth now red-streaked. It was terrible. Feral. The cunning present in her eyes made the deepest parts of me shiver. "Our hearts are curious things. So sentimental and easily misguided. Pull the right strings or snap the correct cords, and poof! Love strangles intelligence, even in the best of us."

I did not wish to speak on matters of the heart with a woman who was drenched in the blood of innocents. I noticed Thomas shifting ever so slightly beside me and fumbled for another distraction. "How did you remove Wilhelm's blood so quickly?"

"With a stolen mortuary apparatus. Then I dumped his body out the window." She took a step toward Thomas and paused, inspecting him as a cat might consider an injured bird hopping about. For some reason, she inclined her head in a show of respect. "Are you impressed, *Alteţă?* Or should I say Prince Dracula?"

Thomas stopped moving and grinned lazily. I noticed the tautness in his muscles, though, and knew he was anything other than a relaxed, bored member of the House of Dracula. "Very charming of you, but bowing before me is entirely unnecessary. Though I do understand the urge to do so. I'm rather regal and impressive. Prince Dracula, however, is not my true title."

I could not believe his posturing appeared to be working. Anastasia swallowed, focus following Thomas's hands as they adjusted his ruined shirt. He almost convinced me that he had donned royal robes and was worthy of being bowed before. Instead of standing in the sodden, filthy clothes he'd been dragged through Hell in.

Anastasia shifted her revolver, aiming directly at Thomas. "Do not mock your own bloodline, Mr. Cresswell. Bad things happen when one turns against their own. It is time to come forth and accept your destiny, Son of the Dragon. It is time for us to merge our bloodlines and reclaim this entire land."

"I don't understand," I said, glancing between them. "Who are you descended from?"

Anastasia threw her shoulders back, head held high. It was an impressive feat considering the gore smeared all over her; yet she did possess a regal air.

"Elizabeth Báthory de Ecsed."

"Of course," Thomas muttered. "Also known as the Countess Dracula."

For a moment no one spoke or moved. I recalled the brief mention of the countess in Radu's class and fought a shiver.

"So you know it's fate." Anastasia's eyes glittered with pride. "You see, I hail from a house equally known for its bloodlust, Audrey Rose. My ancestor bathed in the blood of innocents. She ruled with fear." Anastasia pointed to Thomas. "He and I? We were destined to meet. As we are destined to produce heirs more fearsome than their ancestors. *Destin*. I had no idea the stars had so much planned! You are a minor inconvenience. One easily taken care of."

I didn't so much as breathe. So Anastasia was a displaced heiress in search of her birthright. And she did not care how she reclaimed it, through force or love. If she thought she could hunt Thomas, coerce him into marriage, and murder me in the process, she'd no idea who *I* was.

I clenched my fists, more determined than ever to keep her talking while I plotted our escape. "How did you murder the man on the train—and why?"

My former friend stared at me for a beat, eyes narrowed. I silently prayed that her need to boast would be tempting enough for her to answer my questions without seeing my true motive. "The Order of the Dragon lives. I wanted to cleanse their ranks. These days, they are mostly composed of that inconsequential Dănești line."

She pointed the revolver toward where Prince Nicolae lay, limp as a rag doll, skin discolored from what I assumed was arsenic, punctures now visible on his neck. It appeared as if she'd used his blood the way her ancestor had—by bathing in it, leaving barely enough to keep him alive. If he even still lived. His chest no longer appeared to be rising and falling with breath.

"The man from the train was a high-ranking member. I slipped him a lethal dose of arsenic, then impaled him as he gasped for breath." Anastasia sounded as if she were recalling a dress she had made from fine silks. "I had no idea it was outside your compartment. A happy coincidence. I then raced back to my room. No one noticed the girl with dark hair. Wigs are *distracție excelentă*. I worried that Wilhelm might eventually recognize me, though. He needed to be dealt with immediately."

A memory of that morning flashed across my mind— I had seen a girl with dark hair. She'd cried out for a doctor. I'd been so consumed with the chaos that I hadn't paid attention to her face.

Thomas crossed his arms over his chest, taking on that bored tone once more. "Where is my sister?"

"How should I know? I am not anyone's keeper." Anastasia jerked her chin toward me, then gestured at a weapon on Nicolae's belt. "Give Dracula's heir the knife."

Thomas's eyes widened as he glanced in my direction. I nearly cried with relief. In her fervor to unite their bloodlines, she hadn't realized that she'd just handed us a way to defeat her. My palms grew slick with the rush of nerves.

I pressed the small jeweled dagger into Thomas's hand and held my breath, worried any show of excitement might alert Anastasia to her grievous mistake. She grinned, attention latched onto the blade now residing in Thomas's steady grasp.

"End him," she said to Thomas. "Do it quickly."

"Why poison?" I asked, stalling. There had to be a way out of this that didn't involve murdering Nicolae.

Anastasia pointed the revolver at my throat. It seemed my former friend had considered mutiny after all. She walked to Nicolae and nudged him with her foot, gun still aimed at me.

"Arsenic is a wonder." She bent down, brushing strands of dark hair back from the prince's face. "It's tasteless, colorless, and can be slipped into all manner of food and drink. A young prince never turns down wine, it seems."

"If you're attempting to instill the same fear Vlad

Dracula did in his opponents," Thomas said, "poisoning Nicolae and the others hardly seems frightening."

Anastasia moved a hand to Nicolae's neck, checking for a pulse. "Isn't it, though? Arsenic is used to weaken and incapacitate the victims, not kill. It would have proven too difficult for me to fight young men, and the murders too messy."

"You wanted villagers to believe the stories of Dracula rising," I said, suddenly understanding. "You couldn't very well stab people and then claim their blood had been dined upon by a *strigoi*."

"Legends are meant to inspire fear." Anastasia stood. "They must be larger than the life we lead in order to maintain their lure for generations. *Don't go into the woods after sunset.* We never think of a beautiful princess lurking in the night forest, do we? No. We imagine bloodthirsty demons. Vampires. Night reminds us that we're also prey. We're terrified and thrilled by the prospect of being hunted."

"I still don't understand one thing, though," I said, gaze trailing from Nicolae's limp form to Anastasia's blood-coated body. "Why murder the maid?"

"That particular murder was homage paid to *my* ancestor. Now, then. Thomas," she swung the gun back to my forehead, "end Prince Nicolae's life now. I have hunted down Dracula's heir. We may begin fresh. New.

We will rise as Prince and Countess Dracula. Reclaim both this castle and your life."

Tension coiled around the room, a match ready to set this battle ablaze. Thomas took an unsteady step back, focus flicking from Nicolae to the gun now at my head. I did not want him to do something he'd spend the rest of his life regretting. Thomas Cresswell was not Vlad Dracula. His life had not been built upon creating death, but on solving it. He was a light carving through the darkness like a scythe. But I knew he'd destroy himself to save me and not give it a second thought.

"Why involve Thomas?" I blurted. "If you're the Countess Dracula, why make him kill?"

Anastasia stared at me as if I were the one who no longer made sense. "Thomas is the last male blood relative of the Impaler Lord. It is symbolic to have him end the life of this false prince, reclaim his bloodline, and bring ruin to the academy. No one will want to attend an academy where the students have died gruesomely under mysterious circumstances. Once the academy is no more, we can take it as our rightful home."

"What of the current king and queen?"

"Have you not been paying attention?" Anastasia demanded. "Arsenic will end their lives, too. I'll go through each noble household until Thomas's claim is the only one left. I will succeed in destroying the Order that way, too."

At that proclamation, two cloaked figures stepped forward. They'd been hidden behind the piles of bones surrounding us. I'd thought I'd lost the ability to be surprised, but I gasped when the taller figure flung its hood back and swept the cloak away from its weapons.

Daciana stood before us, clad in breeches and a tunic, wearing the insignia of the dragon along with more knives than Uncle had scalpels in his laboratory. Thomas flashed her an incredulous yet relieved look and kept the jeweled dagger firmly in his grip.

"There won't be any more killing tonight, *Contesă*," she said with a mock bow, a blade now directed toward Anastasia. "Ileana, please disarm her."

The second figure removed its hood, and my breathing stilled. My attention snapped to Thomas, unsure if my mind were playing tricks on me. Perhaps I was having an elaborate nightmare and I'd wake soon, sweaty and tangled in my sheets. His sister and Ileana were... realization crashed through me the same instant it did for Thomas.

He met my gaze and shook his head, an expression of absolute wonder etched into his features. There was something oddly satisfying about him missing a piece of the puzzle for once.

Anastasia glanced from Thomas to Daciana and

Ileana, confusion giving way to anger. She swung her weapon toward Nicolae's chest.

"How dare you?" she screamed, staring at Ileana. "I worked everything out, everything! You—a pitiful maid—have no right!"

"Stand down, Anastasia," Ileana said, in the tone of someone used to giving orders that were followed. "You have *două* seconds before—"

"I have no need to obey you!" Anastasia thrust herself forward, eyes blazing as she pulled the hammer of the gun back to execute Nicolae. But Ileana was faster. Her sword went directly through Anastasia's body. I stared, horrified, as she slid down the blade, licking deep red blood from her lips, and laughed.

"*Ucis...de...o servitoare,*" Anastasia gasped, fresh blood now dripping from her mouth to blend with the red pool on the ground. "A Báthory murdered by a maid. How fitting."

She laughed again, blood bubbling up her throat. No one attempted to help her while she lay dying, asphyxiating on her own life force. It was too late. Like the man she'd murdered on the train, Wilhelm Aldea, the girl from the village and her husband, and the maid Mariana, there was no bringing her back from Death's Dominion now.

It was a sight I knew would haunt me, along with the Ripper murders, for the rest of my life.

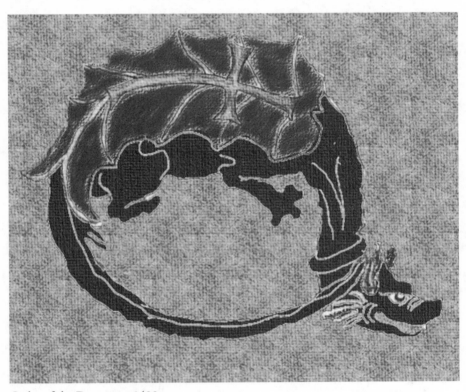

Order of the Dragon, c. 1400s.

FORTY-FOUR
SOCIETAS DRACONISTARUM

CRYPT
CRIPTĂ
BRAN CASTLE
22 DECEMBER 1888

I stared at the blood slowly dripping from the tip of Ileana's sword, words stuffed inside my throat, practically choking me. That was the only reason I hadn't vomited all over Anastasia's impaled body. My friend. I watched the life leave her eyes and was horrified by the serenity that befell her, though her entire body was covered in the black and red of both dried and fresh blood.

Thomas rubbed his hands along my arms, but it wasn't enough to take the chill from deep within my soul. Ileana, the girl I knew as my maid, was part of a secret warrior society and had cut a woman down as if she were spearing a chunk of hard cheese. Right before my very eyes. Though Anastasia was hardly innocent in the matter. I knew Ileana had had no choice and yet... I sank against Thomas, too tired to worry about what anyone might think of my lack of decorum.

"Are you all right, Audrey Rose?" Ileana accepted a cloth from Daciana and wiped down her blade, blood streaking across the silver at first before disappearing with the next swipe.

"Of course," I said automatically.

"All right" was such a relative term. My heart was beating, my body functioning and alive. On the surface I was most certainly all right. It was my mind that wanted to curl up and hibernate from the world and all the harshness within it. I was tired of destruction.

Thomas removed his gaze from Anastasia's body and shifted it toward his sister. I could see his mind whirling around from one fact to the next. It was a way for him to cope with the devastation, I realized. He needed to work the puzzle out to find his calm center amidst a raging storm.

"How?" he asked.

Daciana knew precisely what he was asking. "When I turned eighteen, I received a partial inheritance from Mother. Some of her possessions—jewels, finery, art—and a bundle of letters. At first the letters were just little bits of her... stories of how she met Father. How much she loved and cherished us. Birthday cards she'd prewritten for me. A note for when I married." Ileana brushed a tear from Daciana's cheek. "For a long while, I couldn't bring myself to read more. Then, one snowy afternoon, we were trapped inside. I took out the letters again and read one. Then flipped through toward the end."

"And?" Thomas asked. "Please keep the suspense short."

"Mother told stories of nobles who still believed in the ways of the Order. Who longed for corruption to be eradicated from the governing system. They approached her because of our family ties. Not to become a member herself, but to offer a safe space for them to gather. Do you remember the dragon painting in her chambers?"

Thomas nodded, face grimmer than I'd ever seen it before. I recalled the drawing he'd created on the train, and the story he'd shared about his memory of it.

"It was an honor bestowed upon your family line. And still is," Ileana said quietly.

"The Order would like you to consider offering your services, Thomas," Daciana said. "We need honest people who are unafraid of rooting out the corrupt."

There was an extended moment of silence while Thomas considered this.

"In essence, the Order is simply a vigilante group." He studied his sister and Ileana. "They are not the law, but believe they may uphold it better than the rulers."

"No," Daciana's eyes widened, "we do not believe that at all! The Order simply means to keep the balance. To quite literally maintain order. Power often corrupts. It is a wise man—or woman—who accepts their role as one part of a whole. We are simply a line of defense. The royal family asked for our help."

While Thomas peppered his sister with more questions, Ileana inspected me a bit too closely for comfort.

"We've all endured a long evening, so I'll keep this brief," she interrupted. "I am a high-ranking member of the *Ordo Draconum*. Our mission has always been to maintain order and peace. Once it was for the Dracula family; now it's for nobility and commoners alike. Our loyalty is to our country. Which includes all of our people."

"Ah. I see." Thomas narrowed his eyes. "So Daciana has always been aware of the title you hold, then?"

Ileana nodded. "She's kept my secret, and I hope you both will do the same. Very few know of my association with the Order. I am the first female to be invited into their ranks. Daciana is the second."

"How did you know to infiltrate the castle?" I asked, ignoring the pool of blood at my feet. Part of me wished there was a bag of sawdust to sprinkle about the ground. "I assume you must have been placed here purposely."

"Yes. Due to the arrival of members of the House of

Basarab, I was tasked with infiltrating the staff. After the first murder, in Braşov, the Order felt it necessary to have someone close to the village. I'd also be in a good position to hear rumors going on at the academy. Maids and servants gossip. It seemed like an excellent place to gain information."

I considered this, recalling Radu's lesson about the Order and who made up its ranks. "How did the headmaster not recognize you as nobility?"

Ileana smiled sadly. "Moldoveanu, like most, pays little attention to those in his service. Out of my finery? I become anyone." She lifted a shoulder. "He might be more observant because of his particular skill set, but he is not infallible."

"Why did it take you so long to stop Anastasia?" I asked. "Why wait until now?"

"We didn't know it was her." Daciana moved forward, touching Ileana's arm gently. "We'd been combing the tunnels over the last week or so, hoping to find information. Anastasia was clever. She moved around a lot. We never could locate her."

"I'd thought most of her questions odd. At least worthy of investigating," Ileana added, "but when she was found 'dead,' we didn't know what to make of it. Nicolae seemed suspect again, yet he'd never been present or in the same area as anyone who was murdered. The

Order is not known for solving crimes. We did the best we could by arming ourselves with knowledge. Unfortunately, it wasn't enough."

Prince Nicolae rolled to his side, sputtering up foam. I felt reprehensible for not thinking of him sooner and getting him out of this chamber. Thomas crouched beside him, holding his head up. He flashed a look of concern at Daciana. "He needs a doctor. We need to take him back into the castle. It may already be too late."

Wind gusted through crevices in the mountainside. I shivered as the frigid air wound its way over and through my damp clothing. I'd forgotten that I was standing in my underthings.

Surviving the tunnels seemed as if it were something that had happened to another girl, at another time. Not missing any detail, Thomas pointed at his sister. "Perhaps you might offer Audrey Rose your cloak."

Daciana wrapped it about my shoulders and squeezed me tight.

"Thank you." I breathed in the warmth of the cloak and exhaled the exhaustion settling around me. Watching anyone perish was something I wished to avoid, though I knew better than to believe this would be the last time I encountered violent death.

"Come," Daciana said. "Let's get you near a fire. You both appear ready to collapse."

~⚬~

We stumbled out of the basement morgue, tired, battered, and holding a dying student between us. Standing before us were the headmaster and several guards. Professor Moldoveanu inhaled sharply, then barked out orders. "Take the prince to Percy and have him administer fluids immediately, and treat him for arsenic. He has a tonic he's been working on."

Dăneşti flew to our side and hefted the prince onto a wheeled stretcher. "*Adu doctorul. Acum!* Now!"

Royal guards wheeled Nicolae from the room, the sound of the table screeching all the way down the corridor. I collapsed on the floor, too tired to stand any longer. Thomas folded himself beside me. My partner through Hell. I almost laughed. Liza had been correct once again—Thomas truly would follow me into the bowels of Hades and not bat an eye. Unless he was inappropriately winking, of course.

"I demand to know what is going on in this academy," Moldoveanu ground out. "Why are the two of you covered in filth and gore, dragging the prince through the tunnels?"

I lifted my head and stared at Thomas. I did not know where to even begin. We'd left Daciana and Ileana in the passages. They did not want their identities to be revealed to anyone. I was having a hard time remembering the story we were supposed to give, but I sat up a little as Thomas brushed hair back from my face.

"It's quite a long story," I said. "But the short of it is, Anastasia staged her own death..."

Moldoveanu's sneer faded as I recounted the details of our search in the tunnels. *Poezii Despre Moarte* and the poems it contained. The chambers of death we'd barely escaped. The family lineage of Anastasia and how she wished to hunt Prince Dracula and make him her bridegroom. I left nothing out regarding the arsenic poisonings or the way she impaled certain victims. A tear slid down his face as I relayed the story of his ward's actual death. I pulled out the book of poems and handed it over to him. I hoped to never see it again.

When I finished, Thomas lifted a shoulder. "Seems we ought to get some extra credit. We did stop a murderess from destroying the academy."

Moldoveanu's eyes were no longer watering. They were frozen and dead. "Get back to your rooms and pack your things immediately. I'll decide what to do with you both after the holiday. Your carriage will be waiting at sunrise. Do not show yourselves back here until I say you may return. Which might very well be never."

Without so much as a simple thank-you, the headmaster exited the basement morgue, and we heard the sharp sound of his footsteps echoing his harsh words of farewell.

Thomas offered a hand. "Is it only me, or do you believe he's beginning to like us?"

—

FORTY-FIVE
SWANS AND WOLVES

"Oh! You're both here!"

Daciana moved as quickly down the grand staircase as her beaded gown allowed. It was strange, standing here, surrounded by such beautiful things. Each edge of furniture was dipped in gold and reflected the candlelight. It was stunning in all the right ways. I curtsied politely when she reached us and Daciana did the same.

"It's wonderful to see you under more...civilized circumstances." She kissed my cheeks, then hugged her brother tightly. "I managed to reach Mrs. Harvey before she left for London, but she's upstairs—"

"Napping?" Thomas asked, lips twitching.

"No, you miserable thing," Daciana said. "She's getting

dressed for the ball. Hurry up and get ready. Our guests will be arriving within an hour."

After the horrendous events in the crypt, a ballgown had been the furthest thing from my thoughts. In fact, I'd barely had time to gather my belongings. The headmaster had rushed us out of the castle so quickly we hadn't been able to say good-bye to anyone, let alone go on a shopping excursion. I'd left a note for Noah but wished I could have said farewell in person. I was going to miss him and his sharp mind. Thinking of my classmate brought on darker memories and I tried not to picture Anastasia's impalement and failed.

Daciana tentatively reached out and drew me from those morbid images. Her grip in my hand tightened a bit, giving me strength. "Someone will be up shortly to assist you," she said.

"I didn't bring anything to wear."

I exchanged a nervous glance with Thomas, but Daciana waved it away, a conspiratorial smile lighting her face.

"Nothing to fret over," she said. "Simply a few close friends enjoying Christmas Eve together. Nothing too extravagant. The best dress you brought should do."

The room Daciana had picked out for me was well appointed. It boasted all the finery a royal could want, let alone a lord's daughter.

I stood in the doorway for a moment, taking in the splendor. A fireplace crackled softly in one corner, and I couldn't help walking over to admire the paintings that decorated its elaborate mantel. Flowers and mountains and still-lifes of Bucharest were captured in jewel-toned colors. I stepped closer, inspecting them with interest. Scrawled along the bottom was a familiar name in beautiful script. I recognized his writing immediately.

Thomas James Dorin cel Rău Cresswell.

Smiling to myself, I moved to the large four-poster bed—with a canopy made of gossamer panels—and halted. A familiar box tied with black ribbon was laid out. I'd forgotten to open it while at the academy and had nearly forgotten the day Thomas had tried sneaking it into my chambers. I traced my fingers over the bow, marveling at the smooth, cool silk.

After everything we'd gone through, I couldn't believe Thomas remembered to have it packed. I slowly pulled one end of the ribbon, watching it come undone. Curiosity finally took hold, and I tore into the brown paper wrapping and lifted the lid. Tissue paper crinkled pleasantly as I unveiled the elaborate cloth hidden beneath.

"Oh..."

I held up the brilliant gown from its box, fighting the sudden onslaught of emotion choking me. Thomas had purchased a bit of sunshine and dreams for me. Something full of light to chase away the lingering nightmares. Tiny gemstones winked in the candlelight as I turned it one way, then the next. It was even more lovely than it had been in the window in Braşov. The yellow so pale and creamy, it made me want to sink my teeth into it.

It was one of the most gorgeous garments I'd ever seen. No matter how much death and horror existed, there were still things of beauty left to find. My heart sped up, imagining Thomas sneaking back to the dress shop and having it wrapped. It wasn't the monetary aspect of the gift, but the fact that he'd bought it simply to delight me that stole my breath.

I clutched the gown close and danced around the room, allowing the tulle skirts to swish about as if it were my excited partner. I found I could not wait to show Thomas and perhaps be like a sudden ray of sun to brighten his spirits in return. Mr. Thomas Cresswell might not truly hold the title of prince, but that was perfectly fine. To me, he'd always be the king of my heart.

When Daciana threw a ball, it was no modest event. It was one befitting a queen.

Victoria and the other girls from tea would croon

over the lavish spread of desserts and pastries and fruits and meats piled high enough to feed the entire village of Brașov with its leftovers. The offerings had been molded into shapes of fantastical beasts that I couldn't quite discern from this vantage point. I wished Liza were here to admire them with me. I hadn't received a return letter and squashed a sense of growing unease. All was fine.

I moved around the sweeping balcony, mesmerized by the entertainment taking place in the center of the ballroom. Dancers were crowned with diamond tiaras with shockingly white feathers on each side of their silver-haired temples, looking like swans taking flight.

The bodices of their matching gowns were made up entirely of feathers—white with shades of gray. It was their gloves, however, that drew the most attention as they fluttered about the dance floor. Solid black lace began at their fingertips, transforming into sheer tendrils of smokelike gauze as they coiled tightly around their elbows.

I stood, spellbound, as they gracefully leapt from one foot to the other. Some in the crowd watched, but the majority were lost in conversation.

"Such a pity."

I turned and found Ileana nodding toward the people below. I could not control the gasp that escaped my lips. Gone was the embroidered maid's costume and peasant dress. In their place was a young woman resplendent in a gown elegant enough for a princess.

A butterfly-shaped appliqué stretched its wings across her ample bust, inviting one's gaze to travel to the train fluttering off her shoulders. It was almost as stunning as the person wearing it. I couldn't help but admire this young woman and all she'd done for her beloved land. She was the sort of nobility the world needed. One who didn't fear to tread in frightening places for the sake of her people.

No wonder Daciana was in love with her. It was hard not to admire her courage and drive.

She nodded toward the crowd. "They never stop to enjoy the *magie* going on around them."

"I wasn't expecting quite so many people," I admitted. "When Daciana mentioned a small ball with close friends…" I trailed off as Ileana chuckled. "The Cresswells certainly have a flair for the dramatic. At least I know it's hereditary. Though I do believe Thomas is a bit more theatrical."

"Daciana has her moments as well."

We stood in companionable silence for a bit. There was still one thing I hadn't quite puzzled out. I faced Ileana.

"It was you and Daciana that night in the corridor, removing the body from the tower morgue, wasn't it? You were chanting…"

Ileana nodded slowly.

"Radu mentioned that the Order performed death rites in the woods. Is that what you were doing? Did you know the train victim?"

"Yes." Ileana stared down at the crowd, focus inward. "That was my brother. When I found out Moldoveanu was going to perform a postmortem on him..." She swallowed hard. "It goes against our beliefs. Daciana helped me take his body where it belonged."

"So there *is* a meeting place in the woods?"

A moment passed and I assumed Ileana was weighing her words, deciding how much to share. "There is a sacred location, guarded by wolves. Most don't ever get close to it, thanks to folklore and the occasional bone that's found." A small smile ghosted across her face. "We feed the wolves large animals. They scatter the bones on their own. It provides a good story for the superstitious. No one wants to enrage Vlad Dracula's immortal soul."

"It's a good method of disguise," I said. "I'm sorry about your brother. Losing a sibling is horrid."

"It is. But we can carry their memory with us and draw strength from it." Ileana clutched my gloved hand in her own and squeezed gently. *"Am nevoie de aer.* If you see Daciana, let her know I'll be on the roof. It's too"—she crinkled her nose—"stuffy in here for my tastes."

After waving good-bye, I moved closer to the stairs, working up the nerve to head down.

I stood with my hips pressed against the banister, attention lingering on the crowd of colorfully dressed partygoers. Women wore dresses in greens and golds and all manner of reds, from the deepest evergreen to mulled wine.

I ran my hands down my shimmering bodice. Pale yellow and gold gemstones were carefully sewn onto exquisite fabric, giving the appearance of sunlight on snow. I couldn't deny that I adored the garment and felt like a princess myself. The thought brought on fond memories of the times Grandmama had wrapped me in jeweled saris.

I glanced around the bedazzled room, attention devouring each new shiny treat. Spruce branches hung above windows and mantels, their boughs dusted with glitter. I noticed cleverly placed clusters of mistletoe and steadied my heart.

Perhaps I would indulge in some free behavior myself. If only for one night. The Impaler had been stopped, the academy saved from ruin, and it was time to sit back and enjoy the victory before we found out if we'd passed the assessment course. A letter should arrive soon, and with it word of our fate for the next semester.

A young man cut through the room like a shadow. I watched him weave his way through dancing couples, his destination giving him confidence as he plucked two glasses of punch from a passing tray. He paused at the bottom of the stairs and met my eyes.

Thomas looked every inch the prince he was, whether his claim to the throne was distant or not. My heart sped as he took a sip from his flute but drank me in in larger gulps.

I gathered the layers of my skirts and descended the grand staircase, mindful to keep from tumbling down the steps. For someone who'd claimed to be spending the holiday alone with Mrs. Harvey, I couldn't believe how many guests were milling about. Daciana would put Aunt Amelia to shame with her hosting skills. Half the residents of Bucharest seemed to be in attendance, with more arriving every moment. A quiet little evening with some friends indeed.

As I reached the bottom of the stairs, I spied Mrs. Harvey dancing near the edge of the crowd, cheeks pleasantly flushed.

"You're going to drive everyone quite mad tonight, Wadsworth. Your dance card will be the talk of legends," Thomas said, giving me that half-smile I adored as he offered a glass.

I took a sip, needing all the liquid confidence I could

take in. Bubbles tickled as they danced along my throat. I quickly took another sip.

"Actually, I plan on standing below mistletoe most of the evening."

"Might want to reconsider that, Wadsworth. It's parasitic, you know." Thomas grinned. "Of course, I'll screen potential suitors first if you like. Wouldn't want any of them getting carried away. That's what friends do, right?"

Young women were going to be hanging all over him, too. His dark brown hair was expertly styled, his suit tailored to his lean but well-defined frame, and his leather shoes were shined to perfection.

He was heartbreakingly beautiful.

"You look...average, Cresswell," I said with a mostly straight face, noticing he'd been watching me catalogue every detail. The corners of his mouth twitched. "I expected more, really. Something a bit...princely. I'm disappointed you didn't don a powdered wig."

"Liar."

Ignoring him, I finished off my punch and set it on a passing tray. My head swam with liquid heat, thrumming through my veins as if it were gasoline waiting for the spark to set it ablaze. Thomas tipped his head back and emptied his own glass with surprising speed. I watched him drink in my entire form again, taking liberties to appreciate each curve my gown highlighted. I still couldn't believe he'd gotten it for me.

He stepped closer and placed a large hand around my waist, drawing me into a waltz as the music started up. "We promised each other, remember?"

"Hmm?"

I was having a difficult time concentrating on anything other than his sure footsteps leading me about the room in one intoxicating circle after the next. It was hard to tell if the punch was to blame or if it was entirely the young gentleman before me. I placed one hand on his shoulder and the other in his gloved hand, allowing myself to get swept up in the magic of the song and the fantastical atmosphere. This was a winter wonderland, its contrast extreme against the hell we'd traversed.

"When we were still in London," Thomas brought his lips to my ear, whispering rumbled words and igniting my blood, "we promised. To never lie to one another."

He pressed me closer until there was no decent amount of space left between us. I found I didn't mind as we wove in and threaded through swirling skirts, the crowd of dancers a tapestry of merriment. The rest of the room collapsed into a dream I wasn't paying attention to. There was something better than dreams, something more tangible in my hands. I needed only to reach out and reassure myself that he was solid. He was no ghost from my past.

"You want the truth, Cresswell?" I wrapped my arms around his neck until our bodies were confused about where each one ended. Until the only thought consuming my mind was to bring him even closer, to let him catch fire from me, too. No one seemed to notice my untoward behavior, but even if they had, I doubted I would care in this moment.

"Tell me." Thomas dipped his mouth dangerously close to mine for a beat that drew out a savage chord inside me. He ran his hands down my back, soothing, teasing. "Please."

I hadn't noticed that we'd managed to situate ourselves in an alcove between potted ferns. Their large, fanlike fronds provided a screen from the party raging beyond. We were alone, away from prying eyes, far from society's rules and restrictions.

Thomas tucked a strand of hair behind my ear, expression a bit sad considering where we were. "My mother would have adored you. She always told me I needed a partner. An equal. To never settle for someone who'd simper and defer to my role as husband." He glanced back toward the crowd, eyes misting. "Being here is... difficult. Much more so than I thought it'd be. I see her in everything. It's silly... but I often wonder if she'd be proud. Despite what others say about me. I don't know what she'd think."

I ran my hand down the front of his lapels, tugging him deeper inside the alcove. Darkness made confessions easier—it comforted me in a way the light never could.

"She would be proud," I said. Thomas fidgeted in his suit, attention fixed on the floor. "Do you want to know what I think? The truth?"

"Yes." He gazed unabashedly into my eyes. "Make it scandalous, too. This is a bit too serious for my tastes."

"You look rather..."

My heart sputtered. Thomas was staring intently at me, as if he could divine some secret I'd yet to reveal to myself. I peered into his gold-flecked eyes. In them I saw my own emotions reflected back at me. No walls or games.

"You look like you should stop saying you're going to kiss me, Prince Dracula." He flinched as if my words had stung him. I drew his face back to me. "And just *do* it, Cresswell."

Understanding flashed across his features, and he didn't hesitate to bring his mouth to mine. We stumbled against the wall, the entire length of him encompassing me in his warmth. His hands slid up my frame, knotting themselves in my hair as he deepened our kiss. The corseted world fell away. Restrictions and rules were bindings of the past.

There were only the two of us left standing in a star-filled sky, oblivious to anything but the way our bodies fit together like constellations. He was my match in all ways. I tore my gloves off, allowing my fingers the freedom to trace the planes of his face without hindrance and he replied in kind. His skin was smooth beneath my touch. Thomas drew back, gently caressing my bottom lip with his thumb, his breath no more than a rasp. "Audrey Rose, I—"

I pulled his face to mine and gave his mouth something more interesting to do. Thomas didn't seem to mind the interruption as we explored new ways of communicating.

Eventually, we dragged ourselves out from our secret spot behind the ferns and danced and laughed until both my feet and stomach ached. Tonight wasn't meant for sadness and death, I realized. It was a time to recall how extraordinary it felt to be alive.

Dear Miss Wadsworth,

I'm sure it will come as no surprise, but I must inform you that you did not place in the academy this season. After much thought, I determined that the students who were most deserving during this course were Mr. Noah Hale and Mr. Erik Petrov. They exhibited exemplary behavior as well as forensic skill. Perhaps next time you'll do as you're instructed. Part of one's education includes listening to those of higher rank and experience — something you failed at miserably on more than one occasion.

However, on behalf of the academy, I do offer my sincerest gratitude for your assistance. You might become proficient in forensics with more practice and polish, though that remains to be seen.

I do wish you well.

Sincerely,

Wadim Moldoveanu

Headmaster, Institutului Național de

Criminalistică și Medicină Legală

Academy of Forensic Medicine and Science

EPILOGUE
A THRILLING PROSPECT

CEL RĂU-CRESSWELL RESIDENCE
BUCHAREST, ROMANIA
26 DECEMBER 1888

Prince Nicolae leaned against the settee in the receiving room, face gaunt but back to his normal olive complexion. I'd never been more pleased to see him.

"You're much less corpselike," Thomas said plainly. I couldn't help but laugh. For all the growth I'd witnessed in him, there were still some edges that would never be smoothed out. He turned to me, a furrow in his brow. "What? Does he not appear better?"

"I'm glad you're well, Prince Nicolae. It was..." Calling what he'd been through "awful" felt too mild for what he'd experienced. What we'd all experienced. I inhaled. "It will be quite a story to pass down to our children one day."

"*Mulţumesc.* Just 'Nicolae' is fine." A smile began

but didn't fully expand across his face. "I wanted to thank you both personally. And I wanted to apologize."

He pulled a piece of parchment from the journal he'd been holding and offered it to me. It was the illustration of me—the one where I appeared as if I were the Countess Dracula. I flicked my gaze to his, ignoring the way Thomas snorted from over my shoulder.

"No one believed me," he said simply, holding his palms out by way of explanation. "I'd tried warning my family, and then the current royal court, but they thought me mad. *Nebun*. Then...when Wilhelm died...they still didn't listen. I decided to send threats. I'd hoped they'd take precautions. I assumed if our lineage was being targeted, it was only a matter of time before the king and queen were also threatened." He pointed at the drawing of me. "I thought you were the one to blame. I drew that with the intention of passing it out to villagers. If the academy wouldn't listen... Dăneşti or Moldoveanu...I thought maybe the villagers would dispose of anyone perceived to be a *strigoi*. I'm—I apologize."

Thomas said nothing. I stood and took the prince's gloved hands in my own. "Thank you for the truth. I'm glad we're parting on better terms than when we first met."

"I am, too." Nicolae pushed to his feet, using an

ornate cane, and limped to the door. *"Rămâi cu bine.* Stay well."

A long plain box tied with twine was delivered to my room along with the receipt that afternoon. It was the best Christmas gift I'd ever purchased for myself. Without preamble, I ripped off the twine and opened the lid.

A pair of black breeches were folded along with a silky blouse. My attention fell upon the most precious part of the package: the leather belt strap with gold buckles. When we returned to London, I'd be quite the force to contend with. I hoped Father would be accepting, though perhaps I'd go a bit easy on him at first. I pushed those worries aside and found I couldn't wait to try on the new clothes. I disrobed immediately.

Tugging the breeches up, I secured them around my waist, marveling at the way my silhouette appeared to have been dipped in the finest ink, then laid to dry in the sun. Gentle curves arced over my hips, then tapered into my legs. I pulled the blouse over my head next and secured it with a series of ties in the front before tucking it into my breeches.

The seamstress had crafted a silky shirt, yet it also

had enough structure to keep my assets in place. It was perfectly done.

I ran gloveless hands down the front of the shirt, smoothing away wrinkles as I shifted from side to side in the looking glass. My figure was shown in a way that meant there would be no mistaking me for one of my male classmates when we returned to Uncle's lessons, no matter if I were dressed like one. Part of me wanted to blush at how much of my form was revealed in this ensemble. But mostly I felt like marching around with my head held high. There was a freedom in movement that I rarely experienced with all my layers and bindings.

With effort, I walked away from my reflection and lifted the leather belt from the box. I stepped one limb into it and secured its buckles against my thigh. I slid my scalpel into place and grinned. If I'd felt like blushing before, this was a whole new level of indecency to be toying with. I'd need to wear my apron to avoid whispers and stares. As of now I appeared to be—

"You're stunning."

I flipped around, hand straying to the cool metal of the scalpel sheathed against my thigh. I allowed my fingers to brush against the smooth blade before dropping my hand. "Sneaking into a young woman's sleeping chambers twice in one month is rude even by your lax standards, Cresswell."

"Even when I'm sneaking about my own home this time? And when I've brought a gift?"

He had a feline tilt to his smile as he laid a canvas against the door and stalked into the room, circling me. Unapologetically, he inspected each inch of my ensemble, then stepped close enough for me to feel the heat of his body.

Suddenly feeling shy, I nodded toward the back of the canvas. "May I see it?"

"Please." Thomas swept his arm out. "Indulge your fancies."

I walked over to the painting and turned it around, my breath catching at the sight. A single orchid glittered as if it had been encapsulated in ice. I bent closer, realizing that wasn't correct at all. The orchid actually was a star-speckled sky. Thomas had painted the entire universe within the confines of my favorite flower. A memory of him offering me an orchid during the Ripper investigation crossed my mind.

I leaned the painting against the wall and flicked my gaze up. "How did you know?"

"I..." Thomas swallowed hard, his attention fixed on the painting. "The truth?"

"Please."

"You've got a dress with orchid blossoms embroidered on it. Ribbons in the deepest purple. You favor the color, but not nearly as much as I find myself favoring you." He took a deep breath. "As to the stars? Those are what I prefer. More than medical practices and deductions. The universe is vast. A mathematical equation even I have no hope of solving. For there are no limits to the stars; their numbers are infinite. Which is precisely why I measure my love for you by them. An amount too boundless to count."

Slowly enough to make my heart race, he reached out and pulled a pin from my hair. A section of raven curls fell in a cascading layer down my back as the gold plunked to the floor.

"I am wholly bewitched, Wadsworth." He plucked another pin, then another, releasing my hair entirely from its restraints. There was something intimate about him seeing me with my hair unbound in this private chamber. About his confession. Like a secret language only the two of us knew how to speak.

"Are you implying your feelings are the result of some sort of spell craft, then?" I teased.

"What I mean is…I cannot pretend I'm not…I suppose what I'm saying is it's been a few months." Thomas scratched his brow. "I was hoping to make things a bit more…official. In some capacity. Whichever way you prefer, actually."

"Official in what way?" My heart banged around the inside of my chest, searching for a crack to escape from. I could scarcely believe we were having such a conversation, especially while alone. Though I could also scarcely believe Thomas had practically said "I love you." Which was what I needed to hear again. Just once without prodding.

"You know what way, Wadsworth. I refuse to believe you've misinterpreted my affections. I am wholly in love with you. And it is permanent."

There it was. The admission I'd been craving. He nervously bit his lip, unsure even with all his powers of deductions if I could ever truly love him back. I wanted to remind him of our conversation—about how there was no formula for love—but found my pulse racing for an entirely different reason.

I was ready to accept Mr. Thomas Cresswell's hand. And it terrified and thrilled me at once. He watched as I stood taller and thrust my chin up. If I was going to submit to my own feelings, I needed to be sure of one last thing.

"Will you only ask my father permission to court me?" I needed to know. "What of my feelings? I might fancy Nicolae. You've not asked me directly."

Thomas unflinchingly held my gaze. "If that's true, then tell me and I will never speak of this again. I would never force my presence upon you."

I couldn't help thinking of the detective inspector

who'd worked the Ripper case with us. About his ulterior motives. "It's quite a lovely thought. But for all I know, you've already spoken to my father and a date has been set. Something similar *has* happened before."

"Blackburn was a fool. I believe you should always have a choice in the matter. I wouldn't dream of excluding you from your own life."

"Father would likely be...I'm not sure. He might not approve of such a modern approach. Your asking my permission before his. I thought you cared about his opinion."

Thomas lifted his hand to my face, carefully stroking trails of fire across my jawline. "True, I want your father's approval. But I want your permission. No one else's. This can't work any other way. You are not mine to take." He brushed his lips against mine. Softly, so softly I might have imagined them there. My eyes fluttered shut. He could persuade me to build a steamship to the moon when he kissed me. We could orbit the stars together. "You are yours to give."

I stepped into the circle of his arms and placed a palm against his chest, guiding him toward the tufted chair. He figured out too late that there was something bigger than a cat chasing him; he'd attracted the attention of a lioness. And he was now my prey.

"Then I choose you, Cresswell."

I delighted in the fact that he'd stumbled into the chair, eyes wide. I moved closer, until I was standing before him, and nudged his limb with my knee, teasing.

"It's not polite to play with your meal, Wadsworth. Hasn't—"

"I love you, too." I captured his lips with my own, allowing his arms to circle me and draw me closer still. He opened his mouth to deepen our kiss, and I felt the heavens split open within the universe of my body. I didn't care about Anastasia and her crimes. Or anything other than—

"Much as I hate to break you two up..." Daciana coughed delicately from the doorway. "We have a visitor." She eyed my new outfit and grinned. "You look phenomenal. Very intimidating and 'Bringer of Death.'"

Thomas groaned as I stepped out of his grasp, then shot his sister a withering glare Aunt Amelia would have been proud of. "Bringer of Death is what the villagers will label me if you continue to ruin all of our clandestine moments, Daci. Go entertain your visitor on your own."

Daciana stuck her tongue out at him. "Stop being cranky. It's unbecoming. I'd love to entertain our guest, but I have a feeling Audrey Rose might want to say hello."

Intrigued, I smoothed down the front of my dangerous ensemble. My hair was unbound, but curiosity dragged me from my chambers and down the winding stairs before I could fix it. I halted at the bottom, nearly sending Thomas sprawling to the floor as he bumped into me.

A man with blond hair and familiar gold spectacles paced around the foyer, hands flitting at his sides. It took every bit of my self-control to not jump into his arms.

"Uncle Jonathan? What a lovely surprise! What brings you all the way to Bucharest?"

His attention snapped to me, and I watched his green eyes blink in response to my choice of attire. I was certain the leather scalpel belt around my thigh might cause an embolism, but he took it all in stride. He didn't bat a lash at the state of my hair, which was a miracle in itself. Uncle inspected the young man beside me, then twisted his mustache. I grabbed hold of the banister, knowing from the gesture that his news wasn't good.

Irrational fears flashed before my eyes. "Is everything all right at home? How is Father?"

"He's well." Uncle nodded as if to confirm the fact. "I'm afraid you both may be delayed in returning home, though. I've been summoned to America. There's a troubling forensic case, and I require the assistance of my two best apprentices." He tugged a pocket watch from beneath his traveling cloak. "Our ship sails from Liverpool on New Year's Day. If we're to make it there, we need to leave tonight."

"I'm not sure that's such a wise idea. What does Lord Wadsworth say about it?" Thomas stood straighter, worrying his lip between his teeth. "I suppose my father doesn't care one way or the other. Has anyone been in communication with him?"

Uncle shook his head slightly. "He's traveling, Thomas. You know how hard it is to receive the post, which is why I came myself."

A lock of hair fell across Thomas's brow, and I longed to reach over and smooth both it and his worries away. I gently squeezed his hand before stepping toward my uncle.

"Come on, Cresswell. I'm sure both of our fathers will approve. Besides," I said, my tone turning playful, "I fancy another adventure with you."

A flash of mischief lit his expression. I knew he was recalling the very thing he'd said to me at the end of the Ripper case. "I am rather irresistible, Wadsworth. It's high time you admitted it." He held out his arm, a question in his gaze. "Shall we?"

I glanced at my uncle, noting the smile twitching across his face. I'd always wanted to travel across the pond, and saying no to another case and a trip aboard a luxury cruiser seemed foolish. I focused on Thomas's outstretched arm, knowing he was offering much more than his best manners. He was gifting me with all the love and adventure the universe could provide.

Mr. Thomas Cresswell, last male heir of Prince Dracula, was offering me both his heart and his hand.

Without hesitation, I accepted Thomas's arm and grinned. "To America!"

PRONUNCIATION GUIDE

Aldea	Al-DEE-ah
Anastasia	ah-nuh-STAH-zee-uh
Andrei	AHN-dray
Basarab	bah-sah-RAHB
Braşov	bra-SHOV
cel Rău	chel-RŌ
Cian	KEE-uhn
Daciana	dah-see-AH-nah
Dăneşti	Dah-NESH-tee
Dorin	DOOR-een
Dracul	DRAH-cool
Drăculeşti	Drah-coo-LESH-tee
Erik	AIR-rik
Ileana	ih-lee-AH-nah
Liza	LIE-zah
Mihnea	mee-nah
Mircea	MEER-cha
Moldoveanu	Mol-DAH-vah-nō
Nicolae	NEE-kuh-lie
Noah	NO-ah
Percy	PUR-see
Pricolici	pree-cō-LEECH

PRONUNCIATION GUIDE

Radu	rah-doo
Strigoi	stree-GOY
Țepeș	TE-pesh
Voivode	VOY-vōde
Wallachia	wah-LAH-kee-ah
Wilhelm	VILL-helm

AUTHOR'S NOTE

Historical and creative liberties taken by the author:

As is the beauty of fiction, there are some historical truths at the heart of this story and a lot of imagination added for both embellishment and adventure. Much to my dismay, the *Orient Express* did not stop in Bucharest until early 1889 (a few months after Thomas and Audrey Rose rode it to school during the winter of 1888), but I have always loved the train and couldn't resist opening the novel with it. It was so romantic until that impaled body showed up...

Unfortunately (or maybe not), Bran Castle never was a boarding school or hosted any medical students during its long history. Though popularized in fiction and film, Vlad III (Vlad the Impaler) only passed through the castle during his second reign before attacking Saxons in Braşov. Since it's famously called "Dracula's Castle" (thanks to Bram Stoker's similar description of it, though there are arguments as to whether or not it was the actual castle that inspired his famous vampire tale...which is a story for another time), I decided it would be the perfect location for a serial killer who was pretending to be a vampire.

During the timeframe this novel is set in, Bran Castle had been turned over to the region's forestry department. It was interesting to imagine it as a school of forensic medicine and science in place of the abandoned, disrepair that it fell into for those thirty years until the citizens of Braşov gifted it to Queen Maria of Romania.

Some interior descriptions—like the library—were inspired by the actual cathedral in the castle and were embellished greatly for the story. The entryway with stairs leading up and down and the dragon sconces are from my imagination. I also took the liberty of adding secret hallways and passages and labyrinths beneath the main floors. I liked imagining several ways for Vlad III to escape from this fortress, should any invading armies or unfriendly usurpers make a play for ending his life and seizing control of his beloved country. For more information on the castle and its historical timeline, check out bran-castle.com. There are amazing facts listed there, and the site also offers photographs that are superb.

The Order of the Dragon was truly a secret chivalric order that both Vlad III and his father (Vlad II) were members of. They were really based off of the Crusades, but weren't active during the time of this story. (And they likely wouldn't have had female members, but that wouldn't stop my fearless girls from invading the all-boys club and wielding their swords.)

Facts regarding some science mentioned:
DNA was discovered in 1869 by a Swiss physiological chemist named Friedrich Miescher. He'd called it "nuclein" since he'd discovered it inside the nuclei of white blood cells. Being a student of forensics, and someone who'd read everything she could on the advancements of science, Audrey Rose would have greatly admired him.

Modern drinking straws were patented by Marvin C. Stone in 1888, though the earliest known straw was used by Sumerians in 3,000 B.C.E.

Modern/early feminism: Audrey Rose would have been inspired by books such as Mary Wollstonecraft's *A Vindication of the Rights of Woman,* which was published nearly one hundred years before this adventure in 1792. (In both America and Europe women were fighting for the right to vote, so it wasn't hard to imagine Audrey Rose's mother teaching her these more "modern" ideas that shaped her into pursing forensics in place of securing a marriage.)

Drăculeşti and Dăneşti family names:
Prince Nicolae Aldea and his family members in this story are all fictitious. In fact, most of the surnames are

a nod to the families involved with the dynastic rule of Romania prior to the 1800s. Nicolae was named after Nicolae Alexandru of the House Basarab.

An interesting part of my research was the royal family and how the dynasty could be furthered by placing "bastard" born sons as rulers. I suggest looking up the House of Basarab and the House of Dăneşti if you're interested in in-depth family trees. They were the main lineages of medieval rulers in Wallachia and where inspiration for Thomas and Nicolae's rivalry came from. Both Nicolae and Thomas would not technically be considered princes, since their family had ceased to control this region for quite some time, but, well, it *is* fiction and I love thinking of Thomas as being the anti–Prince Charming of Audrey Rose's dreams. (Who's actually very charming underneath his cool exterior.)

In this story, Thomas's mother's line is descended from Vlad the Impaler through Mihnea cel Rău. (Vlad the Impaler's son.) Mihnea produced heirs, and I imagined Thomas's mother having ties to them.

Countess Elizabeth Báthory is a historical Hungarian noblewoman who remains one of the most prolific female serial killers of all time. She reportedly murdered nearly seven hundred people (mostly her servants) and had both the nicknames The Countess Dracula and The Blood Countess. She was rumored to have bathed in the blood of her victims, which really added to her being compared to Vlad III and a vampire throughout history. Anastasia is named after one of Countess Báthory's children.

Fun tidbit: There's a Romanian folktale where a princess named Ileana is taken captive by monsters and saved by a knight. For this story, I wanted to reimagine her as the heroine of her own tale.

Transylvania:
Transylvania is the historical region of Romania that houses both Braşov and Bran Castle. During this period in history it was called Transleithania and was part of the Lands of the Crown of Saint Stephen, which was ruled by Austria-Hungary. For the sake of this story I kept it to Transylvania and Romania, and I hope that historians and history buffs alike will not be too mad with my embellishments. I have Eastern European roots and tried to do my best with capturing the region and its folklore as accurately as possible.

Any other historical inaccuracies—like forsaking Victorian protocol with hand-holding, and having a weapons belt crafted, et cetera—were done to benefit both the plot and characters for a (hopefully) enjoyable Gothic tale.

ACKNOWLEDGMENTS

Dear reader, thank you for following my characters on their next dark (and bloody) adventure, and for your love of Audrey Rose and Thomas across social media. "Cressworth" is my favorite thing EVER. (Though "Well Worth" also makes me smile.) I ship each of you so hard. Thank you. Thank you. A thousand, million times thank you.

I owe buckets full of gratitude to my super agent, Barbara Poelle, for her talent, sharp eye, the idea of giving Audrey Rose and Thomas an accelerated forensics course, and for her unerring ability to make me laugh throughout a deadline and any other curveball life throws my way. (Remember those months of neurological Lyme treatments and that time my face swelled up and I had a serious lisp before meeting JP?) Thank you for being my warrior, B. I could not have done ANY of this without you...or those fabulous gifs you send me.

To the entire team at IGLA, I'm so happy to have found a home with you. Sean Berard at APA—thank you for escorting *Stalking Jack* on a Grand Tour of

ACKNOWLEDGMENTS

Hollywood. My characters adored the red carpet treatment. Thank you to Danny Baror and Heather Baror-Shapiro, for placing my books in the hands of readers across the world.

Jenny Bak, aka Magical Editor and friend, working together from the start of this novel has been incredible. Your enthusiasm for always making it a little darker and a little creepier brings out all of my super-villain dreams. I swear you are filled with *magie* for making this plot and this story spring to life. Especially after I tried killing it in that first draft. Which is very much in the vein of the undead and the whole Dracula/vampire thing come to think of it...multiple puns intended. I can't help myself! Here's to darker and more magical adventures in book three.

James Patterson, I still cannot thank you enough for changing my life. Cheers to a couple of Newburgh kids who never stopped dreaming! Sasha, Erinn, Gabby, Sabrina, Cat, Tracy, Peggy, Aubrey, Ned, Mike, Katie, and everyone who works for JIMMY books/ Little, Brown and who was involved in the editing, production/sales/art of my work. Thank you for turning this document into a gorgeous work of tangible art and for your dedication to publicity, sales, and marketing, aka championing my book in every way you can. It's a Cresswell approved fact that I totally have the best team in publishing. (Extra shout out to Sasha and Aubrey for helping me polish Thomas's novella into a gorgeous luster while Jenny was out with sweet baby Bak.)

Mom and Dad—I'm not sure I'll ever be able to thank you enough for always encouraging me to be as creative as I dared as a kid and teen. Your belief that I could turn any dream into reality is what gave me the spark to try. Thank you for being there to offer support—and medical jokes/puns—and to help nurse me through the rough patch. Who knew that a girl who wrote about buckets of blood could get so queasy when hers was taken? Vial/Vile will always make me laugh inappropriately; I love you both more than any humble words can say.

Kelli, you're the best sister the world has ever known. Thanks for your extraordinary ability to read and critique the earliest drafts of my work. *Dogwood Lane Boutique* remains my most favorite place to shop for tour clothes (and, let's be honest, #bookstagram props), and I'm so proud of you for slaying your own dreams. And for the family discount…☺

Laura, George, Rod, Jen, Olivia, Uncle Rich, Aunt Marian, and Rich—I love you all and am so lucky to have you. Jacquie, Shannon, Beth—thank you for celebrating ALL of this with me. Ben it's always a blast

ACKNOWLEDGMENTS

whenever you're around and not just because you bring cool toys for the cats.

Simona and Cristina of *Bibliophile Mystery*—*mulțumesc*. Thank you for reading over/correcting my humble attempt at Romanian, and for making sure it was accurate for native speakers of the language. I cannot wait to visit you in Bucharest and Brașov one day soon!

It is absolutely essential in this business to have a squad that's there through it all. Here are just a few of mine: Kelly Zekas, Alex Villasante, Danika Stone, Kristen Orlando, Sarah Nicole Lemon, and Precy Larkins—thank you for reading, messaging, texting encouragement, and offering up advice as wise and brilliant as each of you are.

Traci Chee, your friendship and humor always keep me in great spirits. I still laugh every time I think about crying over Pink the singer instead of the color, and the mass confusion that deadlines wreak on us all. Thank you for your stellar advice on my second draft and for all of our wonderful phone talks, texts, and emails throughout the year. Working on our books together is the stuff dreams are made of, and our friendship is even more kick ass. I'd be lost without you!

Stephanie Garber, you're one of the most magical friends a girl could ever hope for. Our coffee or wine talks are the absolute best! (And our gif game is pretty terrific too. Especially when Stormtroopers in tutus are involved.) I'm pretty sure we're long-lost sisters with how often we finish each other's sentences. Also thank you in advance for a room full of Julians in your next book. You're welcome for that, fellow readers ☺

To Irina, aka Phantom Rin, your illustrations for this series are epic and amazing. Each time I see one of your sketches I pinch myself. Thank you for bringing my characters to life in such deliciously creepy and beautiful ways. I couldn't resist using them as inspiration for Nicolae's drawings and hope I did them justice.

Brittany, aka Candlemaker Extraordinaire, from *Novelly Yours,* thank you for some of the most lavish and amazing book-scented candles around. I'll never get over how gorgeous blood splatter or glittery mica on a candle can be. Shout out to Jessica at *Read and Wonder* for designing the magnetic and quote bookmarks— I love the top hats on Audrey Rose and Thomas! Jess from *Wick and Fable,* your Cresswell tea and Audrey Rose blend give me life.

I'm infinitely grateful for ALL the book bloggers and bookstagrammers out there, and wish a special thank you to: Ava and the Knights of Whitechapel, Kris at *My Friends Are Fiction* (aka my fellow pizza-loving pal), Rachel at *A Perfection Called Books,* Hafsa and Asma at *Icey Books and Icey Designs,* Melissa from *the Reader and the Chef,* Brittany from *Brittany's Book Rambles,* Bridget from *Dark Faerie Tales,* and Stacee aka *Book Junkee* aka my Cresswell cheerleader for adding MORE kissing scenes; I can't thank you all enough for what you do for both myself and my books. Pilar, "Pili," your daily Sherlock gifs are always appreciated, and your adoration of Thomas across the Twitterverse makes him preen even more. He will truly be insufferable by the end of book three.

Sasha Alsberg you are such a gem—thank you for loving Audrey Rose so much and for cheering her on. I am so happy to share the shelves (and an obsession with historical homes) with you! Also, a GIANT thank you to all the booktubers out there who've posted AMAZING videos or have hosted readalongs for both *Stalking Jack the Ripper* and *Hunting Prince Dracula.* I am continually blown away by your love and support of this gritty Victorian world.

Goat posse—Anita, Lori, Bethany, Ashlee, Riley, Precy, Mary, Kalen, Eric, JLo, Lisa, Amy, Michelle, Darke, Justin, Jennifer, Angela, and Suzanne—you are some of the very best people in the world. Much #GoatWub to you all.

Librarians and booksellers: My respect for you is

boundless, much like the infinite numbers of stars in the sky. Books are powerful weapons and you wield them with the utmost care and precision. Thank you for everything you do for both readers and writers across the world.

ABOUT THE AUTHOR

Kerri Maniscalco grew up in a semi-haunted house outside New York City, where her fascination with gothic settings began. In her spare time she reads everything she can get her hands on, cooks all kinds of food with her family and friends, and drinks entirely too much tea while discussing life's finer points with her cats. Her first novel in this series, *Stalking Jack the Ripper,* debuted at #1 on the *New York Times* bestseller list. She's always excited to talk about fictional crushes on Instagram and Twitter @KerriManiscalco. For updates on Cressworth check out KerriManiscalco.com.JIMMY Patterson Books